BABYLON RISING

The EUROPA
CONSPIRACY

BOOKS BY TIM LaHAYE

Tim LaHaye Prophecy Books—Nonfiction

Are We Living in the End Times?
Charting the End Times
Charting the End Times (study guide)
End Times Controversy
Perhaps Today (90-day devotional)
Merciful God of Prophecy
Revelation Unveiled
The Rapture
These Will Not Be Left Behind
Tim LaHaye Prophecy Study Bible: NKJV & KJV
Understanding Bible Prophecy for Yourself
Understanding God's Plan for the Ages (chart)
Bible Prophecy: Quick Reference Guide (booklet)

Tim LaHaye Fiction

Left Behind ® (volume 1)
Tribulation Force (volume 2)
Nicolae (volume 3)
Soul Harvest (volume 4)
Apollyon (volume 5)
Assassins (volume 6)
The Indwelling (volume 7)
The Mark (volume 8)
Desecration (volume 9)
The Remnant (volume 10)
Armageddon (volume 11)
Glorious Appearing (volume 12)

Babylon Rising ® (book 1)
Babylon Rising ® (book 2)

Left Behind ®: The Kids—Youth Fiction Series (volumes 1–40)

The Soul Survivor—Youth Fiction Series

The Mind Siege Project
All the Rave
The Last Dance
Black Friday

Additional Bestselling Books by Tim LaHaye

Spirit-Controlled Temperament
How to Be Happy Though Married
The Act of Marriage
How to Win over Depression
Mind Siege
How to Study the Bible for Yourself

BABYLON RISING

The EUROPA CONSPIRACY

TIM LaHaye

AND BOB PHILLIPS

BANTAM BOOKS

NEW YORK TORONTO LONDON SYDNEY AUCKLAND

BABYLON RISING: THE EUROPA CONSPIRACY
A Bantam Book

PUBLISHING HISTORY
Bantam hardcover edition published October 2005
Bantam trade paperback edition / August 2006

Published by
Bantam Dell
A Division of Random House, Inc.
New York, New York

Library of Congress Catalog Card Number: 2005053550

Bantam Books and the rooster colophon are registered trademarks of Random House, Inc.

ISBN-13: 978-0-553-38400-0
ISBN-10: 0-553-38400-7

Printed in the United States of America
Published simultaneously in Canada

www.bantamdell.com

BVG   10   9   8   7   6   5   4   3   2   1

To all those whose study of Bible prophecy has made them anticipate the revival of the old Roman empire. This scenario shows one possible way it could materialize in our lifetime.

FOREWORD
from Tim LaHaye

One of the End Times prophecies whose fulfillment Bible scholars have anticipated for over a hundred years is the revival of the old Roman Empire. Because that empire was never replaced by another world ruler like the three previous empires mentioned by the great Hebrew prophet Daniel, many have written and predicted that Rome would be reunited in the last days. These expectations are based on Daniel Chapters 2, 7, and 8, the latter verses of Chapter 11, and Revelation 13.

Twenty-five years after World War II scholars really began to get excited with all the talk about the European Common Market, the United States of Europe, the German- and French-inspired banking system, and the Euro dollar that is already in place. I remember how excited prophecy scholars became when the number of European states climbed to eight, some making outlandish claims if it hit ten to coincide with the ten toes or ten crowns of Daniel or the ten heads of

Revelation 13. However, deafening silence has prevailed ever since the numbers exceeded twenty states of Europe, even after the recent setback (which may just be a slowdown), when the people of France and Holland voted against the new European Constitution.

Europe is tired of war! Getting together in a cooperative governmental union makes much better sense to those countries. Peace is much more preferable to the killings that marked Europe even before Napoleon Bonaparte over two hundred years ago. What these European leaders do not realize is that they are playing right into the hands of evil conspirators out to take over the world, or at least, prepare for a world takeover predicted by the prophets of both the Old and New Testament.

The hero of our Babylon Rising series, Dr. Michael Murphy is both a prophecy and archaeology scholar, who knows about the real end-time government and the "Man of Sin," the "Son of Perdition," or as many refer to him, the "Antichrist," who will lead it.

In this fascinating book Murphy goes through hair-raising events to stave off the work of Talon (who may be the most vicious terrorist hit man in fiction history) and the Seven for whom he works. They are trying to establish a One World Government, religion, and commercial systems that will give them control over every man and woman on earth. They may or may not know they are paving the way for this Antichrist, mentioned by so many ancient prophets. Murphy uncovers the secret to his near-miraculous conception, which indicates he may already be a resident of planet Earth. In the process our hero is marked for extinction by the most ruthless group ever assembled.

Little do they realize they are preparing the world for the one man more evil than themselves. Fortunately for humanity, Murphy knows and is primed for action.

BABYLON RISING

The EUROPA
CONSPIRACY

ONE

FIRST THERE WAS a snapping sound...then a combination of rushing wind and sheer terror. One thousand feet of empty space separated Murphy from the raging river and instant death.

For a split second he was suspended in midair like an eagle soaring in the sky. Then gravity took over. Adrenaline surged through his body and his grip tightened on the cable like a vise. Teeth clenched together, barely breathing, all he could do was to desperately hang on.

As Murphy first approached the one-hundred-and-fifty-foot-wide gorge, he could see two cables spanning the void attached to large trees on either side. The first cable was low to the ground; the second, about six feet above. Hanging from the center of the top cable was what looked like a manila envelope twisting in a gentle breeze.

He shook his head. *That must be the prize.*

As Murphy moved closer to the edge, he reached up, grabbed the top cable, and pulled hard. *Very tight.*

Then he carefully leaned out and looked over the edge. The sight of the wild Arkansas River one thousand feet below almost took his breath away.

Do you really want to do this, Murphy? As much as you love adventure, someday Methuselah is going to get you killed.

He carefully surveyed the surroundings, looking for the slightest movement. Although he could see no one, his skin began to crawl with the eerie sensation that he was being observed.

He took several deep breaths then slowly inched his way onto the cables. Holding on to the top cable with both hands and standing on the bottom cable, he bounced up and down to test their strength.

As he ventured out on the cables, he realized that he had two problems: the up-and-down motion and the back-and-forth motion: the back-and-forth motion, in particular, put more weight on his hands when his feet were not directly under his body. If he had to use up his upper body strength to move the seventy-five feet to the center, it would be a very long way back.

It didn't take him long to realize that it was not a good idea to look down at the potential thousand-foot fall.

Keep your mind on the envelope and not swinging back and forth.

It took Murphy almost fifteen minutes to reach the envelope. The closer he got to the center of the gorge, the more his swinging motion of the cables increased and the more his body weight on the lower cable caused the distance between the two cables to stretch.

Even though he was six foot three, his arms were now extended above his head to almost his full reach.

Only three more feet to go, he thought reassuringly.

Murphy smiled to himself as he drove into his reserved parking spot on the Preston University campus. Arriving early gave him some precious minutes alone to gather his thoughts before his classes began.

A good night's sleep . . . great cup of coffee . . . and a bright sunny morning with no clouds in the sky . . . it's great to be alive.

The manicured lawns and lush trees made a striking contrast against the blue sky. The smell of magnolias filled the air. Murphy had grown to love the southern lifestyle. He also had grown to love his classes in biblical archaeology. In three years, they had become some of the most popular courses at the university. He was grateful for the opportunity he had to combine his love for archaeology with his love for the Bible. Everyone seemed to enjoy his lectures. Everyone, that is, except Dean Archer Fallworth.

Murphy glanced up as Shari bounced into the office, her sparkling green eyes alive with energy.

"You seem pretty happy for an assistant who's late to work," Murphy teased.

"I would have been here early if I didn't have to stop to pick up *your* mail," she replied, smiling and dropping a stack of letters, magazines, and a small box on his desk.

The brown-paper-wrapped box caught his attention. It bore no return address, only the name Tyler Scott. There was no sound when he shook it.

Shari was pretending to be busy, but Murphy could see her eyeing the box. It could be some unusual new artifact from a distant land. She was a dedicated archaeologist, and she was extremely curious. Because Murphy loved to tease Shari, he set the box down, picked up his lecture notes, and started to review them.

"Aren't you going to open it?" Shari asked.

"Open what?"

"You know exactly what. Here're some scissors."

Murphy laughed and opened the box. Shari cocked her head, watching, as he drew out an unsigned card, which Murphy read aloud:

> *A gorgeous sight,*
> *A Royal delight.*
> *Travel not at night*
> *But in the daylight.*
> *He's looking for you to come!*
>
> *Beyond the gates*
> *He there awaits.*
> *He's looking for you to come!*
>
> *For he to you, he cannot go.*
> *For him his time is slow.*
> *He's looking for you to come!*
>
> *His name has been caught.*
> *It is Tyler Scott.*
> *He's looking for you to come.*
>
> *Use your brain, don't be a blunder-head.*
> *The Spanish name it for the color red.*
> *He's looking for you to come.*

"That's weird," Shari said, looking puzzled. "What do you think that means?"

"I think it means trouble."

"Trouble?"

"Who else would send a strange riddle and leave it unsigned?"

Shari's look of curiosity changed to a look of anxiousness. "Do you think it is from Methuselah?"

"Good guess, Shari. I wonder what he is planning now."

Murphy was now close enough to reach the manila envelope twisting in the wind. His left hand bore his entire weight on the top cable as he reached out and removed the envelope with his right.

He shoved the envelope down the neck of his shirt for safety, then grabbed the cable again with both hands. After a few deep breaths, he began to walk carefully back across the cables toward his starting point.

"Are you having fun, Dr. Murphy? I know I am," Methuselah's voice boomed out, almost causing Murphy to lose his balance.

Where was the sound coming from? Murphy glanced around, but over the roaring of the waters below and the blood pounding in his ears, he had no clue.

"I think that it has been too easy for you so far. Don't you think so too, Dr. Murphy?"

Murphy tried to speed up his efforts to reach the safety of the canyon wall.

Methuselah's laugh echoed from the nearby rocks. "Slow down, Murphy. There's no need to hurry."

With that, the cable under Murphy's feet gave way. Instantly all of his weight shifted to his hands and arms as he dangled above the gorge.

Working frantically, Murphy was able to swing his legs up and catch the heel of his right foot, then his left, on the upper cable. Now he was hanging above the gorge by his legs and arms.

"How long do you think you can hang on, Dr. Murphy?" Methuselah called out, cackling.

"Long enough to slide across the cable and wring your neck!" Murphy cried.

"Now, now, Doctor. You sound as if you might be upset. Let's see if we can make it a little more interesting for you."

Methuselah's cackling laugh increased, and then the upper cable snapped. Murphy could feel himself falling.

"Do you have any idea what the riddle means?" Shari asked with a puzzled frown as she twirled one of her jet-black pigtails in her fingers.

"No, but I'm sure that it's one of his coded messages. I think we'll have to take it apart piece by piece."

"Well, he does mention 'He's waiting for you to come' five different times. That must be significant."

"It must be a key thought. Let's start with the last stanza. 'Don't be a blunder-head the Spanish name it . . . for the color red.'"

"Could that Spanish word be the name for a state? The state of Colorado?"

"Good, Shari. This Tyler Scott he mentioned has been caught."

"Maybe he has been caught telling a lie or caught with his hand in the cookie jar. Or caught being late to work for picking up some dangerous mail." Shari grinned.

Murphy smiled. "Or maybe he's been caught by the police. Look at the phrase 'his time is slow.' He may be doing time in prison."

"That would tie in with the 'gates' and that 'he cannot go' but you must come to him. How about 'gorgeous sight, a Royal delight'? What's that all about?"

"Hmmm. Colorado—prison—gorgeous sight—a Royal delight."

Murphy paced the floor, repeating those words and brushing his fingers through his hair. Then he stopped suddenly and looked at her.

"I think I've got it."

"Well, don't keep me in suspense. What have you got?"

"When I was a young boy I visited Colorado with my parents. We flew into Denver and rented a car and spent almost a month exploring the state. On one of those trips we went to Colorado Springs and Pike's Peak. From there we went to a town called Pueblo. West of Pueblo is Cañon City. What do you think it is famous for?"

"Cañons?"

"Quick, Shari. No, it's famous for the Cañon City State Penitentiary. It has a bizarre history."

"Bizarre sounds like it's right up Methuselah's alley. It's his kind of place. He should live there permanently."

"It was the home of the Do-It-Yourself Hanging Machine. One of the prisoners designed a self-triggering platform that would eliminate the need for a formal execution. The person who was to die would pull the lever himself. The machine operated through a series of pulleys. The pulleys would put three hundred pounds of pressure on the rope. This would throw the prisoner's body upward and instantly break his neck. Everyone thought that this was an improvement over strangling slowly on the end of a rope."

"Yuk! That doesn't sound like much of an improvement to me," Shari exclaimed.

"Well, the rest of the prisoners on death row didn't like it either. They then installed Colorado's first gas chamber, called Roy's Penthouse, in honor of Roy Best, the warden of the prison.

"Their most famous prisoner was Alfred Packer, the first 'Hannibal the Cannibal.' He was put into prison for eating other people."

"Where do you come up with these things?" Shari knew that Murphy's mind was loaded with strange trivia. Sometimes it drove her crazy. "What does that have to do with the note?"

"I'm getting to that. Near Cañon City is the Royal Gorge... get it? A *gorgeous* sight, a *Royal* delight. The world's highest suspension bridge spans the gorge at the height of 1,053 feet. Feeling the bridge move on its cables and the surface shake under you as cars drive by is quite an experience.

"Next to the bridge is an Aerial Tram with one of the steepest incline railways ever built. In some places the distance between the gorge walls narrows to only thirty feet. It's truly spectacular. They've even built an amusement park there.

"I'll bet you a Sanskrit manuscript that Tyler Scott is a prisoner in the Cañon City State Penitentiary. Shari, call the prison and check if they have an inmate named Tyler Scott. Next week is spring break, and I could do with a little vacation."

Murphy heard a buzz, then the sliding sound of a metal door shutting and locking behind him. He was in a small cubicle with one wooden chair placed in front of an inch-and-a-half-thick glass window. On the wall next to the window was a phone.

Murphy looked around. The drab green paint was chipped and scratched. Names and messages were etched into the old surface. It looked as if it hadn't been painted in twenty years.

After another muffled buzz, Tyler Scott entered the chamber opposite the glass window. Tall and thin, and wearing an orange prison jumpsuit, he looked to be about twenty-seven years of age. His blond hair was uncombed.

Murphy picked up the phone. "My name is Michael Murphy," he told Scott. "I'll get right to the point of my visit. This may sound strange, but I think you may have a message for me. Am I correct?"

"I don't get many visitors. Even my parents stopped coming about a year ago. They keep telling me that I'll never amount to anything. They say that I'm a loser." Depression and despair had etched lines on his young face. "I don't know what this is all about."

"Neither do I," said Murphy.

"A couple of months ago a stranger came to visit me. He told me that a large man named Murphy would probably come and ask for a message. He left some money for me to buy magazines and cigarettes."

"What did he look like?"

"He was tall and in his mid-sixties, with gray hair and lots of wrinkles. He looked like he had been in the sun a lot. Oh, yeah, he walked with a slight limp—I saw it as he got up to go. His voice was different. He sort of laughed and cackled when he talked. Kind of spooky, if you ask me."

"What was the message?"

"I'm all out of cigarettes, mister."

Murphy looked at him and smiled. "I'll leave you some money for them."

"Thanks. He said to go to the north side of the Royal Gorge, past the amusement park. Follow the canyon going west for two miles. The canyon will narrow. Look for the cables. That was it. It didn't make any sense to me."

"It doesn't make any sense to me either. Thanks for your help. What are you in for?"

"Armed robbery. I held up a convenience store."

"How much longer?"

"Three more years. They're teaching me auto mechanics. I hope to get a job when I get out."

"I'm sure you will. Besides the money, I'll leave a book for you with the guards. I think it will help you create a new life for yourself."

On the way out Murphy left some money and a Bible for Tyler Scott. He put a note inside suggesting that the young man start reading in the Gospel of John.

As Murphy drove the ten miles from Cañon City to the Royal Gorge, memories began to flood his mind. He remembered his father taking him on the railroad that ran at the bottom of the gorge. They had eaten lunch on the train and ridden the open-air observation cars to view the canyon from below. His highlight was going over a hanging railroad bridge with the class five rapids below them.

What a great time I had with my dad. If Tyler Scott had had a caring dad, would his life be any different?

Murphy parked his car and put on his day pack as he thought about what he might be facing. He strode across the suspension bridge, proceeded west next to the gorge, leaving the amusement park and people behind him. Soon he was alone.

He had forgotten how beautiful and majestic the Colorado Mountains were. Every now and then he stopped and looked into the gorge. It was quiet. All that could be heard was his boots on the ground, an occasional bird, and the sound of the rapids far below.

I need to do this more often. There's something therapeutic about being alone in God's creation.

Only one end of the top cable was attached to solid ground. Murphy was now swinging above the canyon like a human pendulum. In only moments he would smash into the wall on the other side of the gorge.

With his arms and legs clenched around the cable, Murphy prayed that he'd be able to hang on after the crash. He could make out individual rocks in the wall of stone now.

Then, suddenly, the position of the cable changed. Glancing up, Murphy could see that it had struck a large rock, which broke some of the downward momentum. Murphy's impact on the wall was arms and legs first, not headfirst, and he was able to hold on. But panic gripped him as he swung back from the wall.

"Oh, God! I'm slipping. Help me," he shouted.

After slipping about twenty feet, Murphy was able to stop his fall. His hands were shredded. He knew there was no way he could climb out of the canyon; the top looked to be a hundred feet away. His only hope for survival was to shinny up the cable to the rock outcropping above him—quickly, before his strength faded.

Murphy was almost exhausted by the time he reached the rock outcropping and pulled himself to safety. He lay there for some time, breathing deeply. When his breathing returned to normal, he checked out his surroundings. He was on a flat rock shelf about five feet wide and four feet long. The rest of the outcropping was too steep to stand on. He dragged the cable up and hooked it around a rock. He didn't want to lose his only connection with the top of the gorge.

His bloody hands were shaking violently as he took off his day pack and took out a couple of energy bars and a bottle of water.

Okay, Murphy. You're alive. Calm down.

He could barely unscrew the lid off the water bottle.

I'm getting too old for this. If I could get my hands on Methuselah, I'd kill him. Well, at least beat him till he's almost dead and stop his crazy cackling.

Murphy knew he had to regain his strength to be able to climb to the top of the canyon. After eating the energy bars and drinking the water, he put the pack under his head and lay down to sleep for a little while.

God, thank you for sparing my life. Please give me the strength and courage to climb out of here.

It was the cry of a hawk gliding gently through the canyon that woke Murphy. Sitting up, he tried to assess his situation. His eyes followed the cable to where he could see the edge of the gorge and safety far above him. He knew he couldn't climb that far on a steel cable. Neither could he stay on this ledge, at Methuselah's mercy. He did have a few resources, though.

He took off his belt and made it into a prussic knot, with a loop for his hand to fit into. From the shoulder straps of his day pack he formed two more prussic knots and loops to stand in. After he wove the knots into the cable, steeling himself for what he was about to do, he began the long slow climb to the top of the gorge.

Murphy hung his body weight on his right hand, which was hooked through the loop. He then reached down with his left hand and slid up the prussic knots that were attached to his feet. Then he stood up on the loops and slid the belt up the cable. He continued this process like an inchworm climbing a branch. It took almost an hour and a half for him to work his way to the top.

By the time Murphy pulled himself over the top of the canyon wall and uttered a prayer of thanks, Methuselah was nowhere to be seen—or heard. Perhaps he assumed that Murphy would never make it out alive. Or, more likely, he just got bored.

There must not have been enough excitement for him, Murphy thought dryly.

As he looked around, he saw something at the base of the tree where the cables had been attached. Sitting on a rock was a brass balancing scale. Broken wooden numbers lay in the two pans of the scale. The numbers 1 and 2 had been snapped in half. Part of each one lay in each pan. A three-by-five card was under the scale. Murphy picked it up and read the words.

BABYLON—375 METERS DIRECTLY
NORTHEAST OF THE HEAD

Murphy shook his head. *Methuselah, you're not through with the games yet, are you? Well, at least you had faith in me to live through your stupid tricks.*

Murphy had almost forgotten about the manila envelope in his shirt. Now he pulled it out and opened it carefully. He peered in but couldn't determine what was inside, so he tipped the envelope and poured the contents into his hand.

Plaster?

TWO

The town of Akkad, twenty-three miles from Babylon, 539 B.C.

DARK FIGURES CREPT *stealthily through the sleeping town. Some moved in pairs, but most were alone. Each, however, was fully aware of the danger. At every turn of the streets they glanced around nervously to see if they were being followed. If discovered, they were sure to be beheaded. Yet anger and greed overcame their fear of death and drove them to the meeting.*

It was cold and late at night. The quarter moon and cloud-filled sky created deep shadows. It was the perfect cover they needed. Only an occasional barking dog could be heard.

There were no welcoming lights in the darkened building they approached. After a coded knock, the door opened and they were ushered into a large room lighted with just a few small flickering oil lamps.

Smells of garlic, curry, and body odor permeated the air. Bearded men with nervous dark eyes were seated on Oriental rugs, the flickering light casting eerie shadows on their faces and brightly colored turbans. Some whispered angrily to each other. Others were quiet. Most looked very anxious and apprehensive.

The satrap from the province of Susa, Abd al Rashid, a squat man with bad breath, was the last to enter. Governor Abu Bakar and Governor Husam al Din nodded as he strode in. Everyone looked toward the two governors. Husam al Din was the first to speak.

"We have sources close to King Darius who inform us that he is planning to promote the old Hebrew as his chief administrative officer. We cannot let this happen. If he is placed in charge over us, it will affect our entire operation."

Abu Bakar added, "He is not a man who can be bribed or corrupted. He is too honest. Others have tried and have lost their lives as a result. We must come up with a plan to discredit him to King Darius."

Those opening words caused a soft murmur. Kadar al Kareem raised his hand. "The old Hebrew is faithful to Darius. It is doubtful that we will be able to accuse him of disloyalty. But there may be a way, however. The old man is a follower of Jehovah. His dedicated religious faith can be twisted and used against him. We must convince the king that the old man's God is in some way against Darius."

Daniel was finishing his meal of fruit and bread when his aide came into the room.

"Master, King Darius has sent a messenger with a command. He has asked that you and the other two governors and his one hundred twenty satraps meet in the royal palace in four days from today."

"Did the messenger say what the meeting was about?"

"No, he only mentioned that Darius was going to create a new law. It will be an irrevocable law of the Medes and Persians."

Daniel slowly shook his head. "I hope that he will think through the new law carefully. In my eighty-five years I have seen many kings regret passing a law they cannot change."

————

At the sound of the trumpet, the crowd grew silent. People turned toward the door, clapping as Daniel entered.

Daniel smiled and nodded at the men in multicolored robes as he walked toward his place near the king's throne. He knew in his heart that it was all an act. Although the men in the room were smiling and applauding, he could sense their hatred and jealousy. He had discovered their secret system of corruption. They knew he could expose them at any moment. He was fully aware that these hypocrites were his political enemies.

The royal guard began to file into the large hall from behind the throne. Soon many trumpets began to sound, and everyone rose in silence.

Loud cheers and applause broke forth when King Darius entered, smiling and waving. His gold-embroidered scarlet and blue robes barely covered his short, portly body.

After what seemed to be an eternity, Darius finally sat down and lowered his scepter. "I have been informed that all of you have held a meeting and unanimously came up with a wonderful suggestion," he stated.

What? Daniel had not been part of any meeting. He knew something was wrong.

Smiling broadly, Darius continued, "I appreciate your loyalty and your desire to honor me as your king. Because of that, I'm going to issue a new law that will be in effect for the next thirty days. It will be an unalterable law of the Medes and Persians. It will not be annulled for any reason. For the next thirty days, anyone who prays to any god or man except me will be thrown into the den of lions."

Then Daniel quickly understood their plan.

Darius called for the scribes and signed the decree to the cheers of the audience—except for one man.

The lion collapsed with a roar as Daniel fell onto its back. It took a moment or two for Daniel to catch his breath. After he had gathered his wits, he tried to focus. The only light entering the den came from the hole in the ceiling through which he had just been thrown.

The smell of the lions and their droppings was almost overpowering. It made it hard to breathe. As he looked around he could see the slanted yellow eyes of many surprised cats looking at him. One of the large males began to roar, soon followed by others. The sound was deafening...and terrifying.

Daniel could feel fear surging through his body. He had seen lions before, but only caged. Now there were no bars...only about thirty lions milling about him just a few feet away.

"Dear God, I have faithfully served you. Please give me strength to face death today." Daniel's prayer was interrupted by a voice from above. Darius. Daniel could hear the torment in the king's voice. "Daniel! My heart is in anguish. I tried to save you but I could not. May your God, whom you serve continually, rescue you! Good-bye, my faithful servant."

Before he could respond, he heard another sound—the scraping of the large stone that covered the hole into which he had been thrown. The royal guard was shoving it back into place.

Scribes soon brought melted wax and poured it on one end of the stone. As the wax rolled down off the rock and onto the ground, it formed a puddle. As the wax was drying, Darius and some of his nobles took their rings and made impressions signifying the unalterable law of the Medes and Persians. Anyone who broke the seal and tried to rescue Daniel would be put to death immediately.

With the rock covering the hole, only small shafts of light entered the den. Daniel could hear the lions moving about him. Occasionally one startled him with a roar. When would the attack begin?

For about fifteen minutes he sat in the middle of the den with his arms wrapped around his knees, nervously rocking back and forth and praying. His heart leaped to his throat when the tail of a lion hit him in the face as the large creature walked by.

Half an hour passed before Daniel realized that perhaps the lions were not going to attack him. Slowly he began to move. As he made his way toward a wall, he could feel bones under his feet—human bones. The thought made him want to throw up. Finally he reached the wall and leaned his back against it and listened.

He could hear the lions moving around in the darkness. Occasionally he felt a lion's breath and whiskers on his face as it sniffed him. It was an extremely unnerving experience. He kept anticipating that sharp teeth and pain would follow the warm breath.

Daniel thought back to how he had felt when he first heard Darius's most recent decree. He knew that the satraps and governors had set a trap just for him, because they and he knew that he would not be able to pray to Darius. Jehovah was the only true God of heaven and earth. No one else deserved worship. Especially not some small, overweight man with a large ego and an abundance of pride and arrogance.

He recalled how the delegation of satraps had broken into his room while he was praying. They had grabbed him and brought him to Darius, telling the king that Daniel was praying to Jehovah and asking for His help. The color had drained from Darius's face when he realized that he had sentenced his most faithful leader to death. The king had spent the day in frantic attempts to save Daniel, but finally Darius acknowledged that he could find no way to rescind his original ruling.

Eventually Daniel began to drift off, his thoughts turning to the first time he had come to Babylon.

THREE

"IT SEEMS TO ME I recall someone talking to me last week about being late to work." Shari, dressed in her usual white lab coat, didn't even look up from her microscope when Murphy entered the lab. He knew she was pretending not to smile.

"I'm glad to see that your powers of observation are improving," he answered.

She looked up with a smile. "Say, what's with the scratch on your head?" she asked, concerned. "Was spring break too hard on you?"

"A rock attacked me."

"Right. It just leaped off the ground and rushed at you."

"Well, actually, more like I rushed at it."

Shari looked at him more closely. "How about the scabs on your knuckles? Did you have a boxing match with the rock too?"

"You could say that."

Her good-natured jesting suddenly turned serious. "This doesn't have anything to do with Methuselah, does it?"

Her words sounded just like something Laura would say. Ever since Laura had died, Shari had taken over the job of worrying about him.

Murphy changed the subject. He didn't want to explain his near-death experience. He didn't want her to start saying that he should stay away from Methuselah.

"I've got something for you to look at," he said, handing her a manila envelope.

Shari's curiosity was piqued. She knew that Murphy didn't want to talk about what had happened, so she turned the envelope over in her hands and asked, "What's in it?"

"A little surprise. I want you to tell me what you think."

She poured the contents of the envelope on to a sheet of paper on the worktable. Murphy's encounter with the wall had crushed the plaster. As she looked closely at it, she said, "Oh, by the way, Bob Wagoner called *before you came in late for work*. He said he'd like you to give him a call."

Murphy smiled as he walked to his office.

FOUR

BOB WAVED to Murphy from his usual booth in the back. Murphy smiled and nodded, thinking, *We're all creatures of habit.*

They shook hands and Murphy slid across the green vinyl bench and sat down. The décor of Adam's Apple Diner hadn't changed since it had opened in the late 1970s. And Roseanne, the gray-haired waitress, looked like she had worked there, and eaten lots of food there, since its beginning.

"What's on the menu today?" Bob asked as she approached the table.

"There's lots on the menu, Pastor Bob, but my guess is that you'll have your usual cheeseburger and chili fries."

"You've got me pegged, Roseanne." He threw up his arms in mock surrender.

"And for you, Dr. Murphy? The chicken sandwich?"

"You're a mind reader, Roseanne."

"I'll get your coffee," she said as she waddled off toward the kitchen.

"Well, bring me up to date, Michael. We really haven't had a chance to talk since you got back from your trip to Ararat. Were you able to find the ark?"

Murphy's big smile left his face. Wagoner could sense uneasiness and pain. "Did something go wrong?" he asked, his voice turning somber.

For the next forty minutes Murphy recounted the deaths of his climbing party. He shared the betrayal of Colonel Blake Hodson and Larry Whittaker, the photographer, and how they had killed Professor Reinhold, Mustafa Bayer, Darin Lundquist, and Salvador Valdez, the former Navy SEAL. He then went on to describe how Talon had tried to kill him and how Azgadian had rescued him.

Wagoner listened quietly as he ate his cheeseburger. Not only was he absolutely spellbound by the tragic story, but he knew that Murphy needed to talk. Holding that much pain inside was not healthy.

"How about Vern Peterson, the helicopter pilot? What happened to him?" Wagoner asked when Murphy paused.

"He instinctively knew that something was desperately wrong. He saw the control box in Whittaker's hand and tried to descend away from the radio signals before the bomb blast. He realized that he couldn't escape and leaped out of the helicopter in desperation."

"It's a wonder that he wasn't killed!"

"Well, his fall was broken by a huge snowbank. It softened his landing somewhat, and the snow covered him at the moment of the explosion. When I saw him, he was in the cave with me, Isis, and Azgadian. The guardian of the ark not only rescued me but he brought Peterson to safety."

"Was Vern all right after the drop from the helicopter?"

"At first we thought he only had some bad cuts and a sprained ankle. But he was coughing a lot in the cave, and we realized that he must have some internal bleeding. We got him to a small clinic in Dogubayazit. From there he was transferred to the hospital in Erzurum. He's recovering now in Turkey and should be back in the U.S. sometime this month."

"And the ark? Did you find it?"

Murphy was quiet for a while, then looked around the diner as if checking whether anyone was listening. He leaned toward Wagoner and replied, "It was unbelievable. Fantastic! It was better than anything I could have ever imagined."

Wagoner's eyes grew wide. "You've got to be kidding!" he exclaimed. "You really found it?"

"Yes, Bob. It was there. Half of it was buried in a glacier, but we were able to enter the rest of it."

"Did you bring back some pictures?"

Murphy's eyes lost their sparkle. "Talon destroyed them all. We have no physical evidence. Talon set a charge and started an avalanche that covered the ark with tons of snow. There are now only four living eyewitnesses: myself, Isis, Azgadian, and Talon. It would take a miracle to find the ark now."

Wagoner saw the disappointment on Murphy's face. He decided to change the course of the conversation. "Speaking of Isis, how's she doing?" he asked, smiling slightly.

Murphy smiled back. "She's doing fine. She went back to work at the Parchments of Freedom Foundation. I think she was a little tired after all the trials we went through."

"That's not exactly what I was talking about."

Murphy smiled again. "She's a very attractive woman, Bob."

"Are you interested?"

"Okay, I'm interested. But I feel a little guilty."

"Michael, it's been a year and a half since Laura's death. Stop beating yourself up. Let me ask you a question: What do you think Laura would want you to do? Do you think she would want you to remain single forever?"

"Okay, Bob. I've got your message. Could we change the subject?"

"Did you find anything on the ark?" Wagoner asked. He could sense the excitement on his friend's face. "Well, come on, man! I'm dying to know."

"I must have your word that you won't repeat what I'm going to tell you."

"You've got it, Michael. I'll not say a word."

Murphy proceeded to tell him about the discovery of the brass plates that held the secret of the Philosopher's Stone, a discovery that could eliminate the need for fossil fuels. He talked about the singing sword they found and the vases full of self-lighting crystals.

Wagoner sat there, nodding in amazement. "Where are the brass plates, sword, and crystals now?"

"At the bottom of the Black Sea with Talon. I think he was chewed to pieces by the propeller blades of the ship . . . which made me feel sorry for the ship."

Wagoner made a face. "I can't blame you for having such feelings." He would probably feel the same way if someone had crushed his wife's larynx. "Is there any way to retrieve the plates?"

"There might be if we had a mini-sub and lots of time. However, it'd be like looking for a needle in a haystack."

"Doesn't that ship travel the same route each week?"

"I'm sure it does," Murphy replied. "Why?"

"Couldn't you get the charts of their route? If you had that and the approximate time of day when Talon went overboard, you could narrow the search quite a bit. At least it would be a smaller haystack."

"That's not a bad idea, Bob. And if we had some metal detecting equipment, it might be possible. I don't think the pack has had much time to settle into the sand yet. It might be worth a try."

Murphy glanced at his watch. Time had flown by. "Hey, Bob, I've got to go."

The two men walked out to the parking lot. Wagoner said, "I'd like to pray with you before I leave. I want to pray that God will give you great wisdom and courage. He has evidently called you to some very unique and dangerous tasks. I'm also going to pray about your possible relationship with Isis."

"Thanks, Bob. I appreciate your friendship, and I can certainly use your prayers."

FIVE

WELL, STEPHANIE KOVACS—Ace Reporter, are you happy?

She could see the emptiness in her eyes as she looked in the mirror to put on her lipstick.

Do you like being a mistress? Is it worth the price?

Now she found herself getting angry. She had sold her own pride and self-image for an extravagant lifestyle, for power and influence, and to further her career as a news journalist.

She stood up and shook her head a little. It gave her hair that wild-tiger look that Shane liked. She took one last look at her low-cut black dress that gave maximum exposure to her ample chest. She felt sexy. She smoothed the dress over her slim hips and turned and looked at herself from both sides. Pleased, she left the room.

Barrington was pacing back and forth in front of the penthouse windows when she entered the living room. Behind him the lights of the city sparkled like beautiful jewels in the night.

"What's wrong, Shane?" Stephanie asked. He looked a little startled and slightly embarrassed. Shane Barrington was not the kind of man who liked anyone to think that he could be bothered by anything. Frowning, he said, "I was just thinking about something."

"Between us?" There was a touch of fear in her voice. Even though they had been together for a while, she didn't feel secure in their relationship. Barrington was known for his verbal bursts of anger and had blown up at her on several occasions. He had never hit her, but often she felt that she had to walk on eggshells around him.

"No, no. Of course not. I was just thinking about work. We haven't had a good news story in a couple of weeks. I like to be on top of any breaking events. It's good for the ratings and makes the Barrington Network News lots of money."

Kovacs nodded.

"Say, what ever happened to Professor What's-his-name at Preston University? You know, the one who searches for biblical artifacts," Barrington asked.

"You mean Dr. Michael Murphy?"

"Yeah, yeah. That's the one. Didn't he leave on some kind of search for something?"

Barrington knew full well who Murphy was. He was just trying to play dumb. He didn't want to come across as too interested. That would arouse Stephanie's news reporter curiosity. He also didn't want to reveal the increased pressure that the Seven were putting on him for information. They hadn't heard from Talon after he had come down from Ararat. He had seemed to disappear off the face of the earth.

Immediately a red flag went up in Kovacs's mind. *What's Shane trying to do?* she wondered. *He knows full well who Murphy is and that he's looking for Noah's Ark. He even tried to hire him, but Murphy turned him down. Who's he trying to fool?*

"Yes," Kovacs replied slowly, thinking. "He was looking for Noah's Ark on Mount Ararat."

"Whatever came of that?" Barrington, looking out the windows, appeared to be engrossed in a police helicopter flying with its searchlight on.

"I don't know." *He's after something.* A spark of enthusiasm surged through her. It reminded her of the excitement she felt when following up on investigative leads. Maybe this was the opportunity she had been looking for.

Her mind flashed back to that night when she stepped into the room on top of the Barrington Communications Building. It had been filled with huge sprays of flowers, the carpet sprinkled with rose petals. Barrington had said that it was in appreciation for her hard work and loyalty and that it was to make up for having missed dinner with her. That night a small crack in his armor of secrecy had been exposed. He had told her that some people had found out about his massive debts and less-than-legal creative accounting. They had invested $5 billion into Barrington Communications, and he was now their pawn.

Kovacs had wondered who these powerful people were, but Barrington would say only that they were "hell-bent on establishing a one-world government. And a one-world religion too. And people like Murphy, they see it all coming, in the Bible. So they have to be stopped. Before they can persuade others to resist."

In the time that they had been together, Kovacs had recognized that Barrington was doing something more than just making money. It was more than just fulfilling a power-hungry ego. It was something . . . evil.

I need to get away from this man and his lifestyle, Stephanie recognized. *It's not what I really want. It's empty. Maybe this is where I can make some kind of difference and somehow redeem my poor choices. I can warn Murphy of the danger he is in.*

"Shane, why don't you let me check it out for you? There might be a story that you could use."

Perfect, she took the bait. Barrington grinned to himself. *She's so easy to manipulate.*

"Well, that might give you a change of pace," he said. "If that's something you'd like to do, then go for it. Take one of the cameramen if you need one. You can also use the jet if you like."

You can't let Shane know your true feelings. You need more time to plan your escape from him. You must keep up the masquerade. Kovacs ran over to him and gave him a big hug.

He kissed her. *Great! I'll have a good evening tonight and get the information I need too. Not bad, Barrington. Not bad.*

SIX

"MURPHY, DO YOU HAVE any idea how old that white powder and chips were?"

Shari's green eyes were bright with excitement. She so loved the joy of discovery.

"Let me guess, Shari. Hmmm...at least two thousand years old?"

Shari put her hands on her hips and cocked her head. "You knew, didn't you?" she said accusingly.

"I was only guessing, Shari."

Murphy proceeded to tell her about his vacation in Colorado. When he was finished, she began, "I—"

Murphy put his hand up to stop her. "I know. I know. You're going to tell me I shouldn't have gone."

"You've got that right!"

She knew that it would be a losing battle to go any further. "Well, after all that effort, did you come to any conclusion?" she asked.

"I have to admit, it took me quite a while. The brass scale at the base of the tree was quite a puzzler. Especially with the broken numbers one and two."

"Did the note help?"

"In fact, it did. I kept repeating the phrase over and over in my mind: BABYLON—375 METERS DIRECTLY NORTHEAST OF THE HEAD. Then it hit me. It was referring to the *head* of the golden statue that Nebuchadnezzar built. The same one that was taken to the Parchments of Freedom Foundation. Methuselah was giving me directions to another find. It must be located 375 meters directly northeast of where we found the golden head."

"What do you think it is?"

"Hold on to your pigtails. I think you're going to like this. I think it might be the Handwriting on the Wall that was mentioned in Daniel, Chapter Five."

"You mean the one where God used the fingers and hand of a man to write a message to King Belshazzar? You're crazy. How'd you come up with that?"

"It was the scale with the broken numbers one and two in the pans. Remember what the Handwriting on the Wall said?"

"No, I don't."

"It said '*MENE, MENE, TEKEL, UPHARSIN.*' "

"Oh, that's right. How could I forget? That makes perfect sense. I really understand now."

"Okay, okay. Give me a break. The word *MENE* means numbered. It was repeated twice. That stands for the numbers one and two in the pans. The word *TEKEL* means weighed. That's what the brass scales represented. The word *UPHARSIN* means divided. That's why the numbers were divided into two pieces. Translated into plain English it means: God *numbered* the days of Belshazzar's rule as the king. He found him *weighed* in the balance scales of God's judgment, and he was to be punished by *dividing* his kingdom and giving it to others."

"What about the white powder?"

"It's plaster. In Daniel Chapter Five it says that the handwriting was in the plaster on the wall opposite the lamp stand. I believe that the envelope held some of the plaster off that very wall. If this theory is true, that plaster is over twenty-five hundred years old."

Murphy went to his office and phoned the Parchments of Freedom Foundation for Isis.

He didn't realize how nervous he was until he was placed on hold.

Drumming his fingers on the desk, he thought, *You're like a schoolboy, Murphy. Grow up!*

"Michael." Murphy could hear the excitement in Isis's voice. He smiled, wishing he could drown in her sparkling green eyes. *Pull yourself together!*

"Isis. How are you?"

There was a slight pause. "I'm better now, Michael."

For a moment her words caught him off guard. He wasn't usually tongue-tied but now he struggled to collect his thoughts.

"Isis, I'm in between classes now. I was thinking about you and was wondering if . . . *Okay, you can do this* . . . you might be free Friday and Saturday. I need to fly up to New York. Could you fly up from D.C. and meet for the weekend?"

"That sounds wonderful, Michael."

After hanging up, Isis let out a big breath of air and stared out the window. Just hearing his voice had sent a thrill through her.

SEVEN

MURPHY COULD FEEL his Irish temper rising. The closer he got to the lecture hall, the more irritated he was becoming. It had all started when he pulled up in the parking lot and saw the van with BNN on the side. The thought of Barrington Network News being on campus brought a bad taste to his mouth.

His mind flashed back to the explosion at the church. He remembered trying to comfort Shari over the loss of her brother and Pastor Bob trying to console him over the murder of Laura. A BNN crew had been there. The network seemed always to be butting in at the most inopportune and painful times in a person's life. All the reporters wanted was a big story. They didn't care about people's feelings.

Then his thoughts shifted to the funeral of Hank Baines. He could remember what that reporter, Stephanie Kovacs, had said as she shoved a microphone in front of his face.

"Here at the memorial service for FBI agent Hank Baines, I'm talking with Dr. Michael Murphy of Preston University. Dr. Murphy, you were the last person to see Hank Baines alive, is that right?"

She had tried to pressure him into an emotional response.

"What is it you and Agent Baines were discussing, Dr. Murphy? Have you told the police? Have you told his grieving widow? Tell me, do you feel any sense of responsibility for his death?"

Since that time, Murphy's resentment of news reporters had grown.

Near the entrance to the lecture hall, he could see Stephanie Kovacs sitting on a bench under the magnolia tree. Students were talking with her. Her cameraman was positioning himself for the best shots.

She rose as he approached. "Dr. Murphy. Could I have a moment with you?"

Students were watching, so Murphy did his best to appear cordial. He took a deep breath and said, "What can I do for you, Miss Kovacs?"

"We happened to be in the area and were wondering if it would be possible for us to attend your lecture today?"

Right! Just happened to be in the area. Murphy had suspicions that there was more she was after, but all he said was "Anyone is free to come in, Miss Kovacs."

"Would it be permissible to shoot some video footage?" She flashed her most charming smile.

"I suppose, as long as you don't disturb the class. I prefer to have the students thinking about the topic rather than what they'll look like on the evening news."

"Thank you, Dr. Murphy. We will be quite discreet."

Quite discreet! Now, there's a change. What's with this meek and mild approach?

"Good morning, class. Before we get started today, you may have noticed that we have a celebrity with us—Stephanie Kovacs. Most of you will recognize her as one of BNN's top investigative reporters. She's brought along her cameraman."

The rowdy students clapped, cheered, and whistled. Kovacs acknowledged the din with a smile.

"The cameraman will be moving around taking a few shots. Try not to make faces or hand signs or *you* may be investigated," Murphy warned with a grin.

Everyone laughed.

"That especially goes for you, Clayton."

Clayton Anderson, the class clown, turned his palms up and opened his mouth in mock shock. *Who, me?* he mouthed, pointing at himself.

"Today we will be considering a new subject," Murphy said more seriously. "We'll focus on the ancient city of Babylon. You may want to jot down a few notes. This *will* be on the test."

There was a groan and the sound of notebooks opening.

"As you will recall from the lectures about Noah's Ark, Noah had three sons: Shem, Ham, and Japheth. Ham was the son who violated his father while he was asleep. One of his sons was named Cush, and he had a son named Nimrod."

Murphy could see that some of the students had a questioning look on their faces.

"Stay with me. I need to lay this foundation. In plain English, Nimrod was the great-grandson of Noah. The Bible calls him a great hunter or warrior. His name in Hebrew literally means 'let us rebel.' This can all be found in Genesis Chapter Ten.

"The Jewish historian Josephus identifies Nimrod as the builder of the Tower of Babel. This great tower was built to represent the people's rebellion against God and the setting up of their own power structure. They did not want to come under His influence. It was at the Tower of Babel that God confused the people and created different language groups."

"Dr. Murphy?" Clayton called, raising his hand. "I thought that the Tower of Babel was where King Solomon kept all of his wives."

The class broke out in laughter.

"I'm glad you feel better now, Clayton. May we continue?" Murphy said with a wry smile.

The cameraman was videotaping the entire interaction.

"Nimrod was the founder of Babylon along with a number of other cities. He was also the founder of Baal worship, the world's first organized system of idolatry. The city became famous many years later because of a great king named Nebuchadnezzar, who broke the power of Egypt at the battle of Carchemish and ruled Babylon for forty-five years."

Murphy dimmed the lights and turned on the PowerPoint projector. Up came an artist's re-creation of the city of Babylon.

"Babylon is located about fifty miles south of Baghdad. Have any of you heard about this town in the news lately? Babylon lay on a great plain with a large man-made lake above the city. At the height of Nebuchadnezzar's reign, the gardens of the city were considered one of the wonders of the world. Herodotus estimated that the great wall that circled the city was sixty miles long, encompassing almost two hundred square miles. Some of the walls were eighty feet thick, and many chariots could ride abreast on top of the wall. Two hundred and fifty towers were on the wall. It was estimated that five hundred thousand people lived within the city walls and another seven hundred thousand people in the extended city outside of the walls."

Murphy clicked up another slide.

"Most of the city was made of sun-dried bricks, and most of the bricks carried this inscription:

Nebuchadnezzar, Son of Nabopolazzar, King of Babylon

"I know you're disappointed they didn't have your name on them, Clayton. They would have said King of Jokes."

Everyone laughed and whistled.

Murphy clicked up a slide of an ancient temple. "There were fifty-three temples within the city. The structures were called 'ziggurats.' They consisted of three to seven platforms that grew smaller as they rose in height. The next slide will give you some idea of the size of a ziggurat."

After clicking up another slide, Murphy paused so the students could absorb the information. At their murmurs, he nodded. "Yes, surprising, isn't it? These towers were immense."

BABYLONIAN ZIGGURAT

1st Step: 300 feet by 300 feet by 110 feet high
2nd Step: 260 feet by 260 feet by 60 feet high
3rd Step: 200 feet by 200 feet by 20 feet high
4th Step: 170 feet by 170 feet by 20 feet high
5th Step: 140 feet by 140 feet by 20 feet high
6th Step: 100 feet by 100 feet by 20 feet high
7th Step: 70 feet by 80 feet by 50 feet high
300 Feet Tall—A 30-Story Building

"The next slide will give you some idea of the various gods that the Babylonians worshipped."

BABYLONIAN GODS

Anu	God of the highest heaven
Marduk	National god of the Babylonians
Tiamat	Dragon Goddess
Kingu	Husband of Tiamat
Enlil	God of the weather and storms
Nabu	God of scribal arts
Ishtar	Goddess of love
Ea	God of wisdom
Enurta	God of war
Anshar	Father of heaven
Gaia	Mother Earth
Shamash	God of the sun and justice
Ashur	National god of the Assyrians
Kishar	Father of earth

"Throughout human history, men have talked about various gods. Part of the reason for this is the fact that we can look about us and see the grandeur of creation. We ask, Where did this all come from? Could it have just happened? Did it just pop up from nothing? There must have been some cause. Something or someone started all of this that we call the universe. This is called the question of first cause.

"This leads to the second question. With all the intricate design in nature, was there a designer? Whoever the designer was, they must certainly be smarter than me. These two questions lead to the third and fourth questions: Is there a purpose to life? And can I come to know what this purpose is?"

Murphy paused and glanced at his watch. "Well, I think that's enough for today. It will give you something to think about until we meet again. Make sure that you pick up the reading assignment on your way out."

EIGHT

"DR. MURPHY, I appreciate your taking time to meet with me. And thank you for allowing us to videotape your class," Stephanie Kovacs said as she approached.

Murphy was waiting on the patio of the student center.

"Aren't you going to tape our interview here?" Murphy asked, confused. *Why is she being so nice and polite? This isn't her usual go-for-the-jugular attack.*

"No. I asked the cameraman to put everything away. I just wanted to ask you a few questions without having to worry about camera angles."

"Okay. Shoot."

"May I go back a little? A few months ago you were in the midst of planning an expedition to look for Noah's Ark. Did you in fact go to Ararat?"

"Yes, we did."

"The ark must be a popular subject."

"I'm not clear what you mean."

"Well, I was looking over the reports from the news wire and ran across a recent one about another team that was looking for the ark. It was to be funded by a Christian businessman from California. It seems that he had hired Earth-Link Limited to take some satellite photos of the Ararat region. The article went on to say that the snowmelt on Ararat was the greatest since A.D. 1500. Evidently they had discovered something on the mountain that looked like a wooden structure."

"We had some photos from the past that we thought indicated the same thing," Murphy agreed.

"The businessman put together a team of archaeologists, forensic scientists, geologists, and glaciologists. They were to be led by a guide who had climbed Ararat many times. The guide told the team that there'd been an eyewitness sighting and some photos taken in 1989."

"Yes, we too had heard of that sighting."

"Everything was set for the trip to get started and then the Turkish government shut down their expedition. They wouldn't give them permits. They said that it would be too dangerous because of terrorist threats."

Murphy smiled slightly. "There may be more to the story," he said quietly.

"What do you mean?" Kovacs asked quickly. Her curiosity was a ten on the reporter's Richter scale.

"I think they may have cancelled *all* permits after our expedition."

"Your expedition? Why?"

"Because of the murders."

"What murders?"

For the next hour Murphy related details of the search for the ark and the deaths of the climbing party. He carefully omitted information about Talon, the brass plates, and the special crystals found on the ark. Without evidence, they would only sound like fantasy.

"Did you find the ark?" Kovacs broke in excitedly.

Murphy hesitated before sharing the exciting discovery.

Kovacs thought to herself, *Could there really be an ark? Murphy doesn't seem to be one of those weirdo, right-wing Christian nuts that I've interviewed before. And the murders . . . did Shane have anything to do with them?* She shuddered at the thought.

Back in the office, the ringing phone broke Shari's concentration. Bob Wagoner was calling for Murphy.

"Hi, Pastor Bob," Shari said with a grin. "How are you?"

"Very well, Shari. I saw you sitting at church with Jennifer and Tiffany Baines. How did they seem to you?"

"I think they're making the tough adjustment to the loss of a husband and father. Since they came to know the Lord, they seem to have a peace in the middle of turmoil."

"Yes, we'll all keep praying for them. By the way, how are *you* doing?"

"I'm doing pretty well. I've been reading the Book of Philippians. It's a real encouragement. Especially Chapter Four."

"That's great, Shari. Keep it up. Could I please speak to Michael?"

Wagoner was surprised to hear that Murphy was being interviewed by Stephanie Kovacs.

"Well, tell him to give me a call when he gets a chance. I've got something I'd like to share with him."

"You bet, Pastor Bob. Good to talk with you."

Something in Stephanie Kovacs's tone made Murphy answer her question about the ark. He couldn't quite put his finger on it. She wasn't being as aggressive as usual. She was asking the right questions for a reporter, but he could sense sadness in her normally fiery blue eyes. She listened intently to everything he was saying.

"Let me ask you a question, Stephanie," Murphy said, turning the tables. "What did you think about today's lecture?"

"It was quite interesting. I didn't have any idea that the city of Babylon was as big as you were describing. It's hard to realize that the Babylonians were as advanced in building as they were. I'd like to hear the rest of your lectures."

"You're certainly invited. What did you think about the last part of the presentation—the part about purpose and meaning to life? Have you found purpose and meaning? Are you happy?"

Immediately Kovacs looked away. She didn't know how to handle Murphy's question. Murphy had struck a nerve. She was *not* happy with Barrington. She didn't want to be a mistress. She wanted to be loved for who she was, not what she could do in bed.

Murphy knew it would be best not to press the subject. Sometimes it's better to let an important question seep slowly into a seeker's soul. "Well, Miss Kovacs, I need to get back to my office. My next lecture on Babylon is on Thursday morning. I think you might find it interesting. If you're in town, I encourage you to come."

Murphy was already standing with his hand outstretched. Kovacs wanted to blurt out that he was in danger, but some students were walking toward them. The words just wouldn't come.

Silently she shook his hand, and Murphy walked away.

NINE

AS MURPHY STRODE toward his office, he could see Paul Wallach leaving the next-door lab. Murphy was about to call to him, when Paul turned toward the student parking lot. He seemed to be staring at his feet as he walked.

He doesn't look very happy.

Shari was in tears when Murphy entered the lab. At the sound of his voice, she sobbed and reached for a tissue.

"Paul and I had another argument."

"About?"

"The same thing," she said, wiping her nose. "He keeps talking about his plans to join Barrington Communications when he graduates in May. I *know* it isn't the right thing for him. There is something about Barrington that is evil. I just feel it."

That sounds just like something Laura would have said...only she would have added, "It's just woman's intuition."

"Where does that put you guys with each other?"

"I don't know. Paul is so wrapped up in making money, meeting important people, and having power like Barrington. I won't live that way. There's more to life than selling yourself to the highest bidder. Paul's changing, and I don't like what I see. He used to be more caring to me. Now it's as if he's only interested in making it big. We used to hold hands and walk together and share ideas with each other, and now...Oh, Murphy, I don't know what I should do." Shari paused and took a deep breath. "I'm going for a walk. I need some fresh air."

"Is there anything I can do?" Murphy asked, his concern evident in his voice.

"Just pray for me," Shari said, her voice breaking. "By the way, Bob Wagoner called while you were out. He asked you to get in touch with him."

Murphy sat at his desk and reached for the phone. He was worried about Shari, but he felt sure her strong values would guide her in the right direction. Murphy got straight through to Wagoner, who said, "I have an article you might be interested in—it's about the end of the world."

"What are you talking about?"

Bob laughed. "Last weekend Alma and I took a group of high school students from the church down to Orlando, to Disney World. While there, I was reading the paper when I noticed an article that caught my attention. It's right up your alley. It is about the end times. I clipped it out and brought it back with me. Let me read it to you. It says:

End of the World

Orlando police found an elderly man wandering the streets Tuesday evening. He seemed confused and disoriented. He kept shouting that the end of the world was coming. He claimed that one man would soon rule the world.

Police Sergeant Owen East told reporters that this is the third such incident involving this individual. Each time he seemed more and more agitated. Police escorted the elderly gentleman back to a local nursing home. It is believed that he may be suffering from Alzheimer's.

"That's a good one, Bob. Send it over. I'll add it to my collection," Murphy said with a smile.

TEN

"DID YOU ENJOY your vacation, Talon?"

All of his muscles tensed for a brief moment and anger rushed through his body. Then he relaxed almost as quickly. Years of training to control his emotions took over, and a smile came across his lips. "Vacation?"

"Yes. It seems like you've taken your time about reporting in. We were wondering if you might have taken a vacation."

Talon was annoyed by John Bartholomew's sarcasm. The man's tone sounded like the British headmaster at the boarding school Talon had attended. He had resented being talked down to even as a child. Breathing deeply, he recalled the pleasure he'd had when he slit the tires of the headmaster's car. It caused him to miss an important lecture in Capetown.

Talon's fingers caressed the gargoyles on the arms of his chair as he drew his attention back to the seven people before him. The bloodred cloth covering the long table they sat behind was very appropriate for them.

"I must apologize for my delay," Talon stated. "It seems I had a swimming engagement in the Black Sea." There was no point in telling them that he had fallen off the ship and almost been sliced by the propeller blades. They wouldn't care that he had nearly been killed or that he had had to swim thirteen miles to shore and spend a week in a hospital due to exposure. All they cared about were results and the fulfillment of their plan to rule the world.

"Well, Señor Talon," Mendez said, "we understand that you discovered the fabled Noah's Ark." Even in the dim light Talon could see Mendez smirking behind his neatly trimmed mustache.

"In fact, I did."

Mendez cleared his throat and continued. "Mr. Bartholomew informed us that you made a discovery of some new technology on the ark that will enable us to control all of the world's energy supplies. He said that it would make oil a thing of the past. Is that true?"

"Well, I'm not a scientist. As you know, my specialty is the elimination of people, but I think Noah discovered the Philosopher's Stone."

"The Philosopher's Stone—the ability to change base metals into precious metals?" Mendez exclaimed. "Are you sure?"

"It's only what I heard. I was in the shadows on the ark listening to a conversation between Colonel Hodson, the CIA operative, and Professor Wendell Reinhold from MIT. That was just moments before Hodson snapped Reinhold's neck like a toothpick. I then had the pleasure of taking *his* life."

"What about the Stone?" Bartholomew broke in.

Talon moved slightly. His hands were cold, and he could feel the gargoyles under his fingertips. He knew that the Seven would not be happy with what he was going to say. "The formula for the Philosopher's Stone is written on three bronze metal plates," he explained. "I put them in a backpack along with some curious crystals, a dagger that may have been made of tungsten steel, and other items from the ark. I had them with me when I boarded the ship sailing from Istanbul to Romania."

"*Had* them!" Sir William Merton exclaimed.

Talon controlled himself and smiled slightly. He could feel perspiration forming on his forehead, and his underarms were damp. "I had an encounter with Professor Murphy on the ship, and we got into a fight. The backpack slipped off and was lost."

"What!" General Li slammed his fist onto the table. "I thought you killed Murphy when you caused the avalanche to bury the ark under thousands of tons of snow and ice!"

"He somehow escaped."

"We don't pay you to make mistakes, Talon," said Jakoba Werner, a fleshy German woman with blond hair. "We pay you a vast amount of money to destroy our enemies."

John Bartholomew's tone was chilling. "Maybe we need to find someone else who can do the job."

"I can do it," Talon replied. "I have my own personal scores to settle with Murphy."

"Talk is cheap," Viorica Enesco, an angular woman with a Romanian accent, said. "It is time for action. Show us what you can do."

Bartholomew again spoke. "Is there any way you can recover the backpack?"

"I think so. But it will take time to search the area where I went over into the Black Sea."

"We don't want a geography lesson or excuses, we want the plates," Barrington ground out. "But right now something has come to our attention that needs an immediate response. We have many operatives. One of them monitors all of the newspapers printed by the Barrington Network News. She ran across a small article about an elderly man who talks about the end of the world and a leader who will arise to rule the world. That man must be eliminated."

"What harm can an old man . . . ?" Talon began.

"Enough!" General Li shouted. "We don't pay you to question! Just do it—now! Your very life may depend on it."

ELEVEN

MURPHY PLACED his briefcase on the desk, took out his notes, and surveyed the crowd. His attention was caught by Paul Wallach. He was sitting far back in the lecture hall. *Not in his usual spot. He and Shari must still be at odds.*

Shari was on the other side of the room passing out graded book reports. She didn't notice that Paul was watching her.

Murphy sighed.

"Good morning, class. Let's get under way. You will recall we were talking about the ancient city of Babylon. The Babylonian Empire was very advanced. The Babylonians excelled in the theoretical mathematics of geometry and algebra. They measured time with water and sun clocks. They also measured degrees of angles precisely.

Their numerical system was based on sixty. That's why we have sixty minutes in an hour and 360 degrees in a circle. They also utilized a decimal system and knew about square roots and the value of pi. Their calendar was based on lunar cycles with twelve lunar months. Weights and measures were regulated across the empire, using metal or stone weights in the shape of ducks."

Don West raised his hand. Murphy could always count on Don to add some unique detail. He was the most well-read student in the class.

"Dr. Murphy," Don said, "I was looking up Babylon on the Internet last night. I read that the Babylonians were quite sophisticated in the area of medicine too. It's believed that they had a superb knowledge of human and animal anatomy and physiology. Also, they understood the circulation of blood and the importance of the pulse. The article indicated they even did delicate operations on the eye."

"That's correct, Don. They were very scientific on one hand and very superstitious on the other. The Babylonians were well steeped in divination and witchcraft. They used magic formulae to attempt to read the future. They used drops of water on oil, noting the direction of the wind and the influence of storms. They also made predictions based on which way smoke blew in the air, the way a fire burned, and the position of the stars. To the Babylonians, even abnormal births held some significance for the future. Archaeologists have found stones shaped like sheep livers with incantations inscribed on them. The Babylonians specialized in the observation of animal entrails. They believed that the gods communicated through signs, natural phenomena, and worldly events. For example, the sudden appearance of a lion, the eclipse of the moon, or an unusual dream might portend the future."

Stephanie Kovacs stepped into the lecture hall through a side door. *Curious*, Murphy thought. *Perhaps she really is interested in ancient Babylon.*

"The Babylonians made systematic recordings of the planets and named most of the signs of the zodiac," Murphy continued. "There was a flourishing business of selling charms and amulets to protect people from evil. Almost like how we use a rabbit's foot for good luck today.

"The city of Babylon is very important when it comes to archaeology and Bible prophecy. It is the second most-mentioned city in the Bible. The first is Jerusalem, which is referred to 811 times. Babylon is mentioned 286 times. Both of these cities have great historical importance."

By now Kovacs had found a seat in the back and was looking attentively at Murphy.

"The Book of Daniel and the Book of Revelation both talk a great deal about Babylon. The events of Nebuchadnezzar's dream, Shadrach, Meshach, and Abednego in the fiery furnace, Daniel in the lions' den, and the 'Handwriting on the Wall' at Belshazzar's feast all took place in Babylon."

Murphy paused and casually leaned back against the desk. "You will recall from previous lectures that the Bible talked about Noah's Flood as a judgment against the wickedness. Men could be saved from the judgment of God only by entering the ark of safety. Well, the 'Handwriting on the Wall' at Belshazzar's feast is similar. It was a judgment against King Belshazzar and his wickedness and pride. His kingdom was destroyed, just as the world was destroyed in the Flood. The people of Noah's day were given warnings to turn from their evil ways, and they would not listen. Belshazzar didn't heed the warnings of God when his grandfather was punished by going insane. You'll recall that his grandfather, Nebuchadnezzar, became like a beast and went around on all fours for seven years."

Murphy paused for a moment to let it sink in. "Isn't it strange that we do the same thing today? God gives us warnings. He pleads with us and confronts us. You may ask, 'How does He do this?' He does this through the still small voice of our conscience. Our conscience tells us what is right and what is wrong. If we listen to our conscience and do right, happiness follows. However, if we ignore it, we will face destruction and unhappiness like the people of Noah's day or like Nebuchadnezzar and Belshazzar. Have you heard the still small voice of your conscience speaking? Have you been obeying it or ignoring it?"

Murphy stopped talking, to let his students reflect. Finally the silence was broken by the ringing of the bell, which startled everyone. There was not a lot of talking as the students filed out of the lecture hall. Stephanie Kovacs remained in her seat.

TWELVE

"GOOD MORNING, STEPHANIE," Murphy called up to her. The two of them were alone in the lecture hall. "I didn't see your cameraman."

"I didn't think it would be necessary. I was still in town and thought I'd catch your lecture. Do you have time between classes to talk?"

"Sure. Let's go over to the pond by the student center. There are some benches there and we won't be disturbed. There'll be another class in this room in about fifteen minutes. It will be anything but quiet."

Kovacs turned to Murphy, her face serious. "I need to apologize to you," she said. Her tone lacked its usual cutting edge.

Murphy was caught off guard. "For what?"

"For coming on too strong. As an investigative reporter, I've always approached any story with skepticism. I use my aggression, hoping that it will make the other person nervous and reveal something that would incriminate them. I've tried that with you in the past and you've always answered truthfully. I've watched you under different stressful situations and have come to realize that you aren't some religious nut."

Murphy laughed. "Maybe a little strange . . . but not crazy."

The humor eased the tension a little. Kovacs began to relax and open up. "I've been thinking about what you said in your first lecture. You know, the part about being happy and finding purpose in life. Is it really possible for anyone to be truly happy?"

"Well, I guess that would depend on what you mean by happiness, Stephanie. If you think happiness means having freedom from any conflict with people, I don't think that will ever happen. We'll always encounter disappointments, hurts, and rubs with our family, friends, and fellow workers. That's part of living. Happiness doesn't mean that we'll never get sick or have any financial concerns. There are many ill people who seem to be cheerful, while a lot of healthy people are pessimistic. The same can be said about rich people and poor people. I know some people who have very little when it comes to earthly goods and yet they are content. And there are many rich people who are angry and depressed. We've all heard stories of rich people committing suicide."

Kovacs nodded. She couldn't identify with the suicide part, but she did understand those who are angry and dissatisfied. She was living with one such man.

"Happiness has more to do with attitude," Murphy told her. "Actually, I think happiness is the end result of having a positive attitude toward life, even in the midst of struggles. Someone has said that happiness is like a butterfly. When we chase it, it seems to always elude us. But when we busy ourselves with our responsibilities, the butterfly of happiness lands on our shoulders."

"Well, my butterfly must be taking a vacation," Kovacs said with a wry smile.

Murphy could tell that there was more behind her quick retort. He knew it would be best to let her talk.

"Today, when you mentioned Shadrach, Meshach, and Abednego in the fiery furnace and Daniel in the lions' den, it brought back memories. My grandfather used to tell me stories about them. He was a very religious man. He was warm, caring, and funny. I guess as I think about it now, he was probably a happy man."

"Did you go to church in your younger years?"

"Yes, back in Michigan."

"Do you still go?"

Kovacs paused, then explained, "No. I stopped in junior high school. My father was killed by a drunk driver, and I couldn't understand why a loving God would do such a thing. I guess I got angry with God and stopped going."

"That happens to a lot of people."

"You mentioned judgment and conscience today. That was really heavy. I haven't thought about God using our conscience."

"You sound discouraged."

"More like disillusioned. I don't think it's possible to be happy—at least for me."

"I think that God may be trying to talk to you."

"I'm sorry, Dr. Murphy, but now you *are* beginning to sound like one of those religious nuts. I don't hear voices. It's always bothered me when people say they hear God talking to them. It sounds like they need to be in an insane asylum somewhere."

"Well, let me try to help you understand. Did you ever fly a kite with your father?"

"Yes, many times."

"Do you remember when you would let out the string, how the kite would rise? You could hear the paper rattling in the wind.

Sometimes it would rise so high that it almost disappeared out of sight."

"I remember that."

"When the kite was out of sight, how could you tell that it was still there?"

Kovacs looked a little puzzled for a moment. Then she said slowly, "I guess by the pull of the string. It meant the wind was still blowing the kite."

"Right. That's sort of how it is when God speaks to you," Murphy explained with a smile. "You can't see Him. He is out of sight. And you can't audibly hear His voice because He is too far away. But you can feel His loving tug on the strings of your heart. He does this when you read the Bible. He also does this when you listen to the still small voice of your conscience. That's how God speaks to you."

"That's a different concept from hearing voices."

"Yes, it is. Let me ask you a question. Do you feel the tug of God on the strings of your heart today?"

Stephanie Kovacs's blue eyes began to fill with tears. She turned away from Murphy quickly, but he knew he had given her food for thought.

THIRTEEN

Jerusalem, 605 B.C.

BLOOD-CURDLING CRIES *could be heard everywhere when Nebuchadnezzar's final assault began. With his archers focusing on the soldiers protecting the wall, hundreds of men were dropping in place.*

He had not been successful in the direct use of siege ladders, catapults, or battering rams. His change of strategy took almost a year to complete. Now a dirt ramp up to the lowest part of the wall surrounding Jerusalem provided the breach that was needed.

His well-trained soldiers ran up the ramp, pouring over the wall and into the city. Women and children ran screaming for protection. The army of Jehoiakim fell back as hundreds more were slain. They were no match for the battle-hardened Babylonians. Within half a day it was over.

The smell of death was everywhere. Soldiers stripped the dead of any valuables and left them lying where they had fallen. The living were herded into the temple courtyard. There the elderly, handicapped, and wounded were separated from the women, children, and teenagers. The able-bodied men were killed where they stood.

Nebuchadnezzar and his soldiers looted the city. He let his men take anything they wanted. He kept only the gold and tapestries from the temple. He would bring these trophies back to the treasure house of his god.

Nebuchadnezzar then went to examine the captives. He instructed Ashpenaz, his master of eunuchs, to select young men fourteen to seventeen years of age to be trained as aides for the king's court.

"I want you to pick out only those who are children of King Jehoiakim or the nobles of the city. They must be healthy and without any blemishes. Make sure that they have wisdom, are quick learners, and are widely read in many fields. They must have poise enough to keep silent and still look good in the palace. The women and children who remain are to become servants for the nobles of the court. Leave the elderly, crippled, and wounded to clean up the city. They pose no threat."

Daniel, along with many other lads, was chained together for the long march back to Babylon. During a water stop at the second oasis Daniel had opportunity to talk to others shackled near him.

"My name is Daniel," he murmured. "I am the son of Malkia, the chief judge of the king's court. The barbarians have killed my brother and my parents."

"My name is Hananiah," said the teen standing nearest Daniel. "These are my two brothers, Mishael and Azariah. We are sons of Zephathah. Our father was keeper of the king's treasury. We too have lost our parents. Do you know where they're taking us?"

"I overheard someone say that we were to become slaves in King Nebuchadnezzar's palace."

Mishael nodded toward the man overseeing the slaves. "Do you know anything about him?"

"The soldiers call him Ashpenaz," Daniel explained. "He is master of the king's eunuchs."

Azariah said fearfully, "Does that mean what I think it means?"

"I am afraid so," said Daniel. "But at least they're not going to kill us."

"But, Daniel, don't you want to someday marry and have sons and daughters of your own? How can you stay so calm?"

"Yes, Azariah, I do, but we both know that will never happen now. We must trust ourselves to God. I don't like the idea of becoming a eunuch any more than you do."

Daniel was jolted from his memories when he felt the brushing of soft fur on his face. One of the lions stopped, looked back at him, and sniffed. Daniel froze. He was holding his breath when the lion turned and collapsed right next to him like an overgrown pet. Confused and curious, Daniel slowly reached out his hand and touched the animal's back. It did not move.

I wonder what would happen if I petted it.

Daniel smiled when the large male seemed to enjoy the caress.

I must still be dreaming. This cannot be real.

But it was. He could feel the warmth of the cat's body and the rising and lowering of its chest as it breathed. The heat of the cat's body was almost comforting. Slowly Daniel began to relax. As he started to pray, his memories returned.

Hananiah was the first to see it. "Look!" he exclaimed, nodding toward the north. The other boys turned to see the majestic city of Babylon in the distance.

As they approached, they could see a wide moat circling the city. Merchant boats sailed in the waters that were fed by the great Euphrates River. The wall surrounding Babylon was three hundred feet tall and ran for as far as the eye could see. One of the other captured boys said he heard that the four walls surrounding the city were each fifteen miles long. Never before had any of them seen anything like it.

The farmers in the fields outside the city walls stopped their work as the prisoners in chains marched slowly by. All types of fruits and crops seemed to be growing. Daniel could see workers dipping water jugs into canals. They stopped and pointed at the prisoners, whispering. Were they slaves too? *Daniel wondered.*

The large bridge crossing the moat was covered with wooden beams. The beams could be removed in case the city came under siege. Anyone attacking the city would have to swim the moat, then climb the huge wall. Babylon was impossible to conquer.

The massive gate at the end of the bridge was open. As the prisoners walked forward, Daniel could see that there was an inner wall some distance from the outer wall. The gap between the two huge walls was filled with rubble. No one could cross the gap easily. If invaders somehow scaled the outer wall, they still would have to cross the rubble and scale the inner wall.

Pretty smart, *Daniel thought.*

After passing through a second large gate, the four boys entered the city and gasped. There were wide streets filled with people and carts and chariots with soldiers. They entered on Aa-ibursabu, the festival street, which ran right next to the Arahtu canal. Buildings on either side of the tree-covered avenues rose to over one hundred fifty feet high.

"It looks like they touch the sky," said Hananiah. "They're enormous."

Soon they passed the small temple of Ninip, which extended over both sides of the canal. Next they beheld E-sagila, the magnificently decorated great temple of Belus, dedicated to the god Merodach.

"One of the other slaves told me that the temple treasury holds wondrous articles made from gold and silver. Most of them have been captured by Nebuchadnezzar during his many wars," Mishael said.

They strained their necks as they saw the pyramidlike temple rise to over three hundred feet.

"Can you believe these streets?" Daniel asked. "They're paved with three-foot-square stone slabs. It must have taken many slaves to lift them into place."

Azariah pointed. "Look at the beautiful houses and walls made of sun-dried bricks. The mortar looks like black bitumen. And look! All of the bricks have the names and titles of Nebuchadnezzar imprinted on them."

They marched on toward Qasr, a richly decorated building that covered eleven acres.

Throughout the city they could see enormous colored reliefs of lions, bulls, dragons, and giant serpents. Huge hunting scenes depicted the chase of the lion and the leopard.

They must have many talented craftsmen, *thought Daniel.*

Eventually they passed the Ishtar Gate and the enormous Middle Palace, decorated with cedar and costly woods. The many doors were made of palm, cypress, ebony, and ivory and framed in silver and gold and plated with copper. The thresholds and hinges were of brass.

As the boys passed large statues of Ninus, Semiramis, and Jupiter-belus, Daniel said, "How sad. The Babylonians worship idols made by human hands and not Jehovah, the true God of heaven and earth."

Hananiah and his brothers were awed by the magnificent hanging gardens. Flowers, vines, and trees covered the rising terraces in a breathtaking display.

"I wish our mother was alive," Hananiah said sadly. "Remember how she could coax life out of the sickliest-looking plant?"

"How did they ever figure out the irrigation system?" Mishael asked in wonder. "Those engines that raise the water from the canal to the top of the terraces are unbelievable."

As the days passed, the changes in the boys' lives seemed incredible. Now they were eunuchs. The four boys were grateful, however, that they had had each other to cope with the difficult experience. With the pain behind them, they had to learn how to survive, how to adjust.

Daniel, Hananiah, Mishael, and Azariah soon began their education in the wisdom of the Chaldeans. The first step took place when Mukhtar, the superintendent in charge of their training, changed their names.

"You will no longer be known by your Hebrew names. You must forget your past. I am going to name you after our Babylonian gods."

Oh, great, *thought Daniel.*

"Daniel, you will be called Belteshazzar. Hananiah, I will name you Shadrach. Mishael, you shall be known as Meshach. Azariah, you will be addressed as Abednego. The sooner you realize that you are Babylonians, the happier will be your life. Service in the king's court is better than working in the fields. I too am a slave, you know."

"Mukhtar, will you please grant us a request?" Daniel asked respectfully.

"What do you want?"

"It is the food from the king's table."

"Are you not getting enough?"

"No, no. That is not it. There is too much to eat. It is not what we are used to. It is too rich for us. Is it possible for us to be fed vegetables and water instead?"

"What! You will become sickly and weak. If you lose your health, I will lose my head. The king will kill me for neglecting my responsibilities."

"Would you consider a test for ten days?"

"What kind of test?"

"Feed us only vegetables and water for ten days, and then compare us to the other youths eating from the king's rich food. If we look sickly, then we will eat their food also."

One of the lions roared and swatted a female. She cowered as he yawned and strutted around. Daniel could see his sharp white teeth even in the dim light.

"Jehovah, what is happening?" *he asked aloud.* "Why are you allowing me to live? Is there something you want me to do?"

Daniel's mind began to drift.

"I cannot believe that three years have passed," said Mukhtar. "When you first asked me to feed you only vegetables, I thought you were crazy. But you've been healthier than all of the other youths."

"Our God has given us strength," replied Daniel.

"It must be so. He has also given you wisdom. You have mastered our literature and science. You have shown yourselves to have understanding of dreams and visions. This is good . . . for you will stand before the king this day to be tested. He will ask you many questions to see what you have learned. I know that you will do well, for you are ten times smarter than the other youths I have trained. I am confident that the king will have you join his staff of skilled magicians and wise astrologers."

"We will serve wherever you place us, Mukhtar," Daniel told him. "But if we have any wisdom at all, it has been given to us by Jehovah."

FOURTEEN

"I'M SORRY, SIR, but you'll have to take off your belt and shoes. We're a little backed up today. The terrorist warning is high."

Murphy bit his lower lip and didn't say anything. It had taken him almost an hour to get through the security check.

Oh, boy. Now I get to wait for another hour and forty-five minutes before the flight. Patience was not one of his virtues. He didn't like to wait in lines or sit around the airport. It bothered him not to be active, doing something productive. He reached for his cell phone, dialed 411, and asked for the phone number of the Orlando Police Department.

As he waited for the automated voice to give him the number, Murphy watched people in the waiting room. He could see a young mother struggling with two rowdy little boys. Other people were also frustrated at having to wait. *The events of 9/11 have certainly changed the entire world*, he thought grimly.

He got the number, then selected the option to be connected automatically. Murphy gave the officer who answered his name and asked to be connected to Sergeant Owen East.

"Are you ready to order, sir?"

"Yes, we are." Murphy smiled at Isis. Her green eyes were sparkling, and her beautiful red hair framed her delicate features. She looked like a supermodel who had just stepped off a fashion runway. Who would have thought that she was an academic? Murphy felt like a schoolboy on his first date.

"It's good to see you, Isis," he said in an understatement. "You look great."

Her slight smile and her look almost melted him.

"Oh, by the way, I've got some great news," Murphy told her. "Vern will be returning to the States next week. The doctors in Turkey say that he's almost fully recovered. I talked to him on the phone from the airport."

"That's wonderful! I hope you don't have any more life-and-death adventures planned. I think Ararat was enough excitement to last for a lifetime," Isis said.

Murphy paused.

At his look, she narrowed her eyes. "Does your hesitation mean what I think it means?"

Murphy looked a little sheepish. "I know. I know. But this is a possible archaeological discovery that would help verify the Bible . . . like finding the ark did."

For the rest of the meal, Murphy explained his most recent episode with Methuselah and the contents of the envelope. He concluded, "We could find Belshazzar's famous Handwriting on the Wall. I think that Methuselah was telling us it is in Babylon."

"*We?*"

Murphy smiled. "Yes, *we*. I need your help. You have the expertise to determine the validity of the writing."

"You need my expertise!" Isis's normally soft Scottish brogue sounded a little irritated. Murphy realized that he hadn't communicated what he really wanted to say. He leaned forward, stretched out a hand toward her, and said soberly, "Isis, I want *you* to go with me. Even if we don't find anything, I want you by my side."

FIFTEEN

IT WAS 7:00 P.M. when Murphy drove his old Dodge into the parking lot of the Quiet River Nursing Home.

The gray-haired receptionist greeted him with a smile. He asked for Dr. Harley B. Anderson and was directed to the library, down the hall on the left.

All nursing homes smell the same, Murphy thought as he strode down the corridor.

There was only one person in the small library when Murphy entered. The elderly man seated at the desk had a full head of bushy white hair. He was neatly dressed in a sports shirt and khaki pants, bifocals perched on the tip of his nose. He was deeply engrossed in a book. He didn't look like someone who was out of his mind and not in touch with reality.

"Excuse me, sir. Would you happen to be Dr. Anderson?"

The man lifted his head and paused. Murphy could see Anderson was trying to figure out how a stranger knew his name.

"Yes, I'm Dr. Anderson, young man."

Murphy stuck out his hand. "My name is Dr. Michael Murphy. I'm a professor at Preston University in Raleigh, North Carolina. Do you mind if I join you?"

"Be my guest," the older man answered. "Have we met before? My memory seems to be fading a little."

"No, sir. I became acquainted with you through a newspaper article and a Sergeant East of the Orlando Police Department. The article mentioned something about your concerns over the end of the world."

Anderson sat up quickly. His eyes brightened and the weariness seemed to erase from his face. "What did you say you were a professor of?"

"I didn't say, but I'm a professor of biblical archaeology."

"So you know a lot about the Bible?"

"You might say that. I've studied the Bible for many years."

"Good! Then maybe I've finally found someone who will understand. Let me start at the beginning of the story. I am an embryologist. I was one of the early pioneers in the field of artificial insemination and invitro fertilization. Of course, I've long since retired. Anyway, in 1967, I was working with a gynecologist named Dr. J. M. Talpish on a project in Transylvania, Romania."

As Murphy listened, it didn't take him long to realize that Dr. Anderson was not suffering from Alzheimer's or another brain disorder. The man was as rational as Murphy himself.

Dr. Anderson continued, "We discovered a process to artificially inseminate motile spermatozoa into female eggs outside of the womb. This was done under high-powered microscopes in the laboratory. The fertilized eggs remained in salt solutions in petri dishes until they were implanted into the endometrial lining of the uterus of the birth mother."

"Excuse me, Dr. Anderson, it's my understanding that the first in vitro fertilization and successful birth took place in England in 1978. I believe Drs. Steptoe and Edwards were the first pioneers."

Dr. Anderson frowned. "They were the ones who got the *credit* for being first . . . but Talpish and I were about twelve years ahead of them. We weren't allowed to publish our results or talk to anyone about them."

Murphy was really interested now.

Dr. Anderson continued, hardly taking a breath. He had a secret that he wanted to divulge and Murphy had a listening ear. "We artificially inseminated a donor egg and implanted it into the uterus of a young Gypsy woman, a girl of about eighteen years of age. It was a very strange situation. We were hired by a group of people who identified themselves as Friends of the New World Order. They paid us a great deal of money to artificially inseminate the girl."

"When you say strange, what do you mean?"

"Well, this group of people provided the egg and also the semen. Our job was to put them together and implant an egg into the girl. We were sworn to absolute secrecy. We stayed with the project until the birth of the child. It was a boy. Then—"

"Then what?" Murphy was fascinated.

"My associate, Dr. Talpish, was killed in a mysterious automobile accident. I soon realized that it was *not* an accident. I believe the group of people who hired us had him murdered. To protect myself, I shipped all of my papers and project notes to my daughter in the United States. She placed them into a safe deposit box. I left instructions with her that if I were to die mysteriously she should mail the notes to the newspapers.

"It wasn't long after the death of Dr. Talpish that some of the group that had hired us paid me a visit. I had the feeling that they were going to do something to me, so I spoke up before they had a chance. I told them that I had sent my papers to the United States for safekeeping. They were irate, threatened me. They told me that if I ever said anything to anyone, they would kill my wife and my daughter. And they meant it!"

"Is your family still alive?"

"No, a couple years later my wife passed away. It was a natural death. I then went to live with my daughter. She never married. She died of liver disease about a year ago. Then I came to live in this home."

"Have you heard from the group again?" Murphy asked.

"No, they've left me alone. I think they don't want to stir things up."

"So why are you walking the streets telling your story now?"

"I guess I want to clear my conscience," the old man said. "I think we did something terribly bad. I was able to follow up on the boy the Gypsy woman bore for about five years and then I lost contact. I think the group moved the woman somewhere—or got rid of her. I'm not sure. Recently I started doing some reading about prophecy and the Bible. What I read frightened me. It talked about a coming evil person who would rule the world. The more I read, the more I became convinced that Dr. Talpish and I had possibly helped in the birth of that person. It's all in my papers in the safe deposit box."

Murphy was riveted.

"I've been diagnosed with leukemia; the doctors have given me only a few months to live. My wife and daughter are dead, and I will soon be joining them. What possible harm can the group do to me now?" Dr. Anderson asked with a wry smile. "I want to try to do something to make up for my past actions. I need to alert people of the danger ahead. I feel so guilty, like Judas in the Bible—the one who betrayed Jesus. How can God ever forgive me?"

A look of frustration and fear came over his face.

Murphy could sense the pain that he must have been carrying for years. "God will forgive you," he said emphatically. "He forgives anyone who will come to Him, no matter how wicked or selfish they have been."

"I haven't been concerned about God for my eighty-plus years. It's too late for me now."

"It's never too late. Do you remember the story of Jesus' death on the cross? Two other men were crucified with him that day. They were both thieves. One of them asked Jesus to save him—just minutes before he was to die. Jesus said, 'This day you will be with me in paradise.' The same could be true for you, Dr. Anderson," Murphy said sincerely, "if you would only invite Him into your life."

"Excuse me." The gray-haired receptionist entered the library, smiled at the two men, and said, "I'm sorry, but visiting hours are over. I'm afraid that you'll have to leave now. If you want to continue your conversation with Dr. Anderson, it will have to be tomorrow."

"You must come back tomorrow! I have much more to tell you," Dr. Anderson exclaimed.

Later, back in his motel room, Murphy sat on the bed trying to process his talk with the old doctor.

Could it be true? Could Anderson and his partner have been in on the birth of the Anti-Christ? That would mean that he is alive today . . . about thirty-eight.

Murphy knew that if he was ever going to get to sleep, he'd have to change what he was thinking about. He turned on the television and began to unpack his suitcase. He had just stepped out of the bathroom when something caught his attention.

The announcer said, "We have a late-breaking story. A bizarre animal attack took place today when a Sergeant Owen East, of the Orlando Police Department, was nearly killed by a falcon. Eyewitnesses state that they saw a large bird, which some believe was a falcon, swoop down out of the sky and land on the sergeant. He was leaving work when the incident took place. Another off-duty officer ran to his aid. He was able to beat off the bird with his nightstick. Doctors at Mercy Hospital say that Sergeant East is in critical condition. Dr. Alfred Fordham, the physician in charge, says that the officer's voice box was severely damaged and there was a great deal of blood loss. On another news front—"

That has to be Talon's work!

SIXTEEN

THE BLACK SUV pulled under a willow tree by the curb and stopped. As Talon rolled down the window, classical music could be heard coming from within.

He smiled. *Two for one. This will be a good day.*

He opened up a book by Edgar Allan Poe and began to read.

"Dr. Murphy. I'm so glad to see you," Dr. Anderson said, smiling broadly. "Would you mind if we went for a walk and talked? This nursing home is quite depressing. It's nice to be with someone young whose mind is still good."

"That would be fine, it's a beautiful day. I noticed a small park not far from here. There's a coffee shop next to it. We could get something to drink and maybe even a cinnamon roll."

"You've discovered my weakness. I go there often." Dr. Anderson grinned.

Murphy and Dr. Anderson strolled down the path by the park. Magnificent willows shaded the walkway.

"Dr. Murphy, before you arrived I went to the office at Quiet River. The chief operating officer is a notary. I had him witness this letter." Dr. Anderson handed Murphy a single sheet of paper.

Federated Bank & Trust
New York City, New York

To Whom It May Concern:

The bearer of this letter, Dr. Michael Murphy, has been given permission by me to retrieve items out of my safe deposit box. Because of health conditions, my doctors will not allow me to travel great distances. I therefore have given Dr. Murphy the power of attorney to act on my behalf.

Please afford him your kind assistance. Thank you for your help in this matter.

Most sincerely yours,

Harley B. Anderson

Harley B. Anderson, M.D.
Quiet River Nursing Home

Witnessed by *Lenny H. Harris*
Florida Notary # 12331

"I'm not sure I understand." Murphy looked up at Dr. Anderson, puzzled.

"Dr. Murphy, I don't have a great deal of time left. I need to get that information into the hands of someone who can alert the proper people. I think you are that person. I know that we just met yesterday, but there's something about you I trust. Would you please do this for a dying old man?"

The plea in Anderson's eyes was hard to resist.

"Of course I will," Murphy said. "I'd be happy to help you."

"Thank you so very much. You don't know what that means to me."

Talon turned down the music, rolled up the window, and started the SUV. *Now it's payback time for my little swim in the Black Sea, Dr. Murphy.*

His eyes focused on Murphy and his load of coffee and rolls.

Patience. Just have patience. It's a virtue, you know.

Murphy wasn't aware of the SUV behind him as he came out of the coffee shop. He was looking at Dr. Anderson, who was standing near a park bench. Murphy's hands were loaded with coffee and cinnamon rolls, and he was trying not to drop anything. Only as he neared Dr. Anderson did he notice that something was wrong. The old man's eyes were wide and his mouth was gaping open as he stared at something behind Murphy that terrified him.

Murphy's martial arts training instantly kicked into gear. Dropping the coffee and rolls, he leaped forward, trying to grab for the doctor. As their hands touched, he could hear the roar of the SUV closing in at great speed.

Murphy tried to jump to the side and pull Dr. Anderson with

him, but it was too late. He could feel the doctor being ripped from his grip as the left front fender of the SUV hit the old man and sent him flying in the air. Murphy had moved just far enough away that he bounced off the side of the SUV and rolled away, dazed but alive.

Talon, not bothering to get out of the SUV, believed he had accomplished his task. Pleased, he stepped on the gas and disappeared around a corner. Murphy pulled himself together and limped over to Dr. Anderson. He seemed to still be breathing . . . but it was shallow.

"Doctor! Doctor! Hang on! I'll get some help!"

A feeble hand reached up. Murphy bent until his ear was close to the doctor's mouth. "The key. Around my neck," Dr. Anderson whispered.

Murphy could see a chain around the old man's neck. Blood was oozing out over it.

"I want to be like the thief . . . on the cross," Dr. Anderson murmured before his eyes fluttered closed one last time.

SEVENTEEN

MURPHY KNEW that Levi Abrams was a complicated man. He had been born in Israel and had gone to college in the United States. Then, immediately upon graduation, he had joined the Israeli Army. Tall and muscular, he soon came to the attention of Mossad—Israel's Institute for Intelligence and Special Operations. The group recruited Abrams for top-secret work. Murphy could never get him to talk about what he had done during his years with Mossad.

Although Abrams said that he had retired from Mossad and was now living in the United States, Murphy wasn't too sure. He was too well connected in the Middle East and Arab countries, and he knew too much about current covert operations. Murphy believed that Abrams's job as a security expert for a high-tech company in the Raleigh-Durham area was just a cover. Levi might have just the information Murphy needed, so Murphy phoned his old friend.

"How are you, Michael? I heard about your wrestling match with an SUV," Abrams said as soon as he got on the line.

"How did you hear about that?"

"You'd be surprised what I know, Michael. But if I told you, you know I'd have to kill you." Abrams's grin could be heard in his voice.

Murphy laughed. "I think you'd have a difficult time. I've learned some new karate moves."

"You sound a little cocky for someone who barely escaped with his life. Don't forget you're talking to the master teacher."

"Oh, I beg your pardon, O Great One. Is it possible for a lowly student to get some time with the Great Master?"

"What's on your mind, Michael?"

"Does the name Methuselah ring any bells?"

"What does that old buzzard want now?"

"I think he's given me a clue to another biblical artifact—the Handwriting on the Wall. The one written on Nebuchadnezzar's wall by the hand of God."

"You've got to be kidding, Michael. Do you really trust Methuselah?"

"Not very far. But he *has* led us to some great finds in the past."

"So, how can I help?"

"I need you to pull some strings and help me get back into Iraq. I have to go to Babylon, and you have all the connections."

There was a pause. "Are you serious, Michael? I think you have a death wish. There may not be SUVs trying to run you down, but there are roadside bombs, random mortar attacks, and kidnappings. Do you want to lose your head to a sword?"

Ignoring Abrams's question, Murphy continued, "I'm planning to take Isis with me. She's going to contact the Parchments of Freedom Foundation to see if they'll fund the trip like they did for the Ararat expedition. There's a good chance that they will."

"Oh, great! Now you're going to take a beautiful redheaded

American woman with you. Do you think she won't attract attention? I think you hit your head in your last adventure. Iraq is not
the safest place for civilians."

"Could we at least get together to discuss it?"

"When were you thinking about going?"

"Within a month or two. I'm going to fly up to New York on
some business. Isis is going to fly up from D.C., and we're going to
go over the details."

"Maybe we could get together in New York. Some friends have
asked me to attend to certain matters there."

"Friends?"

There was another pause. "Michael, let's just say that they need
some information to make effective business decisions."

EIGHTEEN

EUGENE SIMPSON GLANCED at his watch as he pulled up next to the Gulfstream IV jet. With a sigh of relief, he shifted the polished ebony Mercedes into park and got out. *Whew!...Just on time.*

He had worked for Barrington Communications for three years and had been late only once. One mistake is all any employee ever had with Shane Barrington, one of the richest and most powerful men in the world.

As Simpson opened the back door, he looked into Barrington's flint-gray eyes. It gave him the chills. He quickly stepped back and stood at attention like a trained soldier. The athletic frame of the coldhearted corporate warrior emerged. He straightened the coat of his $2,500 suit and looked around.

The soft gray hair at his temples whipped around in the slight breeze. Simpson looked at his employer's high cheekbones and thin lips. His large body and confident stance were very imposing.

"Get the bags, Eugene."

It was slightly overcast when the jet put down in Zurich. The damp dark weather matched Barrington's spirit. He was not happy at being there. He was getting a little tired of being ordered around by seven pompous, smug, power-hungry egomaniacs. He'd about had his fill.

Careful, Barrington. They've helped to make you rich and can destroy you too. They do control your purse strings, you know ... at least for now.

He felt his chest and stomach muscles tighten when the chauffeur drove up to take him to the castle.

Why do they always send that creepy driver who has no tongue? Oh, well. At least I don't have to listen to him jabber.

In about fifteen minutes the limousine broke through the low clouds. The sky was blue and the sun shone on the snow-covered Alps. It took about another hour before Barrington could see the gothic spires of the castle in the distance. They didn't look quite as foreboding as the last time he was there.

Maybe I'm getting used to it, he told himself. *If it wasn't for those egomaniacs, this would be a beautiful place to visit.*

The chauffeur let Barrington off in front of the giant wooden door. Inside the large entry hall, he walked past suits of armor standing like lifeless sentries for some medieval king. Torches that usually burned brightly were out. The whole place seemed eerie and uninviting—deserted. His footsteps echoed loudly on the stone floors.

By now he knew the routine. He strode to the large stainless steel door at the south end of the hall, which hissed open to allow him to enter, then hissed shut. He pushed the down button. *All aboard. First stop, Hell.*

It had been Hell, all right. Especially the night he first met Talon as his son Arthur lay on a bed with a breathing mask over his face. He recalled the conversation.

"Talon? What kind of name is that, a first name or a last name?"

He could hear the South African accent like it was yesterday.

"It makes no difference. I use it because it is a tribute to the only serious wound I have ever gotten in my life as a warrior. The first falcon I raised and trained as a boy in South Africa—the last thing I allowed myself to grow attached to—turned on me one day and ripped my index finger off my hand."

Barrington remembered Talon removing the glove of his right hand and displaying what looked like a flesh-colored finger, except where the fingertip should have a nail, the whole tip was honed to a sharp point. The artificial finger was in reality a deadly killing weapon. And Talon used his finger of death quite effectively.

Even as hardened as Barrington was, he shuddered as he remembered Talon using his finger to cut the breathing tube that fed life-giving air to his son, Arthur. Barrington watched silently as his son slowly suffocated to death. He really didn't love the boy, but he was angry with himself. *Why didn't I try to stop Talon? It was cold-blooded murder, and I did nothing to stop it.*

He could feel his fists clenching tightly as the elevator came to a stop and the door hissed open.

Barrington's attention shifted to the ornately carved wooden chair in the center of the darkened room. A light came down from the ceiling and lit it up. He could see the gargoyles on the arms. He remembered grabbing them on other occasions.

Well, let's get this over. Time to take the hot seat.

He sat down in the chair and looked at the long table in front of him covered with the bloodred cloth. No one was seated in the seven chairs behind the table. In the ominous silence, Barrington could hear his own heartbeat.

This is like going to the principal's office in high school. They make you sit outside and sweat for a while before they talk to you. I know their game.

Ten minutes passed before the Seven entered and took their places.

Not very brave. They shine lights in my face so I can't make out who they are. But someday I'll find out. Then we'll see how brave they are.

John Bartholomew was the first to speak. "You're a little late, Mr. Barrington. Do we need to buy you a Swiss watch?"

The sarcastic tone inflamed Barrington. *Just smile and ignore it.* "That might be a good idea. Do you know where I can get one?"

"Are we a little testy today, Mr. Barrington?"

Barrington knew he had better cut out the sarcasm. He was on their turf, and they had the power . . . this time. He was forming his response when General Li spoke.

"Yes, we are very concerned. What was Dr. Murphy doing in Orlando with a Dr. Harley B. Anderson? Our messenger failed to dispatch both of them, and we are quite disturbed."

The voice of a German woman broke in. "We want you to find out more information about this Dr. Michael Murphy. We are not satisfied with what we are getting. What are your plans for procuring this information for us?"

Barrington knew he really was in the hot seat. "I have one of my best investigative reporters following up on Dr. Murphy right now."

"Is that a fact, Mr. Barrington?" came the smooth response of Señor Mendez. "Would that reporter happen to be Stephanie Kovacs?"

How do these people get all this information? Barrington thought angrily.

Mendez continued silkily, "Isn't she also your live-in lover?" The man's voice had an unmistakable smirk in it.

Barrington was desperately trying to think how to respond when Sir William Merton spoke up.

"Can you trust her, Mr. Barrington? We do not have much patience with those who are not loyal," he said, stroking his clerical collar.

Barrington bristled. He didn't like being threatened by anyone—especially by people who hid in the dark. His hands gripped the gargoyles tightly as he said icily, "I can trust her. She always pursues a story to the end. I also have a student in one of Murphy's classes working for me—Paul Wallach. Between these two people, I think you will get the information you need."

"You had better hope so, Mr. Barrington. Your health depends on it," Bartholomew stated firmly.

If someone had talked to me that way when I lived on the streets of Detroit, they wouldn't still be standing, Barrington swore silently.

"Our recommendation is that you watch her very carefully. Are we clear about this?"

Barrington clenched his teeth tighter.

"I didn't hear your response, Mr. Barrington."

Now it had come to a push-and-shove game. The Seven were testing him as to who was in control and who had the power.

"I understand."

"What did you say, Mr. Barrington? I couldn't hear you," Bartholomew repeated.

It was plain to see that they not only wanted submission but they also wanted to humiliate him.

"I said I UNDERSTAND!"

"Well, it's nice to have you on board. And by the way... next time don't be late."

Barrington bit his tongue. His mind was racing as he got up and left. *Who do these people think they are... having me fly all the way across the Atlantic for a short meeting like this! They could have phoned the same information. They just want to let me know who is in control. I don't know how much more of this I'm going to take.*

NINETEEN

MURPHY GLANCED at his watch. *Ten minutes to nine. You'd better get going.*

He finished his last sip of coffee and tossed the cup into a trash container. Then he got up, stretched, gathered his notes, and took a deep breath. The scent of magnolias filled the air. This quiet spot on campus was a haven to think and pray before his classes started.

Many of the students were already seated when he entered the lecture hall. Murphy walked down the stairs to the platform and opened his briefcase. Then he took out his notes and glanced around the room. Shari was talking with two students on one side of the room. Paul Wallach was seated on the other side.

I guess they're still having problems, he thought.

A number of students were gathered in a group toward the back.

"Please take your seats," Murphy announced. "We're going to begin."

As the group began to split up, he saw that they had been gathered around Stephanie Kovacs.

Three lectures in a row. I wonder why she's spending so much time at Preston . . . and in my class.

"Good morning, class. Today we're going to continue our historical look at the great city of Babylon. We have already seen that it was a huge city with majestic buildings, paved streets, drainage systems, and a vast network of irrigation canals. The dimensions of the largest canal can still be traced. It left the Euphrates at Hit and skirted the desert and ran southeast for over four hundred miles to the Persian Gulf, where it emptied into the Bay of Grane. Over the years, the city has been ruled by a number of great leaders, including Hammurabi, Nebuchadnezzar, Cyrus the Great, and Alexander the Great.

"In 539 B.C. the Persians captured Babylon. Later King Xerxes I of Persia destroyed part of the city. From that point on the great city of Babylon began to decline. The writer Dio comments that when Trajan visited Babylon in A.D. 116, he saw 'nothing but mound and stones and ruins.' "

Murphy could see a little bit of a glassy stare as the class began to swim in historical details. *Maybe this will recapture their attention*, he thought with a grin.

"Does the name Saddam Hussein ring any bells with you? Are you aware that Saddam began the rebuilding of the city of Babylon in the early 1980s?"

Murphy turned on the PowerPoint projector. Slides of many new buildings and huge walls were projected at the front of the room.

"This next slide is a quote from Saddam Hussein given in 1979.

"What is most important to me about Nebuchadnezzar is the link between the Arabs' abilities and the liberation of Palestine. Nebuchadnezzar was, after all, an Arab from Iraq, albeit ancient Iraq. Nebuchadnezzar was the one who brought the bound Jewish slaves from Palestine. That is why, whenever I remember Nebuchadnezzar, I like to remind the Arabs—Iraqis in particular—of their historical responsibilities. It is a burden that should not stop them from action, but rather spur them into action because of their history."

Saddam Hussein, 1979
quoted by David Lamb in the *Los Angeles Times*

"Before the war in Iraq and the capture of Saddam Hussein, he had three overriding goals: gaining territory, gaining economic power, and eliminating Israel as a nation. Although he will now never be able to accomplish these objectives, we need to keep our eyes on Iraq and the city of Babylon."

Murphy could see that he had again caught the students' attention.

"In the Bible, the Book of Revelation contains over 404 verses. In Chapters Seventeen and Eighteen there are forty-two verses that deal with what I believe is the literal rebuilt city of Babylon. When you add Revelation Fourteen: Eight and Sixteen: Nineteen, which discuss Babylon's future, you have forty-four verses talking about this city. In other words, it is important enough that ten percent of the Book of Revelation speaks of the fate of Babylon."

"Dr. Murphy, why do you think that Babylon is so important?" Paul Wallach asked.

That's the first time Paul has spoken up in a long time. I'm glad he finally decided to participate.

"That's a good question, Paul. I think it is important because Babylon was the first city where organized rebellion against God took place. We find that in Genesis Chapter Eleven. Babylon was the capital city of the first world ruler, Nimrod. He was also the king of Babylon, as was Nebuchadnezzar, who destroyed the city of Jerusalem and the temple in 586 B.C. Babylon was the city from which four Gentile empires ruled over Jerusalem."

Murphy brought up the next slide on the projector. "Another reason I believe it is important is found in Revelation Seventeen: Five. Look at some pretty strong words from the Apostle John."

> **MYSTERY,**
> **BABYLON THE GREAT**
> **THE MOTHER OF HARLOTS**
> **AND OF THE**
> **ABOMINATIONS OF THE EARTH.**
> Revelation 17:5

"The great historian Arnold Toynbee suggested to his readers that Babylon would be the best place in the world to build a future world cultural metropolis. In fact, there are some who believe that not only will Babylon be a cultural center, but it will become an economic center as well. According to bible prophecy, that center will house the one-world government, one-world religion, and one-world commerce."

Wallach raised his hand again. "Why do they think that Babylon is that important?"

"I think there are a couple of reasons, Paul. An obvious answer is that it is in the center of much of the world's oil production. Oil is one of the driving economic factors for all countries. Another reason would be to help rebuild Iraq in such a way as to placate and ease the tensions in the Arab world. The hope might be to take on a more tolerant view of the various radical groups in the Muslim cultures. In this way they might hope to decrease terrorist activities. However, I don't think a renewal of Babylon will accomplish the desired goal."

Murphy could see that, by now, even Stephanie Kovacs was taking notes.

"Let me come back to the thoughts about Babylon becoming an economic center. For the past few decades, we have witnessed the rise of what is called the European Union. This is a family of democratic European countries that have banded together for the purpose of peace and prosperity. It was initially made up of only six countries: Belgium, Germany, France, Italy, Luxembourg, and the Netherlands. Later they were joined by Denmark, Ireland, and the United Kingdom. Greece joined the group in 1981, and Spain and Portugal in 1986. They were followed by Austria, Finland, and Sweden. Even more countries have applied for membership. Some have referred to this union as the United States of Europe. The European Union is growing and needs large supplies of oil. For that oil, the member nations are beginning to turn their focus toward the Arab countries."

Murphy clicked up another slide. "You will notice on this next slide two mottoes, or slogans. Note the difference between them. This has a lot to do with philosophy and focus."

UNITED STATES OF AMERICA
"UNITED WE STAND."

EUROPEAN UNION
"UNITY IN DIVERSITY."

"By uniting together, members of the European Union have raised the standard of living for Europeans during the last half century. They have been fostering cooperation among the member nations while still promoting diversity. One of the ways they have united is by the establishment of a new monetary system utilizing what is called the euro. This has strengthened Europe's voice in the world's marketplace. In fact, the euro is more stable and valuable than the U.S. dollar. The United States is operating with a $435 billion trade deficit; the European Union, however, can boast a $26 billion trade *surplus*. Together the member nations have a fourteen percent larger economy than the United States. The next slide shows what has already been established by the European Union."

European Union

- European Parliament
- Council of the European Union
- European Commission
- Court of Justice
- Court of Auditors

- European Economic and
  Social Committee
- Committee of the Regions
- European Central Bank
- European Ombudsman
- European Investment Bank
- Europe Day—May 9

"The motto 'Unity in Diversity' is symbolized by a woman riding the back of a large bull. She is holding a flag with ten stars in a circle. The ten stars represent the original ten countries that founded the union. Also riding on the back of the bull are smaller people all waving the flags of the various member nations."

"What does that symbolize?" Don West asked.

"It comes from Greek mythology, Don. According to the legend, Mother Earth and Father Heaven had two children named Cronus and Rhea. Cronus and Rhea produced a son by the name of Zeus. As the story goes, Zeus was watching a young maiden named Europa playing and talking with her girlfriends."

"It doesn't sound like much has changed," said Clayton Anderson. "We're still watching the girls."

The students whistled and catcalled.

"I guess you're the expert, Clayton," Murphy replied, to the amusement of the class.

"If I may continue. Cupid shot one of his arrows into Zeus, and he fell in love with Europa. He transformed himself into a handsome bull of chestnut color with a silver circle on his brow and horns like a crescent moon. Europa and her girlfriends walked up to the bull and petted it. Europa said, 'I bet I could ride the creature. It looks so calm and gentle.' That was her mistake. When she sat on the bull, it got up and ran across the ocean. Europa held on for dear life. Later Zeus married Europa, and they lived on the island of Crete. Their sons became very famous and powerful. Although their names are forgotten, hers is not. It is believed that the continent of Europe was named after Europa. The maiden riding a beast is a reminder of Zeus and Europa. It foreshadows the birth of a continent that will become very famous, powerful, and influential."

As Murphy punched up the next slide, the bell rang. "Hold on a minute, gang. I want to give you a reading assignment for the next session."

There were audible groans from all over the lecture hall.

"I want you to read Chapter Two of the Book of Daniel. It talks about Nebuchadnezzar's dream of a large statue. I think it will help to clarify some issues about the European Union and coming future events."

TWENTY

AS THE STUDENTS were making their way out of the lecture hall, Stephanie Kovacs walked down the steps to the platform where Murphy was putting away his notes.

"Good morning, Stephanie. I was surprised to see you again."

"I was still in town, Dr. Murphy, and I thought I'd catch your lecture again. I enjoyed it. You have some thought-provoking ideas. Do you really think that Babylon will develop into an economic and cultural center?"

"As a matter of fact, I do. I think it will rise to prominence once again as part of fulfilling the various prophecies in the Bible."

"I'm afraid that I'm not well versed in the Bible, let alone in any prophecies. Can you give me an example of what you are talking about?"

Murphy reached into his briefcase and pulled out his Bible. "Let

me read you a passage from the Book of Revelation—Chapter
Eighteen, beginning at Verse Nine. It's talking about how people
around the world will mourn the fall of Babylon.

"The kings of the earth who committed fornication and
lived luxuriously with her will weep and lament for her,
when they see the smoke of her burning standing at a distance
for fear of her torment, saying, 'Alas, Alas, the great city of
Babylon, that mighty city! For in one hour your judgment has
come.' And the merchants of the earth will weep and mourn
over her, for no one buys their merchandise anymore:
merchandise of gold and silver, precious stones and pearls,
fine linen and purple, silk and scarlet, every kind of citron
wood, every kind of object of ivory, every kind of object and
most precious wood, bronze, iron, and marble; and cinnamon
and incense, fragrant oil and frankincense, wine and oil, fine
flour and wheat, cattle and sheep, horses and chariots, and
bodies and souls of men. The fruit that your soul longed for
has gone from you, and all the things which are rich and
splendid have gone from you, and you shall find them no more
at all. The merchants of these things, who became rich by her,
will stand at a distance for fear of her torment, weeping and
wailing, and saying, 'Alas, alas, that great city that was clothed
in fine linen, purple, and scarlet, and adorned with gold and
precious stones and pearls! For in one hour such great riches
came to nothing.' Every shipmaster, all who travel by ship,
sailors, and as many as trade on the sea, stood at a distance
and cried out when they saw the smoke of her burning, saying
'What is like this great city?'

"This prophecy was written by the Apostle John in A.D. 95 after
Babylon had already fallen into ruins. He was talking about a future

destruction that will come to pass. This is especially interesting since Saddam started the rebuilding of Babylon."

"I was fascinated by the symbol of the woman riding the bull as a symbol of the European Union. Do you have any other information about that?"

"Why don't you come to my next lecture and find out?"

"I wish I could, but I'll be out of town," Kovacs responded.

"Well, let's go over to the student center and get a cup of coffee, and I'll fill you in. Do you have the time?"

"Sure." *Maybe this time I'll be able to tell him.*

Kovacs took a sip of coffee and looked around at the students sitting at tables, laughing and flirting with each other. *Those were innocent days. How I wish I could return to them.*

"Where would you like to begin?" Murphy asked.

"Do you mind if I take a few notes?"

"Be my guest."

"Tell me about this statue. I don't understand it."

"Well, it started when King Nebuchadnezzar had a dream about a large statue that had a head of gold, a chest of silver, a body of bronze, legs of iron, and feet of iron and clay mixed together. He couldn't understand this image."

"Neither do I."

"Daniel informed the king that the golden head represented his kingdom and power. The chest and arms of silver stood for the kingdom that was to follow Nebuchadnezzar's. It wouldn't be as strong and influential as his was. That was the Medo-Persian Empire. It would be followed by the Greek Empire, represented by the bronze body. The two legs of iron stood for the Roman Empire, which broke into two sections. The feet of iron and clay mixed together illustrated ten kingdoms that were to come."

"Nebuchadnezzar must have had a bad pizza that night."

Murphy laughed and nodded. "Many Bible scholars believe that the ten toes of the image represent ten kingdoms of the revived Roman Empire. They think that they will arise out of the European Union."

"Didn't you mention that there were more than ten countries in the European Union?"

"Yes, there are more right now. Many people feel that there are other possibilities as to what those ten toes represent. Some think that there will eventually be a merging of several countries together. Others think that the ten toes represent ten regions of world commerce. That's probably the most plausible explanation."

"By regions, what do you mean?" Kovacs got her pen ready.

"It has been suggested that the regions are Europe, the Far East, the Mideast, North America, South America, South Asia, Central Asia, Australia and New Zealand, Southern Africa, and Central Africa. Of course, only time will tell. But right now, we can see the rise of Europe. It's becoming more and more powerful and is beginning to have a stronger voice in world affairs."

"I've heard it said that what the world needs is a world leader. Someone who can bring about peace. Do you believe that this will one day happen?"

"Most certainly! The Bible calls him the Anti-Christ. Some people think he may be alive today. He'll unite the nations at first and seem to bring about peace. However, that's just a ploy. He'll soon become a dictator and take control economically, socially, and spiritually."

"You mean like a Hitler or Stalin, or Mao Zedong?"

"I think he'll be much worse," Murphy said soberly. "The Bible also talks about a rapture, where the believers in God are taken out of the world before a final world war called the battle of Armageddon. Those who don't believe in God will be left behind to go through a period of great tribulation."

"Yes, I've heard that discussed before. It all sounds pretty scary," Kovacs replied. "And pretty unbelievable. Like a novel."

"It doesn't have to be," Murphy told her.

"What do you mean?" Kovacs looked puzzled.

"Well, people don't have to be left behind. All they need to do is ask Christ to come into their lives and change them from the inside out.

"Stephanie, do you remember the last time we talked, I used an illustration about a kite and how God speaks to us through our conscience and through the Bible? Another illustration comes out of the Book of Revelation. It is found in the third chapter and the twentieth verse. It says, *'Look! I have been standing at the door, and I am constantly knocking. If anyone hears me calling him and opens the door, I will come in and fellowship with him and he with me.'*

"It's a picture of Christ standing at the door of your heart. He would like to come in, but He's a gentleman. He won't force His way in. He just patiently knocks and waits for the door to open. He keeps calling and hoping that His still small voice will be heard. He knocks at everyone's heart's door. It is sort of like the pull of the string on the kite. Stephanie, do you hear Him knocking at your heart's door?" Murphy stopped talking.

Kovacs waited a minute before she said, "I'm afraid, Dr. Murphy."

"Afraid of what, Stephanie?"

"Afraid of the changes I would have to make in my lifestyle."

Murphy nodded. "I know. It may not be easy, but God will give you the strength."

"I'm still scared. I don't think I'm ready for that."

"That's okay. God has plenty of time. You can open your heart's door to Him when you are ready. It doesn't have to be in a church or with anyone else present. You can do it when you are all alone. All you have to do is pray a little prayer to Him. Something like this: 'God, I realize that I am a sinner and I have done wrong. I believe that You died on the cross to pay the penalty for my sins. I believe that You rose from the dead to create a new life for me. I would like to experience that new life. Please forgive me. I want to follow You. Please change my life. Please help me to learn to live for You. Thank You for doing this for me. Amen.' "

Stephanie was staring off into space.

"Let me write out a verse for you that I've found helpful. You can memorize it." Murphy wrote out the verse and handed it to Kovacs. They talked about it for a few minutes, then Don West came up to their table.

"Excuse me, Dr. Murphy. I saw Shari Nelson a few minutes ago. She said if I saw you around campus to let you know that you had an important message in your office."

"Thank you, Don."

Murphy turned back to Stephanie. "If you'll excuse me, I think I should attend to this message. Shari doesn't track me down unless it's something urgent."

"Sure, I understand. Maybe we could continue this conversation at another time." *Why do we keep getting interrupted just when I'm going to talk to Dr. Murphy about the danger he is in? It's almost like some force is fighting against me.*

Stephanie sat there watching Murphy walk away. She then looked at the verse he had written down for her.

I have learned the secret of contentment in every situation, whether it be a full stomach or hunger, plenty or want; for I can do everything God asks me to with the help of Christ who gives me the strength and power.

Philippians 4:12-13

TWENTY-ONE

"BOY, YOU'RE IN TROUBLE NOW!" Shari said with a smirk as Murphy entered the office.

Murphy chuckled. With that smirk on her face and her black pigtails, she was a sight to behold. Shari definitely had her own unique style. "Trouble?"

"There's a note on your desk. Dean Archer Fallworth wants to see you in his office at eleven A.M. He sounded a little upset on the phone."

"Do you know what it's about?"

"He didn't say. All he wanted me to do was to make sure that you got the message. He's probably jealous that so many students are taking your class in biblical archaeology. I think he's wound a little too tight."

———

Murphy could feel his stomach tightening as he approached Fallworth's office in the arts and science building. Their working relationship had not been an easy one.

I wonder what he's going to complain about this time.

Fallworth glanced up from his desk as Murphy entered. Fallworth's hand trembled slightly as he tried to keep his facial expression under control. "I want to talk to you about your class," he said curtly. "I understand that you are pushing religion on your students again."

Murphy could feel his temper beginning to simmer. "I'm not quite sure if I understand what you mean. I *am* teaching a course in biblical archaeology, and we discuss religious topics in the process. It's part of the curriculum."

"My sources suggest that you are using your course to push your one-sided views about Christianity. I understand that you are talking against Arabs and putting down other religions."

"I don't know where you are getting your information, Archer. But it's wrong. I share facts and details about many forms of ancient worship from Babylonian gods, to Greek mythology, to Christianity. The students are presented with information and its relationship to archaeology and history. I haven't put down anyone."

"Don't you talk about Christianity more than the other religions?"

"Of course I do, Archer. It's a course in biblical archaeology."

"I think that you're coming across bigoted and intolerant of other people's views."

"Wait a minute!" Both of Murphy's feet were firmly planted on the floor and he was leaning forward. "Just how do you define tolerance?"

Murphy could see Fallworth's neck beginning to get red. "Tolerance is respecting other people's viewpoints and holding them on an equal level with your viewpoints. You should give them equal time to share their concepts and not be judgmental of someone else's beliefs or behaviors."

"That sounds good and politically correct, Archer, but that's not what tolerance means according to the dictionary. Part of what you're saying is true. Yes, we should respect the right of other people to believe what they desire. Not everyone believes the same thing. But I don't have to put what another person believes on the same level as what I believe. That would make truth relative and not absolute."

"Truth *is* relative."

"Is it really? If an Arab terrorist, or a Russian terrorist, or a terrorist from any country blows up innocent children in a school— you're saying that I should hold his beliefs, values, and behaviors on the same level as mine, when I think life is sacred? And because I don't hold and endorse his beliefs on the same level, I'm judgmental and intolerant? That's not how it works."

"That's a good example of what I mean. Look at what you've just done. You have racially profiled terrorists. I think that you're phobic against Arabs and Russians!"

"Whoa! Just a minute, Archer. Because I have strong opinions and convictions that differ from what you believe, that makes me phobic? Is that the game? When I have a different viewpoint, you begin to call me names?"

By now both Murphy and Fallworth were standing.

"You're fanatically phobic on certain issues!" Fallworth exclaimed.

Murphy quashed his desire to suggest that they go outside to settle the issue. *Get control, Murphy. Don't escalate it any more. A soft answer turns away wrath.* He took a deep breath.

"I used Arab and Russian terrorists as an illustration. It was not a put-down of particular groups of people. Those examples are current on television and in the newspapers. You don't read about Eskimo or Polynesian terrorists, do you? I think that tolerance and political correctness have become twisted. Disagreement with someone's beliefs and behaviors is not intolerance, it is discernment and conviction. If we didn't have that, we would have everyone thinking the same way."

"That would be nice for a change rather than your bigoted opinions."

"And who determines which way to think or believe, Archer? Is it you? If anyone disagrees with you, do we then call out the thought police and put them in jail? If we are to hold everyone's beliefs and behaviors on the same level and become tolerant and accepting of them, why don't you hold my opinions on the same level as yours? Why aren't you tolerant of them? Why must I give up what I believe and only approve what you believe in? Don't you see a double standard here? Isn't Preston University a place where ideas are shared and free speech is allowed?"

"Of course free speech is allowed, but not hate speech. Not fanaticism."

"I think you've lost it, Archer. Having convictions, values, and moral standards does not equal fanaticism."

"That's the point. You think you have a corner on truth. You're not sensitive to other people's feelings, nor are you being inclusive of their beliefs."

Murphy could see that they were just going in a circle so he reverted to his usual tactic when frustrated and under verbal attack. He asked a question. "So, what's the bottom line, Archer? What do you want from me?"

"I want your hate speech to end. Your conservative, right-wing, phobic fundamentalist beliefs are disruptive to this university. Christianity should be saved for church; it has no place in the classroom."

"Let me follow your logic. You're equating hate speech with Christianity. And it's okay to use hate speech in the church, but not in the classroom. Am I to assume that you don't see your views as hate speech toward the ideas and beliefs of Christians?"

Fallworth ignored the question. "Murphy, I'd like to see your idiotic archaeology class removed from the school curriculum entirely."

"Well, Archer, I have about a hundred and fifty students who are excited about the class. I don't hear any of them complaining about it. The only complaints come from you, and you haven't attended any of my lectures recently. So much for intellectual honesty."

"Do you know who you're talking to?"

"Yes, I think so. I think I'm talking to a person who had a bad religious experience at some time in his life and is hurt and angry about it. Or maybe you have some moral issues that you are struggling with. It's been my experience that when emotions are out of control for the event going on . . . something else is going on."

"We're through talking, Murphy. Just remember what I said; your job may depend upon it."

"Is that a threat, Archer?"

TWENTY-TWO

MURPHY AND ISIS WERE SEATED at a window table in the Pierre, overlooking Central Park, awaiting Levi Abrams.

Murphy could not take his eyes off Isis. She was stunning. Her long red hair seemed to shimmer like spun gold. Being with such a beautiful woman almost took his breath away.

His heart raced as Isis looked across the table at him and smiled. Murphy glanced out the window, trying to rein in his emotions. He could see the pond, the Wollman Memorial Rink, magnificent trees, and the lights of the city twinkling on the other side of the park.

Isis spoke softly. "There's something lovely about New York in the evening, isn't there?"

"You're right. I think that since 9/11, when the World Trade Center was destroyed, everyone looks a little differently at the city now. It sort of brought everyone together."

Isis focused on Murphy for a moment, watching him gaze out the window. He had a handsome rugged quality about him. He was decisive and straightforward. No pretense at all. He was positive, full of life, and always seeking adventure. He was short on patience and strong on opinions, but she had grown to appreciate his candor and openness. It was infinitely better than some of the other men she had dated, who had no opinions or convictions about anything.

Murphy glanced up and caught Isis looking at him. Something in her eyes, in her whole being, unnerved him. He was trying to think of something to say when he heard a voice.

"So, what are you lovebirds up to?"

Murphy felt a twinge of embarrassment at Levi Abrams's words. He hadn't shared his growing feelings for Isis openly with her yet.

Murphy stood, and the men hugged and clapped each other on the back. Then Abrams bent down and kissed Isis on the cheek. "My, my, but you do look lovely tonight. Michael, I'm glad we could get together. This is a fine spot. It has been a couple of years since I have eaten here."

Fadil stood in the shadows shaking nervously as he watched the street. Nothing seemed strange or out of place. He looked over at the window of Aladdin's Magic Carpet and could see a few people sitting at tables eating dinner. He glanced at his watch, then cautiously crossed the street and entered.

The dim lights made it hard to see who was in the restaurant. The scent of curry filled the air. Fadil made his way to the back and saw familiar faces. He nodded slightly to them and sat down.

Asim was the first to speak. "I'm glad you all could make it tonight. I have received a coded e-mail from Abdul Rachid Makar. He has instructed us to ready ourselves."

"You mean that we no longer have to be sleeping warriors?" Ibrahim asked, excited. "When does our leader want us to strike?"

"Soon, very soon! The infidel dogs will again face the terror of Allah! They thought 9/11 was bad. Won't they be surprised?"

Fadil's voice trembled when he spoke. "Will it be in the morning or in the night?"

Asim looked around and lowered his voice. "It will be in the morning, when the infidels are going to work. Will you be able to disrupt the power grid?"

Fadil nodded.

"Good. I have been informed that the devices are on the way," Asim said. "Most of their security is in the airports, train stations, and government buildings. We will catch them off guard and hurt them greatly."

Everyone lifted his glass. "To the death!"

"That was a wonderful meal, Michael. And to be in the company of such a beautiful lady too. I'm doubly blessed," Abrams said.

They all laughed.

"Michael, tell me about your crazy idea to go back to Babylon." Abrams turned serious now.

"I told you about my encounter with Methuselah and the ancient plaster."

"It was at least twenty-five hundred years old," Isis explained. "I ran a carbon dating test on it in the Parchments of Freedom laboratories."

"I think that Methuselah has found Nebuchadnezzar's Handwriting on the Wall and has given us clues to find it. Could you make arrangements to get us into Iraq?"

"I might be able to. Do you remember Colonel Davis of the U.S. Marines?"

"You mean the one with the bone-crushing handshake?"

"Yes, he's the one. I was told he's still overseeing the guarding of Babylon. I think I can pull some strings. But don't you want to take someone else with you besides just the two of you?"

"Who were you thinking of?"

"Your friend Jassim Amram. The professor of archaeology at the American University in Cairo. He is an expert on Arab culture and identifying ancient artifacts. I think he'd be of great help to you."

"That's a good idea, Levi. And he's the sonar sled expert. Using it can speed up the search process. I think I know about where the spot should be, but sonar would help pinpoint it. I'll call him tomorrow, check his availability, and have him find out about the sonar sled."

"I'll e-mail Colonel Davis and get permission. Do you have funding yet?"

"We're still working on that," Isis replied. "The foundation is excited about the possibility of such a find."

There was a slight pause. "Levi, how about your business? Have you gotten the information you came to New York for?" Murphy knew that he wouldn't be able to discuss details.

"Well, let's just say that we are following up on rumors that an important transaction is about to take place."

"In New York?"

"We're not sure, but there is a strong possibility. I'll be following up on some details here for the next couple of days and then I'm off to Texas," Abrams said.

"Texas? What are you men talking about?" Isis asked, a questioning look on her face.

"Just men talk," Abrams said as he looked at his watch. "I'm sorry but I must run. I need to catch a cab. I have a late appointment this evening."

"No need for that," Murphy told him. "I have a rental car; I'll give you a lift."

"That would be great, Michael. Let me go make a phone call and then we can leave."

"What was that all about?" Isis asked when Abrams had left.

"Terrorists. It sounds like Levi's group"—Murphy raised his eyebrows—"is getting information that there may be another bomb attack in New York."

"Why then is he going to fly to Texas?"

"My guess is that something is going to be smuggled across the Mexican border. It's almost impossible to guard without the National Guard. Rumors are that Mexico is the favorite route for terrorists to enter the United States these days. After they arrive, some go into what's called sleeper cells awaiting orders to strike predetermined targets in the United States."

"You got all that from his conversation?"

"No, not tonight's. I know quite a bit about Levi." Murphy lowered his voice. "I think he's an undercover agent for Mossad here in the States. That's how he's so well connected."

"Are we talking about spy activities?"

"You might say that. I'm just glad he's on the side of the good guys. I'll drop you off at the hotel first, then I'll take Levi to meet his friends."

Isis looked worried. "Michael, I want you to be careful," she said softly.

Murphy hesitated for a moment, then reached across the table and took her hand in his. He was about to make a joking comment but could tell from her look that it would be inappropriate.

He smiled and spoke gently. "I'll be fine. I'll be very careful. I want us to have many more conversations together."

Isis smiled, yet she felt a twinge of fear deep inside.

TWENTY-THREE

MURPHY DROVE NORTH and then turned east on 62nd Street to the FDR Drive.

"Michael, take the toll bridge over to Randalls Island Park and then highway 278 into the Bronx. I need to meet my contact near Hunts Point Market."

Murphy had been to Hunts Point on one other occasion, on the way to the Bronx Zoo with some friends. They wanted him to see one of the largest food distribution centers in the United States. He remembered them saying that it provided produce and meat for more than 15 million people. Tons of food were loaded and unloaded in the teeming market each day. It was a rough-and-tumble place. Many of the men who worked in the market were not the type you'd want to meet in a dark alley. Murphy remembered seeing just about every nationality possible working side by side. *It would be easy for a terrorist to disappear into that crowd*, he recognized.

Abrams broke into his thoughts. "Did you know that a number of famous people came from the Bronx?"

"I know that Yankee Stadium is there. I've been to a number of games."

"Oh, yes, but *people* who came from the Bronx: Regis Philbin, Carl Reiner, and even Colin Powell. I met him in Israel."

"When was that?" asked Murphy.

"When he was head of the Joint Chiefs of Staff. I also heard that the movie actors James Caan and Tony Curtis, along with Bobby Darin, the singer, and Ralph Lauren, the designer and perfume guy, lived there. I think Al Pacino and Neil Simon came from the Bronx too."

"You're a walking trivia book, Levi. Do you have any trivia on the business acquaintances you're looking for?"

Abrams hesitated for a moment. "Michael, turn there at the next corner."

Murphy could tell that his friend wanted to change the subject.

"Michael, slow down now. Turn off your lights and pull over to the curb."

Murphy followed Abrams's request without question.

"See the old car in the next block?"

"The one in front of the old tenement house?"

"Yes, that's Jacob. Quickly turn the dome light on and off."

Murphy did as requested and then waited. After thirty seconds, the brake lights of the old car flashed on and off.

"We can approach," Abrams explained. "After I find out what's happening, you can go back to the hotel, Michael."

Together they walked the block to the old car and got in the backseat.

"Who is that, Levi?" Jacob asked.

"This is my friend Michael Murphy. You can speak freely in front of him. He can be trusted. What have you learned?"

"There are about seven of them," Jacob said. "We have the first names of three, and we're working on the other four. There is a short stocky man with a dark mustache. His name is Asim. He looks like a short Saddam. We think he's their leader. There is a tall thin man named Fadil. He seems to be a very nervous type. The other one is Ibrahim. I think he has a short fuse. He is a very intense person, a true zealot."

"Have you discovered anything about their plans?" asked Abrams.

"We intercepted an e-mail to Asim. It was from Abdul Rachid Makar."

"Makar!"

"Yes, the number-two man in the movement. He's very powerful and demands absolute loyalty. He rules with a strong hand. One of our informants told us that he held a party for his wife and invited his friends. One of those in attendance had stolen a small amount of money from him sometime before."

"Let me guess. He cut off the man's hand."

"No. He cut off the man's head right in front of everyone. He is a very evil man."

"What did the e-mail say?"

"We're still trying to decode it. But we're pretty sure that it is telling them to get ready for a significant attack. We don't know where or when, but it sounds as if it will be soon. It seems to indicate New York."

"That makes sense. It would be a great boost for their movement if they could get through the security defenses a second time. Where's Matthew?"

"Around the corner in a car watching the back entrance."

"Let's get him."

As Abrams, Jacob, and Murphy approached, they could see a man who seemed to be focused on something in front of the car. When Abrams tapped on the driver's window, the man didn't move.

"Something's wrong!" Abrams exclaimed, pulling the door wide. Matthew's eyes were open, but Abrams knew instantly that he was dead. But why was he sitting straight up?

Jacob opened the back door. "Levi. He's been stabbed."

Murphy looked over Jacob's shoulder. Someone must have been in the backseat and run a long knife through the seat and into the man's back. The knife held him in an upright position.

Abrams and Jacob closed the doors and wiped their fingerprints off the door handles.

"Are you just going to leave him there?" Murphy asked.

"Michael, this is the sad part of our business," Abrams explained somberly. "We must leave our friend there. He is undercover and has no identification on him. We cannot remain here for the police or any other agency to find us. We all know the price when we join."

"We've got to move quickly!" Jacob exclaimed. "We can't wait for them to launch an attack. We must stop them before they do something."

"Do you know where they are?"

"They live on the fifth floor on the end, where the light is."

Abrams turned to Murphy. "You must leave. You cannot be found with us. It's too dangerous."

"There're two of you and seven of them, and you're asking me to leave? No way. I'm going with you."

"You're not armed."

"I'll take my chances." Even as he said that, Murphy could recall Isis's worried look. He had promised her he would be careful.

It only took them a couple of minutes to get to the fifth floor. They approached the door quietly, then paused and listened. They could hear a television playing. Jacob opened his jacket and took out a set of lock picks. Slowly he inserted them. Within a few seconds there was a *click* and the men froze.

Abrams drew his gun and whispered, "I don't think they heard it. Let's wait a moment and then go in."

Jacob nodded, put away the picks, and drew his automatic. Both of them screwed on silencers. Murphy could tell that this was not the first time they had worked together. They were like a well-oiled machine.

Abrams nodded and Jacob slowly turned the knob and opened the door. They entered a small hallway that had two doors opposite each other. One door was open, the other closed. A flickering blue light came from the open door along with the sound of the television. They inched down the hallway toward the open door. Abrams looked at Jacob and signaled for him to keep an eye on the closed door. Jacob nodded. Murphy was a couple of feet behind them.

Abrams rounded the corner of the door with his gun ready for action, then paused and surveyed the room. He looked back at Jacob and raised one finger. Jacob nodded. One man was lying on a couch in front of the TV. He had fallen asleep.

Abrams crossed to the couch quickly, put his hand over the man's mouth, and whispered in Arabic, "Don't move." But the startled man did move. As he started to struggle, Abrams hit him with the gun.

That will slow him down a little.

He searched the man for a weapon and found a .32 automatic and a very impressive knife. Abrams recognized it; the special knife had sharp blades on both the top and the bottom. This man must have been a trained assassin.

Abrams nodded to Jacob to go to the closed door. Jacob turned the knob as quietly as possible. The door handle clicked. Anyone in the room might have heard the sound. He waited for a moment and then slowly opened the door.

He had the door partly open when there was a yell in Arabic and the sound of a gunshot. Murphy couldn't see the bullet, but he saw Jacob twisted and yelling. Jacob fell back against the wall in the hallway and collapsed, the gun falling from his hand, blood flowing from his thigh.

Abrams had ducked down and away from the doorway.

The Arab was yelling as he came out of the room. Seeing Jacob on the floor, he swung his gun toward him to finish the job. Then Murphy sprang forward, shouting. The Arab tried to swing the gun in Murphy's direction, but it was too late.

Murphy blocked the gun arm with his left hand. His right came forward with a twisting karate fist into the Arab's left temple. The man fell to the floor unconscious. Murphy kept moving past the door opening.

The sudden silence was shocking. Abrams and Murphy were listening for any sound that might reveal the presence of another terrorist. Jacob was gritting his teeth trying not to make a sound.

Abrams was the first to speak. "Michael, are you all right?"

"I'm fine, but they've shot Jacob."

"I'll be okay," Jacob replied grimly. "Check and see if there is anyone else here."

Abrams and Murphy searched the apartment but found no one else.

As they came back to the hallway, Jacob spoke.

"They're all alone. The others are probably nearby at some bar.

These Muslims are not like the rest. They like their alcohol and women."

Murphy helped Jacob into the living room.

Jacob looked at the man who was on the couch. "Ah, no wonder he fought you. That one is Ibrahim, the uptight zealot. You hit him pretty hard."

Abrams and Murphy stopped the bleeding in Jacob's leg, then searched the apartment. Near the telephone was a clean pad of paper. Abrams picked it up and held it at different angles, studying it in the lamplight.

"Someone wrote on this and removed the note."

He grabbed a pencil and began to lightly brush it back and forth over the pad. Soon fine white lines emerged from the depressions created on the pad by the last note written. It only contained one word.

"Presidio," Abrams read.

"Presidio? There's a military base called Presidio in San Francisco. It's next to the Golden Gate Bridge," Jacob said.

Murphy spoke up. "There is also a sleepy little town called Presidio in Texas. It's on the border between Texas and Mexico. The Rio Grande runs between Presidio on the American side and Ojinaga on the Mexican side. Presidio has grown to about six or seven thousand people due to the amnesty program for undocumented aliens. During the Mexican Revolution, General Pancho Villa used Ojinaga as his headquarters for operations. It would be a perfect place to infiltrate the border."

Murphy had barely gotten the words out of his mouth when the man on the couch regained consciousness and leaped onto Abrams's back, trying to choke him. Instinctively Abrams made a fist with his right hand; at the same moment his left hand came on top of the fist. He twisted slightly and drove his elbow into Ibrahim's stomach. The pain and loss of air made the man bend forward. As his head went down, Abrams turned around and brought his knee up into the terrorist's face, sending him backward against the wall to collapse on the floor, his nose broken and bleeding.

Jacob was crawling toward his automatic, which Murphy had picked up and placed on a table. Abrams was reaching for the gun in his shoulder holster. Ibrahim, dripping blood, looked like a trapped animal, desperate to escape. His eyes darted back and forth from Abrams, to Murphy, then to Jacob on the floor.

Abrams spoke in Arabic. "Tell us about Presidio."

Ibrahim screamed back, "Never, you infidel devils." Then he turned and started to run. Abrams and Murphy both leaped forward, but he was just beyond their reach. He threw himself through the window, yelling "Allah be praised."

Ibrahim landed on the fire escape just outside the window. Now he was bleeding from several cuts caused by broken glass in addition to his broken nose. He scrambled up the stairs toward the roof.

"Michael, make sure Jacob is all right. I'm going after this one," Abrams called over his shoulder.

Murphy grabbed the gun off the table and propped Jacob up against the couch. "Here," he said, "you take the gun in case anyone comes back. I'm going to help Levi."

TWENTY-FOUR

THE SUDDEN ROAR *of the lions startled Daniel out of his thoughts. Two were snarling and fighting with each other. He could hear the clatter of teeth and the slapping of paws against fur. The lion relaxing next to him bolted up with a snort as the two males tumbled toward them.*

Daniel tried to move but was not quick enough. His joints had grown stiff and sore from the den's cold rock floor. He was an elderly man; swiftness of movement was a thing of the past.

The two fighting lions rolled right over him, knocking the wind out of him. He couldn't believe how heavy they were. How ironic to be crushed to death in a lions' den, *Daniel thought. But it was just a brief skirmish. Daniel quickly checked his body for bleeding wounds. He didn't want the lions to smell fresh blood.*

The fight had come on too quickly for Daniel to pray. He had been too shocked to react. But he now found himself thanking God that he had not been injured by the wild beasts.

My friends would be surprised to see me alive, *he thought.* I can't believe this is happening to me.

The strange evening dragged on with Daniel slipping in and out of sleep. He had a hard time separating the reality of the den with the reality of over sixty years of memories of being a Babylonian slave in the king's court. He could hear King Nebuchadnezzar's words as if it had been yesterday.

"Well, Daniel. No doubt I do not need to explain why you are here."

"You have been troubled by a dream, my king. An awesome dream that stirred your spirit, and yet when you awoke, not a fragment, not a shred of it remained. Only an empty echo, like the sound of a word in a strange tongue."

Daniel remembered how this troubled the king.

"You saw a great image, O King. The head of the statue was of gold, wondrously bright, like molten fire, the chest and arms of shining silver like the moon when she is full. The belly and thighs of the statue were of bronze, the legs of iron, the feet of clay and iron mixed."

Even though Daniel foretold of the destruction of Nebuchadnezzar's kingdom, he remembered how the king had rewarded him by making him the chief administrator over all of the wise men of Babylon.

He thought back to how Nebuchadnezzar's heart had become hardened over the years. He would not acknowledge Jehovah, the God of heaven. His pride was too great to give God credit for establishing his kingdom. In his arrogance, the king erected a ninety-cubit-high golden statue in his honor. He acted like he had superhuman power... until that fateful night. The night God struck him with insanity.

―――――

"Master! Master! Wake up!"

Daniel could feel his assistant shaking him.

"What is it? What time is it?"

"Master, the royal guards are at the door. You must come quickly. Something has happened to the king."

Dressing hurriedly, Daniel joined the guards, who had chariots waiting. They rode like the wind to the palace.

What could be wrong with Nebuchadnezzar? He was a very healthy man. Had he been attacked?

As they drove into the palace courtyard, Daniel could see soldiers rushing downstairs with the king's servants following them. Everyone was yelling and screaming. Daniel rushed over to the captain of the guard, who was shouting orders.

"Tarub. What is happening? Where is the king?"

"He's gone mad. One moment he was eating dinner, and the next moment he was tossing food and plates. He growls like a wild animal. We tried to restrain him, but he is extremely powerful. He seems to have the strength of ten men. We locked him in his chambers and called for the astrologers and wise men. A few moments ago he escaped and ran into the fields across the Euphrates. The men are looking for him now. Can you do anything?"

Daniel turned and looked through the gate and out toward the fields. He could see many torches in the distance.

A guard ran up to the captain as Daniel was offering a silent prayer for wisdom.

"Sir. Some of the men have just found the king. He is near the canal that waters the fig trees. Over there to the left, where the torches are gathering."

As he got out of the chariot, Daniel could see the king on the ground circled by soldiers who were keeping a good distance from him. They didn't want to provoke him to run again. Nebuchadnezzar was down on his hands and knees digging in the dirt.

The soldiers parted ranks to let Daniel through. He was well-known as a great man, a man who had the wisdom of the gods. All eyes were on him.

As he moved closer to the king, he could see what Nebuchadnezzar was doing. He was digging up plants and eating the roots. His eyes were wild. Saliva mixed with dirt was dripping from his mouth. He growled as Daniel grew nearer.

Daniel stopped and squatted down, so he would seem less threatening. He began to talk in a very calm and soothing voice. "O King Nebuchadnezzar. What troubles you? I your servant Daniel am here to comfort you. May I have permission to speak?"

Growling loudly, the king threw the plant he was uprooting at Daniel, who fell over backward. Daniel knew the king wouldn't get well until God allowed it to happen.

Yet Daniel remained faithful to the king. Every week for seven years, he'd go out to the fields to visit and try to talk to Nebuchadnezzar. Sometimes he would find field workers throwing rocks at the king, whose hair and nails had grown long. They'd yell and call him names. Daniel would chase them away. He felt sorry for Nebuchadnezzar, a king who lived like an animal.

God humbled Nebuchadnezzar for seven years as he groveled in the dirt in the shadow of his palace. His wits had been scattered to the four corners of the wind. During that period his great kingdom was almost destroyed. It hung together by a thin thread. His jealous neighbors were plotting its overthrow until God brought back his sanity.

"O God. Please keep me humble. Please keep pride from overpowering me. Don't let me forget that You and You alone are the one who puts people up and can take them down just as you did Nebuchadnezzar," Daniel prayed.

TWENTY-FIVE

AS ABRAMS CLIMBED through the broken window, he looked up. He could barely see Ibrahim climbing the fire escape stairs about a floor above. Abrams yelled for the man to stop even though he knew it was useless.

Their shoes made a lot of noise against the steel of the fire escape. Above that sound, Abrams could hear Ibrahim shouting death threats in Arabic.

There were eight stories to the old tenement, and by the time Abrams reached the roof he was breathing heavily. He paused for a second before sticking his head up to see. As he peeked up, he heard the sound of a gunshot and felt the spray of brick next to his face. Instinctively he ducked down.

He must have had a gun hidden on the roof somewhere.

Abrams took out his gun, raised his arm above the wall, and fired three times in the direction of the gunshot. Then he could hear Ibrahim running on the gravel of the roof.

As he popped his head over the wall again, he could see the Arab disappearing around the elevator shaft. He fired and saw a brick explode close to Ibrahim's shoulder. Abrams leaped onto the roof and ran toward the small building. By the time he had reached it, Ibrahim was nowhere to be seen.

Abrams poked his head around the building, staring into the darkness. Just then the zealot fired. Abrams fired off several rounds, and then there was silence.

Murphy was just starting up the fire escape when he heard the first shot.

Maybe there were more Arabs!

He began to climb as fast as he could as gunshots echoed through the night. A battle was taking place, and he had no idea who was winning.

By the time Murphy reached the roof, there was silence. As he peered over the wall, he couldn't see anyone, just a small building. Carefully he made his way over the wall toward the building. He had almost reached it when he heard two muffled shots in the distance—not from the roof. Had they come from the apartment?

Murphy reached the small building and peered around it. Levi Abrams was standing upright, his hands raised. The zealot Ibrahim was yelling at him, "You are going to die, you Jewish pig."

Murphy shouted.

Ibrahim turned at the sound and fired. Both Murphy and Abrams hit the ground. Ibrahim then turned back toward where Abrams had been standing and pulled the trigger, but the gun was empty. Abrams leaped up and rushed forward. His right hand hit the inside wrist of the Arab's gun hand just as his left hand hit the back of the gun hand. The gun went flying.

Ibrahim ducked down as Abrams's body weight came forward. He too had been trained to fight.

The zealot then rose and flipped Abrams onto his back. The wind was knocked out of him.

By now Murphy was running toward the battle. Ibrahim heard him coming, and ran, with Murphy trailing after him. Once he'd regained his breath, Abrams too pursued the terrorist.

It only took a few moments for Ibrahim to reach the edge of the building. He leaped onto the outer wall, then hesitated. The adjacent building was about ten feet away. His only chance for escape was to leap.

Murphy yelled. "Don't do it! You'll never make it!"

Ibrahim briefly crouched down and sprang. His hands were up and his entire body was extended as he crossed the gap, crying "Allah be praised!"

Abrams had just reached the edge in time to see the zealot's hands grasping bricks on the top of the other building. Then the rest of his body hit the wall. The impact jerked his hands free and he began to fall.

Murphy and Abrams watched helplessly as Ibrahim dropped eight stories, desperately flailing his arms and legs. His body hit the alley below with a sickening thud.

Abrams and Murphy looked at each other. There was a split second of silence, and then the same thought seemed to hit both of them at the same time: *Jacob!*

They ran across the roof and back down the fire escape. As they clambered through the window, they could see Jacob on the floor with his eyes closed and the gun in his hand.

At the sound, Jacob opened his eyes and pointed the gun at them.

"You're alive!" Abrams exclaimed.

"Yes. After you left I could hear the gun battle. Then I heard some noise in the hallway. The other Arab must have woken up. I could hear him but couldn't see him. All of a sudden he dashed to the front door. I fired twice but I don't think I hit him."

"We have to get you out of here and to the safe house," Abrams said, reaching down and lifting his partner. Murphy grabbed his other arm, and the three limped to the elevator. They could hear noise behind other doors; some of the other tenants were probably calling the police. But they also knew that no one would leave their apartment to see what was happening—not in this neighborhood. There was too much danger of being shot yourself.

"I'm sorry to get you mixed up in all of this, Michael. You don't need this kind of trouble," Abrams said ruefully.

"I'm just glad I was here to help. When I know terrorists are planning to do something to the country I love, how can I just stand around and do nothing?"

"Michael, after you drop us off at the safe house, get back to your hotel. Act as if nothing happened. We must get information back to our group. I'll try to contact you later. Thanks again for your help—especially on the roof."

"What happened up there?" Murphy asked.

"I guess I got sloppy. During the gun battle Ibrahim yelled and hit the ground like he had been shot. I ran over thinking he'd been wounded. He was just faking and got the drop on me. If you hadn't yelled when you did, I wouldn't be walking out of here now."

Abrams, wearing gloves, went through the dead zealot's pockets, searching for clues. Murphy, holding the flashlight, looked at the body and asked, "What's that on his neck?"

Abrams moved the collar of his shirt slightly. "A crescent moon with a star. You see it on the flags of many Muslim countries."

Murphy got closer and shined the light directly on the tattoo. "No. This is different. Look closely, Levi. In all Muslim symbols, the points of the crescent moon point to the right or up, with a five-pointed star or several stars. This crescent moon is pointing down to a star with six points made up of two triangles, similar to the Star of David. And look at the points of the crescent. Three small lines are coming off each point."

"Yes. I see them. They almost look like claws that are closing in on the Star of David."

"Those aren't claws like a cat's; they look more like the talons of a bird."

Abrams looked up at Murphy. "Are you thinking what I'm thinking?"

Murphy glared at Abrams. "Do you think Talon has Arab terrorists working for him now? How does Presidio tie in to all of this?"

"I don't know, Michael. But I do know I'm going to Texas for sure."

TWENTY-SIX

MURPHY HAD a difficult time going to sleep that night. Adrenaline was still coursing through his system. His mind kept reverting to the evening's events. He could see Matthew sitting up in the car staring into space with a slight trace of blood dripping from his lips.

He could hear Jacob yell as the bullet tore through his leg. He remembered Ibrahim leaping onto Levi's back attempting to choke him to death. He could feel his fist strike the Arab in the temple.

Man, that really hurt, he thought, grimacing as he flexed his knuckles.

He then flashed to Isis's face and her words to be careful. If she only knew how close he had come to death. He thought back to his emotions as he saw Ibrahim attempting to leap through space only to fall to his death . . . and the crescent moon with the talons. Finally he drifted into a restless sleep, thinking about one word: Presidio.

The sound of the phone ringing startled Murphy. It took him a moment to remember where he was. He groped for the receiver, muttered "Hello," and heard the automated voice announcing his seven A.M. wake-up call.

Great! He slammed down the receiver. Then reality hit him. *Breakfast with Isis at eight!*

Murphy had decided that it would be best not to tell Isis what had happened last evening with Abrams just yet. He would wait for a more appropriate time. They had a lot to do today, and he didn't want her to worry. After breakfast, they headed for the Federated Bank & Trust to retrieve the contents of Dr. Anderson's safe deposit box.

In the bank, Murphy spoke with the manager, explained the situation, and handed him the notarized letter with the power of attorney.

"Oh, yes," the manager said. "I've already received a copy of the letter. I also had a phone call with a Mr. Lenny Harris from the Quiet River Nursing Home who explained everything. We were expecting you." The manager took the key from Murphy, retrieved Dr. Anderson's box, and left Murphy and Isis alone in the safe deposit customer room.

Murphy looked at the key the old man had directed him to take as he lay dying. Could the contents of the box be worth Dr. Anderson's life?

Murphy looked at Isis. He could tell that she was excited. She loved new adventures. Slowly he opened the large safe deposit box. It was filled with file folders and a journal. He read the titles aloud as he removed the files from the box one by one.

"The first folder is titled Madame Helena Petrovna Blavatsky—The Theosophical Society. Annie Besant—Lucifer Magazine. Zigana Averna—now, that's a mouthful. Alfred Meinrad—I've heard of him;

he's a scientist. Carmine Anguis. Calinda Anguis. J. M. Talpish. The Friends of the New World Order. The new age. And a handwritten journal. It almost looks like a daily log of some kind."

"I wonder what this is all about."

"I'm not sure. All I know is that when I spoke with Dr. Anderson, he mentioned the end of the world and a one-world leader. This may provide clues to what he was talking about."

"Michael, there's a library right across the street. Let's go over there, where we can spread out, and read through these folders. If we both read, it will speed up the process a little."

"Great idea." Murphy put the folders and the journal into his briefcase, and they left the bank.

As they crossed the street, Isis looked at the old four-story library. It had six tall Roman pillars in front and a set of marble stairs. The soot of many years had turned the white marble a dull gray. Pigeons milled around cooing on the roof and the steps. Carved into the marble above the pillars was this motto:

**THROUGH WISDOM A HOUSE IS BUILT,
AND BY UNDERSTANDING IT IS ESTABLISHED.
PROVERBS 24:3**

A chill went down her spine as Isis looked at the library. Something was wrong. She couldn't put her finger on it. Was it the building itself? Was it something inside the building? Something in the material they were going to examine? Or was it something else? She couldn't shake off her unease. She almost felt that someone was watching them. But when she looked around, she didn't catch anyone looking in their direction. Everything seemed normal—except her feelings.

That's silly, she told herself. *Don't mess up the excitement of Michael's find with women's intuition.*

As they entered the old building, they came into a great hall filled with tables, rows of oak book card catalogs, racks filled with books, and an old information desk. Behind the desk was a dowdy, chubby woman in a white dress with large blue polka dots.

Isis looked up and could see each floor of the library circling the center hall. Anyone standing above could look down on those in the center of the open hall. Behind the railings above, Isis could see stacks and stacks of bookshelves with people milling about. If it had not been for her uneasy feelings, Isis would have enjoyed the library. It made you want to come in and spend the day soaking up great thoughts. If only she could shake off the eerie sensation and relax in the friendly environment of books!

Murphy and Isis climbed the marble stairs and went to the back of the library on the third floor. There they found a secluded table where they could lay out the material and begin to read.

The thousands of books that surrounded them seemed to soak up sound. They could talk softly here without bothering anyone. It was almost like they were in their own little world. It was even a little romantic, just the two of them.

I just wish I didn't have this chilling feeling, Isis thought. *Maybe I should say something to Michael.*

TWENTY-SEVEN

STEPHANIE KOVACS CALLED Shane Barrington from her cell phone. His secretary told her that Barrington was in a meeting and would be back about 4 P.M. *Good*, Kovacs thought. *That will give me about two hours before he'll be back home.* She drove quickly to Barrington Towers, parked in the lower garage, and took the elevator to the top floor.

Although she had her own apartment, she'd been spending most of her time with Barrington at his penthouse. She remembered back to when she first moved in and how excited and how much in love she'd been.

What a fool I was, she told herself.

It was a pleasant arrangement for the first few months, but then the trouble had started. She remembered the night when Barrington spoke those chilling words: *"Promise me you won't do anything foolish so I'd be forced to . . . dispose of you. I've grown very fond of you, Stephanie. I'd hate our relationship to end in tragedy."*

That night fear entered her mind and began to grow like a weed. She knew then that she hadn't really loved Shane Barrington, but had fallen in love with his power and money.

As an investigative reporter, she had the ability to sniff out corruption and shady business transactions. Barrington Communications was beginning to stink. After those first few months, she had begun to ask too many questions about his business dealings, and he didn't like it. It was then that the yelling had begun, punctuated with Barrington hitting the walls or doors with his fist. It took all her negotiating skills to calm him down.

Eventually her fear grew to the point where she was afraid to question anything or to discuss any sensitive subject. Her fear had created distrust, and her lack of security had begun to grow into resentment. She knew that she had to get out of the relationship; this was her opportunity. She could pack all of her things and move back to her apartment. At least they wouldn't be sharing the same bed anymore. She couldn't pretend that everything was okay when inside she was in emotional turmoil. She could no longer sleep with someone she had lost respect for; no amount of money or power could soothe that pain.

Kovacs had closed her last suitcase when she heard what sounded like a key in the door. She panicked, stuffing her bags into the closet and closing the door. Then she ran into the bathroom, where she nervously pretended to put on lipstick. *Maybe he'll think I came home early.*

"Stephanie?" Barrington's voice sounded from the living room.

"I'm in here." She hoped her voice sounded calmer than she felt.

In the mirror, she could see him entering the bedroom.

"I got through early with my meeting and decided not to go back to the office," he said, smiling. "I saw your car in the garage. What are you doing here?"

"I got through a little early myself."

Barrington slid his arms around her waist and looked at her in the mirror. She tried to smile like she was glad to see him, but she was actually repulsed by his touch. He turned her around and kissed her. After he walked away, she trembled in fear.

"How about a steak dinner tonight? I'm hungry," he said. With that he turned and headed for the closet.

"Where would you like to go?" she asked, hoping to distract him. He hesitated before reaching for the door handle. "I don't care. You pick."

He was still looking at Stephanie when he opened the door to the closet and stepped in. He stubbed his toe on her first suitcase and almost fell over the other two.

"What the . . . ?" He paused, trying to process the scene. Then he stepped back and looked at Stephanie, the color draining from her face.

"Is this what I think it is?"

"Shane, I was going to talk to you about this."

"Talk to me. When? After you had run away?!"

Stephanie could see his face darkening in anger.

"I trusted you!" he shouted. "I thought you were loyal. You know how I hate disloyalty."

"Shane, you know we've been having more and more fights. I . . . I just think it would be best if we separated for a little while to let things cool down."

Kovacs was beginning to back toward the living room as Barrington advanced.

"So you're just going to run out," he shouted. "No one runs out on me!" He clenched his fist. The veins in his neck were standing out.

Stephanie started to turn to run but Barrington caught her with his left hand and whirled her around toward him. At the same time, he slapped her, sending her flying across the living room. She tripped on the coffee table, breaking the vase, and rolled off the corner of the sofa onto the floor.

It took a few seconds for her head to clear. There was a ringing in her left ear, and the whole side of her face was stinging, and she could feel an instant headache.

Barrington was furious. He snatched her up and shook her.

"No one runs out on Shane Barrington!" With that he slapped her again, sending her into a lamp that fell over, shattering a large wall mirror.

This time Stephanie could hardly move. She was dazed. She could taste the salty taste of blood, feel the pain inside her mouth where the skin was ripped. As she sat up, her head spun. Blood was dripping from her nose onto her white blouse. She was in too much shock to cry. *Oh, God, please help me.*

Barrington had disappeared into the bedroom but soon emerged with her suitcases. He threw them at her. The first one bounced on the floor and then into her chest, knocking out what breath she had left. The second one bounced off the first case and into her face. Her head flew back, hitting the wall. And then there was blackness.

When Stephanie awoke, she was cold and disoriented. It took her a moment to realize that she was in her BMW in the lower garage of Barrington Towers. Her whole body ached. Slowly she sat up and looked around. The garage was empty except for a few cars. The pain in her face was excruciating. She flipped on the dome light and looked into the rearview mirror. She didn't recognize what she saw. There was blood all over her clothes and in her matted hair. The left side of her face was dark, puffy, and swollen. Her eye was already turning black. She looked like she had just been run over. She ran her tongue across her teeth. One was chipped.

She could see her suitcases in the backseat. Barrington must have put them—and her—in the car. After several deep breaths, she found her purse and fumbled around for the keys. She could only see out of one eye.

I thought he was going to kill me. I can't believe I'm still alive.

As she put the keys in the ignition and started the car, she noticed something on her windshield. She tried to read it but it was written on the outside and was backward. She tried to focus with her right eye. It was written with lipstick. Finally she could make it out. It read: *NO ONE RUNS OUT ON ME!*

Stephanie was glad that it was 4 A.M. and everyone was in bed when she finally got home. She didn't want to run into anyone looking the way she did.

She left the suitcases in the car and went straight to the bathroom. She turned on the water for a tub bath, took some aspirin, and crawled in. The warmth felt soothing and healing. As she finally was able to relax, she began to sob.

After forty-five minutes, the hot water finally ran out. She gathered what energy she had left and dragged herself to bed. The emotional and physical drain had been enormous. She was asleep in a few minutes.

It was three in the afternoon when Stephanie's home phone rang.

"Stephanie, it's Melissa. Are you all right?" Barrington's secretary was whispering.

"I'm not feeling good today. I'm going to take a sick day."

"Stephanie, are you sure you're all right?"

"Why are you whispering, Melissa?"

"I'm away from my desk at another phone."

"Why?"

"I'm afraid. I've never seen Mr. Barrington so mad. He ordered me to clear out your desk and put all of your belongings into boxes. When I asked him why, he yelled at me and said, 'If you want to keep your job, do as I tell you!' He's never acted this way before.

"I overheard him call Lowell Adrian, the human resources director, and tell him that you're fired immediately. Then I heard him say, 'She'll never work for any news organization if I have my way. She's through for good!' "

Kovacs's spirits dropped even lower. Not only had she lost her own self-respect by becoming a mistress, she had broken a power relationship and gotten beaten up as a result. Now she was being blackballed from working for any news media. All possible sources of income were drying up.

Trying to hold back her tears, she said, "Melissa, I appreciate your calling, but you have to get off the phone. If Shane knows that you've called me, you'll lose your job. I can't bear that guilt. Go, and don't call me again. It's too dangerous."

Stephanie began to weep. Her life was falling apart. She was swimming in guilt, fear, frustration, and anger. Emotions surged over her like giant tidal waves. Her life was a mess, and there was nothing she could do about it. She curled up in a ball and cried for an hour. Then the tears were gone and depression began to take hold. She was filled with despair.

It was late in the evening, as Stephanie was curled up in bed, that the first ray of hope poked its head through her dark cloud of depression. A word came into her mind. *Happiness.*

She remembered Dr. Murphy asking if she was happy. She thought back to the time she interviewed him after the loss of his wife. He certainly wasn't happy then, but he did seem to have a peace about him. He said that only God can give peace in the midst of turmoil.

I'm certainly in turmoil·but I don't have any peace. I wonder if there is anything to all this God talk?

Her mind began to drift back to Dr. Murphy's comments about a kite.

"Stephanie, when the kite was out of sight, how could you tell if it was still there?"

"I guess by the pull of the string. It meant the wind was still blowing the kite."

"Right. That's sort of how it is when God speaks to you. You can't see Him. He is out of sight. And you can't audibly hear His voice because He is too far away. But you can feel His loving tug on the strings of your heart. . . . Do you feel the tug of God on the strings of your heart today?"

Gentle tears began to flow from her eyes. *Dear God*, she prayed, *I'm hurting and lonely. I think You are tugging on me trying to get my attention . . . and You've got it. I don't know what to do. I need Your help. I've really made some poor choices, and they've affected my entire life. It's a mess. If You're up there somewhere listening to me, I need Your help.*

I know I am a sinner and I need You to change my life. I can't do it myself. I've tried more than once. I believe You sent Your Son, Jesus, to die for all my wrongdoing. Please forgive me. I'm not sure what this all means, but I feel You knocking at the door of my heart. And I want to open it to You today. Please come in and help me to have peace.

With that, Stephanie cried herself to sleep.

TWENTY-EIGHT

MURPHY OPENED to the first page of the journal, which read "The Journal of Harley B. Anderson." Isis began reading Helena Petrovna Blavatsky's file. Using a colored marking pen, occasionally Murphy highlighted something. The only sound was the turning of pages. After about forty-five minutes, Murphy spoke.

"Isis, listen to this. I've highlighted certain dates and comments in the journal. They give an overview of what it contains.

April 17, 1967
Today J. M. and I were contacted by three men from a group called the Friends of the New World Order. They want us to artificially inseminate a girl for them.

May 22

The group from the Friends of the New World Order again met with J. M. and me and informed us that they have selected the girl to be inseminated.

June 12

We again met with the Friends of the New World Order. They promised to pay for a fully equipped lab. That will cost a great deal. They told us that after the birth of the baby, we could keep the lab and all the equipment for our own use. They said that they had one stipulation—that we would have to keep the entire matter in absolute secrecy. They are very strange.

July 3

J. M. and I met the young woman to be inseminated for the first time. She seemed nice but a little frightened. Her name is Calinda Anguis. She is Romanian, and J. M. had to translate and explain the procedure to her.

July 10

Today we received the sperm and eggs provided by the Friends of the New World Order. They would not tell us who the donors were. Strange!

July 13

J. M. and I completed the procedure of implanting the fertilized egg into Calinda Anguis.

July 20

We examined Calinda Anguis, and everything seems to be going smoothly with no complications.

August 10

Today J. M. and I met with members from the Friends of the New World Order. They again stressed absolute secrecy about Miss Anguis and the entire procedure. They seemed to be very nervous and quite demanding. J. M. and I are very curious.

September 4

J. M. and I met for lunch. He shared his concerns about what we were doing and about all of the secrecy. He has fears that we may be doing something illegal. We both do not care for the people we have met. They seem evil.

September 29

I was able to find out details about the father and mother of Calinda Anguis. The father is Carmine Anguis and the mother's maiden name is Kala Matrinka.

October 14

I received a phone call today from the Friends of the New World Order. They were extremely demanding and firm about the secrecy of what we are doing. I am beginning to agree with J. M. We may be doing something illegal.

October 17

I did some investigating and was able to discover who the egg donor was. Keres Mazikeen.

November 30

I was able to trace down the mother of Keres Mazikeen. She is a lady named Mariana Yakov. She told me her mother's name was Zigana Averna. I am beginning to feel nervous and uncomfortable. J. M. thinks he is being followed.

December 28
The holiday season was uneventful.

January 15, 1968
I have made an amazing discovery. The sperm donor is the famous scientist Alfred Meinrad. It is a very curious situation.

February 7
I was able to uncover information about the great-grand-mother—Zigana Averna. She worked for a woman named Alice Bailey.

February 20
A group from the Friends of the New World Order visited our clinic and talked with Calinda Anguis. J. M. and I were not allowed to be in on the conversation. She seemed very agitated after they left.

March 14
J. M. has found out information about the Friends of the New World Order. He told me that he was very frightened. He told me he would talk about it when he was sure that we would be alone.

March 31
Calinda began contractions around 8:00 P.M.

April 1
The boy is born. The mother and child are doing fine. Members of the Friends of the New World Order came to the hospital. They were very adamant that the boy get the best care possible. They were almost rude to us.

April 29

J. M. has apprehensions about the arrangements with the group. He says that we must talk soon. He sounds very frightened.

May 12

Terrible tragedy—J. M. was killed in an automobile accident. The police said that he was traveling at high speed and could not negotiate a turn in the mountains and drove off a cliff. I am very frightened. J. M. did not like to go to the mountains. He never sped anywhere ... always driving under the speed limit. I feel like I must protect myself. I don't think it was an accident. I believe that he was murdered. I have decided to send all of my notes and papers to my daughter in the United States. I have instructed her to put them in a safe deposit box in an unknown location.

"That does sound very strange, Michael," Isis said thoughtfully. "Who do you think the Friends of the New World Order are?"

"I'm not sure. In my talk with Dr. Anderson before he was killed, he was convinced that they were evil people who had an evil plan of some kind. He even suggested that he might have helped in the birth of the Anti-Christ."

"You mean the Anti-Christ of the Bible that you're always talking about?"

"The same one," Murphy said, soberly.

Isis had grown up in a household where the myths and religions of the world had an almost tangible presence. Her father, an archaeologist, had such a deep interest in the deities of the ancient world that he had named Isis after not one but two goddesses (her middle name was Proserpina).

Like her parents, however, Isis grew up without any kind of christian belief.

But Murphy was different from most Christians she had met.

There was something about him that was genuine, and intellectual, and attractive. The Ararat adventure had shaken all of her ideas about the Bible and religion. She had actually walked on Noah's Ark—there was no doubt about that at all. She had also helped him find Moses's brass serpent and Nebuchadnezzar's golden statue. They were real, and she could touch them. She was beginning to believe that Murphy's faith was real, and the Bible was real, and it frightened her. At some point she would have to make a decision as to whether there is a God or not.

I need to be open-minded. What if there is a real Anti-Christ? The thought made her shudder.

TWENTY-NINE

"MICHAEL, LISTEN TO THIS. I've been reading some of these other folders."

Murphy looked up.

"This Madame Helena Petrovna Blavatsky is very interesing," Isis began. "She was born in 1831 and died in 1891. In 1875 she founded the Theosophical Society. Its logo is an alchemical symbol of a circle formed by a snake eating its tail. Inside the snake circle is a symbol of two interlocking pyramids representing the union of heaven and earth. In the center of the pyramids is an Egyptian ankh. At the top of the pyramid is a circle with an inverted swastika inside of it. As you know, the swastika is a well-known occult symbol believed to have originated in ancient India. The words surrounding the snake say: THERE IS NO RELIGION HIGHER THAN TRUTH. It says that she wrote a book entitled *The Secret Doctrine*."

"I've heard of that book," Murphy said, excited. "Adolf Hitler kept a well-marked copy of it beside his bed. He was a follower of Madame Blavatsky. That must have been where he got the idea of using a swastika for his military uniforms."

"Dr. Anderson lists that she also wrote another book, *Manual for Revolution*."

"Wow! That's something. I've heard of that book too. It was one that Sirhan Sirhan requested while he was in prison for killing Robert Kennedy. This Blavatsky woman had some interesting followers. I've heard it said that she's viewed as one of the greatest occultists in history. She founded Blavatsky Lodge and the Esoteric School."

"It looks like Dr. Anderson did some research on her," Isis said thoughtfully. "He lists that as a child, Blavatsky was restless, impetuous, daring, reckless, and had a fearful temper. He goes on to say that she had a passionate curiosity about the unknown and an unusual interest in the mysterious, weird, and fantastical. She used to scare her playmates by telling them that there were subterranean corridors under their homes that were protected by hunchbacks. It is said that she could cause her playmates to hallucinate. She even claimed to see a Hindu in a white turban. He was her phantom protector. She said that she received her directions from him telepathically. He became her spirit guide."

"She sounds like Shirley MacLaine." Murphy grinned.

"According to Dr. Anderson, she would go into a trance and become a channeler. She was into table rapping, materializations, séances, and had psychic powers and could move objects at will."

Murphy laughed out loud. "She sounds very talented."

"Here's an article that says she led a wild life of wandering the world for about ten years. She was shipwrecked on the island of Spetsai sailing from Greece to Egypt. At one point she went abroad disguised as a man and fought under Garibaldi. She was wounded and left for dead in the battle of Mentana in Russia. And she established the Theosophical Society and wrote those books I mentioned. Dr. Anderson quotes her in one of her writings saying *'Lucifer is divine and terrestrial light, the "Holy Ghost" and "Satan" are one and the same.'*"

"I think her theology was a little messed up."

"Dr. Anderson goes on to say that Madame Blavatsky heavily influenced two women: Annie Besant and Alice Ann Bailey. Besant was an activist in the feminist movement; she was especially involved in birth control. She was generally looked at as a socialist political radical. For ten years she and Alice Ann Bailey published a monthly magazine entitled *Lucifer*."

Murphy made a face. "Today they would probably make the magazine into a television series or at least a Saturday morning cartoon program."

"She was married to Frank Besant at nineteen. He was a clergyman who had traditional views. Those views clashed with her independent spirit, and she left her husband. In the process she rejected Christianity and became an atheist and free thinker. She was instrumental in developing the foundation for the New Age Movement."

Isis turned a page and continued. "Alice Ann Bailey started a number of organizations, including the Lucis Trust, World Goodwill, Triangles, the Ariane School, and New Group World Servers. She compiled twenty-one books with over 10,469 pages of material. She claimed that she wrote them while she was in a trance state. They were dictated to her by her spirit guide, Djwhal Khul the Tibetan. It is from her writings that words like 'reincarnation,' 'astrology,' 'meditation,' 'karma,' and 'nirvana' became popularized."

"Boy, those spirit guides really are into literature, aren't they."

"It says that the Lucis Trust was founded in 1922 under the parent name—LUCIFER PUBLISHING COMPANY. Hey, Michael, just listen to some of the famous people who have belonged to the Lucis Trust: Robert McNamara, Ronald Reagan, Henry Kissinger, David Rockefeller, Paul Volcker, and George Schultz."

"Huh. Isis, did you know that these very men were part of the Council on Foreign Relations? It's the elite group that influenced the founding of the United Nations. I remember that the Lucis Trust was headquartered for many years at the United Nations Plaza. I believe they've moved to somewhere on Wall Street now."

"What do you think about all this, Michael?"

"It sounds like Madame Blavatsky became an occultist and influenced Alice Bailey, who took her work and expanded on it. She in turn started *Lucifer* magazine and other organizations that continued the occult teachings. Her works and organizations then influenced men who started the United Nations. It doesn't make for a pretty picture."

Murphy picked up another folder. "It sounds like those gals were triple-threat charmers for sure. What do you think they had to do with Dr. Anderson?"

"I'm not sure yet. I've got some more reading to do."

THIRTY

JOHN BARTHOLOMEW SMILED to himself. *This is the perfect change of pace. No one will even notice us. It's one of the most crowded cities in the world.*

He was getting tired of meeting in the castle, and Switzerland was too cold. He wanted to enjoy the sun for a change. Besides, Señor Mendez had made arrangements so everyone could fly into Rio de Janeiro on separate planes. He had rented a large villa beyond Copacabana Beach near Rodrigo de Freitas Lagoon. It was a secluded spot where they would be alone and could bask in the sun.

How appropriate, he thought, *to be able to make plans to destroy Christianity, the rule of law, and set the stage for the Anti-Christ in the shadow of Corcovado Mountain with the giant Christ the Redeemer statue on top. Señor Mendez has a sense of humor.*

The meeting began at 10 A.M. on the shady veranda. Jakoba Werner was the first to speak in her thick German accent. Her blond hair was tied back in the usual tight bun. "I would like to commend Señor Mendez for his choice of location. The accommodations and the dinner last night were superb."

"I will second that," said Ganesh Shesha. "This reminds me of a presidential palace fifty kilometers outside Calcutta. I used to visit it often."

"Well, I'm sure that we all appreciate the sun rather than the snow," said Bartholomew. "Let me call this meeting to order. You will recall that at our last meeting, you were all given assignments to work on for our sevenfold plan for world governance. I will report on phase one."

Bartholomew passed out a detailed paper outlining the first phase.

"Let me highlight phase one: the relocation of the United Nations. We have begun to plant the suggestion into the minds of key UN leaders to consider moving the United Nations organization from the United States to Babylon in Iraq. We believe that this move will do several things. First, it will please the Europeans that America is losing its influence. Many European countries already resent U.S. policies and politics. They will think that the Americans are getting what they deserve for trying to control the world. Everyone likes to see the 'big dog' have its ego deflated. It will help to isolate the United States from the rest of the world. Second, the move to Iraq will please the Arabs and help to unite them. It will give them a sense of prestige. They'll believe that they are rising in power, and they'll think that they have some control over their future. It will also help to settle the various factions that are fighting with each other. Rebuilding Babylon will bring back Arab pride and give them all something to focus their energy on. Especially if it becomes the headquarters for the UN."

Viorica Enesco tossed her red hair. In her thick Romanian accent, she asked, "Wouldn't the Europeans object to having the UN in Babylon rather than somewhere in Europe?"

Bartholomew smiled. "Some of them may indeed object. But those in leadership positions will not care. They know that the UN is just window dressing anyway—all talk and no action in the final analysis. The UN would collapse instantly if the United States and the European Union withdrew their funding. The key leaders in Europe know that they have the real financial power and the expertise to control the Arab nations. They would strongly support the Arabs in exchange for lower oil prices. The United States would still have to support the UN or be accused of being Arab-phobic. They will cave in to the political pressure. That will cause a drain on U.S. finances and help to weaken the dollar. A crisis will soon occur that will help to expedite this phase."

Bartholomew gestured to Ganesh Shesha, who smiled slightly. His white teeth stood in sharp contrast to his dark skin.

"Phase two involves an increase in the threats of war. We have begun a plan to create a crisis between India and Pakistan. The threat of a nuclear war will help to cause political turmoil in the United States. It will get their leaders bogged down in time-wasting negotiations and political posturing. We will then send funding to key African warlords. They are egomaniacs already, and they will expand their power. They will begin eliminating their enemies, as they did with the extermination of hundreds of thousands in Rwanda and the fighting in Somalia and the Congo. The funding of certain Muslim factions will enable them to turn their anger toward the Christians in their countries. It will be wonderful to see the United States attempt to settle conflicts on many fronts."

The other six nodded in agreement.

"We have already started stirring up the North Koreans over the nuclear issue," Shesha explained. "We will increase the conflict and cause the United States to deploy more Navy ships and Army personnel to the area. At the same time we will increase the rumors that China is attempting to take over Taiwan. More resources will be drained from the United States. We have already begun to complicate the nuclear threat in Iran. The Americans now have to spend time planning war scenarios for that country. At the right moment we will instigate a combined attack on American consulates around the world. In conjuction with this, we will fund terrorists to make strikes at major seaports like Long Beach, California, and in New York City. The Americans already have a difficult time with security in these areas."

Bartholomew looked at Señor Mendez. "I believe that you are next."

"Yes. The next phase involves the boycott of U.S. trade. Our plan is to shut down the flow of oil to the United States. This will raise the price of gas and anger the people. There will be infighting, and everyone will blame the politicians, who will become protective of their positions. There will be turmoil. It is our hope that this will cause the Americans to begin to use up their oil reserves. This will create the need to drill for oil in Alaska. The environmentalists will fight Congress for endangering protected forests and waterways. Billions of dollars will be spent in attempting to drill for oil and pipe it to refineries. We want to help break the financial back of the only nation that stands in our way of world control."

Everyone clapped. John Bartholomew and Sir William Merton were calling "Here, here."

"We'll then help the European Union to open liberal trade negotiations with South America, Canada, Asia, India, and the African countries," Mendez continued. "They will turn to the EU for support. Nations around the world will begin to kiss up to Europe. At the same time we will tighten restrictions on American goods. The U.S. manufacturers will have to lay off people due to international boycotts. Unemployment demands and welfare checks will begin to drain the American coffers. Retail spending will decrease as the unemployed have to use all of their money just to survive. More people will be laid off in a vicious cycle of no demand and no supply. The citizens will become restless and hostile toward their own democratic government. In some places we will attempt to help create civil unrest. For example, we'll plant rumors that layoffs are being caused because of race and religious convictions. It will be chaotic."

"It sounds very good so far," Viorica Enesco said, smiling. "Now for phase four. This plan is to create medical emergencies. We are funding sleeper cells within the United States. At a given point they will release a smallpox epidemic. This will tie up medical personnel and many dollars. Other sleeper cells will send anthrax packages to local, state, and federal government leaders ... even in small- to medium-size communities. It will create pandemonium! This will tie up police, security, and emergency services all over America. More energy and money will be spent. Then, when the crisis seems to reach its peak, our remaining sleeper cells will bomb key larger hospitals. The Americans have a weakness for caring for the sick and needy. They will rally to their aid and will begin to pull in all their resources to protect their own."

"Isn't this wonderful?" Jakoba Werner said, shifting her weight in her chair and sitting forward. "In phase five, to weaken the U.S. stock market, we will then have the Arab sheikhs begin to move their money out of the U.S. market into the European Union. This will help strengthen the euro and weaken the U.S. dollar. We will tell large foreign stockholders to buy stocks on margin and inflate the market with a false upward trend. People will invest and then we'll have them fail to pay on the margin, causing a drop. We will attempt to cause some quick upward and then downward moves in the market. Investors will become nervous and stop investing. After this happens several times, Americans will begin to look at investing in the more stable European markets. More money will drain out of the United States. We may not be able to collapse the market, but we can greatly weaken it."

"Very good," John Bartholomew said enthusiastically.

Werner continued, "We will infuse money into the Americans' next presidential election. Our plan is to support those candidates who are more liberal and socialistic in their thinking. Once they are in office and world political pressure mounts, they will cave in to the demands of other countries. They will want to be accepted in the global community, not hated. They will seek peace at any cost. Their independence will decrease as they conform to the flow of the coming worldwide society of man."

Everyone turned and looked at General Li, who nodded. "Phase six is unique. It is called the fire plan. With the threats of war, nuclear proliferation, terrorist bombings, boycotting of U.S. trade, the increase in oil prices, the weakening of Wall Street, and medical emergencies—all of America's resources will be stretched to a breaking point. Certain sleeper cells will then start actual fires, beginning near large metropolitan areas. The first priority in firefighting is to protect people, then structures, then forests. As the fires rage in the cities, other sleeper cells will start forest fires near power plants, in the hope of shutting down large power grids. Then they will start fires in the forests surrounding dams. The plan is to cause erosion problems, which will lead to increased runoff, mudslides, and flooding. Hopefully this will damage crops, structures, and transportation."

Everyone nodded in agreement. The plan sounded wonderful to them.

"The U.S. has already been drained financially with the war in Iraq, tornadoes, hurricanes, and flood relief in its own country. They have been helping in relief efforts in Afghanistan and Turkey, and for the tidal wave victims. The weakening of the U.S. economy will affect the entire world. It will strengthen the European economy, and that is exactly what is needed. The only way to conquer a great country like the United States is by dividing it. If we can get it to fight on many fronts, the Americans will finally give up dealing with the rest of the world and will draw in to protect their own. They will become so weak as to no longer be a threat. Especially in the one place we have not yet mentioned: Israel. If we can get the U.S. to cut off aid to Israel, we can destroy and finally eliminate that canker from the face of the earth. The world will be in turmoil and will be crying for a world leader to step in and take control."

Sir William Merton was nodding vigorously. He looked a little warm in his clerical collar. "The seventh phase is to begin the religious movement," he explained. "When the world is in a desperate financial condition, the people will turn to religion for support. Remember, 'religion is the opiate of the masses.' We will begin funding various religious leaders and also begin to call for all faiths to unite. We will push for the universal brotherhood of man. We will support and encourage the homosexual community. Those who oppose them will be ridiculed, threatened, and punished. We can do this by instituting legislation that will take away critical tax advantages for churches and religious organizations. Any who oppose our plan can be accused of hate speech and jailed for nonconformity. That will squelch any opposition. We'll establish a new world religion that will have vast influence over the people." His eyes glowed as he spoke.

John Bartholomew cleared his throat and spoke. "Some parts of these plans are already in place and operating effectively. The rest will come into being soon. So far our plan is coming together. If Talon can carry out his assignments, I believe we will be right on schedule. I think this calls for a toast."

THIRTY-ONE

MURPHY LOOKED UP at Isis as she read, studying her for a moment. There was no question that she was beautiful. Her sparkling green eyes and red hair were striking, but there was more. She was smart, well-read, and could hold her own in almost any conversation. She was fun to be with and was not afraid to try things that were new and different. She was independent and yet at the same time seemed to need his strength. He felt a strong desire to protect her. He knew that he was beginning to recover from Laura's death. He could sense a new love growing, and it felt comfortable . . . and good.

Isis looked up and their eyes met. She smiled, and he fought the urge to reach out and embrace her. After a moment she lowered her eyes and began to read again. Murphy took a deep breath and opened a new folder.

As he picked the folder up, he noticed something about the journal he had just placed on the table. A piece of paper seemed to be sticking out in back. Murphy picked up the journal again and pulled what turned out to be two pages together. On one was a genealogy of the child Dr. Anderson and his partner had helped to create.

"Look at these!" Murphy exclaimed.

"It seems that Dr. Anderson has done some of the work for us already. Let's see what we can find about these people."

Murphy continued, "Anderson writes that Carmine Anguis, the father of the birth mother, was a Gypsy chieftain from the Rom tribe. They are well-known for fortune-telling. I've heard that some of their members built homes that looked like churches. They would then beg on the street—by showing them pictures of the outside of what looked like a cathedral. They would ask them to help build their church. It was really their home. That scam is still happening today. I've seen many of those types of homes in Romania."

"It sounds like a play on people's emotions. Does it say anything about the mother, Kala Matrinka?"

"Dr. Anderson suggests that she may have been a prostitute before becoming Carmine's wife."

"What about Alfred Meinrad?"

"He was a scientist and had a Ph.D. in astrophysics and a second Ph.D. in microbiology. He was a very outspoken atheist and evolutionist. I don't believe he ever married. According to newspaper reports, he was killed in a mysterious automobile accident. He

Traceable Genealogy of THE BOY
Harley B. Anderson, M.D.
Transylvania, Romania
October, 1963

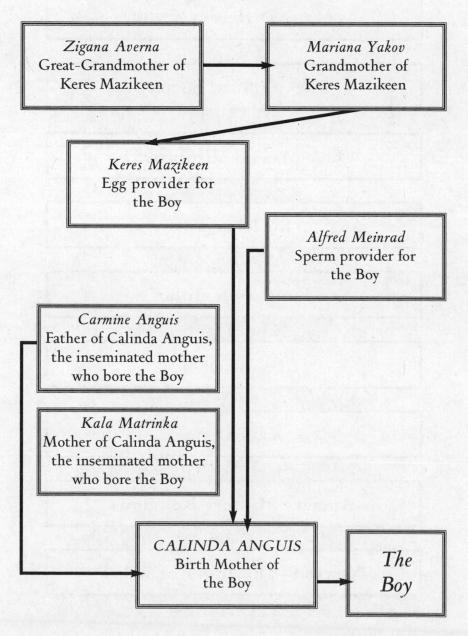

Zigana Averna
Great-Grandmother of
Keres Mazikeen

Mariana Yakov
Grandmother of
Keres Mazikeen

Keres Mazikeen
Egg provider for
the Boy

Alfred Meinrad
Sperm provider for
the Boy

Carmine Anguis
Father of Calinda Anguis,
the inseminated mother
who bore the Boy

Kala Matrinka
Mother of Calinda Anguis,
the inseminated mother
who bore the Boy

CALINDA ANGUIS
Birth Mother of
the Boy

The
Boy

NEW AGE MOVEMENT

Many Different Cults

Theosophical Society

Free Masons/Illuminati

Rosicrucians

Knights Templar

Gnosticism

Kabbalism

Ancient Mystery Religions

Nimrod—The Tower of Babel

was driving in the mountains when all of a sudden he veered off the road and down into a canyon. Does that scenario sound familiar?"

"That's just what happened to Dr. Talpish!" Isis exclaimed thoughtfully. "Michael, you asked me how Madame Blavatsky, Annie Besant, and Alice Ann Bailey tied together with Dr. Anderson. I think I've found it. Look at the genealogy of the Boy. Zigana Averna was the great-grandmother of Keres Mazikeen. Zigana worked as an assistant for all three of the women. First for Blavatsky, then Besant, and finally Bailey. She died sometime in the early 1940s. She was the mother of an illegitimate child named Mariana Yakov. The father's name was Ivan Yakov from Stalingrad. Ivan Yakov was later imprisoned for murder. Mariana Yakov became a prostitute until her mid-thirties, when she married Aaron Mazikeen. Dr. Anderson indicated that he was a drug smuggler and was shot to death in Istanbul. Mariana Yakov gave birth to a girl named Keres Mazikeen. Later Yakov, an alcoholic, died. Mazikeen provided the egg for the Boy. Alfred Meinrad provided the sperm. Calinda Anguis was merely the host body that gave birth to the fertilized egg."

"Wow!" said Murphy. "Dr. Anderson really had to do some investigating to discover all that."

"Yes," Isis agreed. "He goes on to say that Zigana was an expert in table rapping, séances, fortune-telling, and channeling of spirits. She even exceeded Blavatsky in her ability to do signs and wonders. She became a devil worshipper and excelled in corruption of every sort."

"I don't think I would want her baby-sitting the grandchildren."

"Michael, Michael! Listen!" Isis exclaimed, reviewing the genealogy. "You know that I can read and speak many languages."

"Sure. I know that."

"Look at these names. *Zigana Averna*: *Zigana* is Hungarian for 'gypsy,' and *Averna* is Latin for 'queen of the underworld.'

"*Mariana Yakov*: *Mariana* is Russian for 'rebellious,' and *Yakov* is Russian for 'supplanter'—one who takes the place of another.

"*Keres Mazikeen*: *Keres* is Greek for 'evil spirits,' and *Mazikeen* is Jewish for 'elflike beings that can change shapes.'

"*Alfred Meinrad*: *Alfred* is Italian for 'counselor to the elves,' and *Meinrad* is German for 'strong advisor.'

"*Carmine Anguis*: *Carmine* is Latin for 'crimson,' and *Anguis* is Latin for 'dragon.'

"*Kala Matrinka*: *Kala* is Egyptian for 'black,' and *Matrinka* is Egyptian for 'divine mother.'

"And finally *Calinda Anguis*: *Calinda* is Latin for 'fiery,' and *Anguis* is Latin for 'dragon.'

"There's something really spooky about all of this," Isis said softly. "Michael, what do you think the other piece of paper means?"

Murphy looked at the page headed "New Age Movement." "My guess is that Dr. Anderson did some further investigation," he said thoughtfully. "In the Bible, Nimrod was considered the father of all cults against God. He is given credit for instigating the Tower of Babel as a rebellion against God. The various ancient mystery religions came from him. Those gave rise to Kabbalism—something you are hearing about in the news today—Gnosticism, and then the secret societies like Knights Templar, Rosicrucians, Free Masons, and the Illuminati. Anderson must have started with Madame Blavatsky and the Theosophical Society and traced its origins back to Nimrod. No wonder he was feeling guilty and wanted to rectify his errors."

"It sort of sounds like the story of Judas and how he felt remorse for being a traitor to Christ. See, I *do* know a little about the Bible," Isis said with a smile.

"You're right, Isis. It reminds me of a short poem:

"Still as of old
Men by themselves are priced.
For thirty pieces Judas sold
Himself, not Christ."

"Michael, this is becoming very scary."

THIRTY-TWO

RASHAD ENTERED the great hall and paused for a moment as he stroked his beard. A thorough search of so large a building would take some time. He walked over to the card catalog and pretended to be looking up something.

A few minutes later Asim strolled through the doors. He went to the magazine rack, selected one, and then sat down at an empty table. He opened the magazine and held it as if reading. However, his eyes were not focused on the pages; he was looking beyond.

The next to enter was Fadil. No casual observer would have paid any attention to the first two Arabs. They acted quite normal. Fadil, on the other hand, stood out—not his tall thin body, but his nervous mannerisms. He seemed anxious and his body made quick jerking movements. His eyes darted back and forth, and perspiration sheened on his forehead and stained his shirt. He made his way to a bookcase and quickly pulled down a book. He didn't even look at it. He just held it as his eyes searched the room.

Alvena Smidt was deeply engrossed in looking up the difference between "quiddity" and "quidnunc" in the dictionary when she heard a voice.

"Excuse me, madame. But could you assist me?"

At the sound of the voice her eyes brightened. She looked into the face of a light-skinned man with a neatly trimmed mustache, wearing a topcoat and gloves. He was tall and wiry-looking. His emotionless eyes were the type that would make most people shiver. But not Alvena Smidt.

"Don't say another word," she exclaimed. "Let me guess. You're from Cape Town, and you speak Afrikaans."

"You are correct," Talon said, surprised. "How did you know that?"

Smidt took off her glasses and stood up. She adjusted her blue polka-dot dress and approached the counter, smiling broadly.

"I knew it. I just knew it! I was born and raised in Cape Town myself. My parents came from a line of Dutch traders that go back to the 1700s. I can always tell someone who is from South Africa. I guess it's the combination of English and Dutch tones in their voice. At home my parents only spoke Afrikaans, and your voice is much like my father's. It is so good to hear someone from home. I moved to the States after college and have been here ever since."

"That is all very nice, but I was wondering if you could help me."

"Oh, yes. I'd be glad to. Are you needing to look up some book or article? You look like the type of man who loves to read. I bet that you love the classics, don't you? I like classical music. It's so stimulating. Do you—"

He interrupted. "I'm looking for some friends of mine. A man and a woman. They are—"

"Are they from South Africa too? I'd love to meet them. I wonder if they might know any of my family."

"No, they're not from South Africa!" he said firmly. "The man is about my height, six foot three, rugged-looking. The woman is a redhead. Have they been in here?"

"Oh, yes. Who could miss that beautiful woman with the red hair? She looked like a model. Is she a model? And the man with her was so handsome. They made such a striking couple. I thought to myself, now, there's a happy couple. I wonder how many children they have. I just love children. Don't you?"

"Are they still here?" he said through gritted teeth.

"I don't know. But if they are, bring them back to the counter. I'd love to meet them."

"I appreciate your assistance. You're quite solicitous."

Smidt smiled and blushed at the same time. It was not often that she met someone who was polite and knew how to use the English language. Most people would have only said "Thanks for your help." That was okay, but it was so common. She watched him walk away. *It's such a joy to have a conversation with someone who is educated . . . and from South Africa too.*

She continued to watch him as he went over to the short man with the dark mustache at the card catalog. Two other Arab-looking men joined them.

He must be a diplomat or something. I wonder if he speaks Arabic also.

Smidt was about to put her glasses back on when she saw the man look back at her, smiling and nodding. She flushed. He was not only educated, he was good-looking too . . . and she had been lonely for quite some time.

"Michael, I'll be back in a moment," Isis said, rising. "I need to use the ladies' room."

As he watched Isis walk away, Murphy realized that Dr. Anderson's notes might help them discover more clues as to who the Anti-Christ might be. He knew that if what they were reading was true, they probably were in real danger.

Whoever the Friends of The New World Order are, it's certain that they are powerful and have an evil plan. They succeeded in killing Dr. Anderson. Will we be next? Murphy wondered.

Smiling to herself, Isis turned and looked back at Murphy as she walked off in search of the restroom. *When he's focused on something, it would take an earthquake to get his attention.*

After passing row after row of bookshelves, she found a sign saying that the restroom was on the second floor. She did not look down into the great hall as she descended one flight. She didn't see the Arabs talking . . . nor did she notice Talon.

"Rashad, you and Fadil search the right side of the main floor. Asim and I will search the left side. If you find them, do not approach. Pretend that you are just ordinary people in the library. One of you stay in the area and the other come and get me. We will move up one floor at a time. Asim and I will use the elevator as we go up; you two use the stairs. That way they will not get by us."

Talon was about to continue when Asim interrupted.

"Can we not kill them? I want to avenge the death of Ibrahim."

"They will die, but we must be careful. This is a public place, and we don't want people to identify us. I know you want them dead, but there is more at stake here than just the lives of two people. We don't want their deaths to jeopardize our opportunity to kill thousands."

THIRTY-THREE

SHARI WAS SIPPING a cup of coffee at a table near the student center when Paul Wallach walked up. He wasn't quite sure how to begin. He and Shari hadn't seen each other for about a week, and their last conversation did not end well.

"Hi, Paul. Thank you for coming. Do you want to get something to drink?"

"No, I think I'll pass. I just had lunch a little while ago. How've you been?"

Shari paused for a moment. "Not very good," she said truthfully. "I've been crying a lot, Paul, and I finally realized I can't go on feeling this way."

Wallach didn't say a thing. This conversation was going somewhere he really didn't want to go.

"Paul," Shari continued, "do you remember when we used to have discussions about religion?"

"Before the bombing?"

"Yes. At that time you seemed quite interested in looking into the Christian faith. And even after the bombing when I visited you in the hospital and took care of you after you got out, you were interested. But now something's changed. You don't seem to want that to be part of your life."

"I guess it's just not what I thought it would be. I'm finding that my interests are changing," Wallach said quickly.

"Changing?"

"Yeah. I'm focusing my energies on the future," he explained. "It seems to charge my batteries more than church. Don't get me wrong; church is fine for some people—like yourself—but it's just not my thing."

"What is your thing, Paul?"

Wallach began to feel a little uncomfortable. He hadn't really had to put his thoughts into words before. "I mean, I want to get out of school and get started in the business world."

"With Barrington Network News?"

"Yes. Media is an exciting field."

"I think that you may be getting a wrong picture about that world. Barrington's company produces a lot of sleazy programs on television and radio. They go against the moral fabric of society. How can you be a part of that?"

"Barrington also does a lot of good. There are many positive, uplifting programs," Wallach countered.

"Paul, you know that I've always been honest with you and with my feelings. I think that you're being used."

Wallach bristled and began to get defensive. "No one is using me!" he exclaimed.

"Do you think that all the wining and dining and trips to New York in Shane Barrington's jet are because he has a personal interest in you?"

"Yes, I do think so. He lost his son and has sort of adopted me in his place."

"I know that he's paying your tuition and has promised you a job after you graduate."

"Right, and he also pays me for articles that I send in to him."

"Does he print the articles?"

"No."

"What are they about?"

"They're about what I learn in Dr. Murphy's classes."

"And why is Barrington asking you to write them?"

"He says that he wants to evaluate my writing style so he can place me in the proper department after I graduate."

"I think something else is going on," Shari said firmly.

"What do you mean?" Wallach responded, annoyed.

"Why would a billionaire who's known to be an egomaniac suddenly pay the tuition of a college student he never met before? And why would he pay him money to write articles he doesn't print, about archaeology of all things? He doesn't ask to see your writing style on other topics, Paul, does he? Only on what transpires in Dr. Murphy's class? I think he's hiring you to be his personal spy."

"You're just angry because I sometimes challenge your precious Dr. Murphy in class. Not everyone believes in creation, you know," Wallach said angrily.

"It's not that at all, Paul. I'm concerned with your values in life. God doesn't seem to be high on your list. Money, power, and pride seem to be your focus. Those things can be very attractive at first, but in the long run they destroy a person. They don't bring true satisfaction. Jesus said, 'And how do you benefit if you gain the whole world but lose your own soul in the process?' Is anything worth more than your soul?"

"My soul is fine, thank you. I just want to get out of school and start earning some money."

"Why, Paul?"

"That's a crazy question, Shari," Wallach answered, exasperated. "I want money so I can buy things."

"Things?"

"Yeah. Like a car, a house, a boat, or a plasma television... things!"

"Then what?"

"What do you mean?"

"Well, after you buy all the things, then what are you going to do?"

"Have fun!"

"Let me see if I understand," Shari said slowly. "A job earns you money, so you can buy things, so you can have some fun. Right?"

"Right."

"Paul, things don't bring lasting happiness. A car can wear out. A house can burn down. A boat can sink. And a plasma television can break. When that happens, where will your fun be?"

"Everyone has to earn money to live!"

"I don't disagree with working to provide for one's family. But in all of our conversations, you haven't talked about family, or service to the community, or contributing to the nation, or raising children with values that you can pass on. And most of all, you haven't included God in any of the scenarios you've shared with me. Most of your conversations have been self-centered and me-focused. You don't talk about helping others."

Wallach was silent. He didn't quite know how to respond; in his heart of hearts, he recognized that Shari had accurately described his mind-set.

"Paul, there is a something in the book of Second Corinthians I'd like you to think about. It says: '*Do not try to work together as equals with unbelievers, for it cannot be done. How can right and wrong be partners? How can light and darkness live together? How can Christ and the Devil agree? What does a believer have in common with an unbeliever? How can God's temple come to terms with pagan idols? For we are the temple of the living God!*' "

Wallach paused for a moment, trying to process what Shari had just said. "Are you saying that I'm in darkness and on the Devil's side?" he asked angrily.

"Let me try to explain. You and I think differently about God, eternal values, how to conduct one's life, and what's important in life. It's like water and oil. They can't be mixed together. Try as hard as I would like to, it's just not going to happen. If we were to continue our relationship you wouldn't be happy with me and I wouldn't be happy with you." Shari's eyes were beginning to well up with tears.

"I think it's best if we break off seeing each other," she continued. "It's evident that you and I are walking down separate roads. I can't reject all that I believe in and hold dear, no matter how much I care for you. Trying to do so will only end in disaster. I wish it didn't have to end this way, but in the long run it will be the best for both of us." Shari rose and turned away as she finished her sentence. Tears were pouring down her cheeks.

THIRTY-FOUR

WHEN ISIS CAME out of the restroom, she had no idea that Rashad and Fadil had already made it to the second floor. They were slowly walking down one end of the bookshelves, stopping at each aisle to see who might be standing there.

Fadil was a half step behind Rashad. Perspiring more than ever, he kept having to wipe his brow. An accountant by trade, Fadil had only recently been recruited to join one of the sleeper cells. He wanted to help the cause, but he had not been trained to fight and kill like the others. This was all new to him, and he was terrified. He kept thinking about his wife and children at home. What would become of them if he did not return—or if he was caught and imprisoned? Would his family be put into prison also? With thoughts like these whirling through his mind, he had a hard time concentrating on the task at hand.

Isis reached into her pocket and pulled out a piece of paper. On it were her notes from the card catalog earlier in the morning.

```
The Secret Doctrine
by Helena Petrovna Blavatsky
Born 1831 Died 1891
2nd Floor—B section #B12743 Hp. 142
```

She began looking for the B section, focusing on the numbers. She couldn't wait to see what Blavatsky had written. The woman sounded fascinating.

Isis stopped at the end of two rows of shelves and looked up at their numbers. She then checked her paper again.

This is it.

Just as Isis had stopped to look at the shelves' numbers, Rashad and Fadil were at the other end of the aisle looking down. They didn't see her because the shelves blocked her from their view. They continued in the opposite direction as she started looking on the shelves for Blavatsky's book.

After she had found it, Isis headed toward the stairs. At the same moment, Rashad and Fadil entered an aisle far behind her. Isis had already opened the book and was reading it as she walked slowly up the marble stairs. Talon and Asim, on the other side of the library peering among the shelves, did not see her.

As Isis reached the third floor, she turned and looked down into the great hall. She paused for a moment to admire the beauty of the old building and the chandeliers. She was about to turn into the aisle and go back to where Murphy was studying when she saw him. *Talon!*

Terror overwhelmed her. Instinctively she drew back into one of the aisles. Adrenaline surged through her body, her heart raced, and she began breathing heavily. Her mind flashed back to when she had seen Talon on the back of the ship on the Black Sea. She had been certain he would kill her—then Murphy arrived, and Talon and the brass plates went into the ocean. But how did he find them here? And who was with him?

Isis watched as Talon nodded and entered the elevator. She could see the old golden arrow above the elevator door begin to rise to the third floor. As she started to turn toward Murphy, she saw two men starting up the marble stairs. They too looked like Arabs. Could they be here with Talon? Was it they whom he had nodded at? A surge of panic threatened to overwhelm her.

Isis knew that the two men coming up the stairs would not see Murphy immediately. Their table was in a far corner, blocked by bookshelves running the opposite direction. She moved as quietly as she could toward Murphy, and then she heard voices. She quickly turned and stood at the end of an aisle and froze, her heart in her throat. The men were speaking in Arabic. She could understand the dialect.

"They may have already left the library."

"That may be. But we have found out which hotel they are staying at. It's only a matter of time."

Their voices trailed off, as if they were moving farther away. Isis knew that they would soon go farther down the aisle and find Murphy. She also knew that she must not make any sound that could attract their attention.

She worked her way down the aisle to a place where she could see Murphy. How could she get his attention without moving closer or having him speak?

Isis opened Madame Blavatsky's book and tore out the blank

first page. On it she wrote one word: Talon. She then folded the paper like an airplane and tossed it at Murphy.

Murphy was deeply engrossed in Dr. Anderson's journal again when he sensed a slight movement of air and saw a paper airplane glide onto the table. He looked up only to see Isis standing in an aisle some distance from him, eyes wide in terror. She had one finger over her lips. With her other hand she was pointing at the paper airplane.

Murphy knew something was terribly wrong. After unfolding the paper and reading it, he started and half rose. He glanced quickly at Isis. She still had her finger over her lips but was now motioning for him to come toward her. He left the table, stuffing his research notes into his pocket, and tiptoed over to her. She fell into his arms, shaking. She put her hand over his mouth as he began to speak. Quietly she led him down the aisle to the end, where she carefully looked around the corner. She could not see either of the Arab men. They must have gone down an aisle; that meant that soon they'd be working their way back toward them!

Isis grabbed Murphy's hand and led him toward the marble staircase. After glancing around cautiously, they hurried up the stairs to the fourth floor. They had to find a way to escape.

THIRTY-FIVE

AFTER REACHING the fourth floor, Isis and Murphy quickly disappeared into the bookshelves.

"Michael, I'm so scared. There are at least four of them," Isis whispered.

"Tell me what you saw."

Isis explained her first sighting of Talon and the Arab entering the elevator and the conversation she overheard in Arabic. "They'll be up here soon, Michael. What are we going to do?"

"I don't know. Let me look around." Murphy only had a few moments to scout around before Isis whispered.

"I see them coming up the stairs."

"Come back here where the two directions of bookshelves converge. I don't think they'll see us immediately."

Rashad and Fadil split up after reaching the top of the stairs.

Rashad started down the bookshelves that were close to the railing overlooking the great hall. Fadil turned down an aisle and started toward Murphy and Isis.

Murphy whispered, "When he gets near, step into the aisle and say something to him in Arabic." Then Murphy disappeared.

Fadil was caught completely off guard as he approached the end of the aisle. All of a sudden a beautiful woman with red hair stepped in front of him, took a sexy pose, and smiled.

"My, but you are handsome," she murmured. "I'll bet all of the women want to go out with you."

She was close. She was extremely attractive. And she was speaking in Arabic. Fadil did not know how to respond. He had been told not to make contact, only to find out where Murphy and Isis were. He didn't know what to do. He hadn't been trained. Should he grab her? Should he yell? Should he pretend that she was a stranger? As he turned to walk away, he didn't hear Murphy coming.

Murphy fired a quick reverse punch to the Arab's sternum. The surprise and pain took his breath away, and he staggered backward. Fadil's eyes were wide with shock when Murphy struck his temple with an open palm-heel strike. He immediately collapsed to the floor unconscious.

Murphy dragged his body over to a table. He placed Fadil in a chair and made him lie forward as if he had fallen asleep while reading a book.

"That will take care of him. Quick, come with me. I've found a ladder that leads through a crawl hole to the roof. It will take them a little while to figure out where we went."

On the roof, Murphy found a fire escape that ran down the side of the building. "Most likely they'll think we went down the fire escape to the alley, and they'll try to follow us. I've got a better idea."

Isis followed him to a small building that covered the elevator shaft. He pried open the door and looked down. "There's a ladder that goes down the shaft," Murphy explained. "We'll climb down and try to get onto the top of the elevator. Maybe we can ride it to the first floor, then get in and get off in the main lobby, where there are lots of people. We might be able to get lost in the crowd."

It didn't take Rashad very long to find Fadil. At first he thought he was dead, but then could feel a heartbeat. He ran down the aisle toward the great hall. Looking around, he spied Talon and Asim on the fourth floor on the left side of the library. He gave a short shrill whistle and waved. The other two men came running.

Rashad explained about Fadil and said, "I have looked around. I think they must have gone up the ladder in the corner, to the roof."

"Good work," said Talon. "Asim and I will go to the roof. You go down the stairs to the first floor. They may still be hiding in the building."

Mandy and Scott Willard and their grandmother had just gotten on the elevator on the third floor. They had been to the children's area, and each was holding several books. As they pushed the button for the first floor, they heard a thud on the top of the elevator. They all looked up.

To their surprise, a hole in the top of the elevator popped open. They could see the face of a man peering down. The grandmother gasped as the children looked on, wide-eyed.

Murphy dropped into the elevator and smiled. "How are you folks today?"

Murphy then raised his arms upward, and down through the

hole came Isis. She shook her head and ran her fingers through her hair, fluffing it.

"Hello," she said with a smile.

"Who are you?" the boy asked in surprise.

Murphy leaned forward and put his finger to his lips. "Shhh. Can you keep a secret?"

Both children nodded; the grandmother just stood there with her mouth open.

"We're detectives trying to find some top-secret information. Some evil men are after us."

"Cool," said the boy.

"Can you promise not to let them know that we were here?"

Both children nodded vigorously.

"Now, raise your hand and say 'I promise to keep the secret from the evil men,'" Murphy said seriously.

"I promise," both said as they raised their free hands.

By then the doors opened at the first floor and Murphy and Isis exited the elevator. The two children waved good-bye, and the grandmother was still looking on in shocked silence.

They were almost to the front door when Rashad saw them. He ran across the great hall, shoving chairs aside to clear his path.

Alvena Smidt's head jerked up at the commotion. "There's no running in the library!" she called out in a loud whisper. "You must be quiet!"

Rashad didn't even hear her. And if he had, it wouldn't have made a difference. He couldn't let them get away!

Isis had seen the man start to run as they were exiting the front door. "Michael! One of them has seen us."

Murphy grabbed her hand and they ran across the busy street, dodging cars, around the building, and into the alley.

Murphy had Isis hide behind a Dumpster. He grabbed one of the bottles littering the ground and hid behind some boxes.

Rashad could see no movement in the long alley. He drew his gun, and moved forward cautiously, looking left and right. After Rashad had just passed the boxes, Murphy threw the bottle. It crashed on the wall on the opposite side of the alley, and instinctively Rashad turned toward the sound and fired.

That was Murphy's opportunity. Rushing forward, he hit the Arab from behind. The impact sent the gun flying out of his hand and Rashad to the ground. Recovering quickly, he rolled and jumped to his feet.

Murphy could tell that he was facing a trained fighter. They began to circle, sizing each other up. Then the Arab rushed in, ducking, and took out Murphy's feet with a leg sweep. Murphy crashed to the concrete, onto his elbow. Murphy rolled and sprang to his feet only to receive a side kick to the stomach. He fell backward in pain.

He flashed to the face of Terence Li, a young Cantonese archaeology student who had taught Murphy the secret of drunken-man fighting.

"Professor Murphy, when a drunken man falls, he is soft, like a rag. He does not hurt himself. When he stands up, he is hard to hit, like a sapling swaying in the wind. And when he strikes, no one expects it."

Murphy began to stagger, as if he had been seriously injured by the kick. He looked like he would fall over at any second.

Rashad smiled and went in for the kill. He was going to use a tiger claw strike to Murphy's throat and break his larynx. Murphy's head was drooping; he looked too injured even to lift his head.

Rashad lunged with his right arm outstretched. As he moved forward, Murphy glided slightly to the right and planted his foot. At the same time, he drove his right fist around, top center knuckle leading, into the left side of Rashad's neck just under the jawbone. Instantly paralyzed, the Arab dropped to the ground in a heap.

Murphy bent over and looked at him. *That will probably take him about two months to get over*, he thought grimly.

Murphy and Isis straightened their clothing and hid out in the back of a busy coffee shop for three hours before returning to the library. They needed to retrieve Dr. Anderson's folders and journal, but they wanted to be sure the coast was clear. They entered the library carefully, looking all around for Talon and his associates. Seeing none of them, they climbed to the third floor and went back to the table where they had been working. The table was empty, and Murphy's briefcase was gone.

"Do you suppose the library staff picked it up, Michael?" Isis asked, a hopeful note in her voice.

"I certainly hope so. I don't like the alternative."

Alvena Smidt was studying the difference between "primogenitor" and "primogeniture" when Murphy and Isis approached the front desk.

"Excuse me," Murphy said. "We happened to leave some papers on a desk on the third floor. Would any of the library staff have picked them up?"

Smidt looked at Murphy and Isis and smiled. "Why, I'll bet you're the people the gentleman from South Africa was looking for. How did you meet him? Did you go to school in South Africa?"

"South Africa?"

"Oh, yes. The moment I met your friend I could tell he was from South Africa. I guessed that he spoke Afrikaans, and he said I was right. He was well-spoken and quite educated. And he had—"

"Excuse me," Murphy interrupted. "About the papers?"

"Oh, yes. Your friend picked them up for you. He said you forgot your briefcase and he would take it to you. He was such a nice man. Very soft-spoken and polite. He left about three hours ago. Is there anything else I can help you with?"

"No, thank you," Murphy replied, turning from the desk.

———

Murphy and Isis paused on the steps of the library.

"There goes all of our clues about the Anti-Christ," he said in a dejected tone.

Isis didn't say anything. Nothing she could say would bring back Dr. Anderson's notes. Murphy brushed his fingers through his hair. "South Africa," he murmured. "That's interesting. At least we learned something new about Talon. He's from South Africa and he speaks Afrikaans. That may give us a way to track down more information about him."

Isis could see Murphy's expression change as he looked into her eyes. "I'm glad you're safe," he said soberly.

THIRTY-SIX

The night of the attack, Babylon, 539 B.C.

SULAIMAN SLOWLY CLIMBED *the long stairway up to the king's banquet hall. The night was warm and the moon was full. Torches lined both sides of the stairs, and it was easy to see. The smell of jasmine was in the air. He was looking for and alert to any danger that might be lurking in the shadows. As he glanced around he did not see any danger, only laughing couples half drunk with wine and groping each other.*

As captain of the king's royal guard, it was his job to ensure that his men were on duty and not swept up in the debauchery of the evening. It was difficult for young soldiers to stand by watching others indulging themselves and keep their minds on the task of protecting the king and his nobles.

This was not the first time that King Belshazzar had invited his friends to a night of revelry. In fact, these parties were becoming more and more frequent. This was, however, the largest one Sulaiman had seen. The wine was flowing freely among the thousand guests. And tonight the celebration wasn't restricted to the palace—all of Babylon was caught up in the excitement.

"General Azzam," young Captain Hakeem said, saluting. "Do you have any more men you can spare? General Jawhar is pleading for help. He says that we must get the trench dug within the hour. He thinks that he will be able to breach the Euphrates into the marsh above the city. They have about thirty cubits to go."

"Tell him I can give him two thousand." He signaled his aide, gave him the order, and sent the captain running into the night.

General Jawhar, pleased with the reinforcements, sent a message back to General Azzam. The soldiers would be readied. As soon as the water was drained from the moat, a detachment would be sent under the wall. According to the two deserters, Gobryas and Gadatas, there was a secret way into Babylon. Once the troops got in, they would open the main gate and let in the rest of the army.

As Sulaiman entered the great hall, one of the royal guards came running to him. "Sir, the king is calling for you!"

Sulaiman ran to find the king. "I just had a great idea," the king exclaimed. "I remember as a small child that King Nebuchadnezzar took me into the temple treasury of Marduk. He showed magnificent treasures captured in battle—many gold and silver cups taken from the temple of Jehovah in Jerusalem. Go down to the treasury and bring all of the cups to the great hall. I want to serve my guests in those beautiful goblets."

"Yes, O King," Sulaiman said, bowing and turning to leave.

Within fifteen minutes he had returned with servants carrying armloads of gold and silver cups. Soon they were cleaned and filled with wine.

The glittering goblets were passed out to the princes and their wives and concubines. They drunkenly toasted each other and their idols. Their laughter became louder and their toasts more coarse.

Suddenly a loud scream was heard over the din in the great hall.

Everyone turned and looked. Those closest to one side of the great hall could see the fingers of a man's hand writing on the plaster wall. There was no arm or body, just the hand and fingers.

Belshazzar pushed forward so he could see clearly. At the sight of the hand and fingers moving of their own volition, the blood drained from his face. Terrified, he collapsed to the floor, shouting, "Call the magicians! Bring the astrologers! Gather the soothsayers and sorcerers. Get the Chaldeans! Find anyone who can read the handwriting on the wall! I will make the man who can read it the third most powerful ruler in the kingdom. I will dress him in a purple robe and give him royal honor. I will put a gold chain around his neck. I need to know what it says!"

Women ran screaming from the hall, followed by their husbands or lovers.

Sulaiman and the royal guards, their swords drawn, were prepared for battle. They were forming ranks to protect the king. The terror on their ruler's face unnerved the officers and nobles.

Soon the sounds of yelling and screaming reached the queen mother in her chambers. She rushed to the banquet hall to find the king curled up in a a fetal position, sobbing.

"Calm yourself, your majesty," she said firmly, pulling Belshazzar into a sitting position. "There is a man in your kingdom who has within him the spirit of the holy gods. During your father's reign this Daniel was found to be as full of wisdom and understanding as a god himself. He was made chief of all the magicians, astrologers, Chaldeans, and soothsayers of Babylon. Daniel can interpret dreams and explain riddles. He will tell you what the writing means."

THIRTY-SEVEN

ABRAMS DISCOVERED that it was not easy to get to Presidio, Texas. First he had to fly to Dallas, then he took a commuter plane to El Paso, where he rented a car. The two-hundred-and-fifty-mile drive from El Paso took him southeast paralleling the Rio Grande until he reached Esperanza and then east to Van Horn, where he entered the low rolling Sierra Viejas. At Marfa he turned south and drove another fifty miles to the sleepy little town of Presidio on the edge of the Rio Grande. Across the river was the Mexican border town of Ojinaga.

After stopping for gas and directions, Abrams drove through the main business area to a very poor section of the small town. It didn't take him long to find the run-down Pancho Villa Motel. It was surrounded by boarded-up businesses, broken-down homes, and small wooden shacks.

He glanced around to see if anyone was watching. The street had little traffic and no one was out walking during siesta time. Only two beat-up cars were parked in the motel's lot. He parked, walked to the door of room 17, and knocked. The curtain on the window moved slightly and then he heard the *click* of the lock.

A big man with long curly black hair and a full beard opened the door. He had on a dirty T-shirt, exposing muscular arms, and he wore faded and ripped jeans. His sparkling brown eyes didn't fit his worn-out clothing.

"Levi! It's so good to see you again. Come in quickly."

Abrams entered the room and closed the door behind him. "That's some disguise, David," he said, grinning. "Even your wife and children wouldn't recognize you."

"Levi, I'm glad they sent you. This stakeout has been boring."

"Aren't they all?"

"True. I've been living in this mansion for about twenty days. During the daytime I walk about with a gunnysack picking up cans and bottles. The locals think I'm just another wanderer trying to make a few pennies like they do. Then I saw four Arabs move into one of the old sheds down by the river. It doesn't even have any running water. Just an outhouse behind the shed. They must have crossed the border during the night. They have been very low profile, keeping to themselves and going out only for food. Outwardly they look poor and ragged like everyone else . . . until they pull out their cell phones."

"Have you learned anything else?"

"Two days ago I followed two of them. They went to a used car lot in town and bought two old vans. I was watching from a distance. I could see them pull out a wad of cash to pay the dealer. I called the office then. I think they're getting ready to move."

"I've been given the green light to put the pressure on," Abrams said. "Somehow we have to get more information. Is there a way we can get one of them alone?"

"I think so," David replied. "Each day around eight o'clock when it starts to get dark one of them gets into a van and drives to a store. I've been following him in that old Chevy out front. We could probably take him then."

Abrams and David pulled into the store's lot a few moments after the van parked.

"Levi, you stay in the car until we come out. You look a little out of place for around here. I'll take him after he finishes shopping. Then we can go somewhere and interrogate him."

Inside the small store, David quickly spotted the Arab at the far end of one of the aisles. David picked up a box of cereal and pretended to read the label. After a moment he glanced up only to see the Arab staring at him. Although their eyes met only briefly, David could sense that the man was uncomfortable.

Oh, no! He might have made me! David turned and walked away, attempting to look as if he was completely uninterested.

Abrams glanced up when he saw the Arab running out of the store and rushing into the van.

What's going on?

A moment later David was running out of the store. "He made me," he called. "Quick, let's go. Don't lose him!"

The van was squealing out of the parking lot as David climbed in and closed the door. Abrams stepped on the gas.

At one corner the van almost rolled, and the driver could barely maintain control. He sideswiped a parked car and continued. Soon they were on a straight stretch away from town. Abrams attempted to drive alongside the van to force it off the road.

"Levi, he's on a cell phone talking to someone," David shouted.

The words were just out of David's mouth when the Arab swerved, making Abrams step on the brakes.

"Look, Levi! The lights are beginning to flash at that railroad crossing ahead."

The two men could see the lights of the approaching train, but they couldn't tell how fast it was moving.

"I think he's going to try to cross before the train gets there. We'll lose him if he does." Abrams stepped on the gas pedal.

The front of the van crossed the tracks just as the train hit it about midpoint. There was a tremendous crash, and the gas tank exploded.

Abrams braked hard. The two men sat there for a moment, watching a ball of fire being shoved down the track by a long snake.

They could see the train beginning to stop about a quarter of a mile down the track.

"Levi, we've got to get back to that shack," David exclaimed. "He might have called to warn them. We mustn't let them get out of Presidio."

As they approached the shack, they could see three men loading a van. The lights of their car caused the Arabs to run for cover. Abrams stopped about fifty yards from the shack, then he and David jumped out, leaving the headlights on.

One of the Arabs stepped from the shed with a rocket-propelled grenade launcher. With a stream of yellow light, the car was blown backward in a ball of flame.

Both David and Abrams drew their weapons and fired toward the shed. For a moment there was silence.

Abrams picked up an old bottle and tossed it. As soon as it hit the ground, small-arms fire came from the Arabs, aimed at the sound. David and Abrams responded with a volley of shots, and a man yelped in pain.

David whispered. "Do you think we got them?"

"We got someone," Abrams said firmly. "Either that, or they're trying to sucker us to expose ourselves. Let's crawl around and approach them from the rear."

It took the men about seven minutes to crawl behind the shed. As they took up their position, they heard a motor start: the van! They jumped up and started running. The shed was blocking their shot. By the time they had circled the building, it was too late. The van had sped away.

"Quick, David," Abrams called out. "We don't have much time. I can hear sirens in the distance. Someone must have reported the explosion and the sound of gunshots. We've got to check out the shed."

The two men pulled out small flashlights and stepped inside. Two of the Arabs were on the floor, dead. They could see a cache of small arms and some RPG shells, clothing items, and food.

"They must have loaded everything else in the van," David said bitterly.

"I'll take a look at the outhouse and then we must leave. Stay outside and keep an eye out."

Abrams pulled open the door to the ramshackle outhouse and shined his light inside. The odor was repellent.

I hate these things, he thought with distaste.

He stepped onto the wooden floor and looked about. As he turned, he heard a hollow sound under his feet. Shining his light down, he could see that one board didn't have nails in it. He reached down and pulled the board up. Underneath was a metal box. He grabbed the handle, thinking *Well, well, well! What do we have here? I hope it's something that will give some light on where they plan to strike.*

"We've got to go, Levi!" David called. "The sirens are getting close."

Soon both were in the Rio Grande, swimming to the Mexican side, Abrams lugging the metal box.

THIRTY-EIGHT

ABRAMS AND DAVID LOOKED across the river at the remains of the burning car. They could see the fire engines arriving along with some police cars.

"Wait till they go in the shed and find the Arabs and the RPGs. That will cause a stir in quiet old Presidio." David grinned.

"Right now I'm more interested in what's in this box," Abrams answered. "Let's find a cantina where we can explore the contents."

"Right this way, señor," said the owner, staring at Abrams and David in their damp clothes. "Here's a quiet corner where no one will bother you."

"This will do fine," Abrams said, sitting down.

"Is there anything else I can do for you gentlemen?"

"Not right now. We'll order something in a few minutes."

Abrams was about to put the box on the table when he realized that the owner was not leaving. They both looked at him.

Smiling, he said, "Most of my customers are dry when they come in and then get wet later in the night. This is the first time they have come in wet waiting to get dry."

Making a motion with his hand, he continued. "To have a dry booth like this and to have wet Americans sit in it may add to my expenses. I want to keep you protected from catching a very bad cold, señors. I wouldn't want any of my customers to catch a cold either. For a little extra I will ensure that no one will bother you or catch a cold."

"That sounds like a good idea, señor," Abrams replied. "We wouldn't want to catch a cold either. May I add a little contribution for all of your extra effort on our behalf?"

Abrams reached into his wallet, took out two hundred-dollar bills, and folded them into his right hand. He then reached out and shook the owner's hand. Abrams tightened his grip, and the Mexican's smile turned to a look of pain.

"We appreciate all of your extra service, señor. I am sure that no one will catch a cold, aren't you?"

"Sí. Sí, señor. I am sure no one will catch a cold," the man said hurriedly, turning away.

"Come on, Levi. Open it," David exclaimed.

The box, Abrams discovered, wasn't locked. He pushed the button on the side and lifted the lid. The box was filled with stacks of twenty-dollar bills. On top was a plastic sandwich bag with a dollar bill sealed inside. Abrams began to examine the dollar bill as David counted the money.

"Look at this, David!" Abrams said thoughtfully. "Look at the markings on the bill."

David took the bill and peered at it. "That's strange. What do you think those markings mean?"

"I'm not sure, but I have a friend who may be able to help me."

Abrams reached for his waterproof cell phone and punched in some numbers.

It was one o'clock when Murphy heard his cell phone playing a musical tune. He groaned and flipped it open. "Do you have any idea what time it is?" he growled.

"Yes, Michael, I do," Abrams said, smiling. "I'm sorry to wake you, but this is most important."

"I hope it is, Levi. I was just starting into a good dream."

"You can go back to your dreams later," Abrams said with a laugh.

For the next few minutes Abrams recounted everything that had taken place in Presidio. By the time he had finished, Murphy was wide awake.

"Michael, you've always been good at breaking codes and solving mysteries. I need your help with the writing on the dollar bill."

"I'll do my best. What do you see?"

"As you look at the front of the bill, you see a picture of George Washington. To his right there's a green seal. Inside of the seal is a shield. At the top of the shield is a set of scales, and at the bottom is a key. Someone has circled the key in pen. In the open space next to the seal, someone has drawn a crescent moon pointing downward. There are what look like three talons coming off the points of the crescent moon. And below the moon are two pyramids forming a six-pointed star. It is exactly the same as the tattoo on the Arab who fell into the alley."

"It sounds like Talon is again involved in this."

"That's why I called you, Michael. Below the green seal are three letters—R D D," Abrams continued.

"Hmm. That doesn't ring any bells yet, Levi," Murphy mused.

"On the left side of Washington is a black seal with the letter 'L' in the center. Above the seal is the printed statement: *THIS NOTE IS LEGAL TENDER FOR ALL DEBTS, PUBLIC AND PRIVATE.* In between the printed statement and the black seal is someone's name: Lenni Lenape, with Lenni spelled L-E-N-N-I."

"I must still be asleep, Levi. This isn't making any sense."

"I've had this name run through all our sources and through Interpol. We've come up empty. I called them just before calling you."

"Well, let's start with the obvious, Levi. The key is circled. It probably means that this dollar bill is the key or carrier of a coded message. The name of the person is another clue."

"Of course, Michael. We've gotten that far. We're stuck on this person Lenni Lenape. Who is he, and what's his relationship to these Arabs in Texas?"

Murphy ran his fingers through his hair. He got out of bed and began to pace. "That name sounds familiar, Levi. Lenni is a common name, but the spelling you gave isn't, and Lenape is unusual."

"We can't find any Lenni Lenape who has done anything wrong or has been associated with any terrorist groups."

"Levi!" Murphy exclaimed. "I just remembered my history lessons. Lenni Lenape is not a person, it's a *group* of people."

"What are you talking about?"

"Lenni Lenape is the name of a tribe of American Indians. They lived in the wooded areas around Delaware, New Jersey, and New York. They were one of the most civilized and advanced Indian tribes in the United States. The Algonquin Indians called the Lenni Lenape 'Grandfathers' because they had been in the area for such a long time."

"But what does that have to do with the dollar bill?"

"I don't know for sure, Levi, but I can only make a guess. The Lenni Lenape Indians had a large encampment on the top of the New Jersey Palisades. It overlooked the Hudson River."

"I'm sorry, Michael, but you're not making any sense. The Lenni Lenape were Indians in New Jersey?"

"Hold on, I'm coming to it. The site of the original Lenni Lenape encampment is now called Fort Lee. It is from Fort Lee on top of the Palisades that you begin to cross the George Washington Bridge. You travel on highway I-95 from New Jersey to Washington Heights in Upper Manhattan."

"That's it! That's it, Michael. The George Washington Bridge! It must be their target!"

"That would be a terrible target for us! It's one of the busiest bridges in the world. Three hundred thousand vehicles cross the span a day. It's the only fourteen-lane suspension bridge ever built, and it's the thirteenth longest main suspension bridge in the world. It's a National Historic Civil Engineering Landmark."

"I knew you could do it, Michael," Abrams exclaimed. "I need to do some more checking and then we'll pass the information on to all of the agencies involved with homeland security. Go back to bed and try and get some sleep."

"Thanks a lot, Levi. You didn't exactly give me a sleeping pill."

THIRTY-NINE

DAVID LOOKED at Abrams when he finished talking with Murphy. "I got part of the conversation. You think the terrorists may be planning to attack the George Washington Bridge. Do you have any idea how or when?"

"That's still a mystery. The four Arabs in Presidio were part of the plan. Only one of them has escaped. I don't know how this will affect their operation."

"What did Murphy say the three letters under the green seal mean?"

"Oh, David! We got so caught up in the bridge scenario that we didn't pursue it. 'R D D.' I wonder if they're a person's initials?"

"Well, Lenni Lenape wasn't a person. Maybe the letters stand for something else?" David said thoughtfully.

"Let's try to put it together. We've got the George Washington

Bridge starting at Fort Lee and moving toward Manhattan. The operation is being run by Talon and his Arab friends who have tattoos on their necks of a crescent and a star. Their goal is to do something to the bridge."

"Maybe the 'R D D' is the something that they're going to do?"

"It could be. Let's start with the R. 'R' for rapid, or radio, or radical, or raid, or reconnaissance, or retribution, or rifle, or revenge, or—"

"How about radiation?" David put in.

"Now you're talking about a really bad 'R' word."

"Do you think they might have a nuclear device?"

"Well, we know they had a rocket-propelled grenade launcher. That starts with 'R.' Oh, no!"

"What?"

"I wonder if they might be going for a dirty bomb? They're called radiological dispersion devices, you know," Abrams said.

"Levi, I've been with Mossad for years and I still don't understand how a dirty bomb is different from a regular nuclear weapon."

"Well, David, dirty bombs aren't nuclear weapons. Let me try to explain," Abrams said. "A thermonuclear device, like an atom bomb, does tremendous damage. When it explodes it destroys buildings, equipment, and people with a massive fireball and shockwave of heat and pressure that levels everything for more than a mile in each direction. The blast creates radiation that can spread over the city. People in the vicinity of the bomb blast will be annihilated. Those who are a little farther away can be burned with the radiation; they will linger longer, depending on how close they were to the blast."

"You mean it will level an entire city like Hiroshima, Japan, in World War II?" David asked.

"Precisely." Abrams nodded. "The United States and Israel have been worrying about portable nuclear devices—suitcase nukes. They can be fit into a regular suitcase. They are filled with a single mass of plutonium or U-233. A single suitcase nuke could cause a significant explosion ranging from ten to twenty tons.

"The next wonder of war is called the neutron bomb, or ERW, for enhanced radiation weapon. It's a little different from the thermonuclear bomb. It is detonated *above* the battlefield or city being attacked. The central destructive blast is confined to a few hundred yards. However, a massive wave of radiation is sent out from the blast into a much larger area. It kills any living being inside of tanks or buildings without destroying buildings or equipment. The radiation from a thermonuclear bomb can last for a long, long time, but the radiation from the neutron bomb quickly dissipates. It kills the warriors but doesn't damage a country's infrastructure."

"It sounds like the weapon of choice to use in the future," David said in a worried voice.

"I'm afraid it might be. President Jimmy Carter halted the production of neutron devices in 1978. Production later resumed in 1981. It's believed that the Chinese stole the bomb secrets from the United States and exploded their own neutron bomb as early as 1986."

"What does all this have to do with dirty bombs?" David asked.

"Well, I have to lay a foundation so that you'll understand. One more caveat before I jump to the dirty bomb. Have you heard about 'red mercury'?"

"Yes, I've heard of it. Is it a bomb?"

"Not exactly. It's a material called antimony oxide. It's a reddish, dark brown, or purple powder used in combination with heavy hydrogen as a fuel. Uranium or plutonium is used with conventional thermonuclear bombs. But red mercury is a more efficient and cheaper way to make a neutron bomb. It doubles the nuclear yield, with a great reduction in the weight."

"What does that mean?"

"It means that it's possible to make a neutron-type bomb as small as a golf ball. Of course, the initial blast will be smaller, but the radiation area will be pretty large. The Russians developed red mercury. According to Yevgeny Primakov, chief of Russia's External Intelligence Service, red mercury sells for $350,000 a kilo on the open market. The sensors used today in the United States can't detect this type of hand-held nuclear weapon."

"So what is special about a dirty bomb?"

"It's different because it's not triggered by a nuclear explosion, David," Abrams explained. "It uses conventional explosives, like dynamite or fertilizer, combined with radioactive material. The explosion itself is not as big as a nuclear blast. In fact, it will only be as big as the amount of explosives used. However, it still spreads radiation all over the place, and this type of radiation doesn't dissipate quickly. It lasts as long as several years and can extend to decades."

"And terrorists prefer this type of weapon?" David asked.

"Yes, for several reasons. First, dirty bombs are easy to make. Second, the radioactive material for such bombs can be found in most hospitals, universities, even food processing plants! Third, these bombs strike terror in the heart of the general public. People are terrified by the thought of being exposed to radiation. And, last, the long-lasting radioactive material can attach to concrete, metal, what have you. If a city was contaminated by a dirty bomb, many buildings would have to be demolished."

"So dirty bombs are more like weapons of mass *disruption* than mass destruction," David concluded.

"Well, they're both. The explosives destroy and the radiation disrupts. If you ask me, that's what the terrorists are going to use—a dirty bomb!" Abrams said seriously.

FORTY

ALVENA SMIDT FINISHED shopping in her favorite local delicatessen after work. She collected her bundles from Carl, the owner, said good night, and strode outside. It was after nine, and not many people were out on the chilly streets. Smidt was enjoying the night air when she saw a man she recognized walking in her direction. As he got very close she spoke.

"Excuse me. Aren't you the man from Cape Town?" Smidt asked, excited.

Talon looked up and pretended to be surprised. "Why, yes."

"Do you remember me? I'm Alvena Smidt, the librarian. We met today. You were looking for some of your friends. Did you find them? I certainly hope so. I talked with them and they seem like such a nice couple. What are you doing in this neighborhood?"

"I was out visiting some friends. Do you live around here?"

"Yes. Just two blocks in the direction you were coming from."

"A lovely woman like yourself shouldn't be walking the streets alone at this time of night. It might be dangerous."

"Oh, I don't mind. I just got off work. I've lived here for several years, and it's very safe."

"Nevertheless, would you allow me to carry your bag and escort you to your home?"

"Why . . . I . . . I guess so. That would be very kind."

"I don't mind that in the least. I always enjoy an evening stroll," Talon said as he took the bag from Smidt's arms.

It only took them a few minutes to arrive at her apartment. "Well, here we are," she said. "Thank you so very much. It was certainly a surprise to meet you a second time." She was hoping it wouldn't be the last time the two would meet.

"It was my pleasure. Say, would you happen to know if there are any restaurants open now nearby? I'd like a cup of hot tea before going to bed."

"No, I'm afraid not," Alvena Smidt said, frowning. "But I'd be happy to make some tea for you. I live on the fifth floor. I also have some wonderful chocolate éclairs right here." She pointed to the bag Talon held for her.

"I wouldn't want to impose on your kindness," he said seriously.

"Oh, it would be my pleasure," Smidt exclaimed.

Talon wandered around the living room looking at pictures while Smidt prepared the tea and éclairs. When she came out of the kitchen, Talon had removed his coat. They sat and chatted over the tea. She thought it was strange that he had left his gloves on. *His hands must be cold.*

"I must be going now," Talon said, rising and putting on his coat. "That was most kind of you."

"Well, I'm happy that you were in the area. I enjoyed your company. Sometimes it's a little lonely in the evenings. Watching television is not quite like having a stimulating conversation . . . don't you think?"

"My thought precisely."

Smidt walked Talon to the door. "Thank you for coming up."

"Oh, it was my pleasure more than you know." With that, Talon's arms shot out and his hands clasped her throat, his thumbs slowly increasing their pressure on her larynx. He enjoyed looking at his victims as they died.

"I wouldn't want you to tell anyone that you had met me, Alvena. My description and where I come from must remain our little secret. I just can't stand loose ends."

Alvena Smidt's eyes were wide. She couldn't believe this was happening to her. He was a gentleman—a gentleman from her native land! She tried to squirm free but he was too strong. Her whole body was desperate for air. The pain in her throat was unbearable. She could feel herself drifting into unconsciousness. The last thing she saw was a sinister smile.

Talon held on until he was confident she was dead. Then he allowed her body to slump to the floor. He strode over to her handbag, removed all the money and credit cards, and dumped the contents on the floor. Then he opened all of the cupboards, drawers, and closets, and tossed things around, trying to make it look like a robbery.

Before he left he double-checked the apartment. He had forgotten one thing. Hurriedly he washed his teacup and the éclair plate and put them away. He wanted it to appear that she was alone.

Just before he closed the door, he took one more look at Smidt. *I never did like big polka dots.*

FORTY-ONE

MURPHY'S CELL PHONE began to play a musical tune. He held onto the steering wheel with his left hand as he reached over, picked the phone up, and flipped it open. "Murphy here."

"Michael! Where are you right now?" Abrams exclaimed.

"Right now I'm driving out of the parking lot at LaGuardia Airport. I just dropped Isis off. She had an early flight back to Washington. I decided to drive back to Raleigh. I need some alone time to think. Why?"

"We've just gotten some news about the terrorists. We think they're going to attempt to blow up the George Washington Bridge today."

"Today! I'm only about seven miles from the bridge."

"That's why I'm calling, Michael. I was hoping you were still in the area. I'm still in Presidio. Can you help us?"

"Of course."

"Michael," Abrams said seriously, "if something goes wrong . . . you could lose your life."

"I've made my peace with God, Levi. If He wants to take me, I'm ready. I've just turned north onto I-278. The traffic is already terrible. Fill me in on the details. We need to do everything in our power to stop them."

"One of our operatives caught the terrorist that shot Jacob. He persuaded him to cooperate . . . if you know what I mean. Anyway, we believe some members of one of the sleeper cells are transporting two bombs to the bridge."

"*Two* bombs?"

"Yes, we think they're going to attempt to enter from the New Jersey side on both the top and the bottom levels of the bridge. An explosion like that could rip the bridge apart in the center."

"Do you have any idea when it's supposed to happen?"

"We got the impression from the Arab that it was probably going to happen during the early-morning rush hour. You're already in it."

"How can I help?"

"We discovered that the terrorists have rented two Rapid U-Haul trucks. You know, the yellow trucks with the big blue arrow on the side pointing toward the cab, with the large red letters 'Rapid U-Haul.'"

"I know them."

"Well, if you see one entering or on the bridge, it could be one of them. Michael, try to get there as fast as you can. I'll call back with an update. Good luck."

Murphy's tension mounted as he attempted to weave in and out of traffic. Soon there was no way to get around the cars ahead. He was locked in.

The cars reminded him of snails inching their way toward possible death. Murphy wanted to yell at the people to get out of his way. He could feel his frustration and impatience level rising. His emotions were close to the explosion point.

He began to pray.

Norm Huffman and Jim Daniels both came from a long line of law enforcement officers and had become the best of friends. Both of their fathers had been on the New York Police Department, as had their grandfathers. Police work seemed to run in their families. Many of their relatives were on the force, and those who were not policemen became firemen.

After 9/11, their families were concerned about their safety. They were close to retirement, and their wives were begging them to take a less dangerous job. They too felt that they needed a break after years of stress. It was a dangerous business arresting felons, dodging crazy drivers, and handling emergency situations. The events of 9/11 had been the worst disaster they'd ever been through. They had both lost friends and relatives. That deep hurt was almost unbearable. So when they heard about jobs providing security for the George Washington Bridge, they both applied.

They had both gotten the day shift and loved it. Now they could be home each evening with their families. Norm and Jim often barbecued together on the weekends.

Their responsibilities included patrolling the pedestrian path that ran along the Hudson River on the Manhattan side. They started at the south end, walked north, then returned. They could be outdoors and enjoy the beauty of the parkway, they didn't have to worry about traffic, they didn't have to get into fights or be shot at, and they met a lot of nice people walking and jogging. It was a primo job.

Often they would get into conversations with fishermen or people picnicking under the bridge. Many people from out of town walked the area and visited the Little Red Lighthouse at the base of the bridge. The lighthouse had been originally built and installed at Sandy Hook, New Jersey. Dismantled and moved to Jeffrey's Hook in the late 1800s, it was the ideal place to take pictures.

"Just another day in paradise, Norm," Jim said with a broad grin.

"I know. It's a tough job walking next to the river in the sunshine on a clear day. But somebody's got to do it."

"It's kind of quiet today. I don't see many people."

"No, just the maintenance crew and some Rollerbladers over by the lighthouse."

"Maintenance must be working on something. There seems to be more of them than usual."

Norm started to look at the maintenance workers when Jim yelled. "Norm! The two Rollerbladers just went down. They crashed into each other, and they look like they're hurt."

They hurried toward the skaters. Jim was about a hundred feet away when he sensed something was wrong. The two men on the ground looked as if they were Arabs. He had never seen any Arabs skating before. He had a hinky feeling about them.

At the same instant, Norm began to say something about the maintenance crew. He knew most of the men on the crew. He didn't remember any Arabs working in maintenance. Just then their radios sounded with a loud squawk.

"Central Command to all units. Code T! I repeat, Code T!"

Murphy's cell phone rang a second time. It was Levi Abrams.

"Michael, turn on your radio. The news media has gotten ahold of the possible bombing of the bridge. Someone from the FBI must have leaked it. I think there'll be mass panic. No one will want to be caught in another 9/11–type of situation."

Murphy reached to switch on the radio.

"Michael, I don't know what to tell you," Abrams continued, worried. "Bridge security has been alerted. They'll be attempting to get traffic off the bridge and close it down. That is a major operation. The FBI, other police units, and the military are mobilizing just in case our suspicions are correct. The problem is the congestion. Emergency personnel will not be able to get through immediately. Since you don't have a portable radio, you're on your own. You won't know what everyone else is doing. I wish I was there to help."

"I'll try to keep in touch with you by cell phone."

Fadil looked at his watch. His hands were shaking badly. In only a few minutes he would push the button to detonate the explosives that would cut the power to the bridge and shut down the many closed-circuit television cameras. His was a simple job. It was not dangerous. No one could see where he was hiding. He probably wouldn't be caught, yet he was scared to death.

He had told everyone that he believed in jihad, but when it came down to actually doing something about it, that was another thing. The moment of truth was almost upon him. He wanted the American infidels to die, yet he was afraid. Would he be able to escape the effects of the attack? Would he ever see his family again, or would he become a suicide martyr like the heroes of 9/11? He really didn't want to die.

Carla Martin had just driven past the New Jersey–side tower toward Washington Heights when the traffic slowed to a stop.

Now what? she wondered irritably. *Why is everyone stopping on the bridge? I'll be late for my doctor's appointment.*

She bent forward, pushed in another CD, and began to sing

along with the music. She started thinking about her baby—her first. She and her husband, Stan, hadn't been sure if they really wanted to know if it was a boy or a girl, but their curiosity had gotten the better of them. Tony would be born in three months.

After the appointment, I'll pick out the baby crib. What's holding everybody up?

Sharif had overpowered the guard at the tower on the Manhattan side of the bridge. He had convinced the man that he worked for the elevator company and was there to fix a reported problem.

Sharif had shot the guard with a silenced weapon when the man stepped out of the guard booth to check his credentials. After dragging the man back inside the booth, he got the detonators out of the service vehicle he was driving.

His assignment was to lower the elevator to ground level under the bridge. There his fellow terrorists, disguised as maintenance workers, would load explosives into the elevator.

FORTY-TWO

ASIM AND NAJJAR had timed their approach to the bridge precisely. Asim would enter the approach on the top level, and Najjar would approach the lower level. Both were driving large trucks filled with explosives and radioactive materials. They knew that it would be a suicide mission. But they would do anything for the cause . . . even die. Allah would be pleased. They knew that their friends and relatives would not mourn but rejoice. Songs might even be written about their martyrdom.

Talon had given them exact instructions. They were to drive to the center of the bridge and stop where the cables dropped to the closest point above the vehicle traffic. Then they were to get out of their trucks, lift the hoods, and pretend to be having engine trouble. Next they were to slash the trucks' tires, so they would be difficult to move. Finally they were to toss the keys off the bridge.

The power would go out on the bridge and the television cameras would not be able to monitor what was happening. The confusion and traffic would delay the bridge police from arriving at the holdup. And even if they did reach the trucks, they wouldn't be able to move them. Also, no one would realize that a truck was stopped on each level, one above the other. The power of the two simultaneous explosions would be massive. Easily enough to sever the two thirty-six-inch cables on the south side of the bridge.

When the explosion severed the cables, the surface of the bridge would torque downward at the point of the blast. As the bridge twisted, the explosives in the elevator of the tower would be deployed. That would cause the tower and bridge to twist and bend toward the river. Talon hoped that the snapping of the cables, the twisting and weight of the bridge, and the collapsing of one side of the tower would cause the bridge to collapse at midpoint. The attack would be colossal.

Not only would the bridge go down, but radiation would be released that would kill thousands and terrify survivors. One of the main arteries into New York City would be severed. Any possible repairs would cost billions of dollars.

Talon had convinced his Arab crew that this attack would dwarf 9/11 and would go down as one of the greatest single terrorist attacks in history. This thought had pleased them greatly. The $500,000 each man received as payment and insurance for his family also pleased them.

Asim and Najjar each had a detonator. Either man could set off the explosions on both trucks. It was their backup system. If their detonators did not work, Sharif could set them off just before he set off the explosion in the elevator.

Asim's heart was beating fast as he approached the center of the bridge. He braked and turned on his flashing emergency lights. He could hear cars behind him begin honking their horns. The bridge was bumper-to-bumper traffic in the early-morning rush hour.

He got out and lifted the hood. Then he tossed the keys over the railing of the bridge. Next he took out his knife and slashed the tires. Everything was going according to plan.

He looked at his watch and waited, his hand on the detonator.

"Hey! You there! Move your truck!"

The words startled Asim. He turned and looked in the face of an irate commuter who had climbed out of his car.

"I have motor trouble. I cannot move," he said in broken English.

The commuter swore bitterly and shook his fist. "You'd better move this truck!"

Asim pointed at his cell phone. "I am calling for assistance right now."

The man swore again and made hand signs at Asim, then stomped back to his car.

Asim punched in numbers. "Najjar, are you in position?"

"No. The traffic must be a little slower on the lower level. I will be in position in about four minutes. Have patience. Just think, Asim. We will be great martyrs. Allah be praised."

FORTY-THREE

KARA SETTER ARRIVED early. She needed extra time to get things organized and ready for the members of the General Assembly. She loved her job at the United Nations. It gave her the opportunity to meet many important and interesting people from around the world. She was deep in thought as she set out the notebooks with the agenda for the day.

"Good morning, Kara. Are we ready to go?"

She turned and looked into the face of Secretary-General Musa Serapis of Egypt. "Yes, Mr. Serapis. All I need to do is see if the coffee is finished and the rolls are ready. How's your jet lag?"

"It's not too bad."

"I don't know how you do it. How many hours is it from Egypt to New York?"

Before he could answer, the chief of security ran into the room.

"Mr. Secretary, we just got an emergency terrorist warning from the FBI. They suggest that we evacuate the United Nations building immediately."

Secretary-General Serapis and members of the Security Council hurried to the secure room. By the time everyone had arrived, scattered reports about the possible attack were being received. The mention of a possible radiation cloud caused great alarm. After a hasty meeting, it was decided to evacuate the building and send everyone either to their homes or to a safe location. The members also agreed to reconvene at a conference room in Newark International Airport as quickly as they could.

With the memory of 9/11 still fresh in everyone's mind, it was extremely difficult to control the panic in the United Nations building. The delegates, who had been privy to "official" information, attempted to leave in an orderly fashion, but employees and visitors were terrified. All they knew was that there had been a major terrorist alert for New York City.

There was pushing, shoving, and yelling as thousands of employees attempted to leave. Kara Setter was knocked down in the rush and trampled. It was every person for themself.

Everyone who had driven to the city now was attempting to leave at the same time. Tempers flared. The traffic jam was enormous.

Taxi companies no longer answered their phones. All the cabs were tied up shuttling people out of the Washington Heights area. People without transportation ran out into the streets, begging those lucky enough to have a car for a ride.

FORTY-FOUR

SERGEANT HARLAN GRIFFIN and Officer Chris Goodale were about 1,500 feet over the Cross Bronx Expressway observing the traffic flow. They were heading east in their normal morning fly-over in the police helicopter when the alert came over.

"This is control to Air 17. Please be advised that there is a Code T at the George Washington Bridge. Please respond, Code Three."

"Hold on," said Griffin. Immediately he leaned the stick to the right and the helicopter made a sweeping turn to the west.

"Turn on the power!" Goodale shouted.

In only minutes they could see that traffic was jam-packed on the Manhattan side of the bridge. Cars that were facing toward the bridge were locked in place and could not turn around. Traffic moving away from the bridge on the Henry Hudson Parkway, I-95, and

I-87 was hampered from moving forward by other cars attempting to flee the Washington Heights area.

"Look at that mess!" Griffin exclaimed.

"It looks like absolute panic," Goodale responded.

When Norm Huffman and Jim Daniels heard the Code T for *terrorist attack*, they reached for their Glocks. They both knew there was something desperately wrong with two Arab Rollerbladers on the ground and four Arab maintenance workers nearby.

Huffman and Daniels had their hands on their Glocks when the two men on the ground drew weapons and fired. The impact of the bullets against their bulletproof vests knocked the officers backward.

Huffman and Daniels were tough and seasoned veterans. This wasn't their first gun battle. They had just been caught off guard. Instinctively they rolled away from each other, aimed, and fired. The two Rollerbladers did not have the advantage of bulletproof vests. The first skater took a bullet to the head and one more to the sternum. The second one was still trying to get up when he took a bullet in the side that pierced his heart and exited through a lung. Both were dead before they hit the ground.

The firefight had attracted the attention of the four maintenance workers who were about two hundred feet away. They too drew their weapons and aimed. Daniels took a round in his right shoulder. He went down still holding onto his gun.

Huffman hit the ground using the body of one of the terrorists as a shield. Then he began to fire at the workers who were standing near a service vehicle. He had no idea that it was filled with high-powered explosives. Daniels crawled behind the other dead man, shifted his gun to his left hand, and began to fire too.

Goodale was the first to spot the firefight.

"Harlan! To the left at eleven o'clock...near the river...there are two officers down in a gun battle."

Griffin pushed the stick to the left; all of a sudden a terrific ball of flame welled up from the ground.

One of Huffman's bullets had hit the vehicle's gas tank, causing it to ignite. The four terrorists and the truck disappeared in the fireball.

As the service vehicle had been covered only by a thin canvas top, not a metal roof, almost all of the force of the explosives went upward and outward, causing a ball of fire and lots of black smoke.

Griffin and Goodale were stunned. The force of the rushing air from the blast moved their helicopter off course, and it was all Griffin could do to maintain control.

The force of the concussion had thrown Daniels and Huffman backward. They were somewhat protected by the terrorists' bodies and the fact that most of the blast's energy was moving straight up. In shock, they shook their heads, trying to diminish the ringing in their ears.

Shaking and sweating, Fadil pushed the button to ignite the small explosion that blew up the power circuit to the bridge cameras.

After doing so, he dropped the detonator, emerged from the bushes where he had been hiding, and began to walk against traffic along the road away from the bridge. Despite his attempt to look casual, he looked completely out of place.

Kevin Gerber was listening to music on the radio in his car. *This is the worst traffic jam I have ever seen on the George Washington*, he thought.

Out of the corner of his eye he saw movement to the far right. He turned to see a large, well-built man running toward the bridge past the stopped cars.

That's weird. I didn't think they let pedestrians run alongside the roadway.

Gerber continued to listen to the radio for a couple of minutes, tapping his fingers on the steering wheel and singing along. Then he focused on the distance ahead. He could see a man walking away from the bridge toward his line of cars.

What in the world is he doing? Maybe his car's out of gas and he's going to get some. First we have a jogger and now we have a walker ... and both of them in street clothes. Strange.

Gerber continued to tap his fingers. All of a sudden the music was interrupted by a beeping sound.

"This is your emergency radio network. We have been informed that there is a terrorist warning for the George Washington Bridge. The bridge will be closed for the rest of the day. Please seek alternate routes and stay away from the bridge."

Oh, great! And I'm almost on the bridge. Gerber looked around, trying to see if there was any way out of the traffic.

All of a sudden there was a tremendous flash and an explosion on the south side of the bridge. Gerber could see smoke rise up on the other side of the tower.

Then he saw the tall thin Arab-looking man take off running.

What the ... !

Instantly it all fell into place. *He must be part of the terrorist group.*

Gerber turned off the motor and jumped out of his car, in pursuit of the terrorist. Soon the distance between the two men had lessened.

Fadil had no idea that he was being pursued. He had only one thought in mind: to get as far away as he could, as fast as he could.

Fadil didn't hear Gerber until only a few feet separated the men, and by then it was too late. Gerber had leaped into the air in a fly-ing tackle.

Other commuters who had heard the same radio announcement had also put two and two together as they watched one man chasing another. Several climbed out of their cars and followed. No longer would people sit idly by as America was destroyed.

Gerber grabbed Fadil around the waist, and they fell to the ground. Fadil fought like a madman, biting, scratching, and kicking. By then a burly taxi driver had come to Gerber's aid. Soon other men joined in to subdue Fadil, who was screaming in Arabic.

A bridge security team had made it to the south side of the Manhattan tower. Dressed in black SWAT uniforms, they looked ominous. They had keys to the elevator room.

Sharif was unzipping the bag containing the detonators when he heard some noise at the door. He stopped and reached for his auto-matic.

He had just gotten the gun in his hand when the first SWAT offi-cer entered. Sharif swung his arm upward and fired three quick shots. The first bullet hit the officer in the chest, the force knocking him down. The other two shots drove into the wall behind the officer.

The second SWAT man fired five shots into Sharif. Somehow the terrorist lived for almost three minutes before he finally died.

FORTY-FIVE

THE TRAFFIC ON the lower level of the George Washington Bridge was moving very slowly. Sometimes it stopped completely for up to two minutes.

Najjar was getting very anxious. He was still a good two hundred feet from the center of the bridge. He knew that he needed to be directly under Asim on the upper level for the most powerful effect. He wanted to do it right. This was to be his mark in life. He would be remembered for this day.

Move! Move, you filthy Americans! We have history to make today.

Since the age of eight, he had been taught that giving his life for jihad was the most honorable thing he could possibly do. His parents told him that he would one day make them proud by giving his life for his people. He did not fear death; rather he looked forward to it. He could hardly wait for his reward. In a few minutes he would be in paradise.

Buck Wilson had been driving eighteen-wheelers cross-country for over twenty years. He had driven his semitruck in all kinds of weather and through most of the large towns in the United States. He preferred the open road to city traffic. However, he knew better than to get mad during rush-hour traffic. There was no point. Or maybe he didn't really care because it gave him a chance to listen to his favorite country and western music.

I can usually put up with a lot of traffic, but this is ridiculous, Wilson thought. *There must be some major accident on the Washington Heights side of the bridge.*

He began turning the channels of his XM Satellite Radio looking for a New York traffic report. As he did so, he heard a late-breaking news update. "A terrorist alert has been posted for the George Washington Bridge. FBI agents have informed us that they are looking for two Rapid U-Haul trucks. One of the license plates is JRZ738, and the other one is KLM211. The Rapid U-Haul trucks are yellow in color and have a large blue arrow on them with bright red lettering. If you see a vehicle that matches this description on or around the George Washington Bridge, please inform authorities."

Those lily-livered cowards! They only attack innocent women and children! Wilson was looking at the stalled traffic ahead when he spotted a yellow truck. *Could it be one of the trucks the FBI was searching for?*

All lanes of traffic were stopped. Wilson couldn't contain his anger. He left the motor of his truck running, put on the emergency brake, and climbed out. He wasn't sure what he was going to do, but he couldn't just sit there.

He walked in between the stopped vehicles toward the yellow

truck, which was two cars ahead. His heart raced as he glanced at the license plate. He could read all but the last two numbers which were covered by mud.

KLM2.... That's one of them!

He could see the driver of the truck looking at him in the rearview mirror. He would be suspicious and ready for him. Wilson continued to stroll by the truck, not even glancing at the driver. He walked two cars ahead and then stopped. He pretended that he was trying to see what was causing the holdup. Then he threw his arms up in disgust and tapped on the window of the car next to him. The driver rolled down the window, and they talked briefly. Wilson was hoping that the driver of the yellow truck would think that he was just an angry motorist who was frustrated with the slow traffic.

Then Wilson turned and walked back toward the yellow truck, shaking his head. When he got even with the truck, he stopped and knocked on the door. Najjar rolled down the window.

Wilson spoke in a soft voice. "What do you think is holding up the traffic?"

Najjar couldn't really hear because of the noise of all the engines around them. "What?"

Wilson casually stepped up on the running board of the truck. "I said, what do you think is holding up the traffic?" Then Wilson reached into the truck and wrapped an arm around Najjar's neck. He squeezed tightly, lifting and pulling at the same time. Wilson was so strong that he began to pull Najjar out of the truck through the open window. It happened so quickly that the terrorist had no time to reach for the gun that was beside him or the detonator on the passenger seat.

Once Wilson had dragged him out of the truck, Najjar tried to reach for a .32 automatic strapped to his leg. Wilson saw the move and hit him in the jaw. The staggering blow shattered Najjar's jaw-bone.

Murphy was close to the bridge when the traffic finally came to a complete standstill. At almost the same time he heard the radio announcement describing the yellow trucks and giving license numbers. *What if the trucks are already on the bridge? I can't just sit and wait for an explosion!*

Murphy got out of the rental car and started to jog toward the bridge alongside the roadway. It took him about two minutes to reach the bridge entrance. He began to jog across the upper level looking across the traffic for a yellow truck. He had mixed emotions as he ran. On one hand, he hoped that the trucks were not on the bridge. Maybe it would only be a false alarm. On the other hand, if the trucks were on the bridge, he was praying that God would give him the strength and wisdom to stop the attack.

When Murphy neared the center point, he could see a yellow Rapid U-Haul truck stopped on the other side of the bridge, its hood up. He began to weave his way through the stopped cars until he reached the center divider.

No one was in the truck. Someone was looking into the engine compartment, talking on a cell phone.

Murphy climbed over the center divider and wove between the vehicles toward the truck. He could sense people watching his movements. Probably they'd think that he was some driver who had gotten out of his car and was acting irrationally.

Murphy was about two cars away from the Rapid U-Haul when the maintenance workers' vehicle exploded. The shock of the blast caused him to stagger and brace himself between two cars. He looked to his left as a huge ball of fire lifted into the sky followed by a cloud of black smoke. The noise was deafening.

Asim was standing in front of his truck when the blast went off. It took him by surprise. He ran to the edge of the bridge and looked down. Something had gone wrong! He knew that now he couldn't wait for Najjar to get directly under him on the lower level. He would have to hope that he was close enough for the blasts of both trucks to rip the cables and bridge apart.

Asim had just pulled the detonator out of his pocket when Murphy hit him. The detonator slid partway under the car just ahead of the truck.

Asim staggered backward and stopped at the bridge railing. He focused and looked at his adversary. He was not about to let some American infidel stop his mission. It was now life and death. He had to get to the detonator...but first he had to eliminate Murphy.

Asim reached for his switchblade and flipped it open, the sharp blade glittering in the sunlight. People in nearby cars sat wide-eyed as Murphy and Asim began to circle in front of the truck, Murphy dodging Asim's slicing motions.

At one point Asim lunged straight toward Murphy's stomach with the knife. Murphy reacted with a downward block on the terrorist's arm and grabbed his wrist with the same motion and pulled him forward. He stepped to the side, and Asim's knife and hand jammed into the side of a silver Mercedes.

Now it would just be hand to hand. Asim jumped into the air with a double kick that caught Murphy in the chest and knocked him back toward the guardrail. He was trying to regain his breath when Asim hit him in the face and spun him around.

Pull it together! Breathe!... Think! Murphy told himself angrily.

Asim was charging in for the kill. At the last second Murphy dropped to one knee and leaned in toward his attacker. Asim's momentum carried him forward, and he tripped over Murphy's body and crashed into the car ahead, giving Murphy a chance to breathe deeply.

Asim charged again with his head down and his arms outstretched. Murphy jumped up slightly and wrapped his right arm around Asim's neck, then shot both his feet off the ground and dropped straight down with his full body weight on the back of Asim's head. The terrorist did a direct face plant into the asphalt with Murphy on top of him.

It was all over.

Murphy got up and reached under the car ahead for the detonator. Then he tossed it off the bridge into the Hudson River two hundred feet below.

Carla Martin had looked out her side window, two lanes over. She had seen Murphy just as he hit Asim the first time. She had witnessed the entire battle and was horrified. Then she saw the police coming.

It's about time! Grown men are so stupid to get into fights over getting stuck in traffic. I hope that they both get arrested.

She smiled to herself and put in another CD.

It was only moments before the SWAT team arrived. Murphy was handcuffed along with Asim while the police tried to sort out what had happened. They questioned the witnesses in the cars and took Murphy down to headquarters to find out what role he had played in the aborted attack. By 3:30 P.M. everything was sorted out and Murphy was set free.

Murphy was bruised, physically exhausted, and emotionally drained. But he thanked God that the terrorists' plan hadn't succeeded.

FORTY-SIX

The night of the attack, Babylon, 539 B.C.

CAPTAIN HAKEEM *was nearly out of breath as he ran up to General Azzam's tent. The guard stopped him from entering. General Azzam emerged and acknowledged the captain.*

"Sir, I have news from General Jawhar. They'll break through to the river in about fifteen minutes. He asked me to let you know that it's time to prepare the archers. The water will soon be running into the marsh. Within another hour the moat should be drained enough for the men to wade under the wall."

General Azzam nodded and smiled.

It was close to one-thirty in the morning when Daniel climbed up the stairs leading to the great hall. He was walking as fast as his age would allow. He was surprised to not hear music playing. He was even more shocked to not see drunken men and women all around the outer court. Something was different about this banquet.

As Daniel entered the great hall, he saw the king sitting on the floor surrounded by guards and personal aides. Everyone looked terrified, as if they had seen a ghost.

"Are you the one they call the old Hebrew—Daniel?" the king said in a frightened voice. "My grandmother says that you have the spirit of the gods with you. She says that you are filled with enlightenment and wisdom."

"Yes, I am Daniel."

"Look over there! See what is written on the wall! I have called for my wise men and astrologers. I asked them what it meant. They cannot read what it says."

Daniel looked at the wall. He could see the words etched in the plaster:

MENE, MENE, TEKEL, UPHARSIN

"I am told that you are expert in solving mysteries," the king continued. "If you can tell me what it says, I will clothe you with robes of purple. I will give you a golden chain of authority to hang around your neck and make you the third most powerful ruler in the kingdom."

Daniel smiled and bowed politely. "I am not interested in power. You can keep all of your gifts. I am quite satisfied with my woolen robe. You can give your rewards to someone else. As I helped your father in my younger years, I will help you also. It's not from my skill or knowledge that the answer will come. Jehovah will give me the wisdom to tell you what the writing means."

Belshazzar sat forward with his eyes wide, hanging on Daniel's every word.

"For a moment, let me review the life of King Nebuchadnezzar. All of the nations of the world trembled at the sound of his name. They lived in fear of him. He would kill any person or nation that offended him. He was a king of unlimited power and influence. However, he made a great error. He did not acknowledge that God had given him all of his honor and majesty. He became arrogant and proud.

"Because of Nebuchadnezzar's pride, he hardened his heart to God, and God chased him out of his palace into the fields. He roamed the earth like a wild animal for seven years. He lived with the wild donkeys and ate grass like a cow. His body became wet with dew each morning. This continued until at last he acknowledged that the most high God rules over the affairs of men. He is the one who puts up kings and takes them down.

"Now, O King Belshazzar, I am not telling you anything you didn't know. You have heard this story before. You are following in your father's footsteps. You have become proud and lack humility. You have defied the Living God by taking sacred cups from His temple and using them to toast your puny gods. You defiled these cups by giving them to your nobles, their wives, and their concubines. You have praised the gods of wood, stone, silver and gold, and not the God of heaven. Because of this God has written you a message on the wall. I shall now tell you what it says.

"MENE means 'numbered.' God has numbered the days of your reign. In fact, your reign is over.

"TEKEL means 'weighed.' God has weighed you in His balance scales and you have failed His test.

"UPHARSIN means 'divided.' God has divided your kingdom, and it will be given to the Medes and Persians."

Belshazzar sat stunned. He had not expected a message of doom. Everyone in the room was silent, and no one moved. No one had ever spoken that frankly to the king before. They were all expecting the king to order Daniel's death.

Fearing that something more terrifying might happen to him, Belshazzar ordered Daniel to be robed in purple. The golden chain of authority was placed around his neck, and the king proclaimed that Daniel was to become the third most powerful person in the kingdom.

Daniel was apprehensive as he left the palace hours later. He knew that God was going to destroy Belshazzar's kingdom . . . but how?

No one was aware of the soldiers who waded through the moat and under the wall. When they emerged into the city, they pretended they were joining the party as they ran toward the main gate. With all the noise and drunken yelling, no one heard the screams of the guards as they died. Only a few of the people witnessed the opening of the enormous door.

The armies of Generals Azzam and Jawhar, under the orders of Cyrus and Darius the Mede, conquered the great city of Babylon with very little resistance.

Belshazzar was talking with his nobles when enemy soldiers ran into the great hall. Sulaiman was the first to notice them. He yelled to the royal guard, who fought to their last breath trying to defend the king. It was to no avail; all were killed.

The soldiers surrounded Belshazzar and his nobles and held them captive until the generals arrived. Then the generals sat and drank wine as they surveyed their prisoners. At the back of the great hall, two men could be seen talking under a spectacular tapestry.

"Gadates, you haven't counted your golden coins yet," one exclaimed.

"I don't care about the money. This is about revenge."

"Revenge?"

"Yes, Gobrya. Two months ago the king took the entire court hunting for game. My courtier friend brought down a pheasant before the king had done so. Belshazzar became furious. He drew his sword and struck him down in front of everyone. Last week he killed another courtier when one of the nobles commented that he looked handsome. He's a madman! He had to be stopped. I hope that Cyrus's soldiers kill him soon!"

Gadates smiled when he heard General Jawhar give the order to execute the king and the nobles, who begged for mercy. One by one the soldiers killed them, leaving Belshazzar for last. They wanted him to suffer.

FORTY-SEVEN

MUSA SERAPIS COUNTED HEADS. Eight of the twelve representatives of the temporary members of the Security Council had made it to Newark Airport, as had all five permanent members, but the monthly president had not arrived yet.

Serapis spoke. "Under the circumstances, and in light of the fact that the president is not here, do I have your approval to act as temporary chairman?"

Everyone nodded.

Serapis had been the Secretary-General for over a year and was quite well received, especially by the Third World countries. His dislike for U.S. foreign policies was well-known.

For the first hour they discussed emergency plans for the continued operation of the UN and the protection of its employees. The conversation began to change when Permanent Council member Jacques Verney of France spoke.

"We cannot keep on living this way. The people of New York City are terrified. What would have happened if the George Washington Bridge had been blown up? How many people would have died? We need to consider the safety of the members of the United Nations. I think now is the time to consider plan 7216. As you all know, there has been quite a bit of discussion about the possibility of moving the United Nations out of the United States. Because of the global control philosophies of the United States, smaller and less powerful countries have had to resort to terrorism to have their voices heard. These types of terrorist attacks continue to threaten the well-being of all UN employees. I believe these types of attacks will continue as long as the United States continues to follow its godlike dreams to control the world and how it functions."

Permanent members Warren Watson of the United States and Carlton Thorndike of the United Kingdom looked at each other. This was not the first time the subject of moving the United Nations had been brought up. The Middle East, Europe, India, Africa, and South America were becoming increasingly hostile toward the United States. The hostility was also beginning to have a backlash against the United Kingdom for its support of American policies.

Vladimir Karkoff, permanent member from the Russian Federation, said forcefully, "It does not seem like the United States is prepared to deal with terrorists in its own country. The U.S. failure to protect its own people is quite evident. The U.S. inability to prevent such attacks threatens the safety of people in the Russian Federation. I too am in favor of bringing this matter up to the whole assembly for a vote."

Temporary member Salmalin Rajak, from India, said, "I have

talked with many leaders of smaller nations about the imperialistic designs of the United States. They have told me that they are considering a boycott of American products."

Warren Watson countered. "Just where do they think they're going to get the supplies they need, Mr. Rajak? We have been supporting them with 'Food for the Hungry' programs for years. We've spent billions of dollars to help their countries prosper. And look how many American jobs have been outsourced to India. Over the years, we've done nothing but try to help the countries of the world. I can't believe your attitude! Name another country that has helped you as much as the United States."

"The European Union wants to trade with our countries and will help to support them," Rajak replied. "All of Europe and Asia—and most of the world—would rather have the European Union's help than America's help. We think that power has gone to your heads. You think everyone in the world must join America's democratic way of thinking. But who's to say that your way is best? All you want to do is force policies and tariffs on us so that you can exploit us commercially. The United States wants the wealth of all of our nations!"

Rajak paused to collect himself. He realized that he may have come on too strong. He began to moderate his words. "Of course, this does not mean that the United States should not be a member of the United Nations. They are a strong country and should be included. It is just that they should not play such a dominant role. The Americans need to become a little more . . . shall we say tolerant and diplomatic."

Watson, irate, was about to respond when Zet Lu Quang addressed the group. "As a permanent member of the Security Council, I speak on behalf of the People's Republic of China. We also have grave concerns about the United Nations remaining in the America, and especially New York. There has been talk of a UN building being constructed in Geneva, Switzerland, since we already have a headquarters there. Are any other locations being considered? The People's Republic would be most happy to consider the donation of land in our capital city."

Verney responded. "Plan 7216 suggests moving out of the United States. It does not, however, suggest where the final location should be. That must be decided by a vote of the entire body. I've talked with various members of the UN, and there seems to be a positive response to the possibility of moving the United Nations building to Iraq. More specifically, to a city in Iraq with a very ancient history: Babylon. I talked to Helmut Weber, the ambassador from Germany, and his country is most supportive of such a move."

Serapis looked at the assembled group. This was a good opportunity. "I've talked with a number of the leaders of the European Union. They told me that they would support a move to Babylon. The EU would even help to pay off the huge debt the UN has incurred over the years. They also said that they have funds available to help construct a new headquarters."

Everyone smiled and nodded except for Watson and Thorndike, who were fuming. They knew it would not be wise to speak when their emotions were so volatile.

"The EU leaders told me that those funds came as a donation from an anonymous group. Their representatives said that they would pay *all* of the expenses for the construction of a new building," Serapis concluded.

He smiled as he noted a buzz of conversation at his words. He looked toward Jacques Verney. Their eyes met briefly with an imperceptible sign of recognition.

Watson saw the exchange. He felt sure that Serapis and Verney had discussed this topic more than once before. *They're using this recent threat as an excuse to promote the United Nations moving out of the United States.*

Serapis got the group's attention. "Part of our responsibilities is to help promote and preserve world peace. It is our job to agree to general principles and encourage the settling of disputes. I think that moving the United Nations out of America will help to promote world peace. It will be seen as a gesture of reaching out to those smaller nations that do not believe they have a voice. The Arab world and many in Europe will view the move to Iraq as a reaching out to the Muslim community."

Serapis could see many of the members nodding in agreement. He knew he had them in the palm of his hand. "It will reduce tensions worldwide. It may even bring about that lasting peace that we are all looking for. Our children and our grandchildren are depending on us to make the right decision. It is a decision that will lead to the saving of thousands of lives worldwide."

Serapis was beginning to wax eloquent. Watson felt like hitting him rather than listening to him.

"As leaders, we are to look for positive and unique ways to settle disputes among all nations . . . both large and small." Serapis paused for a moment and let his words sink in. Then he asked, "How many of you would like to see this as a topic at our next meeting of the General Assembly?"

All but two hands were raised.

FORTY-EIGHT

THE TRIP BACK TO RALEIGH seemed to drag on and on for
Murphy. It was not so much the miles traveled, but the thought of what
might have happened if the George Washington Bridge had been blown
up. How much devastation would the dirty bombs have caused?

*I'll bet as many as thirty to forty thousand would have been killed by the
blast and radiation.*

Memories began to flood over Murphy as he relived the tragic
events of a bombing at the Preston Community Church. He could
hear the explosion in his mind. He could smell the smoke from the
burning wood. He could taste the ashes on his tongue. He could see
bloodied people and lifeless bodies. And he also could see the sweet
face of Laura as she slowly exhaled her last breath. He relived his anguish at the realization that she was gone and his anger for the man
who had killed her.

More than once Murphy had to pull to the side of the road because his vision was blurred with tears for himself and for those who lost loved ones. He knew their pain. He was emotionally drained when he arrived home that evening.

As Murphy drove to the Preston University campus, he was aware of the struggle of emotions that faced him: Anger at the terrorists and the panic they caused vied with the need for a sense of normality.

How strange life is sometimes. There is so much pain in this world and yet there is also so much beauty.

Murphy recalled the words of King Solomon. They had been a favorite of President Ronald Reagan:

> *To everything there is a season,*
> *A time for every purpose under heaven:*
> *A time to be born,*
> *And a time to die;*
> *A time to plant,*
> *And a time to pluck what is planted;*
> *A time to kill,*
> *And a time to heal;*
> *A time to break down,*
> *And a time to build up;*
> *A time to weep,*
> *And a time to laugh;*
> *A time to mourn,*
> *And a time to dance;*
> *A time to cast away stones,*
> *And a time to gather stones;*
> *A time to embrace, and a time to refrain from embracing;*

A time to gain,
And a time to lose;
A time to keep,
And a time to throw away;
A time to tear,
And a time to sew;
A time to keep silence,
And a time to speak;
A time to love,
And a time to hate;
A time of war,
And a time of peace.

Deep down inside, Murphy knew that it was a time of war—a spiritual war against the powers of darkness.

"Dr. Murphy, I'm so glad to see you. I knew that you were in New York, and I was wondering if you got caught in that terrorist attempt. I was so worried." Shari's usually sparkling green eyes were filled with concern.

"I'm fine, Shari. I was just getting ready to leave New York when I got the word."

"How about Isis?"

"Fortunately, she flew out of La Guardia before the terrorist warning. She's safe back in Washington."

Murphy realized that he could have lost Isis if the terrorist attack had happened and she had been on a later flight. He could hardly bear the thought. He knew that his feelings for Isis were more than just casual.

Shari was riveted as Murphy recounted the events surrounding the attack. Finally Murphy shifted the conversation. "Shari, how are you doing? I know that you were going to have a talk with Paul. How did that go?"

"Good and bad. Bad because we broke up, and that has made me unhappy. It's been a tough few days. And good because it's finally settled. I couldn't continue in a relationship with someone who had different values than me, even though I love him. I knew it wouldn't work in the long run."

"How did Paul take it?"

"I don't think he was surprised. We had discussed it several times before. It's just that it's so final. It's hard to adjust."

Murphy kept silent for a moment. He knew that nothing he could say would ease her immediate pain. "Shari, I'll be praying that God will give you the strength to go through this difficult time."

Shari looked up with tears in her eyes. "Thanks, I need it."

Murphy tapped his fingers while he tried to reach Isis on the phone. His body was filled with a whole host of emotions that were not finding expression.

"Michael, are you all right? Where are you calling from?" Isis exclaimed.

"I'm back in Raleigh. I arrived late last night. I would have called then but I didn't want to wake you up."

Murphy told Isis about the abortive bombing of the George Washington Bridge and his role in deflecting it. Eventually the conversation turned toward the planned search for the Handwriting on the Wall.

"It may be a little more difficult to get into Iraq with all the heightened security. But if they approve, I think we should still go. Are you still game?" he asked.

"I'm game, but a little nervous at the same time," Isis replied.

"Me too. But at least we'll be together, and that's a good thing."

Isis smiled to herself. It *would* be good to be with Michael.

"Have you heard anything from your folks at the Parchments of Freedom Foundation?" he asked. "Are they still interested in helping to fund the expedition?"

"Yes, I talked with our chairman, Harvey Compton, and he has agreed to the project. However, he'd like us to take Dr. Wilfred Bingman along."

"Who's he?"

"He recently joined the foundation. He was a professor of archaeology at Florida State University. I think you'll like him. He's very outgoing and really knows his stuff. You'll have a lot in common."

"The more the merrier. It'll be good to have another archaeologist on the team. I'll contact Jassim Amram to see if he's been able to clear his calendar. With your ability to read ancient languages and all of our experience, we should be able to easily confirm the handwriting if we find it."

"Do you have any doubts, Michael?"

"No, I'm sure it's there. Methuselah wouldn't go to all of the trouble to inform me if it wasn't. I'm just a bit concerned about what we might run into trying to discover it. We haven't had an easy time finding other artifacts. Something usually happens to throw a kink in the works. That's how Methuselah gets his entertainment."

Isis sighed. "You're certainly right about that. Well, at least our lives aren't dull and boring."

Murphy laughed. "I'll contact Levi to see if he has cleared our travel to Iraq. He was also going to see if Colonel Davis of the U.S.

Marines would be able to afford us some protection while we're there. Especially when we travel."

"That would be reassuring. I'd like that."

"I'll call you as soon as I get the green light. I'm looking forward to being with you again, Isis," Murphy murmured.

FORTY-NINE

"OKAY, OKAY. I have to admit it."

Murphy glanced up from his desk with a questioning look. Shari was standing in the doorway holding a box with some mail on top of it. Her head was cocked to one side and there was a smirk on her face.

"Admit what? What are you talking about?"

"Your mail."

"What about it?"

"You've got a really heavy box."

"So?"

"So I have to admit that I'm curious. Let's see what's inside."

Murphy shook his head, smiling. Shari's curiosity was refreshing. Pretending not to care, he looked down at the papers on his desk and said in a bored tone, "Well, if you're so curious, why don't you open it?"

A big smile came over her face. Shari shook the box like it was her Christmas present. "There's something loose inside. It doesn't have a return address on it. And look—the box is almost falling apart."

Murphy smiled at her running commentary. He watched her take a knife and begin to open it. Then he said, "Maybe it's a bomb."

That made her hesitate for a minute and give him a dirty look. She pulled the top off and said in surprise, "It's full of rocks."

"Oh, great! I was wondering when they'd arrive."

"What do you want rocks for?" Shari had scrunched her nose up in distaste.

"Just kidding, Shari. I didn't order any rocks."

"These rocks are smooth like they came out of a river," she said as she placed three- to four-inch rocks on the table. "Look, there's a note."

"Probably from Dean Fallworth. He'd like to stone me to death," Murphy said wryly.

Shari smiled. "The note isn't signed. Some more of your weird mail!"

"What does it say?"

A golden opportunity awaits
Those who appreciate Cabarrus Debates
And search for the Hessian who deserted his session . . .
And later planted a seed which led to the weed of greed.

Murphy sighed. Shari caught the sound and looked up. "What?"
"Methuselah, I'll bet."

"He gets a real kick out of the bizarre, doesn't he? What do you think it means?"

Murphy took the note, ran his fingers through his hair, and began to pace back and forth deep in thought.

"Cabarrus has to be the key."

"Of course, anybody would know that!" Shari said mockingly.

Murphy ignored her sarcasm. "The only thing I can think of is Cabarrus County. According to early North Carolina history, Cabarrus County was named after Stephen Cabarrus, the Speaker of the House of Commons. That must be what the word 'debates' refers to."

"What about the Hessian who deserted his session?" Shari asked.

"The first part is simple," Murphy explained. "A Hessian was a German. But deserting his session is strange. The planting of a seed could refer to real seeds or the seeds of behavior. The 'weed of greed' sounds like an attitude or an action."

"What does all that have to do with river rocks?"

"Cabarrus County...river rock...a German...who plants something...the weed of greed...a golden opportunity," Murphy murmured, thinking. "The Germans had a settlement in Cabarrus County after the Revolutionary War. Most of them had been part of the fighting force that was brought over by the British. Many of them became rural farmers. That may be the reference to the word 'seed.' "

"Okay, but what does that have to do with greed?"

Murphy was silent for a few minutes as he paced back and forth. "Well, try this one on, Shari," he said finally. "There was a Hessian soldier named John Reed who settled in Cabarrus County. He was a deserter from the British Army and moved into the lower Piedmont. He married and started a farm. One Sunday afternoon in 1799, his twelve-year-old son was fishing in Little Meadow Creek on the farm. He saw something shiny in the water and picked it up. He took it home and showed it to his father, who didn't know what it was. For three years they used the object as a door stop."

"Okay, okay. What was it?"

"It was a gold nugget weighing seventeen pounds. John Reed took it into town one day, and a jeweler instantly recognized it. He offered Reed three dollars and fifty cents for the metal. It was worth thousands. Reed later found out that it was gold and made the jeweler pay him more money."

"I would think so."

"Reed and several partners then began to search for more gold in Little Meadow Creek. By 1824 they had taken over $100,000 of gold from the area—that was in 1824 dollars. It was the first documented gold find in the United States. One of their slaves named Peter dug up a gold nugget that weighed twenty-eight pounds. North Carolina was the principal gold-producing state until 1845, when the California Gold Rush started."

"Where do you come up with all of this trivia?"

"It's called reading, Shari. I think that Methuselah is telling us that there is some kind of golden opportunity waiting for us at the Reed Gold Mine. It's located about twenty miles from Charlotte."

Murphy reached the Reed Gold Mine in the afternoon of the next day and bought a ticket for one of the guided tours. Anticipating that he might have to go exploring, he had brought a small flashlight with him.

The tour guide led the group into one of several shafts still open to the general public. Along the way Murphy noticed a number of adjoining shafts that had been blocked off. Murphy purposely let the rest of the group get ahead of him.

At one point he shined his flashlight on some boards and noticed something peculiar. Something had been freshly carved in the old wood; the name Conrad. Murphy studied the name for a moment and looked more closely at the boards. They were loose. He could tell that they had been recently moved. Shining his light past the boards, he could see fresh footprints in the dust of the cave.

I'll bet those are Methuselah's. What does Conrad refer to?

Murphy waited until the tour group had disappeared farther into the shaft and could not hear him.

Conrad? Murphy thought again. *Conrad was the name of John Reed's son who discovered the seventeen-pound gold nugget!*

Murphy followed the footprints in the dust. From the marks, it was clear that someone had walked into the shaft and then walked back out.

Why? What's in the cave? Or what has been left in it?

Murphy moved ahead cautiously. The last time Methuselah had lured him into a cave, he had nearly drowned. He was watching for booby traps or anything that seemed out of place when suddenly the footprints seemed to end. They came up to the wall of the cave where an old signboard was hanging. Peering at it in the light of his flashlight, Murphy could just make out faded words and an arrow pointing to the right.

> Shaft # 23
> Beware of
> Dangerous Gases
> ⟶

What's this all about?

The footprints went up to the wall, seemed to move around, then moved away from the wall and back the way he had come.

Strange.

He studied the sign for a moment then tapped on it. It sounded hollow. Could there be an opening behind the sign? Murphy cautiously touched the sign, then looked down at the dust on the ground. Sure enough, he could see a line that was the same length as the sign.

Methuselah must have taken the sign down, placed it on the floor, and then put it back up. Why?

For the first time in all of his encounters with Methuselah, Murphy suddenly wondered, *Who is this mysterious man? How can I find out more about him?*

Maybe he left some fingerprints. Murphy could copy the prints and have them examined by experts. *But how can I take any prints?*

Murphy searched through his pockets. In one he found a Band-Aid. Carefully he picked up the old signboard by a corner. He then shined his light on the board, front and back, to see if there might be any dusty fingerprints. He could see a good print impression on the right side. He pressed the Band-Aid's adhesive side onto the print, and he put the Band-Aid back inside its envelope, thinking, *I hope I got a good one.*

Murphy was correct, there was a hollow opening behind the sign, about ten inches by ten inches. Murphy shined his light inside. He gasped and drew back, then took a deep breath and shined his light into the hole once more.

Inside he could see a golden cup. A mass of writhing rattlesnakes circled the cup in a ceaseless undulation. They had been disturbed by Murphy removing the sign and shining the light inside. Over the sound of his heart beating loudly, Murphy could hear their tails rattling.

Methuselah certainly wants to make things difficult for me!

Murphy looked around for a stick of some kind but didn't see any. He didn't like the thought of sticking his arm in the hole and grabbing the cup. The snakes would be able to detect the warmth from his arm no matter how slowly he moved. He didn't want to be mistaken for prey.

Then he looked at the sign more closely. It had been made of three boards. He broke off two and began to slide them into the opening, one on each side of the cup. The snakes took their time moving away from the boards. A couple even struck at them. Their quick movements made Murphy jerk. His heart started pounding, and he had to take a deep breath to regain his composure. He felt like he was in the movie *Raiders of the Lost Ark*—and he hated snakes too. Eventually he was able to slide the golden cup toward him, pulling out several of the snakes at the same time. Just then Murphy heard a slight clicking sound. Methuselah had placed some type of electronic triggering device behind the cup, and he hadn't seen it! He hesitated, listening hard. All he could hear was the rattle of the snakes.

Murphy let out a sigh and started to drag the cup toward the opening again. As he did so, he heard another click—this time, above his head.

It must be a delay switch.

The thought barely entered his mind when there was a swish of air and something poured over him. It only took him a second to realize that it was raining rattlesnakes. Methuselah had somehow rigged a box of snakes above his head and camouflaged it well. Murphy froze, his arms still outstretched holding the boards around the cup.

The snakes must have been as surprised as Murphy. None struck at him during their sudden drop. Once they hit the ground, they seemed disoriented.

Some snakes were slithering over his shoes. Others were curled with their tails rattling. Murphy realized that he would have to forget about the cup for the moment. He slowly released the cup from between the boards and withdrew the boards from the hole.

Then Murphy bent over and lowered one board toward his feet. He used it to flip away a snake. Soon he had cleared a safe zone around his feet—no snake was left in striking distance.

Where does Methuselah come up with all this stuff?

Murphy then put the boards back into the hole and used them to inch the cup forward until he could grab it. Once the cup was in his hand, he noticed it had a note inside of it. It read:

> **Good work if you're still alive and haven't been bitten. I'm sorry I couldn't remain to enjoy the show. I had some more important matters to attend to. I really didn't think you would make it this far. You only have a few more tests.**

A few more tests! What does that mean?

"Wow! This is terrific. This cup is really old."

Back at Preston, Murphy was sitting at his desk examining the cup when Shari entered. He briefly summed up his adventure in the mine for her, then said, "My guess is that the cup is as old as the Handwriting on the Wall that we'll soon be looking for."

"Why do you say that?"

"In the fifth chapter of Daniel it is recorded that Belshazzar had a great feast. He wanted to do something unique for his guests, so he had his servants get golden vessels that had been captured from the temple in Jerusalem. He served his guests wine in those sacred vessels. At that very hour God wrote the doom of Belshazzar with his finger on the wall. I think that this cup was one of the golden vessels."

"How does Methuselah find all of these artifacts?" Shari asked in wonder.

"It's beyond me. He has to have some knowledge of the Bible to even know that they are there in the first place."

"Why do you think Methuselah left it for you? It must be worth a ton of money."

"I'm not sure. I think he really wants us to find the Handwriting on the Wall for some reason. He doesn't seem concerned about money in any way. Just setting up the booby traps for me have been quite costly. He's really quite strange. I believe I was able to get one of his fingerprints this time. I've sent it off to be examined. Maybe we can find out who he is!" Murphy exclaimed.

FIFTY

THE TRIP FROM RALEIGH to Richmond, Virginia, to meet Dr. Bingman gave Murphy some time to think about the events of the past few weeks. During the two-hour drive he replayed his adventures with Levi Abrams and the Arabs, the discovery of Dr. Anderson's information about the Anti-Christ, and Talon's pursuit of him and Isis in the library. But he spent the longest time thinking about the aborted terrorist bombing of the George Washington Bridge. Thousands of people could have died, and thousands more could have been affected by the radiation.

It was difficult for Murphy to think about finalizing the plans for an expedition to Babylon with the nation in turmoil, but something inside pushed him onward. He knew that the discovery of the Handwriting on the Wall would be a verification of a much larger picture. If God had judged Belshazzar and his kingdom,

God would one day judge the world. Murphy had the sense that world events were rapidly moving toward a climax...a literal Armageddon.

Murphy was deep in thought when he drove into Capitol Square. The busy traffic had slowed to a stop. He looked up at the Capitol building, designed by Thomas Jefferson before he became the president. Jefferson had modeled it after a Roman temple in Nîmes, France. He could also see the bronze statue of Washington on horseback and the statues of Jefferson Davis, Stonewall Jackson, Robert E. Lee, and other leaders of the Confederacy lining Monument Avenue. Murphy glanced at his watch.

Not bad time. At least I won't be late.

Murphy sat at a table in the café awaiting Dr. Bingman. Murphy always liked to meet people in person—especially if they were planning a potentially dangerous expedition.

Murphy didn't have long to wait. He smiled when he saw Bingman. As the man had explained, he did look like a young Theodore Roosevelt with sandy hair and alert green eyes. He even had a mustache that looked like Roosevelt's. Murphy stood and they shook hands.

"Will, how did you become interested in archaeology?" Murphy asked once the men had seated themselves and ordered lunch.

"As a boy, I always loved history. I devoured books about the Civil War and western heroes. I then came to enjoy studying about ancient history. But it wasn't until I was in the first Persian Gulf War that I really got exposed to ancient artifacts."

"Kuwait?" Murphy asked, curious.

"Yes, why?"

"I was there too. I arrived in January of 1991 as part of Operation Desert Storm under General Norman Schwarzkopf."

"Well, I was a little ahead of you with Desert Shield. Those were interesting days, weren't they?"

"That's putting it mildly," Murphy agreed. "We had expected greater resistance. We only had a few fierce battles."

"While there, I got to see some of the ancient treasures of Iraq," Will Bingman explained. "It prompted me to come back and join an archaeological team. We went on several interesting digs."

"Find anything?"

"Yeah. We were digging in a royal cemetery when we noticed two holes in the ground. We guessed that something made out of wood might have been where the holes were and that the wood had rotted away. We poured plaster of Paris into the holes and let it set, then we carefully dug around the plaster. We had made a perfect cast of a harp. It was great!"

"I would have loved to have seen it, Will."

"Then I came back to the States and seriously studied archaeology. My specialty is resistivity research. We pass an electrical current through the ground to measure electrical resistance of the soil, which is affected by moisture. As you know, stones in ancient buildings contain less moisture than the surrounding ground. Graves and human refuse dumps are really easy to distinguish with all the phosphate content in the soil. How about you?"

"Well, I don't know how much Isis has told you, but my specialty is biblical archaeology. I teach at Preston University in Raleigh."

"Does that mean that you're a follower of Jesus?" Bingman asked.

"Yes, it does."

"Well, isn't that something. Me too. I made a decision to turn to Christ during Desert Shield," Bingman explained. "The sergeant in charge of our platoon always prayed with us before we went out into battle. I watched his life. He seemed to have peace in the midst of war. I questioned him about it, and he told me that true peace came from God through Jesus Christ. That was when I turned my life over to God. I haven't been the same since."

"I think we're going to have a good time together in Iraq, Will," Murphy said, smiling.

"What exactly are we looking for, Michael?"

"The Handwriting on the Wall in Babylon."

"You've got to be kidding. Do you think you know where it is?"

"I've got a good idea. Will, have you been listening to the news about what the United Nations people have been suggesting?"

"You mean moving out of the United States to Babylon. Yes, Michael, I heard that. They say it's because of the fear of future terrorist bombings, but I think it is about good old-fashioned greed. I think they're after the oil."

"You're probably right," Murphy agreed. "Whoever controls the oil controls the destiny of nations that need it. Everything depends on oil. It's a trump card. Countries need oil to run the weapons of war to protect themselves. I think there'll be a showdown over oil."

"Are you talking about the final war in the Valley of Megiddo?" Bingman asked.

"Yes. I think that much of it will be driven by the need to gain control of oil resources. I recently read where scientists estimate that there are from 1,000 to 1,200 billion barrels of oil in proven oil reserves around the world. Saudi Arabia is estimated to have 260 billion barrels, Iraq 113 billion barrels, Iran 100 billion barrels, and Kuwait 97 billion barrels. Between those four countries, that's about fifty-six percent of all the oil in the world. The Middle East will become a focal point in the days ahead."

"Michael, how do you see all of that tying in with Babylon?"

"The second most mentioned city in the Bible, after Jerusalem, is Babylon. The Book of Revelation says that in the last days, Babylon will be destroyed. Before it can be destroyed, it has to be built up. If we can find the Handwriting on the Wall, it's just another proof that the Bible is correct."

Murphy wanted to tell Bingman what he knew about the Anti-Christ, but thought it might be best to hold that for another time. For now, he could see that they would be able to have a good working relationship. Bingman seemed to be a man he could trust. He looked like he could hold his own in any situation.

"I know that Saddam had started rebuilding Babylon but the war in Iraq has put a stop to that," Bingman said. "How could Babylon be built into a major city? It would take years and years."

"I think it could happen very quickly, Will. Remember, Oak Ridge, Tennessee, only had a few people until the government decided to extract uranium-235 isotopes as part of America's efforts to build an atom bomb. The U.S. Army built a complete city for a hundred thousand people in eighteen months. And how about Dubai Internet City in the United Arab Emirates? They started building in 2001 and had buildings ready to move into in twelve months. It can happen faster than you think."

"Well, Michael, I'm ready to go. You've certainly stirred my juices. When do we leave?"

"I'm pulling together the final details. I should be able to tell you in a couple of days."

Murphy's phone rang at 9:30 P.M. Levi Abrams was calling to say that he was being reassigned. They had found something on a terrorist's computer. "It may help us to find out how Talon is tied into all of this and who is funding him," Abrams explained.

"Where are you going?"

"All I can tell you is that there is a small town in Israel called Et Taiyiba. We think the orders for the bombing of the bridge came from there. It's a half-Jewish, half-Arab town. Over the years it's been a site for terrorist activity. Hamas has a headquarters there and has been instrumental in sending suicide bombers into Jerusalem from that location. The Hamas leader Sheikh Yasin is suspected to have links with the Et Taiyiba cell and also with Osama bin Laden. He underwent terrorist training in bin Laden-affiliated camps in Afghanistan. Then he returned to the West Bank and Gaza to establish terrorist cells. Some connection, and some financial support, is going to the Hamas leaders from an outside source. That source may be Talon."

"Now I'm really going to pray for you, Levi. You've got to be very careful. Talon has no conscience. He doesn't care who he kills... he's completely amoral."

"I appreciate that, Michael. Although I don't have the same faith that you do, I can tell you care for my soul. Oh, yes, Michael—Everything is set to go in Iraq. Colonel Davis is ready to assist you in your search. Some of his men will meet you at the Baghdad Airport. After a couple of days there they'll escort you to Babylon. You be very careful too... and take care of Isis. I don't think she is someone you want to lose."

FIFTY-ONE

MURPHY BEGAN the checklist that had almost become second nature to him as a world traveler. He pointed as he ticked items off: *passport . . . visa . . . copies of passport and visa . . . airline tickets . . . cash . . . euros . . . credit cards . . . maps . . . contact phone numbers . . . toilet articles . . . clothes . . . equipment . . . What are you forgetting? You always forget something!*

The phone rang as he was walking to the closet to get his suitcase. It was Cindy at the switchboard at Preston University. Stephanie Kovacs had called, saying it was urgent that she speak with Murphy. "I told her that we have a policy to not give out home phone numbers but that I would pass on the message," Cindy explained.

Murphy took Stephanie Kovacs's phone number and thanked Cindy. *I wonder what this is all about?*

———

After packing his suitcase and placing it in the trunk of his car, he took a moment to try to reach Stephanie Kovacs. She thanked him for calling and said, "Do you have a moment to talk?"

"Sure, what's up?"

She hesitated for a moment. "Forgive me. I'm usually not at a loss for words. I'm not quite sure where to begin. . . . Do you remember when you asked me if I was happy?"

"Yes."

"I haven't been able to get that out of my mind. You touched a sensitive area because I haven't been happy for some time. Anyway, that thought along with your illustration about the kite and Christ knocking at the door to my heart got me thinking."

Murphy started praying. *God, you're working in Stephanie's life. Please give me the right words to say.*

"The past few days have been really hard on me, and I had to make some difficult decisions that have affected my career. I did what you suggested."

"What was that, Stephanie?"

"I prayed to God and asked Him to come into my life and help me through this tough time."

"That's great, Stephanie."

"I don't know how to explain it, but something has changed. I'm not out of my problems yet . . . but I don't feel overwhelmed. I have a kind of peace in the midst of all this stress."

"That's God's specialty. When He changes someone's life, it's like a new birth. He implants a new way of thinking in our mind. He gives us a new attitude and a new perspective in how we view life. He's begun a new work in your life and will continue to help you grow in faith."

"I think you're right. Things *are* looking different. Well, at least most things are."

"What do you mean, most things?"

"I had another reason for calling you, Dr. Murphy. I think you may be in some kind of danger."

"Danger?" Murphy repeated.

"Yes. I'm sure that you know that my relationship with Barrington Communications has been more than just as a news reporter. I . . . I had a personal relationship with Mr. Barrington," Kovacs explained.

"Yes, I'm aware of that."

"For some time we haven't been getting along, and I've been observing how he conducts his business. I became suspicious. He's made a number of quick flights out of the country in the past few months. I sometimes use the same jet for news stories. In passing one day, the pilot mentioned that Mr. Barrington sure made a lot of trips to Switzerland. And in one of our conversations, Shane mentioned that he was working for a group of people who were the financial backers behind Barrington Communications."

"A *group* of people?"

"Yes. I don't know who they are or how many people are in the group; all I know is they are very, very powerful. They have to be to be able to control someone like Shane Barrington."

"What does this have to do with me?"

"One night he said to me, 'You see, these people I work for, these people who own me, are hell-bent on establishing a one-world government. And a one-world religion too. And people like Murphy, they see it all coming, in the Bible. So they have to be stopped. Before they can persuade others to resist.' I think that when he said 'have to be stopped,' he was talking about eliminating you permanently. You must be very careful."

Murphy paused while he was processing what she had said. "Stephanie, I appreciate you alerting me. I'll be on my guard . . . but something concerns me. What if Barrington finds out that you've talked to me? What kind of danger does that put you in?"

"I don't know for sure. All I know is that I've been going against my conscience too long. I have to take a stand for what I know is right. The attempted bombing of the George Washington Bridge challenged me to join with those who stand against evil of every kind. I hope that God will give me the strength."

"I know He will. I have to leave town today, but let me encourage you. Do you have a Bible?"

"No."

"When you get a chance, go to the bookstore and pick up a copy. A good place to start reading is in the Gospel of John. It helps you to understand who Jesus really is. Then try to find a church where you can go and be encouraged and grow in your new faith. And keep on praying. Prayer will become a real source of comfort for you during tough times."

"Thank you, Dr. Murphy. I appreciate your patience with me. And thank you for sharing with me about Christ. It's changed my life."

"Stephanie, you be very careful. I'll try to touch base with you when I return."

FIFTY-TWO

MURPHY COULD FEEL a mixture of emotions as he approached the security check-in station. Security at Dulles International Airport had tightened dramatically since the attempted bombing of the George Washington Bridge. More airport security staff had been added, and the U.S. National Guard was stationed there, fully armed and alert.

I thought security was bad after 9/11. I can't believe we've had to get here three hours earlier than the flight.

As he looked at Isis, he could tell that she was apprehensive. "Are you okay?" he asked.

"I guess. I was just hoping that I wouldn't have to go through one of those patdown searches. I've only had one, and it was humiliating and embarrassing. It was done before they made the screeners use the back of their hands instead of the front of their hands. As a woman you almost feel violated. It's hard to explain to a man. It's just plain awful."

Murphy began to survey the crowd, imagining what he would look for if he were a security guard. Would it be a little old woman with a knitting bag, or would he be drawn to someone from a Middle Eastern descent? After the bombing of the bridge, racial profiling had increased rather than decreased. Everyone was on edge, and many innocent people were being questioned. Tensions were running high.

"I almost feel sorry for those of other cultures who are being looked at as potential terrorists," Murphy began, "but I think there's no way to stop that. Look at us. We're innocent passengers, yet we have to stand in line and be treated like potential terrorists. Everyone is in the same boat. We're just going to have to get used to it. Life will never be the same as it was before 9/11."

As he looked over the crowd, he saw Wilfred Bingman toward the end of the line. Murphy smiled and nodded. *I'm looking forward to getting better acquainted with him.*

While Murphy was putting their luggage in the overhead bins, Isis slid over to the window seat and began to get comfortable. She looked out the window and watched the men loading the plane from below. Murphy sat down in the aisle seat next to her. He didn't like window seats. They were too confining. Besides, he liked to get up and walk around every now and then without climbing over people. He enjoyed traveling to foreign countries and meeting new people, but he hated the long plane flights to get there. Soon Bingman arrived and sat in the aisle seat across from Murphy.

"This has already been a long day, Michael. Can you believe that it's already eleven P.M.? I sure hope we can get some sleep on the way over."

Before attempting to get some sleep, Isis turned to Murphy. "Michael, do you ever think about Noah's Ark?"

"Actually, I think about it a lot. It was the dream of a lifetime to be able to see it and explore it. I'm so angry that Talon covered it with an avalanche and killed some good people in the process."

At his words, Isis thought back to nursing him back to health in the cave.

"I long for the day that I have some time and can get the financial backing to go back to the Black Sea and look for the backpack," Murphy continued. "Those bronze plates and crystals could be a great source of inexpensive energy."

"I think about it too. Growing up, I thought the story of Noah's Ark was a good child's story," Isis said. "I had no idea that it was real. And then to see it in person and to walk on the deck—it was almost beyond description. What scares me is the judgment of God on the wickedness of men. What you say about the Bible seems to be accurate."

"The ark proves it is real, just as the Handwriting on the Wall will."

Isis was quiet for a while. Murphy could tell she was thinking. "Michael, do you think there will ever be an end to all these horrible terrorist bombings? When I think of the thousands of people who could have died at the George Washington Bridge bombing, I'm so saddened."

"I wish I could say yes, but in all honesty I think they will get worse."

"Why do you say that?"

"For several reasons, I guess," Murphy explained. "The nature of man is selfish and often cruel. All you have to do is look at human history to prove that. It's punctuated with war as far back as you can look. In fact, I've read that there have only been three hundred twenty years of recorded human history where no wars were mentioned. There are always men and women who want to control other people."

"Don't you think that the peace talks will do any good?"

"Perhaps. They seem to delay conflict or prevent it for a period of time, but eventually it returns. As we draw closer to the end of days, the Bible suggests that trouble will increase."

"What do you mean, 'the end of days'?" Isis asked, curious.

"It refers to a conversation that Jesus had with his disciples. He told them that one day there would be a judgment for sin and that He would come again to rule the world. I could show you something from the Bible that talks about this if you're interested."

"Yes, Michael, I would like to know more about the end days."

Murphy opened his briefcase and took out a Bible. "Let me show you the conversation. It's found in the Book of Matthew, Chapter Twenty-four. It reads as follows:

Now as He sat on the Mount of Olives, the disciples came to Him privately, saying, "Tell us, when will these things be? And what will be the sign of Your coming, and of the end of the age?"

And Jesus answered and said to them: "Take heed that no one deceives you. For many will come in My name, saying, 'I am the Christ,' and will deceive many. And you will hear of wars and rumors of wars. See that you are not troubled; for all these things must come to pass, but the end is not yet. For nation will rise against nation, and kingdom against kingdom. And there will be famines, pestilences, and earthquakes in various places. All these are the beginning of sorrows.

"Then they will deliver you up to tribulation and kill you, and you will be hated by all nations for My name's sake. And then many will be offended, will betray one another, and will hate one another. Then many false prophets will rise up and deceive many. And because lawlessness

will abound, the love of many will grow cold. But he who endures to the end shall be saved. And this gospel of the kingdom will be preached in all the world as a witness to all the nations, and then the end will come."

"That sounds sort of bleak," Isis concluded.

"Yes and no. The wars, famines, pestilences, and earthquakes are not pleasant at all. Nor is being hated by people or betrayed. The point is that one day all of the evil in the world will come to an end. That will be a great day for those who are ready to see God. You see, it's possible to have peace and hope in the midst of a world filled with turmoil."

"Michael, you keep talking about the judgment of God. You talked about it when we were on Ararat looking for Noah's Ark. You said that the worldwide flood was God's judgment against the wickedness of man. And you've talked about God judging Belshazzar for his evil with the Handwriting on the Wall. That's pretty scary stuff."

"Yes, it is, Isis. You see, most people think that war is terrible. They think that terrorist bombings are hideous . . . and they are. War can cause shortages of food in a country, which creates widespread famine. Most developing nations barely have enough food for their people. It is estimated that half a billion people on earth are seriously malnourished. Famine can also be caused by cyclones, floods, droughts, pests, plant disease, or even tsunamis. We saw this in the Indian Ocean earthquake that created a hundred-foot tidal wave. The findings suggest that it was an earthquake of a 9.3 magnitude."

"It was terrible! I had to stop watching the news for weeks afterward," Isis put in. "It was too emotionally draining. I heard the estimates for loss of life could reach 310,000 people."

"That's true. Earthquakes have killed a lot of people. The earthquake in Syria in A.D. 1201 claimed the lives of more than a million people. The one in Hausien, China, in 1556 killed 850,000. The

Great Chilean earthquake was a 9.5 quake. In fact, the top twenty-five earthquakes have killed more than six million people over the years. Scientists tell us that eighty-one percent of the world's earthquakes take place in what is called the Ring of Fire tectonic plate."

"Why are you telling me all of this?" Isis asked.

"I'll explain in a moment. Let me just mention one more thing. The Bible talks about wars and rumors of wars, famine, and earthquakes. It also talks about pestilences. That doesn't refer to just crop damage. It includes all kinds of diseases. What do you think is the biggest and most devastating disease today?"

"HIV/AIDS."

"Right. It's killed millions, especially in Africa. In Malawi it's estimated that almost twenty percent of the population is afflicted with HIV/AIDS. But have you heard about the new 'super strain' of AIDS called 3-DCRHIV? It was found recently in a forty-year-old man who was a drug user and had hundreds of partners in the past several months. This particular strain has never been seen before. It's unimaginably aggressive and resistant to almost all treatments. Nineteen of the twenty drugs in use today are ineffective against it. But here's the real kicker. In the past, most HIV infections didn't turn into AIDS until nine or ten years later. This new virulent strain moves at lightning speed. From the onset of the HIV infection, it only takes two to three months to develop into a full-blown AIDS case. Another man in San Diego has been diagnosed with this new strain. The news is causing a panic in the gay community."

"I can see why."

"You asked me what was the point of all of this. All of these things are terrible. They unnecessarily destroy human life, and they are of great concern. The question is, if we are overwhelmed by these tragedies . . . shouldn't we be even more concerned with sin, which destroys the human soul and separates us from a holy God? Jesus stated it this way in Matthew, Chapter Ten: '*And do not fear those who kill the body but cannot kill the soul. But rather fear Him who is able to destroy both soul and body in hell.'*"

"I need to think that through, Michael," Isis murmured. "As you know, I don't have a Christian background. All this is new to me."

Murphy nodded. He was falling in love with Isis, and she had not yet come to the point of faith in her life. He did not want to lose her or have her meet God without settling the issue of receiving Christ into her life.

Isis closed her eyes and laid her head on Murphy's shoulder. She felt safe, comfortable, and protected next to him. She had never met anyone quite like him.

What if all he was saying about the end times were true? What if the judgment of God is a reality? I don't think I'm ready for that.

As Isis tried to sleep, Murphy closed his eyes and began to pray.

Murphy was starting to drift off when he heard Bingman speak.

"Michael, have you been to Baghdad before?"

"On one other occasion," Murphy said, shaking himself awake.

"What's it like?"

"Well, it is a large city of about five to six million people. It's the transportation hub for Iraq. It is probably the richest and most economically solid city there. It is the headquarters for the Central Bank of Iraq and the center of financial operations for the country."

"Will it be dangerous for us?"

"It could be, but we'll be escorted by the military, which will provide protection."

"My experience from Desert Shield is that they'll also provide a target for the enemy to shoot at," Bingman said.

"That could happen too. However, I don't think that the military will be taking us into the more dangerous sections of the city.

One of the things you'll notice is the wide streets. They make moving around the city easier."

"What did you think of all the National Guard at Dulles?" Bingman changed the subject.

"They did look impressive."

"Yes, I think the president has the right idea in calling in the Guard and closing all the borders into the United States. However, I think he should have done it earlier. It's sort of like closing the barn door after the cows are already out."

"I think we'll see that his decision is not temporary, Will. Closed borders may very well become part of our national policy in the future. People may demand protection, and the politicians will have to respond."

"To be honest with you, Michael, I think I'd prefer a closed border to having to watch out for terrorists all the time. Does that sound awful?"

"No. A closed border can give better control and a feeling of security. There's nothing wrong with that."

"It won't make us the most popular country by other nations if we do make it more difficult for people to visit," Bingman said pensively.

"Well, a lot of them haven't liked us when we've had an open door policy," Murphy replied. "They like our money and our freedom, and want to live here, yet they hate us at the same time. It is a strange situation."

"I know what you mean. If I were to move to another country, like, say, Romania, I could become a citizen but I would never be a Romanian. But when people come from other countries to the U.S. and become citizens, they become Americans. America is made up of people from hundreds of countries who have blended together. It has truly become the land of the free and those who seek freedom.

That's what our Statue of Liberty is all about. It sure makes me feel proud to be an American."

"You're right, Will. It's the blending together of cultures as one nation that has made us strong. One of the things that will destroy America the fastest is when people from other countries come here and attempt to re-create their own country on American soil. That type of multiculturalism will cause division. President Theodore Roosevelt had strong convictions about that when he said: 'There is no room in this country for hyphenated Americans. . . . The one absolutely certain way of bringing this nation to ruin, of preventing all possibility of continuing to be a nation at all would be to permit it to become a tangle of squabbling nationalities.' "

"Cultural division does increase tension," Bingman agreed. "Just look at where we're going. Look at the infighting and vying for control in Iraq. There's so much tension among the Kurds, the Sunni, and the Shi'i. If democracy is going to work there, they'll have to begin to think of themselves as one nation rather than three cultures fighting for power. Do you think moving the United Nations headquarters to Babylon would help to unite them?"

"It probably will in the short run. But in the long run, I think it's part of a move for a one-world government to be led by the Anti-Christ. The world will be looking for a leader who will promise to lead countries away from war and terrorism. Words of peace will sound very attractive. If you put that together with the hope of eliminating famine, decreasing poverty, protecting the environment, reducing corruption, and instilling universal spiritual harmony among people . . . he could win the world with that message."

"You're probably right, Michael. I wonder how we fit into the picture."

"I think our role is to try to sound a warning about future judgment and share the good news that God has provided a solution to the problems of the world through Jesus. He is the only one who can lead us to peace with God and harmony with our fellow man—not the Anti-Christ. We live in exciting days, Will, and I think they're going to get even more exciting as we draw closer to His return."

There was silence for a while as both men thought about their own roles and responsibilities. Finally Murphy broke the silence.

"Will, tell me a little about yourself. Do you have children?"

"Yes, I have three. Two daughters and a son. Amber, my oldest, is a senior in college. She's studying to be an English teacher. Amy is a sophomore and is planning to go into psychology. Adam is in his senior year of high school. I don't think he has any idea of what he would like to do, other than play football. But when I look back at my own life, I didn't know what I wanted to do either when I graduated from high school."

"It sounds like you have a wonderful family. Do you have any pictures?"

"This is Arlene, my wife," Bingman said, smiling and offering Murphy pictures from his wallet.

"It sounds like and looks like God has blessed you," Murphy said, examining the pictures.

"Yes. When all is said and done, it's your relationship with God and your family that really matters. I don't like to be away from them, but my wife knows how much I like adventure. This is a trip of a lifetime!" Bingman exclaimed.

"Well, I think we might have some excitement waiting for us in Baghdad. It might be good for us to get as much rest as we can," Murphy said.

Bingman nodded and closed his eyes.

Murphy closed his eyes but sleep did not come easily. He was filled with a growing sense of apprehension.

FIFTY-THREE

THE SOUND OF THE CAPTAIN speaking over the loud-speaker woke Isis. She looked over at Murphy, who was reading his Bible.

He glanced at her and smiled. "Looks like you got some sleep."

"I did but I still feel tired."

"Sitting up isn't the most restful sleep position," Murphy agreed.

Isis thought that it didn't really matter how tired she was be-cause she was with Michael...and it would be for a couple of weeks. Just being close to him made her heart beat fast. *I wonder if there's any hope that he's feeling the same way.*

As the plane touched down and began to taxi, Isis was jarred back to reality. Out the window, she could see U.S. Air Force jets, helicopters, and military vehicles everywhere.

———

Murphy, Isis, and Bingman were all surprised at how many people were flying in and out of the Baghdad Airport.

"Well," said Bingman, "I don't know what I expected, but this is a busy place. It's as packed as any airport in the U.S."

"Except there are a lot more military on security watch," Isis replied. "It makes me feel insecure rather than safe. Weird, huh?"

The words were just out of her mouth when a tall U.S. Marine captain approached. He was dressed in crisp desert fatigues and boots, wearing two shoulder holsters. He was flanked by two younger soldiers carrying rifles.

"Are you Dr. Murphy?"

"Yes. And this is Dr. Isis McDonald, and Dr. Wilfred Bingman."

The captain shook hands with everyone. "I'm Captain Michael Drake, and I serve under Colonel Davis, who is stationed in Babylon. He asked me to escort you. I'll assist you through customs and we can then pick up your luggage. Hopefully, it will be a little faster with my help.

"We have hotel rooms reserved for you in the Green Zone. It's safe and well protected. Most of the news reporters and other dignitaries stay there. We won't be leaving for Babylon for a couple of days. We'll be joining a convoy going that direction. It will be safer that way."

"Captain Drake, we were supposed to meet an Egyptian friend in Baghdad, Jassim Amram. He's supposed to travel with us to Babylon. Will he be able to enter the Green Zone?" Murphy asked. "Otherwise I can meet him outside."

"I'm afraid not, sir. We've recently had a rash of bombings and security has tightened down. If he's going to travel with us, we'll have to meet him just outside of the zone.

"Regarding leaving the Green Zone, you will be permitted in and out, but once you leave, you'll no longer be under U.S. military protection. Americans do stand out in a crowd, and in some parts of Baghdad it would be extremely dangerous for you to travel alone."

"I appreciate that word of advice. We'll keep it in mind."

Murphy, Isis, and Bingman were standing just outside of the Green Zone checkpoint as the sun was going down. It had been a very warm day, and they had been able to swim and relax after the long flight of the day before. It wasn't long before an older Mercedes drove up and out stepped Jassim Amram.

"Michael, it is so good to see you!"

Amram was wearing his usual white suit, which hung loosely on his gangly frame. His rich mellifluous laugh rang out as he gave Murphy a big hug.

He then turned toward Isis and smiled. "And the lovely Dr. McDonald." Amram took her hand and gently kissed it.

Bingman held out his hand. "I'm Wilfred Bingman. Nice to meet you."

"Well, come, come. Let's not stand here. I have a good restaurant selected for tonight, and we can discuss this new adventure."

"Jassim, are you sure that it is all right for us to move away from the Green Zone? You know we'll stick out like sore thumbs. Especially Isis with her red hair," Murphy asked, worried.

Amram waved his hand. "Michael, there is no problem. The area that we are going to go to is very safe and the food is excellent."

The men were deep in discussion about the Handwriting on the Wall when Isis began to look around the restaurant. She had felt uncomfortable for most of the evening. She knew that many of the men in the restaurant were looking at her. Although she had draped a scarf over her hair and was wearing long sleeves, she still stood out. The few other women there were looking at her and making comments. The experience was a little unnerving.

I just need to relax, she told herself firmly. *Jassim said it was safe.*

As she glanced around the room, she caught the eyes of an Arab eating by himself nearby. He immediately glanced away. As he turned, she thought she saw something on his neck—a tattoo?

Could it be? He's got the tattoo of an upside-down crescent on his neck with a star below it!

Isis reached out and grasped Murphy's hand under the table. He could tell something was wrong by her firm grip.

He turned and looked at Isis while Bingman and Amram continued their conversation. Isis was looking in the direction of the man who was standing and leaving his table, and she looked frightened.

She leaned over and whispered, "Did you see his tattoo? It was an upside-down crescent with a star under it on the side of his neck."

"Are you sure? How did one of Talon's men find us here?" Murphy exclaimed.

"Well, it is getting late," Amram was saying. "I should get you back to the Green Zone. The military get very suspicious and have a hair trigger on anyone who approaches the zone after ten P.M."

Amram brought up the Handwriting on the Wall as they left the restaurant. Deep in discussion, they didn't notice a dark vehicle approaching slowly.

At the first sound of gunfire, Murphy reached out, pushed Isis to the ground, and covered her with his body. Amram and Bingman also hit the ground as bullets sprayed a brick wall and shattered the restaurant window.

Then Murphy jumped to his feet, pulling Isis with him. "Run!" he shouted, heading for a dark alley next to the restaurant, dragging Isis along with him. Amram and Bingman were also up and running. *Good. None of us has been hit.*

Murphy could hear the screech of brakes behind him. Whoever had shot at them had stopped and was backing up.

As he ran down the alley, Murphy noticed an opening into a courtyard to his left. It was too narrow for a car to follow. The attackers would have to pursue on foot. Murphy turned into the opening, motioning for the others to follow, then ran across a courtyard, into another alley. They began to zigzag through alleys and yards in an attempt to escape. Soon they came to a small street on which there were a number of shops and restaurants.

"Over there!" Amram shouted.

They crossed the street and entered a small restaurant, breathing hard. Every head turned their way as they entered. The group tried to walk nonchalantly to a table at the back, but it was obvious that they were out of place. Pairs of dark eyes followed them, focused on the three white faces. Americans never frequented this local hangout—especially a light-skinned woman with flaming red hair.

Everyone knew that they were in trouble. Was there anyone in the room they could trust?

Murphy, Isis, Bingman, and Amram looked up at the faces that were staring at them. Eventually a short stocky man approached and said something to Amram in Arabic. "The man says that we should follow him," Amram translated.

The stocky man led them through the kitchen, opened a door that led to the alley, and pointed.

Obviously the man was giving them an escape route out the back. Maybe the people in the restaurant wouldn't say anything to those pursuing them. It was worth a chance.

The group walked quickly through several more alleys until they found a place to rest.

"I am so sorry for what has happened," Amram cried. "I can't understand how we were targeted! I will work my way back to the car and come pick you up. Remain here. I will return as soon as I can."

"Be careful, Jassim. Those men are out there somewhere. We'll keep in the shadows until you return," Murphy replied.

After ten minutes, Murphy, Isis, and Bingman heard the sound of people coming up the alley. They froze and waited in the shadows of a doorway. Isis, trembling, grabbed Murphy's arm and stood close to him.

Four men approached, slowed, and finally stopped right in front of the doorway where the Americans were hiding. Then one of the men lit a cigarette. In the flickering light, Murphy could see that one of the men carried an automatic weapon, two had knives, and the fourth had some sort of club. But the light also enabled the Arabs to see them.

The one with the gun yelled and motioned for them to come out of the doorway. Murphy, Isis, and Bingman stepped forward.

The four Arabs began to argue in Arabic. Quietly Isis began to interpret.

"The large one with the knife says that they should kill us right here. The one with the gun is saying no. He thinks we should be taken to their leader for him to decide. The heavy one with the other knife says that they should behead us right now. The small one is arguing that they should have fun with me before they kill me."

Murphy looked at Bingman. Their eyes briefly met, and Bingman gave a slight nod. Murphy knew it was best to move while the Arabs were arguing. He went for the man with the automatic weapon. As he stepped forward, the man started to bring his gun up. Murphy's left hand hit the weapon as it started to fire, deflecting the bullet.

Murphy spun around in one spot, raising his right elbow and

driving it into the gunman's right temple. He was instantly down and out.

Bingman took on the big man with the knife, who lunged straight forward. Bingman sidestepped, pulled off his jacket, and rolled it over his left arm as protection. The Arab lunged a second time, this time trying to stab Bingman in the face.

Bingman blocked the knife with his jacket-covered arm. He drove his right fist in an uppercut motion into the Arab's diaphragm. Then Bingman brought his knee up, breaking the man's nose and shattering his cheekbone. He was through.

Isis decided to take on the small man with the club—the one who wanted to have fun with her. As she started to charge him, he raised the club over his head and shouted, "White whore." Suddenly she dropped down as if she were sliding into home base, raised her left foot, and drove it straight into his groin. The man dropped the club, rolling on the ground and wailing in pain.

Isis picked up the club and was about to hit the Arab when Bingman grabbed her arm. "Allow me," he said, driving his fist into the man's face.

In the meantime, Murphy had taken on the tall Arab with a knife. Murphy dropped down and did a leg sweep, knocking the man's feet out from under him. He then jumped up and drove his heel down on the man's hand that was holding the knife. The Arab screamed as his fingers broke. Then Murphy grabbed the knife, dropped to one knee, and placed the point on the tall man's throat. He could see an upside-down crescent tattoo on the Arab's neck.

"Who sent you after us? Who are you working for?" Murphy cried.

Isis translated. The man only moaned and clutched his broken fingers.

Isis repeated the question as Murphy pushed on the knife, breaking the man's skin and drawing a bead of blood.

Finally the Arab spoke. "The man with the razor finger wants you dead," Isis translated. "He says the people he works for need you eliminated."

"What do you mean, the people he works for?" Murphy asked, pressing his knee into the Arab's belly.

Again Isis translated what was said. "The Seven."

"The who? Who are the Seven?" Murphy asked.

As soon as Isis translated that, a look of absolute terror came over the tall man's face. Murphy knew that the man would die before he would reveal that secret. He tossed the knife away and drove a reverse punch into the man's chest, rendering him unconscious.

Bingman picked up the weapons, took out the automatic's bullet clip, and tossed everything over a wall. Then he threw the bullet clip as far as he could in the other direction.

Murphy ran to Isis, who was wild-eyed and breathing hard. Yet she did not look afraid. She looked like a wild tiger waiting for her next victim. He pulled her in his arms. "Are you okay?"

"I am now," she whispered, hugging him tight.

Murphy was trying to process what had been said. *The man with the razor finger—obviously Talon—works for a group of people called the Seven . . . and they want me dead. Why?*

As Jassim Amram drove up, he could see bodies lying in the alley. Three people were standing. They turned and looked into the lights of his Mercedes. He smiled and sighed with relief when he saw his American friends.

FIFTY-FOUR

STEPHANIE KOVACS TOOK a deep breath before she opened the door. She was on another, likely futile, job interview. *Pull it together girl. Head up. Put on the big smile.*

Maybe this time she'd have more luck. After all, she had known Carlton Morris for years.

Kovacs grabbed a *Newsweek* magazine and sat down, waiting for her appointment. *Five turn-downs this week. I don't have many more options left*, she thought morosely.

She was halfway through an article on terrorism when the office door opened.

"Stephanie Kovacs, how have you been?" Morris called out. With his bifocals perched on the tip of his nose, his untidy curly white hair, and his broad smile, he looked like Santa Claus without the beard.

"Thank you for seeing me, Carlton," Kovacs said soberly.

The typical chitchat did not last long. Morris could see how upset Kovacs was.

"Carlton, I need some help," she began. "I'm out of a job right now, and I was wondering if you might have some openings here at Fox News."

"Yeah, I heard you were no longer working for Barrington Communications. The grapevine—" he broke off, grinning ruefully, then looking sympathetically into Kovacs's eyes. "Stephanie, we've been friends for how many years?"

"About thirteen."

"As your friend, I've got to be completely honest with you. The word is out on the street that Barrington's got it in for you. Last week the president called me into his office and told me if you showed up looking for a job, I was to tell you that nothing was available. My hands are tied. I have to be honest. You're been blackballed. You won't be able to get any job in the East Coast or West Coast markets. You might find a weather reporting job in some small Midwest town, but I doubt it. Shane Barrington is out to ruin you. I'm so sorry."

Kovacs sat there silently for a moment. She had feared something like this would happen when she left Barrington. Yet she had to try to find a job in the field that she loved—and in which she was good.

"I know, Carlton. I don't hold it against you. It's just discouraging. The thought of changing careers in midstream isn't welcome."

"I'm sorry, honey. I wish there was something I could do."

It had not been easy for Kovacs to go to sleep. She had tossed and turned, worrying about her future, for hours. Finally the escape of sleep had come.

Suddenly her eyes popped open and she held her breath. All of her senses were alert. *What was that noise? How long have I been asleep?* She listened, taking only shallow breaths. All was quiet. She glanced over at her digital clock: 2:30 A.M.

She thought she had heard a creak coming from the wooden floor in her living room. But then it was silent. *Is someone there? I locked the door and the windows. I must be having a bad dream.*

She lay there for another ten minutes, listening intently, but she heard nothing. *I've got to check or I'll never get to sleep.* Carefully and quietly, she sat up and slowly opened the drawer of the night-stand next to her bed. She reached in and pulled out a .32 automatic.

Kovacs crept to her open bedroom door, leaned forward, and looked into the living room. It was empty and quiet. Carefully she crossed the living room to the window that looked out on the city. She opened the blinds and peered out into the night. She could see a few lights in the apartment building across the avenue. There was no traffic down in the street.

Maybe a cup of hot chocolate would help me go back to sleep.

She entered the kitchen and looked around. There was nothing out of the ordinary. *You're just being foolish*, she told herself.

Kovacs set the automatic down on the table and walked to the pantry. After a moment's hesitation, she returned to pick up the gun. Then she opened the door to the pantry. She wasn't quite sure what to expect: Would the pantry be empty, or would someone be standing there in the dark?

As she swung the door open, a broom fell out. She almost fired the gun in surprise, then she started laughing. She took the hot chocolate from the shelf, set the gun down on the counter, and started heating water. She then sat down at the table and thought, *What am I going to do about work?*

She didn't hear a sound. All she felt was an iron grip of a glove-covered hand over her mouth and a forearm choking her. His head and mouth were pressing against her right ear.

"I wasn't in the living room or the kitchen, Stephanie," a man's voice taunted. "I had already made it into your bedroom before you woke up. You walked right past me in the dark. Surprise."

Kovacs was terrified. *Who is this? What does he want?*

"I'll let go of you if you promise not to scream. If you do, it will be your last breath. Do you understand?"

Kovacs nodded her head. She didn't recognize the man's voice. It had no trace of emotion in it. Slowly his grip relaxed. She was looking at her automatic on the counter. *Can I distract him enough to get to the gun?*

"Turn around," the voice said.

Kovacs turned and faced a man with bone-white features, a neatly trimmed mustache, and blank eyes that made her shiver. He was thin, but there was no question that he was extremely strong.

"Who are you and what do you want?" she managed.

A thin smile broke across his lips. "Very brave, aren't you? My name is Talon."

As he looked at her, he remembered the first time he had seen the feisty news reporter. It was on television. She had been reporting from Queens, New York, on the discovery of the home of the mastermind of a UN attack.

Talon remembered chuckling as he watched her. *This woman is good*, he thought. *She may have more ice water in her veins than her boss, Barrington, has.*

And now they were meeting face to face.

"You have been very brave in your news reporting, but not very smart. My employers think that you have been just a little too friendly with Dr. Michael Murphy. We've had your phone tapped for some time since you left Shane Barrington."

"What does Dr. Murphy have to do with all this?"

"You like to report the blunt facts in your commentaries. Let me give you the straight scoop. You have become a security leak for Mr.

Barrington. We cannot tolerate your lack of loyalty. You have shared your last communication with Dr. Murphy."

Stephanie could tell she was in deep trouble.

"You see, Ms. Kovacs, it is no fun to stand behind people and choke them to death. Unless, perhaps, you are standing in front of a mirror. The real pleasure comes from looking people in the eye as they die. That way you get to enjoy all the terror and pain that comes into their faces. It makes all the effort worthwhile."

Kovacs had been in many difficult situations as a news reporter, but nothing like this. She could tell that he was deadly serious. She knew that she had to get to the gun to have any chance at all. That would be the only way she would survive.

Talon sensed her muscles tensing for motion. His hands surrounded her throat. He lifted her up to eye level and began to squeeze. Kovacs had no strength to try to fight back. He was squeezing the life out of her. Just as she felt herself drift toward unconsciousness, the grip on her neck loosened and she started to cough.

Then Talon grabbed her hair with his left hand and tilted her head back. At the same time he used his teeth to pull the glove off his right hand. He readied his artificial finger with the razor tip. He would wait for Stephanie to open her eyes before he slit her throat.

"Mr. Barrington, Mr. Barrington, did you see the latest news flash?" Melissa shouted, rushing into his office.

Barrington didn't like to be interrupted when he was planning his morning schedule. "What are you talking about, Melissa?" he asked gruffly.

"Look, I'll turn on the news." Melissa hurried to turn on the television.

"This is Mark Hadley reporting for BNN. I am standing outside of the apartment building of Stephanie Kovacs, a former investigative reporter for Barrington Communications and Network News. Apparently she was murdered early this morning by an unknown assailant. We only have sketchy information at this time, but it looks like her throat was slit. Police investigators are questioning occupants of the apartment building. We will bring you an update on the six o'clock news. This is Mark Hadley bringing you this very sad report about one of our former BNN coworkers."

Barrington stared at the television in shock. His secretary knew it would be best not to say anything. She quietly turned off the television and left the office.

Barrington stared into space, totally confused. A wave of guilt flooded him. Then he began to think back to the good times he had had with Stephanie. He began to realize that he really did care for her . . . maybe even loved her. Sorrow engulfed him as he thought of their last meeting, of how he had beaten her and thrown the suitcases at her. He buried his face in his hands. He had destroyed her career in news reporting and left her with nothing. The realization that the only person he had ever cared about had been murdered infuriated him.

What had the reporter said? "Her throat was slit"?

It took a few minutes before he realized that this could have been the work of only one person: *Talon! And he gets his orders from the Seven*, Barrington thought grimly.

A plan began to form in Barrington's mind.

FIFTY-FIVE

CAPTAIN DRAKE ARRIVED at the hotel early the next morning. He brought desert fatigues for everyone along with bullet-proof flack vests and helmets. While the team changed, he loaded all of their gear into a Hummer for the trip to Babylon.

Murphy saw Isis in the lobby in her military clothes. She whirled around in front of him. "What do you think?" she asked, grinning.

"You make anything you wear look great."

Murphy felt a strong desire to take her in his arms and kiss her. He knew that he'd like to take their relationship to a deeper level, and he thought she did too. He was also aware that the only thing holding him back was their different spiritual outlooks.

Isis looked at Murphy and smiled. "I didn't realize how tired and sore I was until the alarm went off this morning."

Murphy nodded. "I guess late-night battles in dark alleys do have a way of getting to you. I'm a little sore this morning too. I couldn't believe how you fought back last night. I'm just glad that nothing more serious happened. I wouldn't want to lose you."

Isis looked at Murphy and smiled. It was the kind of smile that would melt any man.

When the three Hummers pulled through the Green Zone security checkpoint, Murphy could see Jassim Amram standing on a corner next to his luggage.

"Captain Drake, that's the Egyptian friend I mentioned—Mr. Amram. The one wearing the white suit."

"I brought a change of clothes and protective gear for him also. He can change when we catch up with the convoy going to Babylon. All of the vehicles will be following a Buffalo."

"A water buffalo?" asked Isis.

Captain Drake laughed. "No, ma'am. I'm talking about an EOD."

"EOD?"

"Excuse me, ma'am. An explosive ordnance disposal vehicle. It's a special heavyweight armored vehicle that can withstand roadside bombs."

"Do you think we'll encounter a roadside bomb on the trip?" Isis couldn't keep the anxiety out of her voice.

"I certainly hope not. The Buffalo has been designed to go ahead of the troops and clear a safe path. Wait till you see it. It's about twenty-five feet long and stands almost nine feet high. It's covered with armor plate on all sides and on the top. It also has extra-thick steel on the bottom, where a blast might occur. It rides on six Michelin run-flat tires. They can keep driving even with damaged tires."

"Don't the explosions endanger the driver?" Isis asked.

"Actually there is more than just a driver. A Buffalo can hold up to ten soldiers. No one's been seriously injured yet. Because the vehicle is so high off the ground, the force of the explosion disperses to the sides. The front end sometimes lifts off the ground from the power of the explosion. Those riding inside say it's quite an experience to drive over IEDs—improvised explosive devices—and keep moving."

"I've heard about those vehicles," Murphy said. "Don't they have some kind of arm that can dig in the ground?"

"Yes, sir. It is called a spork. It's a remotely controlled hydraulic arm. The arm ends in a pitchfork type of instrument that incorporates a video camera. The spork is controlled by a joystick that allows for precise and accurate control. Sometimes a pitchfork gets blown off during an explosion. But they can be repaired, usually within forty-eight to seventy-two hours."

"At least men are not losing their lives."

"Yes, sir. If you look up ahead, you can see the Buffalo beginning to pull out and move ahead of the convoy. When we get to Babylon, I'll give you a tour of it."

Murphy looked over at Bingman, who seemed deep in thought. "What are you thinking about, Will?"

"I was thinking about Iraq and how much the Islam faith plays a part in politics and daily life of the people. What do you think?"

"I think faith does play a large part. It's been estimated that one in every five people in the world is a Muslim. It's one of the fastest-growing religions on earth," Murphy explained. "Muslims are united on the Shahadah, the profession of faith. They all believe there is no God but Allah and that Mohammed is His prophet. They are also united when they build their mosques, which all face east, toward Mecca. After that, they aren't homogenous. Their daily practice and philosophical beliefs vary in different parts of the world."

"What about this talk of a jihad? What's that all about?" Bingman asked.

"Well, the Arabic meaning of the word is 'exerted effort.' It means exerting effort to change oneself for the better. It can also mean physically standing against or fighting oppressors, if necessary. It's the latter definition that has created quite a stir. It's not just fighting against an occupation army, it's fighting against what is perceived to be injustice and anything that might disagree with one's faith. Mohammed suggested to his followers, 'Do not obey the *kafireen*— those who reject the truth—but wage jihad with the Qur'an against them.' This is the concept that has many Westerners worried."

"Does that mean if I don't believe what they do, they want me dead?"

"Some in the Muslim faith have suggested that. They see themselves in a 'holy war' with nonbelievers. I've heard reports of many responding to the calls for jihad. For example, some men have left their homes and fought in Afghanistan, Iraq, and elsewhere."

"Do all Muslims believe that way?"

"No, but extremists and terrorists have taken the term 'jihad' and used it as a cry for all-out war against anyone who does not hold to their faith and beliefs. They've twisted the original Arabic meaning of 'fight only those who fight you' to justify terrorism against innocent civilians and children. They've put a spin on the text and used it for their own personal agendas," Murphy concluded grimly.

"That sounds scary. I wonder how many feel that way."

"No one knows for sure. The problem is amplified whenever Muslim leaders do not speak out against terrorist activities. Their silence gives the impression that they may approve of them. This doesn't help their cause."

"Yeah, that bothered me too. When I drive by one of their mosques, I wonder what they're doing in there. Are they planning the overthrow of the United States? Do they want to destroy my family?"

"Many Muslims do not believe that way at all, Will," Murphy explained. "They love the United States and support it, but the average Westerner doesn't know this. They're not sure who they can trust. This lack of trust creates disharmony between groups. It causes the Muslims to draw away from non-Muslims and vice versa. It can have a devastating worldwide effect. It is a philosophical clash of societies and beliefs. This type of clash and distrust can foster war. Just like what's happening right here in Iraq."

Their conversation was interrupted by a loud explosion, a ball of flame, and a pillar of black smoke. The Hummer stopped abruptly. The Buffalo at the head of the convoy was bouncing up and down.

Soldiers were piling out of their vehicles with their weapons ready. There was yelling, and vehicles were repositioned in case of a firefight.

Captain Drake was the first to speak. "Well, that was a good example of what the Buffalo can do. There must have been a bomb in the car up ahead."

He spoke as if it were a casual, everyday event. The Buffalo backed out of the blazing inferno, stopped for a moment, then drove forward and lifted the car off the ground. It set the burning car to the side of the road then continued on toward Babylon.

Soldiers climbed back in their Hummers and the convey continued.

"It must take some special type of soldier to drive one of those Buffalos," Murphy said.

"Yes, sir. Those are very special Marines. They love their jobs and look forward to each day's new adventure. The rest of us consider them heroes. They're risking their lives to save ours."

FIFTY-SIX

ONE OF THE LIONS *rolled over and dropped a paw onto Daniel's leg. He woke up instantly. It took a moment for him to gather his thoughts. He had almost forgotten he was in a den of lions. The weight of the paw on his leg brought him back to reality.*

Slowly and gently he removed the paw and smiled. No one would believe this story. No one had ever been thrown to the lions and lived to tell the tale.

He thought back to another time when he was startled awake. It was when the great city of Babylon fell to the armies of Azzam and Jawhar. He had arrived home and fallen into a restless sleep after interpreting the Handwriting on the Wall for Belshazzar.

Suddenly soldiers broke into his home carrying torches, their swords drawn. They rushed toward his bed as he sat up. The tip of one sword touched his chest. A soldier held a torch to his face. He made some comment, and the other soldier withdrew the sword. Then they searched the house and left as quickly as they had come. Daniel had no idea what they were looking for. Obviously they thought he was too old to present any danger.

"Kasim, did you taste the wine for the king this evening?" Tamir asked.

"No, he went to bed without any wine or food. He ordered everyone out, even the entertainers. He looked very ill."

"Is the king sick?"

"No, I don't mean that type of ill look. He seemed both sad and angry at the same time. For a while I stayed outside of his door and listened. I could hear him moaning and groaning and talking to himself."

"What's wrong?"

"I think he's angry over a decision to throw the old Hebrew into the lion's pit. He seemed very agitated. Watch it, Tamir. Don't make any mistakes in your baking. He might take it out on you."

At the sound of the large stone being removed from the hole in the ceiling, all the lions jumped up. Light glared down from the hole.

Daniel put his hand up to shade his eyes. He could see the lions looking up, saliva dripping from their mouths. Was it time to be fed? Only their tails twitched back and forth. They didn't seem to pay any attention to him as he rose.

"O Daniel, servant of the living God, was your God, whom you worship continually, able to deliver you from the lions?" a voice called down from above.

Daniel recognized the voice of Darius. He could tell from the king's tone that he did not expect an answer.

"Your Majesty, life forever! My God has sent His angel to shut the lions' mouths. They did not touch me or harm me. It is proof of my innocence and faithfulness to you."

Daniel could hear the king dancing around and shouting for joy. Then the guards lowered a rope and pulled Daniel from the den. Just before he reached the opening, Daniel took one last look at the wild animals that had been gentle with him. He smiled and thanked God.

Darius had his physicians examine Daniel for any injuries. None were found. Soon Darius's joy turned to anger. He was outraged that he had been tricked into putting Daniel in the den. Darius summoned the general of his army.

"I want you to round up all of the satraps and governors Abu Bakar and Husam al Din. Bring their wives and children with them. The lions are hungry and need to be fed. I want you to put in a new family every three days. Make sure that Abu Bakar and Husam al Din are last. I want them to have time to think about their failed attempt to kill Daniel.

"Now I want to make a decree to all of the people of the kingdom. It should read that everyone in the empire shall tremble and fear before the God of Daniel. He is the living, unchanging God whose kingdom shall never be destroyed and whose power shall never end. He delivers His people, preserving them from harm; He does great miracles in heaven and earth; it is He who delivered Daniel from the power of the lions."

The first family did not touch the floor before the lions tore them apart.

FIFTY-SEVEN

"IT'S KIND OF BARREN out here," Bingman said as they drove farther out of Baghdad.

"You're right about that," Murphy responded. "There're some grass and weeds and palm trees, and a lot of open space. If it weren't for the Euphrates River running through Babylon, it would be more like a desert—more like the rest of the country."

They were silent as they watched the shepherds, a few roadside stands, and people moving in and out of small adobe homes near the river. Every now and then they could see fishermen in boats casting their nets.

"What are those buildings up ahead?" Bingman asked.

"That's Al Hillah," Captain Drake replied. "It's a small town right next to the site of the original Babylon. The Marines have set up a base there and send out daily patrols. We've also been instructed to guard and prevent any looting that might go on at local archaeological sites."

Murphy spoke up. "I've heard that there's been massive looting of museums and archaeological relics. Many of them are being sold on the black market."

"Yes, sir, that's true. It's a quick way for poor Iraqis to make some big money. We've done a good job at discouraging the theft, but occasionally they get away with something. Now we only allow those with archaeological permits, like yourselves, to get near any of the sites."

"The town has certainly grown since we were last here," Murphy said, looking around.

"Yes, sir. For some reason we've had a lot of dignitaries come and visit Babylon. A new hotel is being built, and businesses are moving in. I've even heard talk of investors coming into the area and buying up land."

"Why do you think that is happening?" Isis asked.

"I don't know for sure, ma'am. I have heard there might be a possibility of the United Nations moving here. But I can't for the life of me see why. This is not the hottest attraction in Iraq, in my opinion."

"Yet Babylon does have a long and glorious history," Isis said. "It was the home of the great King Nebuchadnezzar and the Hanging Gardens of Babylon, one of the Seven Wonders of the World."

"Yes, ma'am. And maybe it will have a glorious future if enough people get excited about it. In fact, there's a group of a dozen UN representatives in town now. We've been taking them all around. They've been looking at water supplies, building sites, and meeting with Iraqi businessmen and government leaders. It looks like they might be serious."

Bingman turned to Murphy and pointed. "What's that in the distance?"

"That's part of the ancient structures near where we'll be

exploring. Look over to your left. You can see the buildings that Saddam was in the process of reconstructing. Some of the arches are forty feet tall. Tomorrow you may get a chance to see the ancient roadway that leads to Babylon. It has a fence on either side to preserve the pavement, which dates back to 400 B.C."

"Michael, when you were here last, did you have a chance to explore the ruins?" Bingman asked eagerly.

"A little," Murphy replied. "Most of our efforts were directed at finding Nebuchadnezzar's golden head."

"Did you see any of the bricks that had Nebuchadnezzar's name on them? I've read that he had his name on most of the exposed brick surfaces."

"Yes, I did see his name on many of the bricks. But listen to this. Saddam had *his* name put on the new bricks that were added to the original foundation. He wanted to get the credit for rebuilding Babylon."

"Will Colonel Davis be on hand to meet us?" Amram asked the captain.

"No, sir. He's out on a mission and won't arrive back until late this evening. He'll meet you in the morning. Is there something I can help you with?"

"I was just wondering if he received my message about borrowing the sonar sled. We used it when we were here last time to find the hollow opening into the chamber where the golden head was found."

"I believe he did, sir. I know that I saw our men checking it out before I went to Baghdad to pick you up."

"That's good news, Captain. That will save us a lot of unnecessary digging."

FIFTY-EIGHT

ISIS WAS LOOKING forward to an exciting day. She was eager to get started in the hunt for the Handwriting on the Wall.

She was halfway through the mess line for breakfast when she had the eerie feeling that she was being watched. Murphy smiled as he noticed her discomfort.

"Is there something wrong?" he asked, grinning.

"I feel like I'm being stared at."

"Of course you are. Turn around."

About two hundred Marines were looking her direction. They smiled in unison when they noticed her looking into the room. It took her a moment to gain composure, she then smiled, waved, and turned around, grabbing her tray.

After getting their food, they turned and looked for a place to sit. Immediately six Marines jumped to their feet, grabbed their trays, and stepped back, waving their arms for them to sit down. Isis flushed but acknowledged their compliment and sat down with the team.

"That's embarrassing," she said.

The men laughed.

Murphy, Isis, Bingman, and Amram were deep in conversation about the expedition when all of a sudden the Marines jumped up.

A deep voice shouted, "Attention."

"At ease, men. Continue eating."

They turned to see the tanned, rugged face of Colonel Davis. Beneath his aviator shades, his steel blue eyes were sparkling and alert. The muscles on his forearm rippled as he shook hands with everyone, his grip like steel. He was the type of soldier you'd want on your side in a battle.

"Welcome to Babylon," Davis said. "I'm happy to see that you all arrived safely. I have your sonar sled ready, and I've assigned Captain Drake to assist you. He has a platoon of men at your disposal. Please do not hesitate to call on them for any assistance. They'll instantly respond. These are some of the best Marines in Iraq."

Murphy was drawn to the colonel's command presence. He could tell that Davis's men would follow wherever he led.

"Thank you, sir, we appreciate all that you're doing to make our expedition a success. When we were here last time, you assisted us with a bulldozer. Would that be available this time?" Murphy asked.

"By all means ... except we'll have to be very careful as we use it. We have strict orders not to damage any ancient artifacts. I'm sorry that I won't be able to be with you today. I'm scheduled for some meetings with a group from the United Nations."

"Of course," Murphy said. "Thank you again for all of your help, Colonel."

"If Methuselah's directions are accurate, it shouldn't be too difficult to find the Handwriting on the Wall," Murphy said, reaching into his pocket and pulling out the three-by-five card that Methuselah had left for him. He read aloud to the group, which now included Marines with shovels who were waiting for orders.

> ## BABYLON—375 METERS DIRECTLY NORTHEAST OF THE HEAD

Jassim Amram was looking around for the site where they found Nebuchadnezzar's golden head. "It looks like it's been covered over since we were last here. I think it is in this general area. We'll have to use the sonar sled to find the spot."

Captain Drake had the men sweep the area. It took almost two hours before they found the spot.

"Michael, I will use my compass and pace off three hundred seventy-five meters toward the northeast. Look over there," Amram said, pointing. "I'll bet it is very close to those old ruins."

"Captain Drake, if you and your men could follow Mr. Amram, I think he'll need some help," Murphy said.

After several hours of looking, a spot was located and the sonar sled was turned on. The Marines dragged the sled back and forth until it registered a void in the ground. They then dragged the sled in a crisscross fashion to pinpoint the void.

"Dr. Murphy, I think we can use the bulldozer to remove some of this sand. We won't drive over the void in case it collapses on us. We'll just drag the sand away."

"Fine, Captain. I think that's the safest way to operate."

The sonar sled estimated the depth of the sand to the point of the void at about eighteen inches. Marines with shovels were brought in to do the more careful digging.

Soon a sound of metal scraping on rock could be heard. Another fifteen minutes of digging exposed the top of a square capstone with a large metal ring on each corner.

Bingman stepped forward. "I'll bet they put poles through the rings and sets of men lifted it into place," he exclaimed. "It's got to be the covering of some type of chamber."

Murphy called for the backhoe, and chains were attached to the four rings. "This will be a little easier than having teams of men trying to lift it," he explained, smiling.

Soon the backhoe was lifting the stone. There was a slight hiss, then a musty smell escaped from the opening. Murphy and the team brought their flashlights and shined them down.

"Look," Isis exclaimed. "A set of stairs! I'll be that this was a back entrance. It's not wide enough to be the main passageway."

"Let's go in!" Bingman's voice was filled with excitement. "I don't think there'll be any of Nebuchadnezzar's guards hiding in this hole."

"We still need to be careful," Murphy cautioned. "We want to be sure that nothing will collapse on us. Captain Drake, you can tell your men to rest while we go exploring."

"Yes, sir. Are you sure that you don't want some of us to accompany you?"

"Thank you, but I don't think that will be necessary."

Murphy entered the acrid pit first, followed by Isis, Amram, and

Bingman. The stairs continued down for about thirty feet and then stopped in a ten-by-ten chamber with about a seven-foot ceiling. Murphy shined his light around.

"Three tunnels split off the chamber. We can go right, left, or straight ahead."

Bingman's voice could be heard in the background. "Decisions, decisions, decisions. You choose, Murphy. We can always come back here and try a different one."

"Did you bring your bread crumbs, Will?"

"No, but I do have my knife, and I can scrape arrows on the wall."

"That will really preserve the archaeological site," Isis exclaimed.

"It sure beats getting lost."

Murphy laughed. "Let's try it for a while without marking the walls. I think all we'll have to do is follow our footprints in the dust. Let's try the tunnel to the right."

Isis shined her light down to check that she could see her footprints. They were clear in the dust. She felt relieved. She didn't like the idea of getting lost in a maze of tunnels.

She was about to follow Murphy when something caught her eye—other footprints. They came from the tunnel to the left and entered the tunnel that was straight ahead. They seemed to return to the same direction they came from. "Michael!" she called. "Come back here for a moment. I think I've found something."

Murphy returned and Isis shined her light on the footprints.

Murphy brushed his hand through his hair. "They're large prints. Probably a man who weighs about two hundred pounds."

"How would you know that, Michael? Are you Sherlock Holmes?" Amram asked.

"By deduction Dr. Watson. The shoe size is close to my size and I weigh about one ninety-five. The impression created is very similar to mine except for the print pattern on the sole of the boot. And look there! Whoever it is walks with a slight limp. Can you see a lit-tle drag mark from the side of the footprint?"

"I beg your pardon, you *are* Sherlock Holmes. Now tell us who it is and you will win a copy of *The Hound of the Baskervilles*."

"My guess is that it's Methuselah. When I was at the Cañon City Penitentiary, I talked with an inmate named Tyler Scott. He de-scribed Methuselah to me. He said he was about my size and walked with a slight limp. I later received a golden cup from Methuselah. The only way that Methuselah could know about the location of the Handwriting on the Wall and the cup was to have been here before us. I think those are his footprints."

"It looks like I may owe you a copy of the *Baskervilles*," Amram said seriously.

"Well, I'll collect later. For now, let's follow these footprints and see where they lead. They'll be better than bread crumbs or marking on a wall."

The team followed the tracks for another ten minutes until they came to a spot where the tunnel forked. Tracks came and went out of both of the forks.

"So far, so good, Michael. You pick," Bingman said.

"Let's go to the left."

Another ten minutes of exploring brought them to a flat wall.

"The tunnel ends here," Isis said, discouraged.

"It *seems* to end here," Murphy replied after looking around. "Look at the floor. The prints look like they go *under* the wall. I'll bet this is some kind of a back door. Will, you and Jassim help me push on the wall."

All three men put their shoulders to the wall and pushed. Slowly the wall seemed to pivot to the left and open.

"Well, we've learned something else about Methuselah," Murphy said with a grunt.

"What's that?" Isis asked.

"We now know that he's a very strong man. He pushed the wall door open all by himself."

As the team moved through the opening and shined their lights around, they couldn't believe their eyes.

"This must have been the temple treasury!" Murphy exclaimed. "Look at all the gold and silver. There are hundreds of plates, goblets, cups, and eating utensils."

Isis was shining her light on the walls. "Look at the ornate golden shields!"

Amram was scooping his hands through some coins. "This is indeed a king's ransom." He got out his camera and began to photograph the precious relics.

"It's an unbelievable archaeological find!" Bingman cried. "I've never seen anything like it in my life."

Murphy looked at one of the golden cups. "I'll bet this is where Methuselah got the golden cup from."

"It doesn't look like he took very much," Isis said. "Just who is this guy, anyway?"

"Well, I've never actually met him, you know, but I have heard him. He laughs with a high-pitched cackling laugh. I know he has a weird sense of humor. He enjoys putting me into life-threatening situations. He must be independently wealthy, because he creates expensive and elaborate traps for me and he doesn't take any artifacts like the ones that are in this room. He understands the Bible and must believe in stories like Daniel and the lions' den and Noah and the ark. And he has told me that my training is almost done—whatever that means. Oh, and by the way, I have one of his fingerprints and am trying to see if I can get a match somewhere. That's about all I know."

"That's enough to give someone a nightmare," Bingman murmured.

"That's a good way to put it, Will. Methuselah *is* a nightmare."

"Well, maybe your nightmare will come to an end if we go back and find out what's at the end of the other tunnel," Amram said encouragingly.

FIFTY-NINE

"WE'LL LEAVE the wall door open for now," Murphy said. "After we explore the other fork in the tunnel, we can return with the soldiers and retrieve the relics in the temple treasury."

"I can't believe it hasn't been looted before now," Bingman said excitedly. "I feel like a kid in a candy shop. I want to see it all and examine every piece. It's not every day a person discovers something like this."

"I know what you mean, Will, but I think it would be good for us to see what else might be down here," Murphy said indulgently.

It took the expedition team about twenty minutes to retrace their steps back to the fork and then follow the other tunnel, which ended in a dead end.

"This looks like the same type of wall we just came from," Amram said. "I'll bet that it too is a secret door."

"One way to find out," Murphy said, putting a shoulder to the wall. Even with Bingman and Amram's help, it didn't budge. "I know this has to open like the other one," Murphy said through gritted teeth. "We'll just have to keep working it loose."

Finally after forty minutes and a lot of sweat, the wall door gave way. The team stepped into an enormous room. It was so large that their flashlights could not shine through the darkness and reflect off a back wall.

"This is huge!" Amram exclaimed. "Can you believe what they were able to do without modern tools?"

"Look at the stone tables." Bingman was pointing at a marble table with marble benches; dozens of other tables surrounded him.

"Probably a dining room of some kind," Murphy concluded, shining his light straight up. "The ceiling looks about sixteen to eighteen feet high. It's a little hard to tell in this light."

"Look at the painted murals on the ceiling," Isis exclaimed, focusing her light off to the left.

"This must be Belshazzar's banquet hall," Murphy cried. "I have a feeling that we're going to discover the Handwriting on the Wall very soon. Jassim, do you have the camera?"

"Of course. That is why you have brought a smart Egyptian like me along."

"Let's spread out and see if we can find anything."

It wasn't long before the team could hear Bingman yelling. "Come over here. I think I have found Belshazzar's throne."

Murphy was the first reach Bingman. "You may be right," he said firmly. "Look right there. It's a raised platform with three steps."

Murphy walked up the stairs and approached a wall. In front of the wall were the remains of a marble throne surrounded by three smaller thrones.

"I'll bet this is where Belshazzar and his wives or top officials sat," Isis said.

"Probably his wives," Murphy replied. "In Daniel, Chapter Five, it states that he brought golden vessels for his wives and concubines to drink from. They were the golden cups that were taken from the temple in Jerusalem. This desecration was the final straw that caused God to write a message for him on the wall."

They all shined their lights on the wall behind the thrones.

"I don't see anything," Isis said, disappointment evident in her tone.

Murphy told her, "If Belshazzar was sitting on the throne at the time of the writing, I'll bet it's on the other side of the room, where he could watch the armless hand scratch a message."

"Well, let's go see, Mr. Sherlock Holmes. You have been right so far," Amram said.

The team worked their way to the other side of the room, stepping carefully around broken marble blocks.

"Let's do this together," Murphy advised. "Let's all raise our lights at the same time and see what we might discover. We're looking for four words in Babylonian script: the words *Mene, Mene, Tekel, Upharsin*. On the count of three. One. Two. Three."

Four flashlights brightened the ancient wall. It was definitely covered with some type of plaster. Large and small cracks could be seen along with chunks of missing plaster. Everyone was searching for something that looked like a word amid the many cracks.

"Look! To the right," Amram cried. "Is that part of a word?"

All lights turned to where the Egyptian was pointing.

Isis stepped forward to examine the wall more closely. "Yes, I think it is," she concluded. "There are chunks of plaster missing, but I think I can read it. It says 'ene, Tekel, Uphars—' This is it! The first *Mene* is missing along with the first letter of the second *Mene*.

The *Tekel* is quite clear, and two letters are missing off of the back end of *Upharsin*."

Murphy, Amram, and Bingman all shouted at the same time. A strange echo could be heard in the ancient chamber. Amram took out the camera and began taking shots from every possible angle.

After a few minutes, Murphy sat down on one of the marble benches and was silent.

"What's wrong, Michael? Aren't you happy?" Isis asked. "You've found the Handwriting on the Wall!"

"I have mixed emotions. Yes, this is an unbelievable archaeological find, Isis—one of the greatest to date. It's like finding Noah's Ark again. It proves the validity of the Bible and strengthens my faith."

"But . . . ?"

"But I'm wondering what will happen when we share this news with the world. Will people believe it? Will this discovery really change anyone's behavior? Will people understand the importance and significance of God's coming judgment? I feel like I've been standing outside of a building that's on fire. I yell for the people to come out and be saved from the flames, yet they ignore the warnings of smoke, heat, and my pleas."

Isis wasn't sure what to say. She knew she herself was one of those people he was talking about who had been ignoring the messages. She had actually walked on the ark, and now she had actually seen the Handwriting on the Wall . . . and still she hadn't made a decision.

Why haven't I? she thought.

"Michael, archaeologists from all over the world will want to see this, and the room full of temple treasures." Bingman could barely contain his enthusiasm.

Murphy started to speak, then stopped and listened. A sound

like tanks driving over an empty building rushed toward them. Instinctively Murphy knew what it was.

The earthquake hit with lightning speed. Everyone was knocked to the ground. The sound inside the room was terrifying. Murphy got to one knee and shined his light toward the ceiling. Dust and debris were dropping from the ceiling. He looked around for Isis. She was on the floor trying to figure out what had just happened.

As he shined his light toward the ceiling above her, Murphy could see an enormous section beginning to loosen. Isis was just beginning to get her feet under her when Murphy hit her with a body block and sent her flying like a rag doll. At the same instant, a large stone landed where she had been.

Murphy rolled to his feet and ran to her. She was gasping for breath. Murphy took her in his arms. "I'm so sorry. I'm so sorry. But I had to do it."

He pointed to where she had been standing. A wedge-shaped rock had been driven into the floor.

Isis was still disoriented.

"We've got to get out of here," Murphy called out. "If there are any aftershocks, we might not make it. The whole ceiling could collapse and the tunnels could be buried."

Murphy helped Isis up and yelled. "Bingman! Jassim! Are you okay?"

"I'm all right," yelled Bingman, "but Jassim has been hurt. I think he has a broken leg. I can support him on his bad side and he can sort of drag along with his good leg. Let's get out of this place before it changes from a banquet hall to a tomb!"

Murphy turned to Isis. "Are you able to walk?"

"I think so."

"Grab my hand and don't let go."

The dust in the air made it hard to breathe. Murphy picked up his flashlight and began to help Isis across the room toward the entrance. He stopped for a moment and shined his light back into the room. Bingman was supporting Amram, who had a pained look on his face. They were about ten feet behind.

"Will, are you going to be able to make it?"

"We had it worse in Desert Storm. Keep moving."

The trip back to the surface seemed to take forever. They were almost to the chamber that had three tunnels when Captain Drake and his men appeared. "Are you all right, sir?"

"We're okay, but one of the team is injured. Maybe your men could assist him. I think he has a broken leg."

The Marines behind the captain didn't need an order. Rushing past Murphy and Isis, they ran to Jassim Amram. The first Marine grabbed Amram's arms, turned around, and laid him across his back in a piggyback position. He bent forward slightly, holding the injured man's arms over his shoulders. Two other Marines went behind and picked up part of his weight, supporting the broken leg the best they could.

Amram yelled a few times in pain. The Marines ignored his shouts. Getting out quickly was more important than any momentary pain.

Then they began to creep forward as quickly as they could in the tight tunnel. Captain Drake led the way with a bright-beam flashlight.

As they reached the base of the stairway to the surface, Jassim Amram yelled again. "The camera! I left it where the Marines picked me up!"

"I'll get it," Bingman cried. "We also need the pictures to prove the existence of the Handwriting on the Wall. It will only take a couple of minutes. It's not very far back."

Murphy yelled again, but it was of no use. Bingman was off and running. Murphy grabbed Isis's hand and started up the stairs.

"Where is your other team member?" asked Captain Drake, who had gone on ahead.

"He went back for the camera. He wouldn't listen to me."

"It sounds like he was trained to complete the mission, sir. Rescue the people first, then rescue the information."

About two minutes had passed when all of a sudden there was another gigantic rumble, and everyone was knocked to the ground again. An aftershock!

Murphy was up and running toward the staircase. As he arrived, a cloud of dust and air came out of the hole. He grabbed a light and shined it down. Dirt covered most of the stairs. It looked as if the complete tunnel system had collapsed, obliterating the room of temple treasures and Belshazzar's banquet hall. There was absolutely no hope that Will could have survived.

He was wondering what he was going to tell Will's wife and children, when he felt a tap on his shoulder. He spun round and there was Bingham—his clothes torn and dusty—with a huge grin on his face. In his hand he held the camera, battered but intact.

"Looking for this, Murphy?" he asked.

SIXTY

EVERYONE AT BARRINGTON Network News was walking on eggshells. Ever since the death of Stephanie Kovacs, Barrington had seemed to lose some of his focus. He wasn't attending to the daily details of the operation as he did in the past.

Melissa, his secretary and assistant, had stepped in to act as a go-between for the staff and Barrington. She seemed to be the only one he trusted, and she protected him from unnecessary intruders.

He had always been a difficult man to work for, but now he was completely unpredictable. He fired two top-level managers who questioned one of his decisions. Even though they were right, he didn't like to be challenged in any way. He was a walking time bomb.

Stephanie's death had hurt him more than he realized. His hurt had turned to anger, and his anger had turned to hatred. Now that hatred was beginning to settle into the strange world of revenge. It seemed to occupy his every waking thought.

Barrington buzzed Melissa and asked her to come into his office.

Barrington had his chair turned toward the windows. The fingers of his hands were pressed together in front of him like a steeple and were propping up his chin. He looked deep in thought.

"Melissa," he said, "I want you to get some information for me from the finance department. I want to know how much actual cash we have on hand. I don't want to know the value of all our assets in buildings, land, and equipment. I want to know about actual cash that we could use on a quick turnaround. Oh, yes, get those bean counters to let me know how much money I can get the banks to loan me. And how much lead time the paperwork would require."

Melissa knew better than to ask why. "Mr. Barrington? I've had five phone calls from Paul Wallach from Preston University. He'd like to get together with you for a short meeting."

"What does he want?"

"He won't tell me, sir. He just insists that he needs to talk with you."

Barrington sighed, looking disgusted.

"Set him up for Friday at three P.M. After that meeting I'm leaving. I have some planning to do."

When he entered the office, Paul Wallach could tell that Barrington seemed preoccupied. He thanked the older man for seeing him, then asked, School is almost over for me, and I was wondering when I will begin working for you. I graduate the latter part of May."

Barrington just sat there looking at Paul . . . or maybe through him.

"I was curious as to what my responsibilities would be. We really haven't had a chance to talk much about it after you gave me the assignment of reporting on Dr. Murphy's archaeology class. How have you liked my writing so far? What does the future hold for me with the Barrington Network News?"

Barrington just sat there in silence. Wallach found the pause almost unbearable.

"Well, Paul," Barrington finally said, "I have a reputation for speaking frankly. Are you ready for a man-to-man talk?"

"I . . . I'm not sure. What do you mean?"

"I mean we're going to have one today. Number one: There'll be no starting date. Number two: You won't get a salary. Number three: You won't have any responsibilities. Number four: Your writing stinks. Number five: I only used you to get information on Murphy. I didn't care about your writing style. Number six: Your scholarship is discontinued. And number seven: You're a fool."

Paul was in shock. "But, Mr. Barrington," he sputtered. "You told me that you thought of me as a son."

"That was just to get you to do what I wanted. I needed information about Murphy. But now I don't care about him. And I don't need you anymore."

"But, Mr. Barrington—"

Barrington cut him off. "If you want to know the truth, Paul, you haven't got skills enough to drive a nail—let alone survive in this kind of business. Let me give it to you straight. I'll spell it out slowly so you'll understand: You're fired as of today."

Wallach sat there stunned. He had thought of Barrington as a father, and now his world was collapsing.

Barrington sat there looking at him with a cold, glassy stare.
Wallach slowly got to his feet and walked out of the room.

Paul Wallach was devastated. He had put all of his eggs in one bas-
ket, and now it had been dropped. His future was gone.

He was hurt and angry. He felt used and dirty. How could he
have been so gullible and stupid?

He began to think back to when he first met Shane Barrington.
He'd been in the hospital, after being injured in the church bombing. He remembered Shari's reaction to Barrington: Shari hadn't
trusted him from the very start.

Then he recalled how Barrington had come to the Preston
University campus and offered him a job. He had paid Paul twenty
dollars an hour to write summaries of Dr. Murphy's classes. As a
struggling student, Paul could use the money. And Barrington had
seemed so interested in him. But Shari had questioned Barrington's
motives then also.

*Why should the head of Barrington Communications be interested in your
work?* she'd asked. *You're a student, Paul, not a world-famous professor.*

Paul was enveloped in a deep depression. Both the present and
the future were in turmoil. He had come to depend on Barrington's
stipend, and now he was being cut off without a cent. His planned
career had been demolished, his personal self-esteem was destroyed,
and he had lost Shari, the woman he had grown to love.

He realized that he had been on the merry-go-round of success
and had looked only for the brass ring of happiness. He thought it
could be found in money, prestige, power, and influence. Now he realized that his life was hollow and empty, and he was alone.

SIXTY-ONE

THE MARINE BASE at Al Hillah was in full emergency mode when the expedition team arrived back. Marines were running, collecting gear, and troops were being loaded into vehicles filled with emergency medical supplies.

Colonel Davis was standing in front of the command tent giving orders to his officers. He approached as the team got out of the Hummers.

"All hell has broken loose around here. Our men are responding to the calls for help in Al Hillah and the towns surrounding Babylon. Many homes and business buildings have collapsed. Quite a few people have been killed, and many more are injured or trapped. Dr. Murphy, we're in a tragic situation right now."

"I understand." Murphy's mind flashed back to the devastation of the church bombing and the injured people. He could still see

Laura in the hospital as she breathed her last breath. "How widespread do you think the damage is?"

"This has been a big one. Central command has reported that it was a 9.5 quake."

"That's as big as the great quake in Chile!"

"The first aftershock registered at 8.2 on the Richter scale. I'm sure more will follow. The epicenter of the quake is in the heart of the Syrian desert, about a hundred fifty miles west of the town of Al Habbariyah. Emergency teams are on their way now. There's also been damage in Baghdad, Karbala, An Jajaf, and at least twenty other small towns. Central command said that the effects of the quake were even felt in Basra, four hundred fifty miles to the east."

"Is there anything we can do to help?"

"Thank you. If you could assist Captain Drake and his platoon, that would be great. The International Red Cross, the Red Crescent, and other emergency relief organizations are mobilizing."

In the mess tent, Murphy watched as Isis slowly collected food and a beverage. She looked physically and emotionally spent. As they sat down at a table, she turned to him and began to cry. He embraced her, whispering softly until she had cried herself out.

"This has been a terrible day, Michael," Isis murmured. "The excitement of our discoveries, then Jassim's injury and thinking Will was dead . . . and now the death of so many in Al Hillah. I can't get it all out of my mind. I close my eyes and I can still see women screaming and slapping their faces in grief as they sit by dead relatives. I can hear the yelling of the men frantically digging for loved ones buried under the rubble. These people have suffered so much pain and hurt with the wars and now this earthquake. How can a loving God allow it all to happen?"

Murphy nodded. "In times like these there are no easy answers. A passage in Romans, Chapter Eight, talks a little about this." He reached for the pocket-size New Testament he carried. "Let me read you what it says.

"Yet what we suffer now is nothing compared to the glory He will give us later. For all creation is waiting patiently and hopefully for that future day when God will resurrect His children. For on that day thorns and thistles, sin, death, and decay—the things that overcame the world against its will at God's command—will all disappear, and the world around us will share in the glorious freedom from sin which God's children enjoy.

"For we know that even the things of nature, like animals and plants, suffer in sickness and death as they await this great event.

"And even we Christians, although we have the Holy Spirit within us as a foretaste of future glory, also groan to be released from pain and suffering. We, too, wait anxiously for that day when God will give us our full rights as His children, including the new bodies He has promised us—bodies that will never be sick again and will never die."

"In the Garden of Eden, when man disobeyed, it started a chain reaction of sin, death, and decay. From that day until now, we have been overcome by misery, war, and natural disasters like floods, tornados, and earthquakes. It is not a pretty sight. All of nature and mankind itself groans under this curse. It's painful . . . as it's been today digging through the rubble searching for people.

"But one day all the suffering in the world is going to end and there will be no more crying. That's what the Bible teaches. But first there will be a judgment of all wrong. That's the message of Noah and the ark and the Handwriting on the Wall. God sent Jesus to bear judgment for us so that we might go free. That's the good news. A new day is coming and we need to be prepared for it. One day God will wipe away all tears."

Just then a Marine tapped Murphy on the shoulder. "I'm sorry to cut into your conversation, sir, but they received a message in the control tent from a Levi Abrams. He asked that you call him on his cell phone as soon as possible."

"Thank you, Sergeant."

"I wonder what he wants?" Isis said.

"He knows that we're in Babylon. He's probably just checking up to see how we are."

Surprisingly, the cell phone connection was clear, and Murphy was able to reach Abrams immediately. Abrams was calling to check how the team fared in the quake. After expressing regrets over Amram's injury, Abrams said, "I'm in Israel right now—about two hundred fifty miles west of the epicenter."

"This ranks as one of the largest recorded earthquakes," Murphy said.

"It's caused terrible devastation. Did it hamper your search? Were you able to find what you were looking for?"

"Yes, Levi, we did find the Handwriting on the Wall. Isis is organizing an exhibition of photographs we took that prove it."

"You're kidding. What a find, Michael!" Abrams exclaimed.

"I'd like to talk to you about it someday."

"How about in the next couple of days?"

"What do you mean?"

"Michael, some of the terrorists involved with the attempted bombing of the George Washington Bridge have been traced to a small Israeli-Arab town called Et Taiyiba, just south of the Sea of

Galilee in the Jordan Valley. We've had difficulty there before. Israeli soldiers recently raided a Hamas hideout in there and uncovered an extensive Hamas network that had ties to Gaza. They were responsible for a number of attacks and suicide bombings in Israel."

"Are you saying that Hamas is responsible for the bridge attempt?"

"We don't think they were *directly* responsible. We think that another group based in Europe recruited Hamas terrorists. We think the New York attack had two purposes. One was to strike back at the U.S., and the other was to earn money for their war with Israel. We interrogated some of the terrorists that were caught in New York . . . and guess what, Michael? They had the upside-down crescent on their necks with the talons on them."

Murphy felt an immediate rush of anger. "Levi, our team was attacked in Baghdad. We escaped, but one of the attackers referred to a group of people called the Seven. I wonder if they're the group based in Europe. If that's true, then my guess is that Talon works for them."

"You may be right, Michael. Is there any way you could fly into Tel Aviv and drive up to Et Taiyiba to assist us? You have quite a bit of information about this Talon fellow."

"Yes. Bingham needs to get back to his wife and kids. Jassim needs to get back to Egypt to recover from his broken leg. And Isis— well, Isis is worn down. It's been a difficult time for her. I'd feel much better if she were back home, safe. I'll make the arrangements ASAP."

Jassim Amram was struggling along on crutches as he entered the airport in Baghdad. He was followed by a porter carrying his luggage. Murphy and Isis were saying good-bye before she joined Amram on the flight out of Iraq.

"Michael, I'm worried about you in Israel," Isis said, looking deeply into his eyes. "You seem to have a magnetic attraction for people who are trying to harm you."

Murphy could hear her protective tone. He smiled and grabbed her hand. "I'll be very careful. I have a strong reason for returning."

He paused for a moment, then slowly and gently pulled her to him. He wrapped his arms around her and held her close, then lowered his lips to hers.

SIXTY-TWO

MURPHY CLOSED his eyes and tried to sleep, but much-needed rest eluded him. He kept thinking about the devastation caused by the earthquake. Bingham's miraculous escape from the tunnel had been a joyful surprise, but many had suffered—and were still suffering—from the effects of the quake.

I just don't understand it all. God, You've got to help me through this.

His thoughts were interrupted by a stewardess passing out Israeli customs entry slips. He filled his form out, then closed his eyes again. This time, new thoughts came into his mind. He could see Isis at the airport standing in front of him with a worried look in her eyes. *She's so strong in character, so filled with energy, and so beautiful. And yet she's also so vulnerable.* He wanted to protect her and keep her safe.

The drone of the jet engines and the memory of finally kissing Isis began to relax him, and at last Murphy rested.

Israeli security forces were everywhere when Murphy exited the plane. He was glad that he only had his carry-on bags and didn't have to fight the crowds getting their luggage at the carousels. All that he had to do was to get his rental car.

As he walked through the airport, he could see a number of teams of humanitarian aid personnel wearing bright colored T-shirts. Good-hearted people around the world were rallying in support of those devastated by the earthquake.

Murphy followed the coastal highway north out of Tel Aviv till it turned east over the Samarian Hills, toward Nazareth. He noticed that there were more wheat fields, barley fields, and olive groves since he had last been there. He began to think about Nazareth and the Lake of Galilee. Most of Jesus' life and ministry had taken place in the region.

As he drove through the rolling hills, his mind flashed back to the miracles of Jesus. Cana of Galilee was the site of his first miracle; there Jesus had turned water into wine. In fact, twenty-five of Jesus' thirty-three great miracles were done in the Galilean area.

If only this were a pleasure trip, where Isis and I could follow the footsteps of Jesus to Nazareth, Capernaum, Bethsaida, Gennesaret, and Tiberias. I'd love to show her where Jesus preached the Sermon on the Mount.

Murphy used his cell phone to call Abrams when he was about twenty minutes out of Nazareth. "My plan is to get some gas there and then head south toward Et Taiyiba," Murphy said.

"Let me make a suggestion," Abrams replied. "Why don't we meet in Nazareth for an early dinner. It will only take me about a half an hour to get there. Meeting there will be less conspicuous. Et Taiyiba is a small town with many eyes and ears.

"When you stop for gas in Nazareth, ask for directions to the Elmasharef Restaurant. It is a quiet and out-of-the-way place… and the food is great."

Murphy had forgotten how narrow and traffic-filled the streets of Nazareth were. It was certainly a clash between ancient pathways and modern asphalt.

It took him a number of wrong turns before he found Elmasharef. *Oh, great! There it is, but where am I going to find a parking space?*

Then he saw a young Arab boy waving his hands excitedly. The boy was pointing to a parking place. Murphy smiled. *He wants to make some money. Great! I love to see someone hustle.*

"I will guard your car for you, mister. No one will bother it while I am here."

Murphy was surprised at how good the boy's English was. "That's a good offer. I'll take you up on it. I will give you a nice reward when I return."

The boy smiled and nodded. "I will do a good job."

In the restaurant, Murphy got a table and sat down as he waited for Abrams to arrive. His thoughts turned to the strange events of the past weeks. *Why did Methuselah want him to find the Handwriting on the Wall? Why was Dr. Anderson killed? How does everything tie in with the George Washington Bridge near tragedy? Was the group that Stephanie Kovacs said controlled Barrington the same people Levi had discovered in Europe? Could that group be the Seven the Arab in the alley mentioned?*

Murphy pondered these questions, then rose to greet Levi Abrams, who had just arrived.

It was late in the afternoon as Talon drove the Jeep up the secluded dirt road. The passenger's side held two cages. Two dogs hung their heads over the side of the Jeep, breathing in all the different smells carried on the wind. Occasionally they barked with excitement.

Finally, the Jeep stopped near the top of a hill. The dogs jumped down and began to explore. Then Talon got the cages and placed them on the hood of the Jeep.

He removed a falcon from each cage, then untied the thin leather head covers they wore and gazed into their eyes. It had been some time since Talon had given his hunters the opportunity to polish their skills.

The falcons looked at Talon and the two dogs, surveying their surroundings. Nothing escaped their sharp eyes.

"Well, my pretties, are you ready for a little exercise? I want you to keep in practice." With that, Talon released the falcons. They took off, caught the thermals, and began to rise effortlessly in the sky. Soon they looked like small floating dots high in the air.

For a few minutes he watched them as they circled. Then he glanced toward the dogs. They were about one hundred and fifty yards away chasing some unknown scent.

Talon looked far up into the sky. He made a fist with one finger sticking out. He then hit that fist into the palm of his other hand. It was the signal to attack. Almost instantly one of the falcons was diving toward the earth aiming for the lead dog.

The dog was completely unaware of the danger it was in. The falcon's talons sunk into the dog's left eye and face. It screamed in pain and rolled away. It tried to get to its feet, at the same time attempting to wipe away the pain. Then there was a loud fluttering and flapping of wings as the falcon struck again, this time blinding the dog in the right eye. The third strike took the dog down, and the falcon went for the soft tissue of the neck. The dog's screams lasted only a few seconds.

The other dog wasn't sure whether to approach the commotion or to run away. Then Talon made a fist with two fingers pointing out and hit it into the palm of his other hand.

The second falcon took out the other dog in a matter of seconds.

Talon smiled. His pets hadn't lost any of their killing abilities. Then he clapped his hands and the birds returned to his leather-covered arms.

"Well, my pretties, I can tell that you still enjoy the hunt and kill. Very soon I will provide you with a couple of new targets."

In the restaurant, Murphy and Abrams were catching up. "It's been a rough few days," Murphy said. "All the devastation brought to mind Laura's death and the church bombing, and all the people who died while we were looking for the ark. It's also discouraging to have the ark covered with an avalanche and an earthquake burying the Handwriting on the Wall and all of the treasures of Belshazzar's temple."

"But, Michael, you are alive, Bingham is alive, and Isis is alive," Abrams said encouragingly. "The living must go on."

"I understand, Levi. I'm just disappointed. If you could have been there when we walked on the ark, even you might believe what the Bible says. These discoveries just help to verify what I know and believe in my heart is true."

"I wish I could be a man of faith like you. I'm just not there yet."

"Well, keep an open mind, Levi. If you seek to find truth, it will end up finding you. God has a way of pursuing like a hound dog. He's even been called the Hound of Heaven. I think He may be on your trail."

"I hope so, Michael. I hope so."

"Speaking of trails, Levi, fill me in on what you've discovered so far."

"As I mentioned, we caught several of the terrorists involved with the George Washington Bridge incident. One gave us a lead about a group of people who are heading up some kind of operation out of Europe. We also confiscated a laptop computer that gave us information about the terrorist cell in Et Taiyiba. And, as I said, all of the terrorists we captured had the upside-down crescent on their necks. We believe that Talon is using these terrorists to do some of his dirty work. We think Talon may be in the area as we speak."

"What gives you that idea?"

"Yusef and Alona, two undercover Mossad operatives. We sent them to Et Taiyiba as soon as we got the information off the laptop. They've been monitoring the activities of the cell made up of men tattooed with the upside-down crescents. They noticed a light-skinned man with dark hair talking with members of the cell. He had a neatly trimmed mustache and always wore gloves... even when it was hot."

"That sounds like Talon."

"Our plan is to take them the next time they get together."

"I'd like to be part of that operation."

"That's our idea. We want you to take a look at the man we think is Talon. You've seen him face to face and can make the ID."

"I'll be looking forward to that," Murphy said grimly. "We have a score to settle. He's the one who killed Laura and tried to kill Isis and many others."

"We also have another undercover operative named Gabrielle who's been in the Jordan Valley working with the emergency aid teams. She ran across a man named Dr. Brian Lehman from the United States."

"Boy, that name sure sounds familiar."

"You may have run across him, Michael. He's a geophysicist."

"That's right. He is one of the leading experts on earthquakes. What's he doing here?" Murphy asked.

"That's what Gabrielle wanted to know too. She got into a conversation with him about the earthquake damage. It seems that he came over from the United States to check out our earthquake sensing station in Eilat. It's part of the Geophysical Institute of Israel. She got the impression that he had discovered something highly unusual."

"What's that got to do with Talon?"

"While talking with Dr. Lehman, she noticed a man with a mustache watching them. He stood out because he was with two Arab-looking gentlemen. She thought he might be an American but wasn't sure. She became very suspicious."

"I wonder what Talon wants with Dr. Lehman."

"We don't know either, but we plan to find out. We can't overlook any leads or details at this point. There's too much at stake. We've set up a meeting with Dr. Lehman tomorrow. He'll be out in the field doing some drilling. Are you up for it?"

"That's why I'm here."

SIXTY-THREE

IT WAS MIDMORNING when Abrams and Murphy turned onto the dirt road in their battered pickup truck. They had chosen that vehicle so as not to attract attention to their visit.

Soon the road started to zigzag up a small mountain. As they topped the ridge, they could see a well-drilling rig in the valley below. One man was on the rig, and two others were standing by a white pickup truck. In another ten minutes they were at the site.

Abrams was the first to speak, introducing himself and Murphy. Dr. Lehman greeted them, then introduced Kasib Tahir, who was in charge of the well drilling, and Zahid Yaman, on the well-drilling truck.

Dr. Lehman looked at Murphy. "I've heard your name before. Aren't you an archaeologist?"

"Yes, sir. And I've also read some of your work on geology."

Soon the men got down to business.

"A friend of ours mentioned that you may have made an unusual geological discovery of some kind," Abrams said.

"Yes, I think I have," Lehman replied. "When the earthquake occurred, I happened to be in Tel Aviv. I immediately drove to Eilat, where the Geophysical Institute of Israel has an earthquake station drilled into Mount Amram, north of the city. It is drilled into precambrian granite porphyry and rhyolitic quartz porphyry. The sensor is installed in a special casing in a locked vault. The readings were most interesting. I then hired a well-drilling rig to take core samples of the earth movement along the fault line."

Lehman turned and pointed. "You can see that we've already drilled three other core samples in the valley."

"But it looks like you've discovered oil," Murphy observed.

"That's just it. We have. And there shouldn't be oil in this area."

"How can that be? Is that a result of the earthquake?" Murphy asked.

"I believe it is, Dr. Murphy. Let me try to explain. Surrounding the entire Arabian Peninsula is the Arabian tectonic plate. This includes the countries of Bahrain, Qatar, Kuwait, Yemen, Oman, Saudi Arabia, Iraq, Jordan, Syria, Lebanon, the United Arab Emirates, and Israel. Actually, it splits Israel in half right here in the Jordan Valley."

"Yes, I'm aware of that. It's part of the Great Rift Valley geological fault system that joins the African tectonic plate. It follows the Jordan River, which flows southward through the Sea of Galilee to the Dead Sea."

"That's correct," Lehman said. "To the northeast it splits Iran from Iraq along the base of the Lugros Mountains in Iran. That is where the Eurasian plate joins. Directly north is the Alpide belt, one of three major seismic belts of earth. It stretches from its western terminus in the Atlantic Ocean, through the Iberian Peninsula and the northern Mediterranean Sea. It crosses over through Turkey, Armenia, northern Iran, the Himalayas, and finally down through Burma to the East Indies. It is estimated that eighteen percent of all earthquakes occur along the Alpide belt."

"Excuse me, Doctors," Abrams broke in. "I would appreciate it if you could explain in lay terms. I am not a geologist. What's all of this talk about?"

Murphy spoke up. "Levi, imagine an oval line drawn around the Arabian Peninsula. Sort of like an egg with the large part down and the small part up. Now imagine a jagged fracture line moving east and west from one side of the oval to the other. Or a horizontal crack in the top part of the egg. The recent quake in the Syrian desert caused a fracture from the Jordan Valley where we are . . . all the way over to the Persian Gulf."

"That's a good illustration," Lehman said. "The Syrian desert earthquake was not just a surface quake. It was a *deep* quake. By that I mean it created a crack in the earth's surface at least twenty-five miles deep. And the energy and power created by the quake would be equal to all the explosives used during World War II combined—including the atomic bombs."

"I'm impressed," Abrams said.

Lehman continued. "To the best of my knowledge, the crack runs a moderately jagged line between the thirty-second and thirty-third parallels. That is from below the Sea of Galilee, across the Syrian desert toward Babylon, and then dropping down toward the gulf. I believe that oil from Iraq and the Persian Gulf region is seeping into this crack. That's why we're discovering oil in an area where there should be no oil."

"What are you smiling at, Levi?" Murphy asked.

"Michael, I find the thought of Israel being able to tap into Iraqi oil fields a little ironic."

Talon crawled forward and carefully lifted his head between two rocks. He focused his binoculars on the valley below. Slowly he scanned the valley from the three capped wells to the well-drilling rig.

One on the rig and four by the white truck. Dr. Murphy, I've had just about enough of you and your friend Abrams. It is time to end this game.

Abrams's smiled disappeared. He became quite serious as he asked, "Dr. Lehman, how many people have you talked with about your theory?"

"Let me see." Lehman looked thoughtful. "I talked with a young lady named Gabrielle, both of you, and of course the well drillers. No one else as yet. We've been too busy drilling and taking core samples."

"That's great," Abrams said, relieved. "I think that this information needs to be handled very carefully. If the news media got ahold of it...it could forment an absolute uproar in the Arab world. It could lay the groundwork for war."

"Oh, excuse me," Lehman continued. "There was one other person. It was later in the afternoon after I talked with Gabrielle. He was a man in his mid-forties, with a mustache and a slight English accent. However, I don't think he was from Great Britain or Australia."

Murphy and Abrams looked at each other.

"He said that he was just a traveler visiting the Holy Land. He asked me what we were doing. I told him we were drilling core samples to see the extent of the earthquake. Then Kasib yelled from the well-drilling rig that they had hit oil. The man and I went over to the rig to see what all the excitement was about. He may have overheard our conversation and my discussing the theory with Kasib. I don't know for sure. We were too excited. If fact, I remember that later, I turned around to look for him but he was gone. He seemed very friendly. I'm sure that he won't tell anyone."

"Tell me, Dr. Lehman," Murphy said. "Was the man wearing gloves despite the heat?"

When Lehman said yes, Murphy and Abrams both raised their eyebrows. Talon!

Abrams spent some time with Lehman discussing the importance of his discovery and how it could negatively affect the political status between the Israelis and the Arabs. After Lehman promised that he would speak to no one until his theory could be proven valid, Abrams and Murphy headed back to Et Taiyiba.

It was late in the afternoon when Dr. Lehman saw a weather-beaten Land Rover driving over the ridge and heading for the valley.

More visitors! We've certainly been busy today.

As the Land Rover pulled to a stop, Dr. Lehman walked toward it. He recognized the Holy Land traveler with a mustache and smiled. "Hello, there. I didn't know you were still in the area."

Talon shook his hand and asked, "How is your work coming along?"

"We're doing fine. By the way, did you share news of our discovery with anyone?"

"No. Why do you ask?"

"I'd appreciate it if you could keep it to yourself. We aren't sure of the extent of our find yet. We wouldn't want to create a stir that might give some false hopes or cause political problems. I'm sure that you understand the importance of that."

"Oh, yes. I understand far more than you know! I promise to keep it a secret between you and me. In fact, the fewer people who know, the better it is."

"I agree."

"I'm glad that you do. I think that it would be good to narrow the number of people who know even further."

"What? I don't understand." Lehman looked puzzled.

Talon reached forward, grabbed Dr. Lehman's right arm, and spun him. At the same time he circled his right forearm under the doctor's chin, pressing against his throat. Pulling Lehman toward him, Talon increased the pressure on his neck as he whispered, "No one will find out about your little discovery, Dr. Lehman. It will be our secret."

Lehman's eyes were wide in shock and disbelief. He tried to claw at Talon's arm, but it was like an iron vice choking off his breath. The last thing he saw was Kasib climbing off the well-drilling rig and running to his aid.

Talon saw him too. He finished off Lehman with a quick twist. There was a slight cracking sound and Lehman fell to the ground. Talon then made a fist with one finger and hit it into the palm of his left hand.

Kasib was about ten feet away when the falcon hit him. He was completely blindsided. The bird gouged his right eye and ripped the flesh of his cheek as Kasib screamed in pain. Both hands came up to his injured eye as he staggered. Then, with a flapping and fluttering, the bird severed Kasib's jugular vein. He went down to his knees choking on his own blood, then falling face forward in the dust.

Zahid had seen what happened. He grabbed a wrench as he ran toward Talon. At least he could defend himself and take revenge for the savage murders.

Talon could sense the man's determination. He pounded his fist twice into his hand. Zahid glanced from the man to the sky, where, from the left, he caught a glimpse of a falcon. He swung the wrench with both hands like a baseball bat.

The wrench caught the falcon full in the chest. There was no scream, just a thud and feathers flying everywhere. Talon, shocked, shouted as he saw one of his pretties explode in front of him.

The second falcon was not far behind the first one in its attack. However, Zahid's turn to strike the first falcon made the second one miss its mark. It barely ripped open the scalp on the back of the man's head. Zahid was twisting and turning and waving his arms as the bird came at him a second time. Zahid's arm hit the bird's wing, breaking it. The falcon's talons ripped at his chest.

Man and bird fell to the ground in a heap. Zahid rolled onto the bird and crushed it, then picked it up by the legs and began to beat it on the ground in a frenzy.

Talon, horrified at the loss of his birds, walked up behind Zahid and shot him in the back of the head.

SIXTY-FOUR

MURPHY AND ABRAMS MET for breakfast and to make plans for the day.

"You know, Michael, I had a hard time going to sleep last night. I kept thinking about Dr. Lehman's discovery. It could easily become a catalyst for sparking war against Israel."

"Funny you should mention it. I had the same worry. If Dr. Lehman is correct about Israel being able to get Arab oil, there's going to be big-time trouble."

"It certainly won't help the problem of anti-Semitism."

"I think that's putting it mildly, Levi. I was just reading an article put out by the U.S. State Department. It talked about the seminar on anti-Semitism put on by the United Nations, the Global Anti-Semitism Review Act signed by the president, and the comments of the Swiss Observatory of Religions in Lausanne."

"Why were you reading that, Michael?"

"Well, you know that I believe we're living in the last days before the return of Christ. The Bible indicates that in the last days, there will be an increase in animosity toward Israel. Even the Swiss Observatory of Religions acknowledges that there's been an increase in anti-Semitism during the last decade. Over thirty European countries have indicated that there's been a rise in vandalism and desecration of Jewish cemeteries and fire bombings of synagogues. There is also an increase in racist publications against the Jews and a new anti-Semitism in Britain and other countries. This is especially seen in the Arab newspapers like *Al Manar*, and on Arab news networks like *Al Jazeera* and *Al Arabiya*. Hate language against Israel is on the rise. This is one of the reasons that I believe that we are moving toward God's final Judgment Day."

"You know, Michael, I love the United States and believe in what it stands for . . . but I must confess that I sense the same thing in America. There are a lot of stereotypes, cartoons, and caricatures about Jews."

"I don't like to admit it, but you're right, Levi. Anti-Semitism has deep roots in the United States. I think they revolve around four concepts. Many people think that the Jewish community has clandestine control of the government, the media, international business, and the financial world. There is a growing criticism of Israeli policies . . . especially against the Palestinians. The growing worldwide Muslim population has strong feelings against Jews. This is a continuation of the long-standing conflict between Arab nations and Israel going all the way back to Abraham. And there has been a growing criticism of the United States over globalization that spills over onto Israel. This sort of visceral anti-Americanism is affecting many countries around the world. The Jews in general are identified with America, and many people also have a prejudicial dislike for Jews as a race."

"That's a good way to put it, Michael. An ancient Arab proverb says, 'My enemy's enemy is my friend.' I know that many Arab countries make friends with anyone who is against the United States or Israel. We are not only being condemned for our policies but for who we are as people."

"I don't have any easy answers for a very complex problem, Levi. I'm just glad we're friends. All I do know for sure is that this has been a problem in the past and it seems to be on the rise today. Dr. Lehman's discovery of oil only adds to the mix."

Talon looked into the rearview mirror of the Land Rover as he drove through the narrow streets. He watched with anticipation. *Come on. Come on. I know you're there.*

Then he saw the front end of the old green van as it rounded the corner behind him.

You're keeping a good distance . . . but you need to learn to be more subtle. They just don't make spies like they used to.

He smiled to himself and continued until he reached the outskirts of Et Taiyiba. He drove along a deserted street of what looked to be abandoned buildings. He then pulled up in front of an old two-story warehouse with a storefront. On either side of the weather-beaten double doors were large display windows containing a few decaying mannequins.

Four Arabs stood outside of the double doors, deep in conversation and gesturing widely.

They stopped talking and straightened when Talon pulled up and got out of the Land Rover. His very presence seemed to command attention. They acknowledged him with slight nods, no smiles or handshakes. Obviously they were all frightened of him.

One of the Arabs climbed into the Land Rover and parked it around the corner, then returned to the group.

Murphy laughed as Abrams's cell phone began to play the theme from the movie *Exodus*.

Abrams spoke quickly into the phone. "Set lookouts on all of the entrances and exits. We'll be there shortly.

"That was Uri," he told Murphy. "He's followed the man with the mustache to an old warehouse section of Et Taiyiba. There he met four Arabs, and they went into a storefront building. Isaac, Judah, and Gabrielle are with Uri. I think this could be our final showdown with Talon and his crew. I can't wait to put him behind bars! I've never seen anyone who loves to kill as much as he does."

Soon Abrams and Murphy pulled up behind a green van. They got out of their old pickup and entered the back of the van. Abrams introduced Murphy to Uri, then asked, "Has anyone come out since you called?"

"No. The building has a set of double front doors, a side door, and a back door. Isaac, Judah, and Gabrielle are watching them. No one has left."

"Do you have an extra gun?"

"Of course. What kind would you like?"

"Give one of the automatics to Dr. Murphy. We all need to be armed."

They approached the storefront carefully and glanced in. Some natural light from the street penetrated the building. They could see no movement or lights inside.

"They must be in the back," Abrams said. "Uri, radio Isaac, Judah, and Gabrielle and tell them to remain in position unless called for backup. Tell them to stay put even if they hear shots. We don't want anyone to escape. Especially the man with the mustache. He's very cunning, so be alert."

Abrams tried the front door; it was locked. Uri handed Abrams a set of lock picks, and in moments the door was unlocked.

"Pretty cool," Murphy exclaimed.

"Tricks of the trade," Abrams said modestly.

Stepping inside, they paused and listened. They could hear no sounds. With guns drawn, they headed toward a door behind an old dusty counter. They opened it carefully. When no shots greeted them, they stepped cautiously into the warehouse. Rows of shelving filled with cardboard boxes lined the room. Wooden crates were stacked in the aisles. A window in the back let in some light.

Abrams whispered, "Michael, you go down the right aisle. Uri, you go down the left. I'll take the center. Be careful and stay alert. Remember that they could be hiding behind the crates. No talking."

Murphy had moved forward about thirty feet when he heard a slight sound coming from behind a crate up ahead. He approached carefully and quietly. Was his archenemy, Talon, behind the crate, or one of the other terrorists? He had to be ready!

He had just started around the edge of the crate when there was a yowl and a cat ran across his feet. Murphy was so startled, he almost pulled the trigger.

Well, that's one more reason to hate cats. You either love them or hate them . . . there's no neutral ground.

Anyone in the building would have heard the cat's yowl.

Just then there was the sound of a shot. It ricocheted off a steel shelving support near Uri's head. Instantly he dropped to the floor and fired toward the sound. Then he rolled behind a nearby crate.

Abrams and Murphy were fired on at almost the same time. They too dropped and rolled toward protection. Soon shots were zigzagging through the warehouse. Murphy lifted his hand over the crate he was hiding behind and fired toward the unknown shooter. There was silence. Each group was listening for sounds from their adversaries.

"Well, Dr. Murphy we meet again."

A chill went down Murphy's back when he heard Talon's voice.

"I'm going to try to make it our last meeting," Murphy replied firmly.

"It probably will be yours, Dr. Murphy. You haven't been very adept at protecting yourself or your women. Especially your wife, Laura," Talon said with a sneer.

Murphy could feel his anger rising... along with his desire for revenge.

Careful, Murphy. He's trying to get you upset so you will become careless. Don't fall for it.

Abrams was trying to position himself to see where Talon's voice was coming from when another shot was fired. Then there was another silence.

Uri began to make his way over toward Abrams in the center aisle. Murphy held his position.

Isaac, Judah, and Gabrielle heard the gunshots. Their first desire was to come to the aid of the men inside, but, as ordered, they held their positions and watched the doors.

Isaac barely saw the flash of light. Something streaked by and shattered the left window next to the double doors. At almost the same instant an explosion inside the storefront shattered the other three windows and blew out the double doors. A fire was beginning to rage inside.

It must have been an RPG!

Isaac grabbed for his radio. "Isaac to Judah and Gabrielle . . . I think they just fired a rocket-propelled grenade into the storefront. Hold your positions; you've got your orders. No one is to escape."

Isaac picked up his rifle and emerged from a second, gray, van that was parked across the street from the warehouse. He looked through the high-powered scope in the direction from which the RPG came. He was searching the windows of an adjacent building for the shooter.

He saw some slight movement in a building on a diagonal from the storefront. As he began to focus, he heard tires squealing and looked toward the sound.

The Land Rover, with Talon driving, was turning the corner of the warehouse and was heading in Isaac's direction. He glanced up at the window once more. He could see a man rising and aiming a second RPG. Isaac lifted his rifle to his shoulder, took aim, and fired. His shot was a split second too late. The man at the window had already fired the RPG.

The Arab seemed to leap backward as the bullet entered his chest in an instant kill.

The second RPG went in through the blown-out front doors, bounced slightly on the floor, and penetrated the door behind the counter before it went off in the warehouse. A flash could be seen inside. Flames were beginning to engulf the entire structure.

Isaac was turning back toward the Land Rover. Talon squeezed the trigger of his handheld machine gun as he and the four terrorists passed.

Isaac felt a bullet tear through the meaty portion of his left thigh about four inches below his groin. He immediately went down from the force, his rifle flying from his hands. He instinctively reached for his shoulder holster, pulled out his Glock, and began to fire.

"Isaac . . . Isaac. Come in. What is happening?"

Judah and Gabrielle ran toward the front of the building. They had just reached Isaac when the first blast went off. The concussion knocked them down.

The old warehouse was beginning to collapse. Then suddenly four more blasts were triggered simultaneously.

For a second the building seemed to hang in space, then it collapsed. Smoke and dust filled the air.

Judah and Gabrielle knew that nothing could be done for anyone inside the building. They turned their attention back to Isaac. Judah applied pressure on the wound to stop the flow of blood while Gabrielle called for help.

SIXTY-FIVE

"SEÑOR BARTHOLOMEW, I must commend you on your wonderful sense of timing. You couldn't have planned our meeting for any better date. It looks like we will end just in time for the Grand Prix. You do know it is the last true street-circuit Formula 1 World Championship. I'm looking forward to attending. Thank you for your selection," Mendez said with a smile.

"Yes, I agree with Señor Mendez," Viorica Enesco put it. "A marvelous choice. The yachts in the harbor are magnificent, and they are only matched by the fantastic weather. I love to come to Monaco at this time of year. It is one of the most exciting cities in the world, and the cuisine is spectacular."

The Seven had gathered together in a villa on the cliffs overlooking the French Mediterranean. All seated on a picturesque veranda surrounded by lush vegetation and a spectacular view of the ocean, they were sipping wine and reviewing their plan.

General Li was the first to speak. "It is unfortunate that we were foiled in our plan to destroy the George Washington Bridge. That Dr. Michael Murphy and his friend Levi Abrams have become thorns in our flesh."

"That is true, General Li," Sir William Merton agreed. "They did stop the attack, but remember, they did not stop the ensuing panic and terror. It was enough of a threat to make the members of the United Nations vote to move out of the United States to Babylon. The details may have been clouded, but the end result was the same. And that is cause for a toast."

Everyone touched their wineglasses together.

"I agree," General Li said, with a slight smile. "I am just disappointed that there was not more damage. Destruction of the bridge would have cost the arrogant Americans much in the way of dollars and would have shaken their pride at being able to stop terrorist attacks in their own country."

"But we have more attacks planned," Ganesh Shesha told the general. "You may get your wish sooner than you think."

Jakoba Werner smiled as she freed her blond hair from a bun. Her chubby cheeks were red. "I think we all can be happy," she exclaimed. "Soon the new United Nations building will be erected in Babylon. The Arabs are thrilled at the thought of hosting the UN. And by funding the construction through the European Union, as we have planned, the Arab countries will be obligated to Europe. The European Union will be seen as the 'good guys.' Our representatives are already negotiating with Saudi Arabia, Iran, and Iraq for reduced oil prices because of our support. It will help to strengthen the euro and devaluate the U.S. dollar even more. We have even convinced the Arabs to raise oil prices to the United States. This will force them to drill in Alaska, which will infuriate the environmentalists. Everything is falling into place."

"I agree with Jakoba," John Bartholomew stated. "We've even been able to corrupt some UN members. It's wonderful to see how money can buy almost anything. We helped them to secretly open Swiss bank accounts. Little do they know that we can siphon funds out of those accounts! The money comes from us to them, then we take it back from them. Isn't the world of banking wonderful? They're simple pawns on our chessboard."

"By the way, I know that you've been working on it . . . have you been able to figure out a way to siphon money from numbered accounts left by the Nazis in World War II?" Sir William asked.

Bartholomew smiled. "Of course—not only their accounts, but many more. We have ways to persuade the bank officials to work with us. All we have to do is show them pictures of their families and ask if they would like to keep them alive. It seems to have a wonderful way of convincing people to cooperate. We should be happy with how fast we've grown in power. Soon we'll be in control of everything that is happening in the world."

Everyone clapped.

Viorica Enesco was rubbing her finger around the top of her wineglass and staring at the ocean.

"What are you thinking about, Viorica?" Bartholomew asked.

"I was thinking about Talon. He seems to have stepped up to the challenge of eliminating those who hamper our movement. He took care of Stephanie Kovacs, who was leaking information to Dr. Murphy. He also was able to retrieve the notes and materials of Dr. Anderson before Murphy could make them public. He was successful in causing nationwide panic in the United States over the George Washington Bridge attack. And I understand that he is working diligently to try to destroy Dr. Murphy. Maybe a bonus would be appropriate."

They all agreed. Then Señor Mendez spoke up. "We do have one loose cannon."

Everyone turned and looked at him.

"Methuselah. He is a very powerful man. Not only is he wealthy and powerful . . . he is very angry at the loss of his family. He found out that we were behind the downing of the aircraft they were riding in. He wants to thwart our plans in any way he can. He wants revenge! That's why he's helping Murphy. We need to work on a plan to deal with him."

Everyone nodded, their eyes suddenly worried.

Bartholomew spoke up. "Methuselah knows too much about us and our growing power. We don't want him ruining everything. What should also concern us is, did Murphy or that McDonald woman read any of the papers of Dr. Anderson? Just how much does he know about the Boy and our plans for him? Methuselah and Murphy *both* need to be eliminated."

"I think we need to focus a little," Sir William said, running a finger around his clerical collar. "I think that we need to send Talon back to the Black Sea. There is some unfinished business with the valuable items that were found on the ark. Potassium 40 may still prove to lengthen life, and we need to discover the secrets of the bronze plates and the crystals. We also need to start initiating our plan to set the stage for a new religious movement. The 1960s were successful in convincing everyone that God was dead—a significant challenge to the evangelicals. Then in the latter part of the 1970s, the concept of the occult began to grow aided by all of the Saturday cartoon shows about demons, witches, ghosts, wizards, and supernatural heroes. We now have a whole generation that is tired of the God-is-dead talk and the emptiness it brings. They have been softened as children to accept the occult. They are ripe for a religious leader who will talk about the brotherhood of man and peace for the world."

"I agree," Bartholomew said, nodding. "We need to begin to talk of uniting the many faiths. You know, the all-roads-lead-to-Rome concept or the spokes-of-the-wheel theory, where all religions are like spokes that lead to God as the hub. We need to begin to step up our activities in this area."

"We have had a good start with the attempt to redefine Christmas and other religious holidays like Easter," Ganesh Shesha said. "We need to continue to promote tolerance and more laws about hate speech. We need to stop the Christians from pushing any of their thoughts about God onto others. Christianity is a cancer that needs to be eliminated if we are to be successful."

Everyone nodded.

"Don't forget people like Michael Murphy," Jakoba Werner said. "It is people like him and the religious right who are really dangerous. They know too much about the Bible and what it really teaches. They are dangerous because they are unafraid and are able to convince others to follow them. We don't need him or people like him to hamper our ability to create the environment for the Boy."

Bartholomew spoke up. "I think that it may be time for the Friends of the New World Order to begin to go public. We need to use the media to get our message out. The foundation for the European Union is solid and growing—Europa is rising."

SIXTY-SIX

WHEN THE FIRST RPG exploded in the storefront, the shock knocked Uri and Murphy to the ground.

Uri was the first to speak. "Dr. Murphy, are you all right?"

"Yes, just surprised. I smell smoke. The blast must have started a fire."

Uri was almost to Abrams's position. "Levi, are you all right?"

There was no response.

"Dr. Murphy! Levi was hit by the last shot. He's bleeding from a head wound."

"Is he alive?" Murphy asked, sidestepping debris as he hurried down the aisle toward the two men.

Murphy was about halfway down the aisle when the second RPG blasted into the warehouse.

Uri was bending over Abrams when it exploded. The blast killed him instantly; his body protected Abrams from further injury. The boxes shielded Murphy from shrapnel, but the concussion knocked him down, dazed with a terrible ringing in his ears.

Murphy struggled to his feet and frantically began to pull debris off Uri and Abrams. When he saw the extent of Uri's injuries, he was sure the Mossad agent was dead, but he felt for a pulse anyway. There was none. He then looked at Levi Abrams. His chest was moving up and down. As Murphy began to remove the shelving that was pinning his friend, he thought angrily, *A trap . . . it was all a trap! Talon knew we were coming and set us up!*

Murphy, sensing that something else might be in store for them, wanted to get Abrams out of the building.

They must have had a secret exit of some kind. I'll bet it's near where they were shooting from.

By now the fire that began with the blast of the second RPG was beginning to spread rapidly. Smoke was filling the air, making it difficult to see and hard to breathe.

Soon Murphy could see where the shots had been fired from. Talon and his men had set up a barrier of crates, behind which they had lain in wait.

Murphy leaned over one of the crates and saw an open trapdoor that he felt sure must lead to a tunnel. Staying low to the floor to avoid the smoke, he dragged Abrams to the hole. He climbed in first, then grabbed Abrams and pulled him down into a six-foot by six-foot area shored up with boards. On one side of the area was a crawl tunnel about three feet in diameter.

This must have been an emergency exit for the terrorists.

Murphy lay Abrams in the tunnel on his back, headfirst. He then took off his belt and Abrams's and hooked them together to form a circle. He looped the circle under his friend's back and armpits. Then Murphy crawled into the circle of belts.

Murphy knew that it would be difficult to drag Abrams through a tight tunnel. He was two hundred pounds of dead weight. But if he lifted up with his arms and back, Murphy could raise Abrams off the ground. He could then straddle him, drag him, and crawl forward at the same time with the help of the looped belts.

Murphy had just started crawling forward when the first blast in the storefront went off. The earth shook. Particles of dirt began to rain down on him. The fear of being trapped in a collapsing tunnel overwhelmed Murphy. He began to crawl as fast as he could, praying for God's help at the same time.

Another blast rocked the earth, causing Murphy to fall on top of Abrams. Murphy struggled up as quickly as he could and started dragging his friend when part of the tunnel collapsed on their legs. He couldn't move forward.

The dust from the cave-in made breathing almost impossible. Murphy, coughing, pulled his T-shirt up to cover his nose and mouth like a makeshift filter. He waited several minutes for the dust to begin to settle and to get his bearings.

Murphy rotated the two belts so he could unhook them. He then tried to crawl forward, pulling hard against the dirt covering his feet. After much effort, he finally broke loose.

He then crawled forward past Abrams into the tunnel ahead. Somehow he had to turn around and face the other direction to dig his friend free—if he was still alive.

The crawl tunnel had narrowed in the area where Murphy had to turn around. In the total darkness of the tunnel, fear began to creep into his mind. Murphy began to draw his legs up in an attempt to turn around. He soon began to feel wedged in the tunnel. His back was pressed against the side and sharp rocks were poking his flesh.

When he was at the halfway point of turning, his foot got stuck on a rock and he could not move it. Murphy found it difficult to breathe. He was stuck. He couldn't move forward or backward. His leg muscles were on the verge of cramping. Panic caused his heart to pound.

Murphy's mind flashed back to his childhood when he was in the Boy Scouts. His troop was camping in the mountains on a cold night. He crawled into his mummy sleeping bag, curling up in a ball in an attempt to stay warm.

Somehow during the night, his body had gotten completely turned around. His feet ended up toward the head of the bag and his head was at the bottom.

He remembered how he had felt when he realized that he couldn't reach the zipper and free himself. He knew that he'd have to turn around inside the bag to get to the breathing hole at the top.

He had gotten stuck then too at the halfway point in turning around. The cloth of the bag caught on his heels, and he couldn't move forward or back. It was then that he had first experienced the absolute terror of claustrophobia. He didn't know what it was called at that time. All he knew was that he was stuck with little air and no hope of rescue. No matter how much he strained to break free from the cloth that wrapped around him, he could not. The mummy bag had taken on new meaning—it had felt like the bag of death.

Murphy's claustrophobia had never left him . . . and now he was trapped again. He wanted to scream and yell and break free from the grip of the dark tunnel, but the walls would not move.

As a child he had talked to himself . . . to not fight the bag and to slow down his breathing . . . to gain control of his emotions.

Murphy tried to relax. Because of his curled-up position, he had to take very short, shallow breaths. His chest was unable to expand to its fullest.

He forced himself to relax, and after a time the terror and panic gave way to rational thinking.

My heel is caught. I've got to free it somehow.

Slowly and methodically he worked his hand and arm down toward his heel.

If I can only move my foot a little, it may come loose.

His fingers barely touched the top of the heel of his boots.

Just a little more.

That "little more" caused his chest to compress. Panic returned now that he was wedged even tighter.

Relax, Murphy. Relax. Breathe slowly.

It took another thirty seconds before he tried to move his arm and hand lower. He was now able to feel a small rock that was the problem. With his fingers, he moved the rock back and forth until it shifted slightly and then broke free. His heel moved.

As he paused to breathe deeply, he found himself praying and thanking God for that small miracle.

Murphy was finally able to stretch out his legs and lay full length in the tunnel. Precious life-giving air filled his lungs.

As he felt control returning, he turned on his stomach and reached for Levi Abrams's head. The dirt and dust of the tunnel had helped the blood to clot; the wound didn't seem to be bleeding as much. He reached his hand over his friend's mouth and nose. He could feel the warm air of his shallow breathing.

Thank you, God, for keeping my friend alive. Thank you for helping me to get unstuck.

Murphy crawled forward. His fingers scrabbled through the dirt and rocks as he struggled to free Abrams's legs from the rubble trapping them. It took Murphy over two hours to loosen Abrams's legs. His fingers were sore and bleeding.

He then backed into the tunnel until he could grab his friend's arms, and he began to pull. Abrams's body slowly slid over the loose gravel. Murphy then backed up again and pulled once more.

It's working!

Murphy had been pulling and sliding for about ten minutes when the gravity of the situation hit him. He was in a dark tunnel with no light. He was backing feetfirst into the unknown. He was not sure just how badly Abrams had been injured. And he had no idea if the rest of the tunnel was passable. What if they were trapped forever?

He tried to shake those thoughts out of his mind. While he was still alive, there was hope, and hope gave him the strength to keep going.

As he pulled and slid Levi, his mind began to drift toward Isis. Would he ever see her again? Would he finally be able to tell her that he loved her? How he wished he could break free from his narrow tomb, once again to see the light . . . once again to breathe fresh air . . . once again to hold her in his arms.

ABOUT THE AUTHORS

DR. TIM LAHAYE is a renowned prophecy scholar, minister, and author. His Left Behind ® series is the bestselling Christian fiction series of all time. He and his wife, Beverly, live in southern California. They have four children and nine grandchildren.

BOB PHILLIPS, PH.D., is the author of more than eighty books. He is a licensed counselor and executive director for the Pointman Leadership Institute.